WHAT OTHERS ARE SAYING ABOUT
From the Mouth of Elijah

From the Mouth of Elijah is an invigorating tale of courage, love, and sacrifice. Masterfully woven, it takes the reader on an exciting journey, a quest to discover sacred truths and an exploration of the greatest promise ever given—salvation through Christ Jesus. Guiding us on this journey is a company of wonderful characters; some are old and dear friends, while others are new acquaintances that are rapidly finding their places in our hearts. Together, they face the darkest storm yet, clinging only to their faith in Jehovah-Yasha. *From the Mouth of Elijah* is truly a must-read!

—**Megan Garber** (Age 15)

Debilitating devastation, creeping corruption, heart-wrenching sacrifices, and love fiercer than the fires of hell—welcome to *From the Mouth of Elijah*. From the first line of the opening poem to the final period on the final page, I was riveted to this roller coaster of soaring inspiration and heart-crushing grief. Bryan Davis has once again woven a masterpiece, taking us on the journey from death to life, from doubt to hope, from fear to faith, all in a quest for truth and love. Prepare to experience the path of Christ: This epic tale refuses to flinch from the glaring light of true sacrifice. And be warned: You never saw this coming!

—**Ethan Alldredge** (Age 21)

In one word, this book is . . . exhilarating! Mr. Davis's second book in the Children of the Bard series is an edge-of-your-seat thrill ride featuring fantastic locales, surprises around every turn, wit and humor, gripping characters, and a well-crafted story that sets the stage for the battle that is yet to come. Grab onto Apollo and hang on tight, cause it's a ride you WON'T want to miss!

—**Blake Murphy** (Age 19)

From the Mouth of Elijah is another amazing adventure! I couldn't put the book down! The thrilling twists in the plot will leave you guessing what happens next. The spiritual depth is as deep and compelling in this book as it is in all the other books in the series. Bryan Davis has again created a masterpiece that you won't want to miss reading.

—**Caresse Hassoldt** (Age 14)

Bryan Davis has once again left me speechless with this new masterfully written addition to the Children of the Bard saga. *From the Mouth of Elijah* is a thrilling adventure that will change your perspective on life, love, and the true meaning of sacrifice. Who will make the ultimate sacrifice? The answer is a twist you did not see coming. Just make sure you have a box of tissues handy as you embark on the journey.

—**Crystal Watson** (Age 20)

When I want a book that has action, humor, love, and dragons, I know to pick up a Bryan Davis book. Mr. Davis flawlessly transitions from one scene to the next, and as I read, I can just see the characters and where they are. *From the Mouth of Elijah* gives a whole new depth to what we've already learned about Mr. Davis's dragon drama. I finished it in two days and read through it again the next. You won't want to put this book down, even when you finish it!

—**Leah Kahkola** (Age 16)

From the Mouth of Elijah has certainly earned its place in my heart. The lessons it teaches are irreplaceable. God will always be with us, no matter what. I recommend this book to anyone and everyone who loves a great adventure but also wants to learn a lesson about life and what we live for. Or better yet, whom we live for.

—**Allison Strickler** (Age 18)

Mr. Davis has once again created a masterpiece. Like all of his other books, it made me laugh and cry. I stayed up most of the night reading this book. This is his best book yet in the Children of the Bard series!

—**Savannah Wright** (Age 13)

This book threw me through a volcano of emotions, from beaming in pride of all the characters to almost crying. I must say that *From the Mouth of Elijah* is the best Bryan Davis book to date. Not only am I left wanting more, but I don't know if I can even wait for the next book!

—**Dan Lupo** (Age 13)

Bryan Davis has done it again! In the pages of *From the Mouth of Elijah* danger and suspense lurk around every corner. It is impossible to put this book down. It will have you turning every page with excitement. This has to be one of the best books out of the Dragons in Our Midst and Oracles of Fire series so far.

—**Kathleen Vanvolkenburg** (Age 15)

From the Mouth of Elijah will keep you hooked from the first word till the end. It will challenge you, make you laugh and cry, and show you new and wonderful things about the God we serve. You will be encouraged to take up your spiritual sword and go into war as you fight for the greater good.

—**Josh Benda** (Age 19)

Children of the Bard 2

from the Mouth of Elijah

Bryan Davis

LIVING
INK
BOOKS
Writing Worth Reading

From the Mouth of Elijah
Volume 2 in the Children of the Bard® series
Copyright © 2012 by Bryan Davis
Published by Living Ink Books, an imprint of AMG Publishers
6815 Shallowford Rd.
Chattanooga, Tennessee 37421

Printed Edition ISBN 13: 978-0-89957-881-1
Printed Edition ISBN 10: 0-89957-881-0
EPUB Edition ISBN 13: 978-1-61715-379-2
Mobi Edition ISBN 13: 978-1-61715-108-8
ePDF Edition ISBN 13: 978-1-61715-044-9

First printing—June 2012

CHILDREN OF THE BARD, ORACLES OF FIRE, and DRAGONS IN OUR MIDST are registered trademarks of AMG Publishers.

Cover designed by Bright Boy Design, Inc., Chattanooga, Tennessee.

Interior design and typesetting by Reider Publishing Services, West Hollywood, California.

Edited and proofread by Susie Davis, Sharon Neal, and Rick Steele.

French phrases provided by Sofia Becker.

Printed in the United States of America
17 16 15 14 13 12 –V– 7 6 5 4 3 2 1

CONTENTS

ELIJAH'S FIRE

Deception lives disguised in smiles
From nobles, preachers, kings;
Disease in words, deception's snare
In choir robes it sings.

The cause, the cure, they come as twins
In voluntary breaths;
For one a theft, from one a gift,
Both suffocating deaths.

Will fires burn the sacrifice
To spread a cooling breeze?
Will death defeat another death
For those on bended knees?

And so the valiant march to war
Without a sword in hand;
Their weapon rests in silent sighs.
A prayer their only stand.

When sacrificed in blistered wind,
The cure is scattered yon.
Our faithful servants rise again;
Their night has reached its dawn.

And now they march with swords of light
To rescue from the mire,
Corralling misled lambs with love,
Rebuking wolves with fire.

Strip off your scarlet-tainted robes;
To truth forever kneel.
The cure must start with sharpened blades
To cut, then stitch and heal.

O God of truth, O Lord of fire,
Come purge polluted lands.
We plead for healing flames of truth;
We grasp your bleeding hands.

CHAPTER

MOUNT ELIJAH

Matt sprawled in the mud next to Walter. Five armed prison guards surrounded him, one with a rifle pointed at his head. The other four shifted their aims wildly at dragons orbiting outside an encircling firestorm. Flames crackled. Steam billowed. Dragons and men screamed.

Walter belly crawled through the mire, whispering, "Get ready. I'm calling for backup through the tooth transmitter."

"Go for it." Matt looked for Lauren. In the center of the circle, she stood on top of a tank alongside Joran and Selah as they tried to create a protective sound barrier around themselves using Joran's lyre. Another tank sat behind the first, abandoned.

"Makaidos!" Walter barked. "Give us some firepower."

"Gladly." A stream of orange shot from Makaidos and slammed into one of the surrounding soldiers. As flames engulfed his body, a volley of fireballs sizzled in. Two other soldiers dove out of the way and splashed into the mud.

"Matt! Now!" Walter leaped to his feet and punched a soldier in the jaw, sending him flying backwards. Matt swept a leg under the last standing guard. He toppled, slammed his head against the empty tank, and fell limply over Matt's legs.

While Walter ran toward the tank, Matt rolled the unconscious guard to the side and snatched up his rifle. Dripping muddy water, he stood in the hot quagmire and tried to orient himself while voices buzzed in his tooth.

"Thanks for waiting," Walter said. "Let's do it!"

"Matt didn't come. He doesn't know the barrier's ready."

Matt blinked. Lauren's voice, but it was warped and fuzzy. He shook his head, slinging away muddy water and clearing his ears.

"Matt!" Walter called. "Did you hear Lauren? We're all set! Get up here!"

"On my way." Matt leaped toward the tank, but his foot snagged on something. He fell forward and slid through the muck.

2

A gun pressed against his head. "Don't move," a soldier called toward the tank, "or I'll put a bullet through him!"

Walter's voice returned to Matt's jaw. "Keep holding it, Lauren. It might be Matt's ticket back up here."

Atop the tank, Lauren raised her arm. A rope dangled from her wrist. "I don't think I could untie it if I wanted to."

Matt followed the rope from Lauren's wrist to his waist. They were still attached. The knot was too tight. This could be trouble.

"I will take him from here," a woman hissed. Something jerked upward on Matt's collar and hauled him to his feet. A dagger pressed against his throat. The woman called out, her arm wrapped tightly around his waist and her mouth next to his ear. "Give me Lauren. If you do, she and hero boy will both live. If you don't, I will kill him immediately."

Matt tensed. Semiramis! He couldn't let this witch wannabe use him as bait to catch Lauren. "Wrap them in the barrier!" he shouted to Walter. "Don't trust a word she says!"

The rear tank submerged into the liquefying mud, creating a vacuum wind that sucked the surrounding men into a dark void where the tank once sat. The swirling suction pulled Matt and Semiramis toward the hole, but the rope tightened and kept them from falling in. As the ground dissolved all around, Semiramis hung on to Matt's waist, the dagger still at his throat, and shouted toward Walter and Lauren. "What is your answer?"

Walter made a twirling motion with his finger. "Joran, wrap Lauren and Selah and yourself up."

"We can't leave Matt!" Lauren pulled the rope, but the vacuum held him in its grip. "I *won't* leave Matt!"

Like a powerful broom, the wind swept men, mud, and guns into the growing void, leaving only one tank, its riders, and Matt and Semiramis hovering inches over melting soil.

With violent flames spinning all around, Walter shouted at Lauren. "Do what I say! Now! I'll hang on to the rope."

"But—"

"No buts." Walter turned to Joran. "I'm counting on you to save Lauren and Selah. Like I said, wrap them and yourself in your barrier."

Joran responded, but the wind batted his words away.

"Of course not. I'm going to try to save Matt." Walter looked again at Semiramis. "Ease up on that dagger, and we'll talk. In the meantime, I'm going to protect the kids."

Still atop the tank, Joran held a rod in the air and began walking around Lauren. Then he and Selah crouched with her, as if inside an invisible tent.

3

Walter grasped the rope with both hands and leaned back against the pull. "Why should I believe you'd let them live?"

"I have information to trade. I know Arramos's plans. It will prove that I am not in league with him and that I will not harm Matt or Lauren."

"Arramos? What are his plans?"

"Promise to give me Lauren, and I will tell you."

Matt shouted, "Don't do it! I'm not about to let anyone put Lauren in danger."

"You heard him," Walter said.

"Don't take me for a fool. They are minors, children of your best friend. The decision is yours, not Matt's."

Walter grimaced against the rope's pull. "There must be a reason you want Lauren so badly. I can't believe you're going to let yourself plunge into an unknown world."

"I know what I'm doing. You have five seconds to decide." As the blade cut into Matt's throat, Semiramis spoke softly into his ear. "Give me Lauren, and I will help you save both Earth and Second Eden."

He growled, "I wouldn't trade her safety for your promises to save any world." Trying not to move a muscle, he whispered into the transmitter. "Lauren, the rope's still tied to my waist. You and Walter can reel me in. Don't worry about Semiramis cutting me. I've been trained to handle this. Just do something that'll distract her for a split second."

Lauren jumped up and shouted, "Semiramis!"

Semiramis flinched. Matt shoved her arm back, grabbed her dagger, and thrust an elbow into her ribs. The vacuum ripped her away.

Still clutching the dagger, Matt continued hanging by the rope in midair, the wind batting him around. Lauren and Walter pulled at the rope's opposite end, their faces taut.

"It's slipping!" Walter called. "Hang on!"

Lauren leaned back, slowly sinking with the tank. "I am!"

Gasping for breath, Matt groped for something to grab, any-thing he could brace with to keep the pressure off Walter and Lau-ren. In seconds, everyone on the tank would be swallowed by the bubbling lava. They still had time to protect themselves in the bar-rier, but not if they kept trying to save him.

Matt waved both arms. "Let me go! Save yourselves!"

The tank eased lower. Hot gasses shot up from the melting metal. Her face twisting in pain, Lauren shouted, "Never! If you go, I'm going with you!"

Matt gazed at her. Such determination. Such love. She really would give her life to save him.

He glanced at the knot. The last time he dangled from a rope, a hate-filled foster sister stood at the other end, a prankster who wanted him to suffer. Lauren was the opposite of Darcy. She was light and love, everything a real sister ought to be. He couldn't let her die.

He set the dagger against the rope and whispered into the transmitter. "I love you, Lauren. It was great being your brother, even for just a little while."

He sliced through the rope. With a twang, the line snapped toward Lauren. Matt flew away and sailed through the air. With the dagger still in his grip, he forced his arms not to flail. He hur-tled nearly parallel to an expanse of black rocks that lay a hundred feet below. Plumes of steam erupted from fissures, some rocketing high and brushing scalding white fingers against his skin. Crash-ing down there would either tear his body to pieces or boil his blood, maybe both.

A huge lake came into view, the shore not far away. His arms instinctively flapped, as if swimming toward the water. When his

5

momentum eased, his angle bent toward the steaming rocks. Only seconds remained to impact.

With his chest toward the ground, he locked his arms against his sides, closed his eyes, and held his breath. He skidded across water for a split second, then plunged into its depths. Pain shot through his head—ripping, throbbing torture, like a full-body vise crushing his skull. Water gushed into his mouth. He swallowed to keep it from leaking into his lungs. It tasted earthy, yet fresh.

Once his descent stopped, he opened his eyes. Dark water filled his vision, hot and stinging. Which way was up? It seemed impossible to tell.

While he slid the dagger safely behind his belt, he let out a bubble and watched it rise. With a two-armed flap and a vicious kick, he swam in that direction. The pressure eased, but his lungs ached for air. The water grew brighter, still scalding.

6

Soon, the surface appeared, blocked by floating horizontal cylinders that allowed light through undulating gaps. He pushed into a gap and broke through in the midst of a sea of floating logs, a hazy, moonlit sky above. He sucked in a deep breath. The air scraped his throat and burned his lungs. He coughed violently, but each draw of new air made it worse. Still hacking, he stripped off his jacket and held it over his nose and mouth while treading water with one arm. Now the spasms brought in cleaner air, though it was still tinged with a bitter bite.

He grabbed a log, then snapped his hand back. Sparks rose from the stripped bark, apparently a recent burn victim. He set his hand in the water to cool the sting. No real damage—probably just a bit red. Maybe he had hit one of these logs when he entered, explaining the head and body aches.

As his breathing slowed, he searched for the shoreline, but darkness and smoke veiled the view in every direction. A curtain of ash floated from the sky like dirty snow, adding to the haze. Was it dark during the battle at the prison? Every memory fogged, possibly a sign of a concussion. With his limbs aching, he wouldn't be able to tread water for much longer, and the fumes would do him in sooner or later. They were already causing dizziness.

He chose a log that had been completely stripped of all branches, slid his hand underneath, and turned it. As it rotated, it hissed, and vapor rose from the newly cooled sections. When the hissing stopped, he repeated the process with another stripped log, then another. After cooling five logs, he pushed them side by side, threw his jacket over them with the sleeves spread out, and hoisted himself on board, quickly hugging them together.

Bobbing with the logs, he grabbed a jacket sleeve, tossed it over his face, and hugged the logs again. As he breathed through the filter, he closed his eyes. Making plans now would be a lot easier—fewer worries about drowning. Obviously he was no longer anywhere near the prison, so yelling for help made no sense, and it would make things worse if the wrong people heard him.

The improvised raft's up-and-down drift added to the dizziness. It might be better to rest for a while longer until the feeling went away. Taking slow breaths through the sleeve, he let his body relax. Soon, an image came to mind, Lauren sitting in the copilot's seat of an airplane, the very same place he had sat when flying with Walter not long ago, though now their father was the pilot. The two were talking—garbled words, too warped to figure out, something about underborns, magnetic ore, and Apollo, but most of the conversation died in the buzz of the propeller.

After a while, Matt blinked his eyes open. Still bobbing, he pushed his face out from under his jacket. The sky was brighter now and the fumes less dense. A haze-coated sun hovered fairly close to the horizon, giving evidence that morning had broken not long ago. Sleep had helped. The dizziness had gone away.

Turning carefully, he searched for the shore across the log-cluttered lake. About a hundred yards away, the greenish-blue water met a field of dark ground where steam spewed in bursts from invisible holes. Beyond them, a volcano sent billowing clouds of gray into the sky, dotted with sparkling embers. From the volcano's decapitated top, lava oozed down every visible side, some of it hardening before it reached the bottom of the slope, as if trying to rebuild what the eruption had blown away.

He looked in the opposite direction. No sign of shore that way, just a sea of water, logs, and smoke.

Keeping the jacket over his mouth and an arm on one of the logs, Matt let himself into the water and paddled and kicked toward shore. As he progressed, the water grew hotter and hotter, likely affected by the superheated lava field. Soon it might be too hot to go on, but staying in the lake meant sure death. He couldn't swim forever.

After several minutes, he found traction on the lake bottom and trudged toward shore. Just a few steps ahead, a woman lay on her back in shallow water with her face barely above the surface. A coat of ash had covered her torso, making her look scorched, perhaps dead. Dressed in a camouflage uniform, she had to be Semiramis.

Matt sloshed to her and dropped to his knees at her side. Semiramis was breathing, but the fumes would probably finish her off soon.

He let his shoulders sag. Rescuing her might be stupid, but how could he leave a woman to die? It would be heartless. Besides, she might have some idea about where they were and how to escape. With the water seemingly ready to boil, too much time here would make them both part of this lava stew.

Holding his breath, he dropped the jacket and stripped off his shirt, leaving only a thin black T-shirt. After wiping away some of the ash from Semiramis's lips and eyelids, he laid the outer shirt over her mouth and nose. She coughed and shook her head, but Matt kept the wet filter in place.

"Stay calm. I'm trying to save your life." He set the jacket over his mouth again, muffling his words. "Not that you deserve it."

"Help me …" Opening her eyes, she held the shirt over her mouth. "Help me sit."

Matt set a hand behind her back and pushed her to a sitting position. She coughed several times, sucking air between coughs.

While he waited, blood trickled from his dagger wound down to his chest. Pain blurred his vision. The entire world spun one way, then another, as if riding on a yoyo. His danger alarm simmered in his stomach, like a stewing pot on low heat. Maybe it was just the volcano … and maybe not.

9

Matt climbed to his feet and stood in calf-deep water, fighting to keep his balance. He panted through the jacket. Smoke veiled the area, a gray shroud that spun in the swirling air. Cooling breezes cut through his saturated clothes, but his dragon-endowed body heat pushed back the chill.

As the mind fog dissolved, the scene clarified. Between his vantage point and the volcano lay an expanse of lava rock, bare and steaming. Far to the right within the expanse, fallen trees stripped of all greenery lay in burning heaps, some covered with boulders. It seemed that the volcano had blown its top and sent a storm of stones in every direction, knocking down trees before sending a cascade of lava to burn them.

The volcano continued spewing smoke and ash, and the breeze stirred the drizzling gray flakes into tighter swirls, making the lava field look like a postapocalyptic movie set. What was this place?

A Pacific-rim island? That seemed impossible. Just moments ago he battled prison guards in Arizona.

He set a finger on his jaw and listened. No chatter from Lauren, Walter, or anyone else. He ran his tongue across the tooth transmitter. It was still there. Maybe the impact and hot water ruined it, or else he had flown too far, but weren't the transmitters supposed to work from miles and miles away?

Semiramis's spasms finally settled. "Help me," she said, lifting a hand.

After Matt helped her stand and steady herself, he looked her over. Rips in her camo uniform exposed gory scratches on her shoulders and arms, though her dripping hair partially covered some of the wounds. Maybe she slammed into shallow water and scraped herself on the lakebed.

Still holding the jacket over his nose and mouth, he set his free hand on the dagger's hilt. "Do you have any idea where we are?"

As she scanned the devastation, her eyes widened. "Arramos! That cunning serpent!"

"Arramos? You mentioned that name to Walter."

"He is a dragon, Satan himself. I knew he had plans for destruction, but this?" She shook her head. "I am appalled at his malice, though by now I shouldn't be surprised."

A stiff wind from the lake pushed the fumes toward the volcano, cleansing the immediate area. Matt lowered his jacket and breathed freely. Although still carrying a burning flavor, the air seemed safe. "What do you mean?"

She slid her filter down, draped it over her shoulder, and sniffed. Apparently satisfied that the air was safe, she lifted her tresses, revealing a deep gouge in her other shoulder. "I will trade information for your healing touch. I know you healed your mother with skin-to-skin contact."

Matt concealed a cringe. Touching this woman might feel like licking a toad, but the information could be worth it. Using the dagger, he sliced away part of her filter, dipped the rag in the water, and dabbed the shoulder wound. "I might be crazy to help you, but go ahead and talk. I'll see what I can do with this cut."

"Healing is in your heart, not just your hands." Her smile seemed almost genuine. "It is who you are."

"Fine. Whatever." After wiping away ashen grime, he massaged the wound with a bare fingertip. "Just tell me what you know."

"First ..." She winced at the pressure. "First, you must understand that the enemy we're dealing with is as old as the Earth itself. His schemes run far deeper than you can imagine, and his goals are not what you might expect."

Using the rag again, he swabbed the wound. Although the pressure raised some blood, the cut appeared to be sealing. "Well, I thought maybe his goals were falling apart. At least it looked like Lauren was protected from the lava in time, and the dragons were winning the battle."

11

Semiramis half closed an eye. "Did you really think winning that pathetic battle was the goal? Was Arramos really concerned about keeping Bonnie in prison? Oh, yes, Satan was curious about her genetics, so he arranged laboratory experiments to investigate, though he likely understood more about her components than any mortal could ever discover." She laughed. "You must admit that is a humorous proposition."

Matt stopped the massage. "Get to the point. I'm not in a laughing mood."

"Very well." While Matt continued sealing the cut, Semiramis spread her arm toward the volcano. "Take in the lovely scenery while I explain."

"And skip the theatrics, too."

Semiramis crossed her arms and smirked. "Well, well. Testy, aren't we?"

He jabbed a finger at her. "Just can it! I'm not a stupid kid who can't recognize manipulation. My sister used to …" He bit his lip. That was revealing too much.

"Ah!" Semiramis nodded slowly. "I understand now. A man who has been stabbed with a blade of treachery is the quickest to recognize its glimmer, especially when it is wielded by a woman. I will remember this sensitivity and avoid rubbing salt in the wound."

Matt looked away, grumbling, "You sound like the villain in a bad novel I read last week."

"You're a reader? I thought you were a fighter, the macho type who reads only the sports page."

Matt forced himself to stay calm. Too many of his barracks mates were exactly as she described, giving everyone in his company a bad reputation. No sense arguing about it now, though. "You'd be surprised."

"I'll take your word for it and move along." Semiramis cleared her throat. "Elam was worried that Tamiel was using your mother as bait to capture Lauren so he could harness her ability to find the purity ovulum. Then, when you saw that the prison was anticipating an attack from Second Eden, you decided that the entire plot was to kill Elam, Sapphira, and the dragons. Am I correct?"

"Well … yeah." He rubbed the edge of the cut, stopping a trickle of blood. "It seemed pretty obvious."

She stared straight into his eyes. "We checked on you, Matt. You have been trained in military combat strategy, and you excelled in war simulations. Tell me, why might an enemy intentionally draw as many of its opponents' troops and weapons to a battlefield?"

Looking past her, Matt imagined a similar scenario in the academy's war games. His team sent scouts in the opposite direction that their unit actually marched. The diversion worked perfectly, leaving the opposition's base open. "So the enemy could attack a place that's left unguarded."

"Exactly. Second Eden sent most of its finest warriors, dragons and humans alike, to do battle at a remote prison in northern Arizona. Of course, we had to set up an advanced weapons system in order to make it look like our reason to draw them there was to destroy them, but Arramos is not so foolish as to think the greatest dragons would be so easily defeated. He *is* a dragon. He knows their power. If we had defeated them, all the better, but I'm sure you wondered why our defenses were so ill prepared. For example, the laser battery was never fully manned. Did you seriously think that removing the control gloves could stop one of my son's weapons? Not only that, the guards who fought within the ring of fire were poorly trained, and the reinforcements were delayed."

"I thought the problems were because the blizzard—"

"The blizzard?" As dark flakes collected on her head, her voice grew animated. "Honestly, Matt, do you think that bad weather could foil the plans of Satan? Haven't you heard that he is the prince of the power of the air? The blizzard was a ruse. The weather conditions masked the poor preparation and incompetence of the prison personnel. If not for the blizzard, a wise general like Elam would have seen right through the façade. In fact, I think he was suspicious. I wouldn't be surprised at all if he and the dragons are even now hurrying away to Second Eden, assuming they have secured their victory."

Matt replayed the events in his mind. It did seem as if the dragons and their company routed their more modern opponents easily, maybe too easily. And if the reinforcements were so late in coming, maybe never even arriving at all, could Captain Boone have known all along? Might his friendliness have been part of the ploy? "Okay. I grant your point."

"So you must have concluded that Arramos's real target was Second Eden, a direct assault."

"Makes sense. But why? And how?"

She bent her brow, surveying the devastation again. "This I don't know. Arramos knows I hate him, so he never divulged his ultimate plan or motivation. I suspected the diversion, but, of course, I couldn't tell Elam."

"You played along so you could get Lauren."

Semiramis replied in a lilting singsong. "'Tis true. I admit to coveting Lauren's gift."

Matt growled. "I should have left you to boil."

"And then you would be lost here." Semiramis patted his cheek. "Oh, Matt, you are such a heroic young man. You did the right thing, and you need not worry about your sister. Although I care nothing for Elam or the dragons, I will protect Lauren to the death. She is essential for my plan to restore myself and my son. Just trust me."

Matt looked her in the eye. With auburn hair and angular features, she appeared to be an older version of Darcy. "I'd just as soon trust a drunken Nazi."

"And you complain about my theatrics." Semiramis let out a humming laugh. "It's a good thing you're stuck with me. It's the only way you'll learn to trust me."

"Stuck with you? Why?"

"Because we're here." She extended a hand toward the volcano. "We are in Second Eden."

Matt let his gaze shift from the smoking mountain to the burning stacks of debris in the deforested landscape. "I got the impression Second Eden was like a paradise. This place is … well … a disaster zone."

"It looks very little like it did before, but this is why I am sure of where we are." She intertwined her fingers. "I am completely solid. On Earth I was immaterial until a portal to Second Eden opened, and now that they are all likely closed again, I am still solid, proving that we stand in Second Eden, such as it is." She nodded toward the volcano. "That is Mount Elijah. Although it has blown off its cone, I recognize the shape of its slopes. Elam imprisoned me in this region for more than fifteen years, so I know it well. I felt many tremors during the latter part of my captivity, giving me reason to believe that Mount Elijah would soon awaken from its dormancy. There is a superstition regarding what causes it to erupt. I shudder to think that someone might have fallen in."

"It erupts if someone falls in?"

"As I said, it's a superstition, but the image is chilling all the same."

Matt shivered in spite of the rising heat. During the battle, many guards were swept into the crater, but that couldn't really trigger an eruption. "So you want revenge against Elam for imprisoning you. That's why you allied yourself with Arramos."

"My disdain for Elam doesn't compare with my hatred for Arramos. The self-important serpent brutally tortured my son and permanently maimed him, and I will do anything to kill that beast. That's why I long to be restored. In my present state, I have little power, but if I were to become what I once was, I could do battle with him." Looking again at the volcano, she let her shoulders sag. "I thought I knew what he was up to, but his plans were more diabolical than I realized. He didn't mean to conquer Second Eden with Earth's military; he meant to destroy it."

15

Matt blinked at the falling ash. "So, if Arramos is powerful enough to make a blizzard, why did he have to draw Elam and the dragons to the prison? If he made this volcano explode, why didn't he do it while everyone was in Second Eden and kill them all in one stroke?"

"You ask good questions, and I have already pondered them myself. Although Arramos has great power in your world, he has little to no influence in Second Eden. My guess is that he used someone here to gain access to the volcano, and he or she could not get that access until the warriors were gone."

Matt nodded. An inside job. But who among the Second Edeners would be that treacherous? And who could cause a volcano to explode? If Semiramis had been in Second Eden, she would have been the obvious choice, but she was on Earth the whole time.

His muscle aches eased, and the sting from the cut in his throat lessened, though it throbbed enough to bring fresh reminders of this witch's malevolence. Using her to figure out what was going on would be nauseating, but there seemed to be no choice. Maybe playing along would cause her to spill more information, though trying to beat her at her own game could be risky.

Semiramis touched the gash on her shoulder. "I feel much better. Your healing powers are remarkable."

"That's good. … I suppose."

She slid her hand into his. Her touch seemed electric, but he forced himself not to jerk away. "Matt, we need to work together. Will you decide to trust me?"

"Well …" Pretending to be her friend would be like holding hands with a demoness, but it might be worth it. He returned the grasp, refusing to cringe. "I guess we won't survive any other way, will we?"

16

Her smile thinned into a barely visible line. "I see that your training included pragmatism. We do what we must to survive. And don't worry about my desire to find Lauren. As I said, it's in my best interests to protect her."

"At this point, I don't have much choice."

"Well, let me provide you with a piece of information that might make it an easier choice." She compressed his hand. "I assume you know about Tamiel."

"I do. What about him?"

"He is Arramos's number one henchman. Because of his alliance with the devil, Tamiel is powerful, cruel, and murderous. Yet, he has one weakness, and I will tell you about it to enhance your trust in me."

"So I can use the weakness against him?"

"No, Matt, not at all. I am telling you so that you will be sure to *prevent* that weakness from being exploited."

Squinting, Matt shook his head. "Now you're not making any sense."

"Am I not?" Semiramis released his hand and grasped his chin. Her expression suddenly shifted to a serious aspect. "Matt Bannister, hear me now. The real reason I am telling you this is because I want Lauren kept alive. Since my motivations are selfish, maybe you will believe me. If Lauren touches Tamiel with skin-to-skin contact, he and she will both die." She let go of his chin. "That is his only weakness, and they both know about it."

Matt studied Semiramis's eyes. She definitely seemed sincere, and the selfish motivation agreed with known facts. Yet, why hadn't Lauren mentioned Tamiel's weakness?

"Okay. Telling me that does help." He began marching in place in the water. With the heat scalding his skin, they had to get moving. "What do we do now?"

Semiramis turned her head slowly, scanning the lava field. "We have to find shelter where we can talk safely. Another shift in the wind, and we'll be dead. We're lucky to be alive as it is."

"Where do you propose that we go?"

She pointed toward the volcano. "The Valley of Shadows lies well to the left of the mountain. It is encircled by highlands, which should have protected it from lava and flying rocks and perhaps even the poisonous fumes. If this lake is merely an expansion of the river that once flowed into that valley, we could follow the current downstream and find safety. Even if the volcano's fumes are there, the valley has Keelvar leaves, which provide a natural filter."

Matt fixed his gaze on her and tried to mimic her sincere expression. It seemed that they hoped to deceive each other, and they both saw through the veils. It would be almost impossible to out-con this con woman, especially while trusting her guidance. Yet, enemy combatants could work together for a while to save themselves, even if they planned to kill each other later.

He nodded. "Lead the way."

"Very well." She picked up his shirt from her shoulder. "And thank you for this. You could have suffocated me with it."

Several sarcastic replies shot through Matt's mind, but he let them fade. With another nod, he said, "I hope I made the right choice."

Smiling, she walked parallel to the shore in knee-deep water. "You won't regret this, Matt. Your trust, as fragile as it is, in spite of all that I have done to you, proves your character as a noble warrior who would never hold a grudge against a defeated enemy, especially when we have a common enemy, the enemy of all souls, the devil himself."

As Matt walked next to her in the hot water, he pushed aside logs along the way. Her boot-licking praise seemed calculated to drip like acid, like a mocking parrot daring him to call her bluff. Still, he couldn't stand around and wait for a deadly cloud to finish him off. Finding this sheltered valley was probably his only option.

Soon, the shoreline bent to the right. The lake narrowed into a wide river, and a logjam between two piles of boulders blocked the flow. Semiramis stopped at the jam. Matt joined her, and both stood in thigh-deep water, hotter than before. On the other side of the jam, a stream of lava trickled down the channel where water once ran, an extension of a wider lava flow on higher ground that originated at the volcano.

"A dead end?" Matt asked.

"Maybe." Semiramis looked at the steaming ground. "Most of the lava went south and west. We were heading east, and now we're turning southward. The river used to flow through this channel, and it spilled into the valley. But the ground is too hot to walk on. We'll have to find another way."

"How far is the valley from here?"

"On foot? An hour, maybe."

Matt smacked his lips. More bitterness. The fumes were returning. "We might be dead in an hour."

"Do you have a suggestion?"

Matt nudged a log with his foot. "Let's clear the jam and follow the river. We could even ride a log and get there faster."

Semiramis shook her head. "Dangerous. Very dangerous."

"No more dangerous than standing out here."

She set the shirt over her mouth. "Agreed. It's getting worse."

Matt handed Semiramis his jacket, climbed over the pile, and looked for a key log, one that would loosen the rest if removed. He walked partway down the opposite side and, balancing near the superheated riverbed, pushed his shoulder against a likely candidate.

19

As the log shifted, the entire pile vibrated. Water spilled through widening gaps and into the channel. With a loud sizzle, steam shot up from the contact points—water striking lava, creating an instant boil.

Something metallic glimmered in one of the gaps. Matt reached in and pulled out a spyglass, the kind that expands and collapses like an accordion. He climbed over the pile to the lake side and showed it to Semiramis. "No rust. Someone dropped it recently."

"I recognize this." She rubbed a finger along an etching on one side. "This is Hebrew. It says, 'Enoch.'"

"Enoch?" He stared at the odd lettering. "Do you know someone named Enoch?"

"I do, but this was passed down from him to someone else, likely a victim of Mount Elijah."

"Maybe the person who made it erupt? Arramos's conspirator?"

"Not likely. The owner of this spyglass has no such power." She looked out over the lake. "I wonder if she survived."

Matt coughed. The choking fumes were getting thicker by the second. "Well, *we* won't survive if I don't get these logs unjammed."

Semiramis took the spyglass. "Be careful."

"Just find a log cool enough to ride on and get ready." He climbed over the pile again and studied the key log, still jammed tightly. Could he get it out and escape the rush? Maybe. There was only one way to find out.

He grabbed the log and gave it another hard shove. The pile trembled. A new fountain of water sprang from a gap, then another. More sizzling erupted in the channel, and fresh steam rocketed into the sky. Several logs moved, and the fountains expanded into torrents.

Matt scrambled up the logs, but he slipped on the wet, shifting debris. The pile swelled and groaned. More water spewed. The dam was about to burst.

He leaped and reached for a protruding log, but it swung away. Something grabbed his wrist and pulled. His entire body flew up and over the top of the pile.

"Hang on!" Semiramis shouted.

Matt found himself straddling a log with Semiramis's arms embracing his waist from behind. The dam burst wide open. Water cascaded into the channel. Like an arrow shot from a bow, Matt and Semiramis catapulted into the river's wild flow. He grabbed the log with both hands and held his breath. Semiramis's strong arms nearly crushed his ribs. As they rushed downstream, white vapor shot through huge bubbles on the river's surface, as if a hundred mouths opened at the same time to belch steam.

The log bounced and rocked. Hot water sloshed and splashed over their bodies, but at least the steamy ride cleared the air. They could breathe easily again.

After a few minutes, the bounces settled, and the water cooled, though vapor continued to rise from the surface, creating thick fog. When Semiramis's grip relaxed, Matt looked back. She was now wearing his jacket, and the end of the spyglass protruded from a pocket.

He relaxed his muscles. "Thanks for saving me."

"My pleasure, Matt." She laid her head on his back. "Perhaps you will soon decide to trust me."

Matt cringed. This manipulator knew her craft. He couldn't escape from her embrace, and she knew it.

"Drink water while you can," she said as she slid the spyglass into his lap. "It's cool enough to refresh your body. We don't know when we'll have another opportunity to hydrate."

21

"Good point." After pushing one end of the spyglass into his pocket, Matt dipped a cupped hand into the flow and drank, repeating the process several times. Semiramis did the same, glancing at him now and then with a smile. Again, everything seemed calculated, vicious. The look was probably meant to mock rather than to gain favor.

Soon, the current accelerated. Soupy fog flew past their faces, keeping their skin moist and preventing a view beyond the next few yards.

A flapping sound penetrated the veil of mist, like someone shaking a blanket.

"A dragon," Semiramis said.

"A dragon? How can you tell?"

"Trust me. I have heard enough dragon wings to know." She swiveled her head this way and that, as if following the flight of an erratic fly. "It might be Arramos."

"Do you think he saw us?"

"I doubt it, but we should take cover. Be ready to jump to the side."

Matt tried to stare through the mist to find a place to leap, but it was no use. The cloud was just too thick. "Isn't the ground still too hot to walk on?"

"Maybe, but this river dives into the valley in a treacherous plunge. I'm not sure which danger is greater."

Matt looked straight ahead, but the fog blocked that direction as well. "How far of a drop is it?"

"Far enough to worry about. I don't remember how deep it is where the water falls. If it is deep enough, we might survive."

Matt let his fingers drag in the water. "Most of the logs went ahead of us, and some are still behind us. We might get sandwiched between them and—"

Their log dropped from underneath their legs. They flew into open air, then plunged through the fog. Still hanging on to Matt, Semiramis screamed. Matt flailed his arms, trying to shift into a feet-first entry.

The flapping sound returned. Something sharp dug into Matt's shoulders and yanked upward. Pain ripped down his spine, and Semiramis's weight pulling on his back added to the torture.

He looked up. A huge body hovered overhead, and the tips of dragon wings came into view at each side in a rhythmic beat.

He gulped. *Arramos!*

23

THE JOURNEY BEGINS

Bonnie stepped through a shimmering blue curtain and into a small room with floor-standing shelves filled with old books. Between the shelves, colorful murals decorated an alabaster background, depicting fruited vines draped over a long picket fence.

At the back of the room, a lantern sat on a rectangular hardwood table. Two benches, one on each of the longer sides, made it look like an informal dining table. The lantern burned without a flicker, though the hint of spent oil proved it to be a real flame instead of a heavenly light. In this anteroom to Heaven's altar, a blend of temporal and eternal, it could have been either one.

Padding lightly on her Nikes, she walked across a floor of old oak, expecting creaks, but it didn't make a sound. When she reached the table, she pulled the cuffs of her sweatshirt and straightened her sleeves, then smoothed out the wrinkles in her jeans. With a quick brush of her fingers, she combed through her

frazzled hair. The flight from her prison to the Bridgelands had been rough and windy. It would be polite to freshen up for the dear old prophet.

She lifted a hefty book from the tabletop and tried to read the title, but the letters on the cover were oddly shaped and indecipherable. The pages within appeared to be made of parchment, slightly yellowed and wrinkled. It raised memories of many other books, like Dad Bannister's *Fama Regis* as well as Abaddon's resurrection journal.

She laid the book down, drew in her wings, and sat on the closer bench. On the back wall, between two tall shelves, a door with a metal lift-latch stood closed. No sounds emanated from the other side. The room, perhaps just big enough for a small dragon to squeeze into, was perfectly quiet.

She swiveled and looked through the sheer curtain she had passed through. Although tinted blue, the scene on the other side was clear. Tamiel stood on a grassy meadow, his wings spread, his hands behind his back, and his foot tapping. The curtains narrowed inch by inch until they disappeared. Another mural took their place, a painting of the fence's open gate and a narrow path leading to it from the front and rear.

Bonnie blew a sigh. Being out of Tamiel's sight was such a relief! Even the pain from the candlestone embedded in her body had stopped. Still, it could come roaring back at any moment. Time would tell.

She ran a finger along the table. Filled with knots and shallow ruts, it appeared to have been made from roughly cut pine, perhaps many years ago. Who had sat here over the centuries? Prophets? Angels? Jesus himself?

The rear door's latch lifted. Enoch entered and slid onto the bench opposite Bonnie, leaving the door open to a view of rows of people kneeling at altars. The sounds of whispered chatter and song wafted in along with a sweet aroma—spring flowers on a dew-kissed morning. She inhaled deeply. How wonderful! The sensations of Heaven had no equal on Earth. Nothing even compared.

With his shoulders drooping, Enoch laid his forearms on the table and stared straight at her. A two-day white stubble covered his chin and cheeks, complementing his wispy mustache and proving that he was still a living human, not a permanent resident of Heaven. "Greetings, precious one."

Bonnie smiled. "Greetings, good prophet. You seem down."

"Oh, don't mind the sagging features of a thousands-of-years-old man. I am merely tired."

She covered his folded hands with her own and looked into his eyes. "It has been a long journey, hasn't it?"

"Indeed, but listening to the sounds of praying saints always gives me energy to continue." He nodded toward the open door. "If only more people could get a glimpse of Heaven, maybe they wouldn't scorn the idea of God as they do."

"I'm not so sure, good prophet." She wrinkled her nose. Should she go on? Her years in prison enduring torture proved time and again that those who scorn the truth would continue to scorn even if they walked next to those prayer benches for days on end. She sighed and added, "People choose blindness even in the brightest lights. I have seen it happen too many times."

"I suppose you're right." Enoch withdrew one hand and patted hers. "Speaking of journeys, from what I have seen and been told, it seems that your journey has just begun."

"I'm getting that impression, but maybe you could give me more information." Bonnie spread out her wings, hoping to block Tamiel's view just in case he could still see inside. "Tamiel hasn't

27

told me much. He just said that I would start in Paradise and slowly descend into Perdition."

"I heard every word." Enoch pursed his lips and spoke in a singsong cadence. "Every second of suffering will help me corrupt this world, and Elohim will have no choice but to administer justice, this time with a judgment far worse than a flood."

Bonnie cringed at Enoch's impersonation, obviously intended to mock the brutal demon. "That's exactly what Tamiel said. Were you watching from your viewing room?"

Enoch chuckled. "I have been watching you and many of your friends almost constantly for a number of years."

A red-haired young woman poked her head through the doorway while holding onto the frame. "Hi, Bonnie!"

"Karen?" Tears flooded Bonnie's eyes. "It is you, isn't it?"

Karen nodded briskly, her smile broad and tight. "I can't come in, but an angel told me you were here. I just wanted to say hi and I love you."

Bonnie shot to her feet, but Enoch grasped her wrist. "Reunion times will come, dear, and embraces will abound. Be at peace."

"I love you, too." Bonnie bit her lip. What else was there to say?

"Bye for now." Karen slipped away, leaving only the sounds of prayer and singing in her wake.

Bonnie settled back to her seat. If only she could follow Karen and live in peaceful bliss for all eternity. But no. That would have to wait. There was too much to do.

She looked again at Enoch. "Well, if you've been watching me during the past fifteen years, it must have been boring. I haven't done much of anything, and I haven't been able to get news all that time. And now that I'm out of prison ..." She glanced back toward Tamiel. "Sort of out of prison … I don't know where Billy is or my children or my mother. I don't know who's alive or dead."

"Billy and Lauren are looking for you and are quite safe, but I have not seen Matt or Irene lately." Enoch ran a finger along the spine of the book. "I can provide an update about others, especially concerning who has died. Some people have passed away whom you know quite well."

Bonnie swallowed. "Okay. I'm ready."

"Your good friend Sir Patrick is now with us in Heaven. He died at the ripe old age of … well, many more than one thousand years. Because of the persecution inflicted by the Enforcers, Patrick's wife, Ruth, went into hiding with their son, and no one has heard from them since. As I remember, he should be about Matt and Lauren's age."

"Do you know where they are?"

"If you mean Patrick …" He gestured with his head toward the door. "I saw him in there a few moments ago."

Bonnie peeked that way. If Patrick were to make an appearance, that would be amazing. "I really meant Ruth and her son."

Enoch shook his head. "It is difficult to gain access when I have no idea where to begin looking. I do, however, have news about Shiloh and her children. They were on Second Eden, but just before the attack on the prison facility, Gabriel moved them to an Earth hiding place, telling only Elam, and he is not one to give away secrets."

"I'll be sure to keep the secret, too." Bonnie took in a breath. "Has anyone else died?"

"Let's see …" Enoch stroked his chin. "Derrick, the blind lad who helped you dive into the candlestone."

Bonnie's heart thumped. "Not Derrick! When? How?"

29

"After you last saw him in the underground laboratory, he went to live with a relative in Florida where he became interested in overseas missions. He joined a team in Indonesia shortly after you and Billy married. He hoped to help blind children learn Braille. While he was there, terrorists slaughtered the entire team and left only one witness alive, an Indonesian who told of Derrick's fearlessness as he tried to protect one of the children. His heart for the little ones was big, indeed."

Bonnie lowered her head. "Yes ... it was." She ventured another peek at the door. Derrick might be close by as well.

After a moment of silence, Enoch grasped her hand. "Let's talk about life instead of death."

"Yes." Bonnie brushed a tear away. "Let's do that."

"Well, Dikaios is in the Bridgelands, living at peace while he awaits his master's call to ride to Earth. He brought Ember with him, and they are now mates."

"I was wondering about the Bridgelands. I didn't want to ask Tamiel about it, but I thought that place collapsed when the worlds merged."

"It did collapse." Enoch waved a hand. "Restoring a world is a trifling matter to the Almighty."

"I should have known." Bonnie gave him a prodding nod. "Please go on."

"Well, let's see. Charles Hamilton's daughter Elizabeth is in London and is doing splendidly. She gave birth to a daughter about the time you went to prison, so Jennifer would be fifteen years old now."

Bonnie raised her brow. "Jennifer?"

"Yes. Does that name trouble you?"

"Old memories." She shook her head. "It's nothing."

"Well, as you might expect, Jennifer is quite intelligent. Not an Ashley-type super genius, of course, but she is already attending

Oxford." Enoch raised a finger. "Speaking of Ashley, her adoptive sisters, Monique and company, are all doing well, as is Walter's sister, Shelly."

"That's wonderful to hear." A hint of pain from the candlestone pricked Bonnie's heart. She shifted her body to alleviate pressure. "After being locked up for so long, hearing news, whether good or bad, is like feeling a fresh breeze, but I suppose we should turn to the pressing topics—Tamiel and what he wants me to do."

"Indeed, but it is a foul wind rather than a fresh breeze." Enoch released Bonnie's hand. "Shall I remind you of Tamiel's reason for bringing you here?"

"No, I'm trying to get his voice out of my mind."

"I don't blame you, but in order to understand why I agreed to this meeting, you must remember Tamiel's purpose. You see, he knows I could call upon angels to rescue you from him, so he is taking a risk in bringing you to me. Yet, he also needs me to encourage you to acquiesce and go on this journey without hesitation, so he is willing to take that risk."

Bonnie furrowed her brow. "Are you saying I should submit to him?"

"Not to him, but rather to the journey. What you can accomplish is too crucial to prevent."

"What can I accomplish?"

Enoch tapped a finger on the table for each point. "Rescuing the lost. Healing the wounded. Saving your loved ones from destruction. Probably more."

"Why would Tamiel want me to do those things?"

"Tamiel doesn't care about the good you will do as long as you suffer along the way."

Bonnie laid a hand on her chest. "But when I suffer, my song suffers, and the world will rot from within."

31

"This is true, and you have the freedom to refuse. Just say the word. The candlestone will be removed, and you will go free, though Tamiel will also be free, and he will continue to wreak havoc on Earth. Such was our agreement with him before he arrived with you."

"Then I really do have a choice."

"You do, but you need all available information before you make that choice." Enoch fanned the pages of his book before propping it open near the back. "I suppose you were wondering why this is here."

She gazed at the weathered paper's crinkled edges. "It did cross my mind."

"It's to help you remember something." He rotated the book toward her. "Do you recognize this kind of writing?"

Bonnie peered at the page. Oddly shaped characters had been scattered haphazardly across the parchment from edge to edge, tiny drawings of a long-legged bird, a coiled snake, a palm tree, and others.

She touched the bird. A vibration made her jerk back. Wings fluttered, and a miniature heron extended a long leg and stepped up on the page, then morphed into a tall, lanky man pacing with a smoking pipe in his mouth.

"Abaddon's writing," Bonnie said, "like what I saw in his res-urrection book."

"Correct. This is a novel from Abaddon's library. I heard he keeps his resurrection book on a table in the main chamber."

"He does." Bonnie drew a mental image of that mysterious place with its ornate table, event-predicting hourglass, and eggs on wooden stands. "Why are you reminding me of that place?"

"To give you an idea of what you might be doing should you choose to go on this journey. There is a buzz in Heaven about using Abaddon's Lair as a refuge of some sort. You know Abaddon's ways, and you were able to conquer him with wisdom and courage. So perhaps you could lead refugees there, or perhaps the leader might be someone you could equip to face Abaddon. Very few in this world are as wise as you are."

She fingered the cover's binding, worn and frayed. "I could do that, but what does this have to do with my choice?"

"It's just an example of how you might help people in a way that no one else can."

"But which is worse?" She let her tone grow animated. "If I choose to avoid the journey, lives might be lost. If I go on the journey and my song suffers as a result, maybe more lives will be lost because of worldwide corruption. Why should I contribute to a plan that will make the world even worse than it already is?"

"The plan will not *make* anyone worse," Enoch said. "No one in the world will submit to corruption except by choice. If your song is warped or taken away, people will have lost a helpful influence, but to succumb to temptation would still be their decision. On the other hand, those you would meet on your journey are true victims who can benefit greatly from your help." He stroked his chin. "Well, perhaps it would be better to show you what I mean. The proverb is true that a picture is worth a thousand words."

"I should see the suffering before I decide."

Enoch nodded. "A harbinger of the future might provide a sobering influence on the present."

"But I can't see the future. That's impossible."

"True, but you can see into the present, and that could make all the difference."

She blinked at him. "How?"

"When you became an Oracle of Fire, you gained a new ability. Although you are not the variety who sprouted from plants, and you are not able to produce fire, you do possess an important characteristic. Oracles are able to see things that normal people cannot, and you do so while you dream."

Bonnie nodded. "I saw Joran and Selah, but that was the past, not the present."

Enoch closed the book, making the pipe-smoking man disappear. As its wrinkled pages pressed together, it seemed to exhale. "You are a dream oracle, so you can see both. Your daughter is one as well."

Bonnie touched the title on the book's cover. Like smoke rising from a fire, dark lettering lifted off the page, spelling out *Sherlock Holmes.*

"If I became a dream oracle after I was born, how could I have passed it on to Lauren? It's not genetic, is it?"

"Acquired traits are not normally passed down to future generations, but this quality became a part of you. The fire you endured from Abaddon altered your genetics. When the song was infused in your body, you became a bard, a prophetic singer. So your children are blessed with special gifts other children of anthrozils never possessed. Still, Lauren won't be able to control hers until she is taught."

She tapped her chest. "How do I control mine? I didn't choose to dream about Joran and Selah."

"Quite true. Dreams that come during sleep are unpredictable. For you, some night dreams will reflect reality, and some will not, so you cannot always rely on them." He touched her hand. "Yet, you can rely on those that come while you are awake, while you are resting, at peace, and focusing on the word of God. If what you see agrees with that word, since you are a dream oracle, you can be confident in the vision."

She looked at his wrinkled finger, still touching her hand. "I wasn't at peace when I dreamed about Joran and Selah."

"Those were sleep dreams. Again, such dreams are unpredictable. They might or might not provide insight into reality." Enoch drew his hand away and again fingered the book's spine. "Joran and Selah have served a great purpose and will decrease, but I suspect that God still has an important duty for them to perform. I don't think he would have let them suffer for so long just to spin a protective sound barrier."

"I think I understand." Bonnie gazed at Enoch's shadow, cast on the table by the lantern. "So now if I am to make an informed decision, I should try to dream while awake, try to see what's happening to my loved ones."

"If you dare. I expect that the bait will be difficult to refuse."

"Choosing ignorance is the coward's way." She focused on the lantern and let her mind relax. Pain from the injected candlestone flared, but the weakness it caused helped every muscle unwind. All the years in prison had provided a lesson in how to rest in spite of pain and turmoil. If not for that, survival would have been impossible.

Soon, ribbons of light flowed from the lantern. After swirling for a moment, they coalesced in a full-color hologram that floated above the flame. In the image, Matt, now the size of a soldier action figure, flew away from a volcano and plunged into a lake. As he swam to the surface, lines of pain dug into his forehead. Even the bubbles pouring from his nose and mouth looked real.

Bonnie rolled her fingers into a fist. *Come on, Matt! You can make it!*

Finally, he broke the surface. During the next few minutes, he trudged to shore in a devastated land, rode on a log with Semiramis, and hurtled over a waterfall, the series of events flashing by more quickly than real time. Just as a dragon's claws knifed into his shoulders, the colors mixed together and retreated into the lantern.

Bonnie blinked at the flame. "What happened? Why won't it show more?"

"I assume you saw a vision."

She looked up at Enoch. "You didn't?"

He shook his head. "You are the dream oracle, not I."

"Matt was in trouble, but it all went by so fast, it couldn't have been the present, and the vision stopped before I could see what happened to him."

"What you witnessed was probably a series of past events that continued to the exact present moment, and that is when the vision stopped. Of course, it could have slowed down to show the new present events as they unfolded, so the truncation might be something of a lure to draw you to help your son." Enoch rubbed the book's cover. He seemed nervous, unsure if his counsel was right or wrong. "It won't be the first time God has used a dream to call for someone's help."

She slid the lantern closer and gazed at its undulating flame. "Let me get this straight. These visions come only from God, right?"

"That is my understanding."

She refocused on him. "Then God is the one who didn't want me to see past the end of the vision."

"I assume so. Why do you ask?"

"It means that God is allowing the bait to work. He wants me to go on the journey."

"I expected as much, but I had to allow you to come to that conclusion on your own. A coerced sacrifice has no value." Enoch drummed his fingers on the book, a sad expression on his withered face. "At least this revelation proves an important fact. The forces of evil hold sway for a season, and they will influence many. Perhaps even your loved ones will try to stop you from continuing in

36

this quest, but God's ultimate purpose is never thwarted. I will try to help you if I can, though I think my hands will be tied."

"I understand." She firmed her lips. "It seems that my hands are also tied, but I've gotten used to it."

Enoch pushed Bonnie's sleeve up past her elbow, revealing needle marks. Some were red and raw from the recent prison medical experiments, while others had faded to tiny dots, remnants of her father's experiments from twenty years earlier. "All bonds are temporary for those who cherish freedom," he said. "Love has set us all free, but ultimate liberty often takes time to realize."

Bonnie stared at the old prophet. It would be wonderful to sit and talk with him for hours, but Matt couldn't wait. Still, there was one more item to learn. Someone else needed help. "Speaking of bonds, can you tell me what happened to Thomas and Mariel? I heard that Kaylee and Dallas found them, and back when my children were born, you said that Billy and I were supposed to—"

37

"I said, 'Be sure that your offspring forge friendships with the others, especially Listener, Thomas, and Mariel. It is clear that their paths, should they choose the way of faith and righteousness, will lead them toward many adventures.'"

"Right, but we never got to see Thomas and Mariel. They went into hiding when the Enforcers started their crusades, and no one heard from them again."

"Nor have I. Their disappearance is a mystery. I have not been able to find either one in my chamber's viewer."

Bonnie fingered a depression within a knot in the wood. "I think Tamiel has them now, but I don't know what he's planning to do."

"Then I assume you must free them from their bonds. If Tamiel is involved, you can be sure that they will be part of the bait that lures you to sacrifice."

"So be it." She leaned over the table and kissed Enoch's forehead. "I bid you farewell, good prophet. Maybe the next time I see you I'll be able to stay in Heaven."

His features sagged further. "And maybe someday I will be able to enter fully."

"Enter fully?"

He waved a hand. "Never mind. You should get going."

"Yes, I have to help Matt."

"Mrs. Bannister!"

Bonnie turned toward the voice. A tall man with wild white hair took the same pose Karen had, his smile wide and his eyes bright.

"Professor!"

"I'm here, too, Bonnie." Another white-haired head appeared, peeking around the professor's body, a young woman with bright blue eyes.

"Acacia!"

Acacia stepped to the center of the doorway, revealing a silky white dress that flowed from her neck to her knees, radiant and roomy. "I am dedicating my time at the prayer altar to your journey."

"And I am praying for William, though I am certain your name will creep into my prayers from time to time." The professor pushed his hand through his hair. It morphed to brown, and his wrinkles smoothed over. "This is my normal appearance here. I thought you might like to see it so you'll recognize me when you arrive."

Bonnie stared. The professor looked no older than twenty-five, and his eyes shone as clearly as did Acacia's.

Chuckling, Enoch rose and reached for the door. "I think we've had enough of this." As he began closing it, Acacia and the professor waved.

"I love you," they said in unison.

When the door clicked shut, Bonnie brushed tears from her cheeks with her sleeve. "I … I guess I'd better hurry." She stepped over the bench and backed toward the front entry. "What do I have to do to leave?"

Enoch nodded toward the wall. "Just walk through the mural. The gate is open."

Bonnie turned and strode right through the gate. A bright light flashed, but it quickly dispersed. She now stood in the Bridgelands meadow next to Tamiel. With short, curly black hair, rail-thin frame, and androgynous face, he looked like a badly drawn cartoon. Yet, there was nothing funny about this demonic spirit.

He flapped his wings slowly. "Shall I assume that you are ready to embark on your journey?"

She nodded but said nothing. Talking to this foul beast never accomplished anything beneficial. Besides, the embedded candlestone continued flaring, bringing new pain and weakness.

"Seeing that you don't want to have a conversation …" He gestured toward her wings. "Can I trust you to fly with me? My guess is that your talk with Enoch has convinced you to go without coercion."

Lowering her head, Bonnie stared at the ground and nodded.

"Excellent." He stepped in front of her and spread out his wings. "We will now go to your next destination. Stay close. I expect to fly through an area of low visibility."

When he lifted into the air, Bonnie beat her wings and followed. Flying at about fifty feet aboveground, they zoomed across the meadow, past a series of hills and dales, and over a deep chasm. "I have been told of Matt's trials," Tamiel called as he closed in on a cloud bank. "He is a brave young man, but he is involved in a

39

crisis that is over his head. He will need your help. You are far more experienced in dealing with unearthly dangers."

Bonnie fumed. Tamiel's words were as convincing as a politician's promises. He caused the problem and now feigned concern. Whom did he think he was fooling?

They pierced the clouds and continued flying, both silent. After a few minutes, they descended over a lake and landed on a pebbly beach near its edge. "Stay here," Tamiel said as he drew in his wings. "I will return in a moment."

Bonnie folded in her own wings. "Where are you going?"

"Ah! You can speak!" He pointed away from the lake. "The southern wall of Heaven's great city. I need permission from a certain angel to open a portal out in the midst of this lake."

"Can you …" She shook her head. "Never mind."

"You want me to ask about the condition of a loved one." Tamiel's face took on a concerned aspect. "Which one?"

"As if you didn't know. You probably caused his trouble."

"Caused Matt's trouble?" He shook his head. "No, Bonnie, not at all. I am merely using the circumstances. Although I will benefit greatly, I am but a knight in this game of chess. Soon you will learn who is behind this carefully orchestrated plot, a plan developed long before any of the pawns you know ever took a breath."

She crossed her arms over her chest. "Care to explain further?"

"My pleasure." His grotesque smile seemed calculated to produce nausea. It worked quite well. "At one time, you thought your former principal was the evil force behind the persecution of dragons. Yet later you discovered that Morgan controlled his puppet strings. This unmasking brought assurance that you had exposed the true devilish schemer, until, of course, you learned about Semiramis and Mardon and their plot to unite Earth and Hades. Finally, the truth had emerged. The assault by ancient warriors on

Heaven's gates had to be the ultimate reason behind all the cruel plans, but again you found out that this was but another step in a bigger plan."

He laughed. "What fool really thinks a human army could break down the barrier to Paradise? This was but a ploy to bring the remaining dragons to Second Eden, and it was comical watching all the effort put forth by your husband and his stalwart friends as they carried out exactly what we had hoped for. They became unwitting allies, pawns for our side, if you will. Such is the narrow vision that blind passion brings. It incites action without regard for wisdom. It makes a man move a boulder without asking why it is in his path."

"You can cut the insults. Just stick to the facts."

A scowl flashed across his face but quickly eased into a snobbish smirk. "That your allies are stupid is a crucial fact. We will continue using their mistakes for our benefit."

Bonnie kept her arms tightly crossed. "This is all Arramos's doing, isn't it? He planned everything."

"Of course. He used Devin, Morgan, Semiramis, and Mardon, and now he will use you to create chaos on the Earth. Only this time, his pawn will realize that she is a pawn for her own opposition, and every step along the way she will wonder what effects her sacrificial acts are having in her world."

Bonnie kept her face slack. Even this demon's words were designed to choke the song. She couldn't let his caustic bile singe her resolve. "You said you were going to ask permission to open a portal. I suggest you get on with it."

"Gladly." He offered another hideous smile, then spread his wings and lifted into the air.

As he flew low to the ground, Bonnie looked beyond him. A wall with three gates stood about fifty yards away. The middle gate,

41

shining and ivory white, swung open, and a brilliant glow poured out over the beach, as if inviting a lost wanderer to enter and walk on the street inside, a street of transparent gold, sparkling and reflective.

A winged man dressed in white met Tamiel at the gate. While the two conversed, Bonnie turned toward the lake. How could anyone bear to behold the splendor of that glorious city without rushing to its welcoming embrace? Oh, the joy a few hours in that radiant paradise had conceived! And the sounds of ecstatic chatter and dancing feet still echoed to this day. She took in a long breath and let it out slowly. Someday she would go back, but for now, she would have to be content with the journey ahead.

She gazed again at the lake. Mist hovered over the glassy surface, and Heaven's glow cast her winged shadow across the water. The shadow from one wing overlapped a rowboat that floated near the shore, tied to a stake embedded in a boulder.

Stinging pain pulsed in her chest. The tiny candlestone had migrated and lodged somewhere near her heart. Before she visited Enoch, the candlestone would deliver a jolt every few minutes, sometimes gentle, sometimes strong, but always enough to interrupt her heart's rhythm for several seconds. It was definitely on a rampage now.

Each heart flutter brought back a nightmarish memory, the day she blocked the energy field at the portal door, allowing Shiloh to escape from the sixth circle of Hades. That jolt caused a torturous fibrillation that eventually led to death, but the nightmare ended when she awoke in Heaven.

Tears welled in her eyes. The cost of the journey would be high, but there was no choice. Maybe Tamiel was right. Maybe corruption would come. Someone else would have to worry about that. She had to do what any good mother would do. She had to rescue her son.

CHAPTER

CORRUPTION

Gabriel sat atop a snow-covered hill, his body enclosed in his wings as he stared at the landscape—low, rolling hills and sporadic trees, some evergreen and some deciduous. At a dip between two hills, light radiated, the rising sun coloring a retreating cloud bank with streaks of purple and orange. The blizzard they had endured now assaulted regions far away, but it had ushered in a polar air mass—icy temperatures and bitter winds.

He pulled his phone from his pocket and texted Larry, firing through the keys with both thumbs. "Dawn has arrived. Portal still closed. Will update in two hours." Fortunately, everyone's phones had been altered to use a tooth-transmitter protocol that employed new encryption. Now that the prison-escape mission was over, the security change allowed them to remove the annoying chips from between their molars. The phones didn't buzz painfully, no one could trace their communications, and Adam even programmed speed dials for instant messages like "Emergency," "Going to silence," and "Can't talk, but listen in."

Gabriel rose to his feet and shook frost from his wings. Unfortunately, the four layers of clothing, including jeans and a hip-length coat, weren't quite enough to keep the frigid air out. Still, it was time to get going. With dawn breaking, Sapphira would want to try the portal again. If the military discovered their presence, they would be sitting ducks. They had to get to Second Eden as soon as possible.

Legossi slept at his side, her wings covering her head. The hilltop extended dozens of feet in all directions, big enough for several dragons and a convenient spot for a portal, though vulnerable to attack by air. Assigning one human and one dragon for lookout duty made sense. They could take turns sleeping. Since everyone had been through an exhausting ordeal, no one could stay awake for very long.

44

Gabriel stepped into a huge footprint in the snow—Yereq's. The wind hadn't yet concealed it. When they arrived earlier, they expected to find Yereq on guard at the portal, but a long trail of footprints proved that he had left. No one knew why, and contacting him proved fruitless.

Gabriel nudged Legossi's flank with his shoe. "Come on, sleepyhead. It's time to start a fire."

Her wing slid away from her face, revealing a pair of fiery eyes. "A sleepyhead, am I? I recall a certain winged human snoring so loudly the field mice had to wear earmuffs."

"That's just because it's so cold." Gabriel spread out his wings. "Last one to the portal is a flying reptile."

"But I *am* a flying reptile."

"Exactly." With a quick flurry, he flew down the slope to a stand of trees that bordered a meandering stream no wider than two running leaps. Thin ice ran along the stream's edges, not enough to obstruct the swift, shallow flow. The dragons had melted the snow in the area and dried most of the mud, providing a decent place to rest.

Elam and Sapphira knelt together next to a bare oak tree, their heads bowed. As they held hands, firelets ran along Sapphira's radiant face, then down her Second Eden soldier's uniform—green trousers and burnt orange tunic with an emblazoned dragon symbol over a long-sleeved red shirt. She wore a lacy coif over her white hair, but it seemed undisturbed by the fire. The flames crawled close to Elam's hand, terminating at her wrist. He, too, wore the soldier's uniform, though a thick coat hid all but the green trousers.

Gabriel stopped behind them. No need to interrupt. They knew the situation. Preparation in prayer was more important than haste.

About ten steps away, Makaidos and Thigocia slept under the stripped boughs of a larger oak. With their necks snaked together and their wings overlapped, if not for their differing colors, it would be impossible to tell where one dragon ended and the other began. Roxil slept within a wing's length, her respirations lifting and lowering her body in a steady rhythm. Without clothes or coat, it seemed that the dragons ought to be shivering, but their inner fires kept them warm.

A beating of wings sounded, Legossi flying overhead, apparently on patrol. Her vigilance rarely took a break.

Makaidos started at the noise. He and Thigocia untangled and rose to their haunches. Roxil lifted her head and snorted a puff of smoke, as if coughing to clear a bit of congestion.

After yawning and stretching his wings, Makaidos aimed his pulsing red eyes at Gabriel. "Any word from Second Eden?"

"Nothing." Gabriel gestured with his thumb. "If the portal's still at the top of the hill, no one's knocking on the door."

45

"I cannot understand," Roxil said as she shuffled closer. "Karrick is trustworthy, and he is now an expert at opening and closing that portal. Why would he close it unless something was terribly wrong?"

Elam walked their way, hand in hand with Sapphira. With her hair now uncovered, its whiteness shone in the rising sun, and her eyes glittered like the bluest of sapphires.

"We'll have to risk trying again to open it from this side," Elam said as he looked skyward. "Any sign of potential interference?"

Gabriel raised a pair of fingers. "I saw two airplanes and three choppers during the night, all far away. If the military picked up the portal opening yesterday, they're not showing any signs of doing anything about it."

"That's what worries me." Elam stooped, grabbed a stick, and began drawing in a patch of mud. "Our operation was too easy, much too easy."

"Easy?" Gabriel gave his wings a snapping whip. "Legossi and I got shot by guns. Roxil was nailed by a tank. Sir Barlow and Portia and Matt were all sucked into who-knows-where. We needed help from two kids from thousands of years ago to survive. And we were all nearly killed anyway. I wouldn't call that easy."

"I believe," Makaidos said, "that Elam is referring to the level of opposition and readiness we encountered, not to the amount of suffering we endured."

"Right, Makaidos. The presence of that laser battery proved that they knew we were coming." Elam began making a series of marks in the mud, as if counting. "They have jets. They have missiles. They have assault helicopters. They have special ops units. But what did they bring out? A few tanks and a ragtag group of ill-equipped prison guards." He snapped the stick in half. "It doesn't make sense. Even a blizzard shouldn't have kept special ops away."

Makaidos extended his neck and brought his head close to Elam. "You fear a diversion, do you not? An attack on Second Eden?"

Elam nodded. "How else do you explain Karrick's absence?"

"Maybe he sensed danger and closed the portal," Roxil said, "and now he is hesitant to open it from the Second Eden side."

Makaidos bobbed his head. "Your reasoning is sound. The only option is to try again. We were probably too injured and exhausted to break through last night. Now that we are rested, perhaps we will be able to crack the lock."

"If not …" Elam straightened. "We'll have to use a backdoor portal."

Sapphira took his hand again. "From the museum room? The one that leads up the throat of the volcano?"

"That's what I was thinking. Mount Elijah is dangerous, but someone might be able to fly through the heat quickly enough."

47

"You say someone …" Gabriel pointed at himself. "But you mean me. A dragon couldn't reach that portal. The door to get into the room is too small."

"Yes, I did mean you." Elam patted Gabriel's shoulder. "Are you up for it?"

"Flying into superheated air over an active volcano while knowing I could plunge into boiling lava at any second?" Grinning, Gabriel thumped his chest. "Bring it on!"

Elam smiled. "Thanks for the humor. We can use a little levity."

"Since I'm going to risk scalding my backside, do you mind answering a question that's been bugging me?"

"I'll do my best."

Gabriel waved a wing toward the others. "It's pretty obvious that you chose only nonnatives of Second Eden for this mission, but you really never said why. Valiant is the greatest of warriors, and Listener isn't far behind. I know you want them to guard the villages, but still …"

"I know what you mean." Elam sighed and began walking toward the portal hill. "Come with me, and I will try to explain."

"I'll summon Legossi." Sapphira kissed Elam's cheek. "I'll ride her to the hilltop and meet you there."

After Sapphira left, Elam and Gabriel continued a slow march toward the hill. "I have lived for thousands of years," Elam said as the ground transitioned from mud to snow-covered grass. "I have seen the most courageous, sacrificial people this world can produce, but I have also seen the most depraved, hideous monsters who have ever walked in human disguise."

Gabriel kicked through the snow. "I know what you mean. We both knew Sir Patrick, but we both had to endure Devin and Morgan."

"Exactly my point." Elam pushed a hand into his pocket. "People who are born and raised here are exposed to a wide spectrum of influences, for good or for evil. On Second Eden, most of the citizens have never experienced evil on a long-term basis. Flint raised a short-lived rebellion until Abraham banished him, and the armies from the past attacked, but their influence lasted only hours. These were huge, explosive events that were overt, easy to recognize as evil, so Second Edeners weren't affected. They have never faced the subtle, deceptive influences here on Earth, so I can't predict what the effect on them would be."

"What about their companions?" Gabriel asked. "Wouldn't they counter the evil influences?"

"I thought of that, but …" Elam looked up, his eyes following the flight of an eagle.

"But what?"

Elam shook his head. "If you don't mind, let's drop the subject. Since we needed warriors in both places, it made the most sense to me to leave the natives in Second Eden. No use taking a chance."

"That's fine, but speaking of warriors, any word from Yereq?"

"I was going to ask you that." Elam's brow lifted. "Did you follow the footprints?"

Gabriel patted a flashlight hooked to his belt. "During the night, but I lost the trail. I can try again now that we have daylight."

"Sounds good. Let's try opening the portal first, then we'll hunt for Yereq."

After Gabriel and Elam scaled the hill, they walked onto its flat, circular top. Sapphira stood at the center, and the four dragons lined up in front of her, their planned alignment for a potential portal opening. Gabriel and Elam parted, Gabriel walking to the left side of the top and Elam taking his place a few paces from Sapphira. When everyone was in position, Elam raised a hand. "On my signal, give it everything you've got."

49

The second he lowered his hand, the dragons blasted streams of flames around Sapphira as if trying to draw an arch over her body. Sapphira shouted, "Ignite!" She burst into flames, raised her arms, and began weaving the multiple infernos together as if stirring the fire-filled air into a vortex.

Soon, a spinning wall of orange enveloped her body. The dragons continued spewing flames, each one taking a rest in turn. The heat intensified. The snow melted. With scalding air swirling all around, Gabriel backed to the edge of the hilltop and unzipped his coat. Elam retreated only a few steps, apparently able to withstand the barrage of heat.

After several minutes, the dragons' fire began to ebb. Legossi finished with a sputter and a cough. Thigocia's flames ended with a puff of sparks and smoke. Roxil laid her head on the ground and exhaled heavily. Finally, Makaidos wheezed, and his fire fell as sparkling spittle.

Sapphira kept the vortex spinning, but after several seconds, the cylinder thinned out and dispersed. She collapsed to a sitting position and gasped for breath. With each spasm, her fiery coat faded.

Elam leaped to her side and helped her rise, using a sleeve to protect his hand.

"It's locked tight." Looking at him, Sapphira twirled a finger. "While it was spinning, I could feel a portal, so it's still here."

Makaidos lifted his head. "I sense danger."

"So do I." Thigocia spread out her wings. "I do not know if I have the strength to investigate."

"I hear something." Elam set a hand to his ear. "Rumbling?"

"I'm on it." Gabriel shot into the air and began a quick orbit over the hilltop. To the east, four black helicopters closed in. Their nearly invisible blades sent rippling sound waves pounding into his chest. With underside-mounted guns and under-wing missiles, these flyers weren't coming for a friendly chat.

He dropped toward the hilltop, shouting, "Choppers! And they're loaded for dragon!"

"How many?" Makaidos asked.

"I saw four, but that doesn't mean more won't come."

Legossi struggled to her haunches. "We have to strike first. If they get into attack formation—"

"No!" Makaidos shook his head hard. "We are too weak, and they are too many."

"Not to mention too fast," Gabriel said. "They'll be here any second."

Elam raised a hand. "We have no choice but to surrender. Just keep your wits about you. I doubt that they're here to murder us. They probably want access to Second Eden, and we have no way to give that to them."

When the helicopters arrived, they formed a semicircle about thirty feet overhead and hovered in place.

Gabriel wrapped his wings around himself and blinked at the whipping wind. Flying with flexible wings in this frigid vortex would be impossible, even for a dragon.

A man in the far-right helicopter barked through a loud-speaker. "Open the portal!"

Elam spread out his arms and shouted, "We can't! It's locked!"

A hail of bullets drilled into the ground near his feet, but Elam didn't flinch.

"Don't lie. We detected an open portal here not long ago. Give us access, and no one will get hurt."

"Listen, genius!" Gabriel yelled, lifting a fist. "If we could open the portal, we wouldn't still be here! Do you think we just waited around in the Arctic for you to show up? What's your IQ? A single digit?"

For a moment, the chopper blades and engines provided the only sounds. The dragons and humans on the hilltop, all shivering in the icy blast, stared at the buzzing hoverers.

Finally, the voice returned. "We are sending a team down. Do not resist their actions."

A metallic box, black and rectangular, fell from the door of the same helicopter and landed in the mud with a thudding splash. Shaped like an oversized coffin, a human could easily fit inside.

A rope dropped from the door and another from the opposite side, as well as a long chain and hook. Three men in military garb slid to the ground, each one with an automatic rifle in hand.

Two of the men opened the box and waited. The third man walked toward Sapphira, though with a hesitant gait. "Get in the box," he said, gesturing with his rifle.

51

Sapphira glanced at Elam, wind-blown fire rising from her hands and hair. He leaped in front of her. "You can't have her!"

The loudspeaker sounded again. "You'll get her back as soon as you give us access to Second Eden."

As the pounding gusts whipped through his hair, Elam glared at the helicopter. "Forget it! Sapphira is not a negotiating chip. You can't have her."

"Surrender her, or we will kill everyone except for her and you, and then we'll take her anyway."

Elam looked at Makaidos. The king of the dragons stared back at him, as if communicating silently. Roxil looked on, shuffling toward Makaidos, though she appeared weak and sluggish.

Gabriel edged close to Legossi and spoke with just enough volume to overcome the whirring blades. "Is Elam stalling until you dragons can recover?"

"I hope so." Anger spiced Legossi's low, rumbling voice. "We should not give up Sapphira without a fight. All of Second Eden is at stake."

"Agreed."

Elam turned back to the helicopter. "Give me another minute to think about—"

"Kill the winged guy," the loudspeaker said.

The soldier closest to Sapphira lifted his gun. Sapphira pointed at him and shouted, "Ignite!"

His uniform burst into flames. As he dropped to the mud, Sapphira pointed at the other two. With shouts of "Ignite!" she set their clothes on fire. Pivoting, she cast the same command at all four helicopters. Lightning-like sparks covered their metal skins, but nothing caught fire.

A trio of pops sounded from the leftmost helicopter. Bullets zinged into Gabriel's foreleg and thigh. Pain roared up his spine and shredded his balance. He collapsed and writhed in the mud.

With a beat of her wings, Legossi leaped toward the attacking helicopter, leading with a fireball. Her flames splashed over its windshield. She grabbed a landing runner with her teeth and twisted as if trying to sling the helicopter to the ground. Her tail and a wing slammed into the blades, slicing them and sending the chopper into a spinning plunge near the edge of the hilltop. It crashed in a mangled heap and exploded, launching a fireball that rocketed into the sky.

Just as Makaidos, Thigocia, and Roxil spread out their wings to attack, two other helicopters fired a storm of bullets. With a series of sickening thumps, the three dragons dropped to their bellies and moved no more.

As the first attack helicopter burned, Legossi struggled to disentangle herself from the fiery wreckage. A third helicopter launched a missile. With a whoosh and a trail of smoke, it zoomed toward Legossi. She beat her truncated wings, slinging blood, but they provided no lift. The missile slammed into her chest and exploded.

Gabriel covered his face with a wing. Debris pelted the outer surface, sounding like the splatter of flesh and blood. He gagged, then swallowed down bile. This was all too terrible to be true.

After a few seconds, he drew his wing back. Legossi and the helicopter were gone, likely blown over the edge. More soldiers dropped from the remaining three helicopters. They wrestled Sapphira away from Elam, smacked him to the ground with the butt of a rifle, and escorted her to the box.

Sapphira went peaceably, apparently realizing that Elam would suffer even more if she resisted. She stepped into the box and lay on her back, her hands folded over her waist. Like a funeral director closing a coffin, one of the soldiers lowered the lid, his face expressionless.

As they fastened a series of padlocks around the seam, Elam struggled to his feet, his fists balled, but he staggered like a man on a storm-tossed boat.

Gabriel crawled toward him on his elbows, dragging his legs. If he so much as wiggled a wing, they would probably finish him off. "Elam," he grunted, "let her go. We'll regroup. We'll find a way."

"Never!" Elam trudged toward Sapphira. "I can't let them have her!"

The soldiers wrapped a chain around the box, and the helicopter began reeling it up. One of the soldiers kicked Elam in the stomach, sending him sprawling. He then aimed his rifle at Gabriel and shouted, "Sweet dreams, freak!"

A pop sounded. Pain ripped into Gabriel's head. As the world grew dark, he reached into his pocket and pressed the emergency button on his phone. Then the entire hilltop dissolved in a field of blackness.

54

Bonnie tapped her foot on the sand. How long would Tamiel take? He and the angel had conferred for a long time. Why would a being of light and a being of darkness have so much to talk about?

She focused on the lake, an expanse that displayed a perfect mirror—smooth and placid. Yes ... placid. Just have patience, and all would be well.

Soon a winged shadow appeared next to hers, growing as approaching footfalls crunched on the gravelly sand. She didn't bother to look. Tamiel had returned. "Did you ask about Matt?"

"He is alive, at least for the time being, but it seems that he has been captured by a dragon. I advise haste." Tamiel stopped at her side and folded in his wings. "But first, I have something for you."

Keeping her face toward the lake, she glanced at him. He held a gun in his hand, transparent like the candlestone shooters the prison guards used, though smaller than most pistols. It looked more like a plastic toy than a real gun. Yet, a glow of white light swirled in the casing with sparkles embedded in the vortex, proving it to be much more. "What is it?"

"It's a device Mardon and I invented." He laid it in her hand. "I'm sure you know about a dragon's regeneracy dome."

"I do." A stream of light flowed from her hand into the gun. The inner glow strengthened, and the swirl accelerated. The candlestone in her chest pulsed, creating a new jolt that sent her heart into an erratic rhythm. She gasped for breath. The pain would ease soon … she hoped.

"This gun," Tamiel said in a professorial tone, "absorbs light energy in a dynamo of sorts. When you press the barrel against someone's skin and pull the trigger, it injects the energy into the person and causes regeneration, much like a dragon's dome does for a dragon."

55

"Then this isn't a weapon at all." Bonnie set a hand against her chest. Her heart still thumped wildly. "It's a healing device."

"Only for the target." Tamiel pressed a rocker switch on the gun's casing. The tiny spinning wheel behind the trigger mechanism slowed, though it retained its brightness. "It's off now. You should notice relief."

Bonnie's heart settled. As she took in a deep breath, she glared at the gun. It didn't take an Ashley brain to figure out what it was doing. "It absorbs energy from me, doesn't it?"

"Indeed. The candlestone I injected into you is a transmitter. It collects your energy and sends it to the receiver in this gun. As long as the switch is off, however, it will cause you no harm."

"What's its purpose?"

"Healing. It allows you to become like Ashley and Matt, though much more efficient and at a great expense to your health. During your journey, you will find those who need healing, and you will have the opportunity to provide it. Also, the gun's trigger mechanism is locked with a genetic key and will not shoot unless you are holding it. You must deliver the energy yourself."

Bonnie glared at him. "And the more people I heal, the more I suffer, and the more I suffer, the more my song gets weakened, and the more my song gets weakened, the more the world gets corrupted."

"Your wisdom is a credit to you. Few would discern the reason for my devices so quickly."

She forced her facial muscles to relax. Taming her emotions had to be a priority. "I have been through enough to know that a demon bearing a beautiful gift has a venomous serpent in his other hand."

"Well stated and correct when referring to most of my fellows, but I hide nothing. I am open and honest about my goals. That is why I am able to see you."

"See me?"

Tamiel chuckled. "How soon you forget, but you have no time to ponder this riddle. If you want to help your son, you need to leave right away."

"Spoken by the one who is using his suffering to hurt billions of people. You're a deceiver in spite of your claims."

"Not at all. I freely admitted my purpose, and I will tell you more." Tamiel's face darkened, and the tips of fangs protruded over his bottom lip. "Eliminate all thoughts of leaving this journey. I will make sure there are many others who need your help. You will be very sorry if you fail to heed my warning."

Bonnie forced herself to maintain eye contact. She mustn't show fear. Giving this demon any hint that she couldn't stand up to him would be a big mistake.

"Also," Tamiel continued, the fangs receding, "I advise charging the inner energy cell as much as possible now."

"Why?"

He nodded toward the lake. "The candlestone has no power over you in Second Eden, so it will not send energy to the regeneracy gun while you are in that realm. Whatever energy is stored in the gun is still yours. That is, you will not feel drained until the gun is used on someone else. But every time you use it, you will feel an echo of the power drainage, and that process will eventually bring exhaustion. Any recharge will cause pain in your heart but not exhaustion, so the two processes will have differing effects."

"I know what a demon's gifts do," Bonnie said. "They always hurt more than they help. What will be the long-term effects on someone I heal?"

"There is no hidden time bomb, if that is what you mean. I want you to have confidence in your healing power. If it proved to be a sham, you would quickly put a stop to your journey, and you know how disappointed that would make me."

Hiding her revulsion, Bonnie looked at the gun. Although Tamiel's attitude was disgusting, the idea that this device could help someone made it attractive. Yet, it was easy to see how it could become a self-applied leech, a way to bleed her dry as she couldn't resist the urge to provide a healing touch. Already it felt like a ball and chain.

"But back to my original point," Tamiel continued. "Since a recharge cannot occur while you are in Second Eden, you need to do it now."

Bonnie nodded. During her battle with Devin in Second Eden, she had overcome the candlestone's ability to weaken her. Yet, in the prison on Earth, the candlestones again drained her energy. The reason for the difference remained a mystery. "So that's why the boat's here. If I charge the gun now, the pain won't allow me to fly over the lake."

"At least not for a while, and I am sure you want to leave as soon as possible." Backing away, Tamiel blew her a kiss. "Bon voyage, Bonnie Bannister."

Bonnie took in a deep breath. The urge to gag was overwhelming. "If you're trying to disgust me, you're doing a good job."

"It is all part of the plan to warp your song with every suffering moment." He spread his wings. "While you till the soil, I will sow the seeds of corruption. Together we will bring about a reaping of the harvest, and blood will run deep and wide throughout the land … thanks to you."

Bonnie chewed her lip. More words of exasperation begged to fly, but they would just make things worse. With anger delivering a burst of energy, she marched to the boat, untied it, and shoved it into the lake, jumping in with the same motion. A current caught the boat and pushed it speedily onward.

Not bothering to look back, she sat on a narrow bench and stared into the mist. Second Eden lay out there somewhere, and Matt was in trouble, at least if the images the hologram had displayed were timely and if Tamiel spoke the truth.

Bonnie lifted the regeneracy gun and pressed the switch. It flashed to life. The candlestone within throbbed. As her heart ached with wild, vibrating thumps, she shifted to the floor of the boat and curled on her side, collapsing her wings to fit. How long could she let the gun absorb her energy? The balance between two necessities seemed impossible to guess. She needed enough energy in the gun to help Matt and any other Second Eden survivors, but if too much drained into the gun now, using it while in Second Eden would leave her too exhausted to get through the rest of the journey.

She pressed the side of the gun against her chest. With a whisper, she called out, "Father, guide this boat to Second Eden at the speed you choose. When I enter, the candlestone within will stop draining me, so I trust you to bring about the perfect timing. Now I know why you granted me protection from its power in Second Eden and not anywhere else. My weakness here before the portal will be strength for others, and my strength in that land will be healing. Your wisdom never fails."

Bonnie closed her eyes. As her heart pounded through one painful throb after another, the boat floated on. The image of dragon claws digging into Matt's body flashed again and again, ripping his flesh without mercy. Blood poured, and Matt screamed in agony. It was so terrible!

59

She waved a hand to cast it away. This vision wasn't from a dream. It did no good to allow an image of fear a moment of notice. It would just harm her song.

After taking a deep breath, she whispered, "Holy Father, grant me peace. If there is a dream you want me to consider, bring it to my mind as I slumber. I trust you to be my transmitter, and in you I will rest." Seconds later, she drifted into a dreamless sleep.

A Healer's Touch

"Arramos!" Semiramis wailed. "Don't kill me! I can still be of service to you!"

A shrill whistle sounded from the dragon but nothing more.

Matt grimaced. Every beat of the dragon's wings shot more pain into his shoulders as it rose and fell in its awkward flight. After hovering in a circular pattern for a moment, it steadily descended toward a rocky beach on the western side of the river beyond the waterfall's splash point. A young woman with dark pigtails stood near the shoreline, backing away as they drew closer. She whistled and pointed at a sandy spot. "Put them there!"

The dragon suddenly swooped. The claws withdrew from Matt's shoulders. He and Semiramis dropped onto the sand and rolled to a stop near the woman's feet.

Biting his lip to keep from groaning, Matt sat up. The point of a sword hovered within an inch of his nose. Nearby, a purple dragon landed in a trot. Beating its wings, it skittered toward them over rocks and sand.

At the other end of the sword, the woman clutched its hilt. Mist from the splash point sprayed over her narrow face, speckling her cheeks with droplets. Tall, lean, and wiry, she looked like a toned athlete. "Who are you?" she growled. "I can see you are not from Second Eden."

Matt swallowed. Although she appeared to be in her late teens, she carried the aspect of a seasoned warrior. "Matt. Matt Fletch— I mean Matt Bannister." He glanced at Semiramis, who now sat next to him. "This is—"

"I know who she is." The woman shifted the sword and pricked Semiramis's nose. "Do you remember who *I* am?"

Semiramis inched away on her bottom. "You look familiar. I know many residents of Second Eden, though not all of them by name."

"Listener!" someone called from a point closer to the waterfall. "Is there a problem?" A black male teenager stood in front of the spray, his own sword drawn. With his feet set firmly on the beach sand, his arms flexed, and his trousers and belted tunic fitting close to his trim waist, he matched Listener's warrior presence.

"Nothing I can't handle." Listener kept her sword pointed at Semiramis. "How is Albatross?"

"His bleeding is worse." The young man slid his sword into a belt scabbard. "I'll need help fashioning a bandage for compression."

"I'll be there in a minute."

When the young man turned and walked into the spray, Semiramis whispered, "You're Listener? Angel's daughter?"

Listener nodded. "I will deal with you in a moment. Right now, I have to tend to someone." She slid her own sword into a leather sheath at her side and blew a sharp whistle. "Grackle! Guard these villains while I—"

"I'm not a villain." Matt pushed on the sand to get up, but Listener shoved him back in place with a bare foot. An egg-like orb appeared from behind her head and hovered in place next to her ear. It flashed red, then dimmed.

"Semiramis is the worst of villains," Listener said, angling her eyes toward the egg. "He was traveling with her, and I remember my lessons well. Corruption is more contagious than any disease."

Matt shook his head. "I'm not traveling with her by choice. I was—"

"And you have my spyglass." Listener snatched it from Matt's pocket and snapped it into a holster on her belt. "A Vacant stole it just a few days ago."

"A Vacant?" Matt gave her a curious look.

"A Vacant is a—" The floating egg zipped in front of her eyes, again flashing red. When the light ebbed, she nodded. "True. We must first establish common ground before we explain our alliances and enemies."

Matt glanced at the orb, now floating toward her ear. Apparently this woman didn't care to explain it. "I found your spyglass in a logjam by the lake. I didn't know who it belonged to. And Semiramis isn't my friend. We were kind of thrown together. The only reason we were riding that log was to survive."

"Is that so?" Listener bent one eyebrow low. "You called yourself Matt Bannister. Are you related to Billy Bannister?"

Matt nodded vigorously. "I'm his son! And I have dragon traits. I'm a healer. If you have a wounded friend, maybe I can help him."

Her skeptical stare deepened. "Neither Billy nor his wife had the gift of healing."

"I know. My father can breathe fire and sense danger. I inherited the danger-sensing part, but I guess I got the healing ability somewhere else down the line."

The orb floated in front of her eyes and emitted a series of blue flashes, as if speaking to her. She nodded in response, then drew the sword and pointed at Matt again. "I will test your words. Lead the way to the waterfall. I will tell you what to do when we get there." She swung back toward the dragon. "If Semiramis moves, you know what to do."

While the dragon shuffled closer, Matt climbed to his feet. The claw wounds in his shoulders throbbed, and every muscle ached, but this wasn't the time to worry about pain. Someone else needed help, and Listener needed to be convinced. Although he had healed his mother, convincing himself that he could do it again would be hard enough.

As he walked toward the waterfall, the roar of the cascading river heightened. The young man who had called earlier was nowhere in sight, though impressions in the wet sand led directly into the wall of spray. Matt kept his focus straight ahead. What was that floating egg all about? Studying it more might help, but the point of a sword close behind discouraged further thought of that idea.

When he drew within ten steps of the spray, Listener called, "Walk through the left side of the mist, just to the right of the round stone."

Matt spotted the stone, a hunk of granite the size and shape of a bowling ball. "You chose a good hiding place. I can't see anything past the spray."

"We weren't really trying to hide there. Up until a little while before you came, the river wasn't running, so our cave was easier to see. Then a bunch of logs fell over the cliff with a surge of water. That's why I sent Grackle up there to find out what happened. You're lucky he's so fast."

Matt massaged one of his wounded shoulders. "I guess getting clawed is better than getting crushed."

"Perhaps after you prove your healing abilities, you will heal yourself." She prodded his back with a prick of the blade. "Keep going."

"All right. All right." He walked through the warm spray and into a well-lit cave, illuminated by three torches embedded in sand. Six children knelt around a dragon that lay on its side, all with their hands pressed together and their fingertips touching their chins. Little flashing eggs floated about their heads, one per child, all emitting dim blue lights. The young man crouched near the dragon's belly between its forelegs and back legs. Now wearing a form-fitting T-shirt, he spread his outer long-sleeved tunic over the scales on the dragon's side. His dark biceps flexing, he began unbuckling his belt while an orb similar to Listener's hovered near his closely cropped hair. "Since Listener brought you in here, I assume you are a friend."

Matt extended his hand. "I am a friend. My name is Matt Bannister."

"I'm not convinced yet," Listener said as she joined them, "but he'll have a chance to prove his story."

"Oh, Listener, don't be so suspicious." The young man flashed a bright smile and shook Matt's hand. "My name is Eagle. I am pleased to meet you, Matt."

Matt returned the smile. "Is that a nickname for having eyes like an Eagle?"

"A nickname?" Eagle tilted his head, blinking. "It's my real name."

Listener nudged Eagle's arm with her knee. "His companion gave it to him. Our companions suggest our names, which always correspond to something about us, either physically or spiritually."

Matt glanced at Listener's orb, then at Eagle's. Might those eggs be their companions? Maybe, but it felt stupid to ask.

65

"Enough chatter." Listener nodded toward the dragon. "We must tend to Albatross."

Eagle pulled the tunic away. "I was thinking about using this as a bandage by securing it with my belt, but I don't think it's big enough to wrap around."

The dragon's eyelids fluttered, and its body heaved shallow gasps. Blood dripped from a gash in its ribs, and soot coated its scales, making its color hard to determine, though several splotches of white broke through.

One of the children, a girl no more than six years old, stroked the dragon's scaly skin. As her egg floated in front of her nose, tears trickled from her wide eyes and down her dirty cheeks. "Are you a dragon doctor?" she asked Matt, her tiny voice barely audible over the waterfall's roar. Still holding their palms together, the children stared at him hopefully.

"Not really a dragon doctor." Matt laid a hand on the little girl's shoulder. "But I'll see what I can do to help."

She tilted her head and rubbed her cheek over his knuckles. "I hope you can. A lot of people think Albatross isn't brave, but he is. I know he is."

"I believe you." Matt knelt to Eagle's right, his hip touching the dragon's forelegs. "Was Albatross trying to protect you?"

The little girl nodded. "While I was riding him."

Listener crouched close to the dragon's neck, the sword propped on her shoulder. "Albatross is a kind and gentle passenger dragon. If you heal him, I will believe your story."

"I am looking forward to hearing this story," Eagle said, "but I will be patient. If you are a dragon doctor, proceed by all means."

"I'll do my best." Matt laid a hand over the gash. Moist heat radiated from within. "What hit him?"

"A boulder." Listener touched a stream of blood near the wound. "Because of the way Mount Elijah rumbled and shook the ground, Valiant, our historian and expert in nature, thought an eruption was coming that would be far worse than any we had experienced, so he loaded as many women and children as our flying hospital could safely hold and sent it into the sky."

"A flying hospital?"

"Yes." She spread out her arms. "It has wings, like Earth's airplanes. We had a bigger hospital, but we modified it into a smaller one with wings to make it more versatile. It's probably not the best time to give you details."

Matt nodded. "You're right. Go on."

"Then Valiant gathered the remaining children he could find quickly and sent us to this valley, charging Eagle and me with the responsibility of seeing them to safety. Albatross carried Eagle and four children, and Grackle carried three children and me, though he labored greatly because of his age. In fact, both dragons were overloaded and had to rest every few minutes. By the time we reached Adam's Marsh, the entire top of the mountain exploded, and stones flew everywhere. One struck Albatross, and although he faltered for a moment, he recovered and flew on. Both dragons had to rise into the clouds to avoid the storm, so we couldn't see anything or breathe clean air until we dove into the valley. When we landed, Albatross collapsed, spilling his passengers. One boy was dead, his skull fractured by a stone."

Eagle held up an arm, revealing bloody wounds from his palm down to his elbow. "I blocked as many stones as I could, but …" His voice cracked. "But one got through."

Matt grimaced. Eagle took quite a barrage for these kids. At home, he'd get a medal. Anyone who would sacrifice like that was a hero in his book.

"I held Merit in place on Albatross for quite some time." Eagle nodded toward the back of the cave. "Though in vain."

Matt looked that way. Near the wall, rocks had been piled up in the shape of a small human body. "Merit," he whispered. "Poor kid."

"A fine boy. We all loved him." Tears sparkling in his bright eyes, Eagle continued. "After we landed, Grackle and the rest of us worked together to get Albatross into this cave because he was having trouble breathing. We thought the air might be cleaner here."

"Good idea." Matt nodded toward the cave entrance. "Semiramis said there are leaves that filter the air."

Listener chimed in. "Keelvar leaves, but I have not yet looked for any. Besides, it takes an expert like Valiant to identify them. They look like one of the more common varieties."

"Valiant. He must be a very important man."

"Not only is he our revered historian, he is the leader of one of the villages, supremely capable and highly respected by all." She smiled at Eagle. "And he is Eagle's father."

Eagle returned the smile. "Thank you for the gracious assessment. Of course, I agree, as any proud son would."

Matt added a smile of his own. Hanging around these two would lift anyone's spirits. "I'd better see what I can do to help this dragon." He pushed his fingers into the wound and massaged a cracked rib. The hole seemed to go no deeper. The dragon's collapse was likely due to loss of blood rather than organ damage.

While he worked, he glanced at the onlookers, all staring at him wide-eyed. Their floating eggs hovered in place, each one motionless as they, too, seemed mesmerized. Matt cleared his throat. Maybe it would be best to make small talk to settle his nerves. "Why did Valiant choose Elijah for the volcano's name?"

Listener and Eagle looked at each other, both smiling. "You tell him," Eagle said. "My own estimation of my father's wisdom might wear out our visitor's ears."

"Wisdom is never a burden." Listener focused on Matt, her face turning somber. "A prophet from your world said in your holy scriptures, 'Behold, I will send you Elijah the prophet before the coming of the great and dreadful day of the Lord, and he shall turn the hearts of the fathers to the children, and the hearts of the children to their fathers, lest I come and smite the earth with a curse.'"

"I don't think I've heard that before." Matt continued the massage. So far, nothing had changed. Maybe his healing touch hadn't kicked in yet. "You have an excellent memory."

"I remember everything I hear. That's one of the reasons my name is Listener."

"Okay." Matt gazed into her eyes. How old might she be? Eighteen? Twenty? "I still don't get the connection. What's a volcano got to do with fathers and their children?"

"Oh, yes, of course. You wouldn't know." Listener drew in the air with a finger. "Because of trails cut into the side, the volcano was once very easy to climb in spite of its height. Years ago, it was a tradition for fathers to hike with their children to the summit, though that practice later stopped when our prophet plugged the hole leading into the volcano's throat, though it was later unplugged for reasons I won't go into. You see, our prophet thought it was too dangerous, that children might be tempted to go there by themselves, which is true, but others talked about an old saying that if a person were to fall into Elijah's mouth, he would surely spew them out with great wrath."

"Do you believe that?"

Listener glanced at Eagle before answering. "There is some evidence. The last time Elijah erupted, maybe sixteen or seventeen years ago during a time the mouth was not plugged, I was watching the mountain through my spyglass, and I saw someone fall into the crater. Since the volcano's top was mostly intact at the time, I was

69

surprised that I was able to see it happen, though the spyglass is known to allow visions beyond normal perception, at least for me."

Still massaging, Matt let out a whistle. "That must have been scary for a little girl."

"Little?" Listener shrugged. "I might be older than you think."

Eagle grinned. "Our people say Listener came out of her pod old. Even before she could talk, she wanted to be a doctor. She analyzes everything."

"Before I could talk?" Listener's countenance grew dark. "My ability to speak was greatly delayed, but that story would take too long to tell."

"That's fine." Matt gave her a prompting nod. "Is there more to the volcano story?"

"Yes." Her smile returning, she seemed pleased to switch the topic. "When the parents and children arrived on the mountaintop, they would look out over the land of Second Eden and give thanks for the creation the Father of Lights bestowed. Then they would gaze into the mountain's throat at the fire in its belly and shudder together. Fathers would remind their children that although the Father of Lights is filled with love in providing a wonderful world in which to live, he also reserves wrath for those who rebel against him.

"During those days, our people had no rebellion in our midst, so the children had no knowledge of the potential for punishment. On that mountain, the contrast between beauty and death provided a vivid illustration of love versus the danger of abandoning that love, and the experience fostered a lasting bond between father and child that we all cherish."

Matt felt his mouth drop open. How many young women on Earth could speak with such eloquence and wisdom? Listener was amazing.

Her head drooped. "Now that Elijah has exploded and done such damage, some are wondering if the great and dreadful day of the Lord is coming or has already come. Perhaps your world or our world is being smitten with a curse."

"Right. The damage." Matt shook his attention away from Listener and concentrated his energy on the dragon's wound. "Have you heard from anyone at your home?"

"Not yet. Grackle flew over my village and brought back a report. Although his ability to communicate is limited to a series of whistles, he was able to tell of great destruction. There are some survivors, but his language has no numbers beyond the thumping of his tail. After several thumps, I told him to stop. My knowledge of the number wasn't important enough to tire him out."

Matt's fingers tingled. Healing energy flowed. The crack in the rib was finally sealing. "It sounds like this really was the worst eruption ever."

71

"Without a doubt. This is the first time Elijah has literally exploded. Lava from eruptions flows away from our villages, but we could not avoid the storm of boulders. We are blessed that Valiant was wise enough to predict the catastrophe."

"That's for sure." Matt gave Eagle another glance. His proud smile proved that respect for his father abounded. He seemed content to stay silent while Listener did most of the talking, perhaps a sign of respect. Maybe she really was older than she looked.

Matt slowly withdrew his fingers, sealing the puncture wound along the way. "Could there be a cause other than someone falling in?"

"There were other signs." Listener pointed a finger upward and twirled it in place. "Just before Elijah exploded, we saw a circle of fire around the top, like a wall of flames spinning and spinning. It reminded me of Abraham's wall, though his didn't spin, but I suppose you wouldn't know anything about that portion of our history."

"A spinning wall of fire," Matt whispered.

"And just before that, bright flashes of light shot into the sky." She lifted her sword. "I have seen Excalibur summon a similar light, and I have read about laser beams on Earth. The light shooting from Mount Elijah made me think of them."

Matt stared at her egg again. A pair of eyelike slits appeared, blinking at her. "Back on Earth," he said, "I was involved in a battle at a prison, and we had spinning fire and laser beams. They must have appeared here in your world when the portal opened. Maybe all that energy …" He let his words trail away. Could it be? Did the energy that opened the portal actually cause the explosion? Of course, the superstition about people falling into the volcano was nonsense, but a huge concentration of energy might make anything blow its top.

He turned toward the cave opening. Back on the river's beach, Semiramis sat in a slouch under Grackle's watchful eye. Maybe Semiramis was right. Arramos did hatch a scheme to destroy Second Eden, though not with an invasion. He brought Sapphira to Earth so she could unwittingly send the energy from the lasers and her own firestorm into the volcano. The scheme was brilliant, a master stroke. Even Semiramis didn't know the depths of his diabolical plan. And could there yet be more disaster in store?

For the next few minutes, Matt continued massaging the dragon's wound while telling Listener and Eagle the prison-escape story, including the disappearance of the laser weapons and Portia as well as the zapping of Sir Barlow. As they and the children listened in silence, their eyes blinked or widened with the story's ups and downs, and their eggs flickered in kind. Sometimes the children whispered to their eggs, as if responding to the flashes within. Although bizarre, the communication seemed normal to them.

When he finished, he ran his fingers along the dragon's newly sealed wound. "So I think Portia might have transported here before I did, and maybe Sir Barlow as well, but if the laser weapons were right over the volcano's mouth, they might have dropped in."

Listener nodded. "And there would be no way to find them, unless there was, you might say, a back door in the portal."

He wiped his bloody hand on his shirt. "What do you mean?"

"At one time, Mount Elijah's throat was a portal that led to a chamber that we called—"

Her orb flashed several times, first red, then blue.

Listener firmed her lips. "You're right. I have said too much. We will have to pray for the best."

The young girl piped up. "Will Albatross be all right?"

"I think so." Matt again ran a finger along the seal. "See? He's not bleeding, and once his blood supply replenishes and he rests for a while, he'll probably wake up."

The girl clapped her hands. "Good! You *are* a dragon doctor!"

The other children buzzed with excitement, their eggs flashing in time with their gleeful bouncing.

"It seems that the young ones believe in you." Listener rose to her feet and backed away, her sword again pointing at Matt. Light from the cave opening shone on her slender form. "Come. We will now deal with you and your traveling cohort."

Matt cocked his head. "But the wound is closed. You can see that for yourself."

"The hole is gone, yes, but Albatross is not yet healed."

"Then how do you think the wound sealed? Glue?" He showed her his blood-stained fingers. "I did it with these."

73

"Listener," Eagle said, still kneeling next to Matt, "maybe we should consider—"

"Neither of you knows Semiramis the way I do." Listener's face remained calm, no hint of anger or joy as she addressed Matt. "I read about witchery in many forms. I will grant that you might be ignorant of that wicked sorceress's history, but since you traveled here with her, I have to stay vigilant. She is too dangerous to keep in our company, but as for Matt Bannister, I will keep my options open." She gestured with the sword toward the opening. "Go. I will follow. Eagle, kindly stay here and see to the needs of the children and Albatross."

Eagle nodded, his expression apologetic as he looked at Matt. "I will."

Rising, Matt rolled his eyes. "If you say so." As he passed, he scanned her from top to bottom. Her shoulder-length pigtails made her look like a preteen, but her hardened face and steely eyes told a different story, one that agreed with the toned muscles in the forearm that gripped the sword. Her shirt and pants, cut to fit close to her narrow frame, appeared to be made of some kind of soft leather, though it was probably nearly as tough as she was.

When they walked through the wall of spray and emerged into the light, Listener strode past him and marched straight ahead, her sword pointing at Semiramis. "Now that Albatross appears to be healing, it's time to deal with this evil—" She halted, blinking as she cocked her head. "I hear something."

Matt joined her and listened. The splashing noises drowned out any competing sounds. "What is it?"

"A melody." Her voice took on a mysterious tone. "A song that begs for words."

"Where is it coming from?"

74

Listener stepped into the shallows and looked at the top of the falls. Water and an occasional log gushed over the ledge, flew through the air, and tumbled to the splash point.

Matt winced. With every thump and crack of a splintering log, he pictured himself smacking into the stone landing. The cost of claw wounds didn't seem so high anymore.

"It's getting closer." Listener spun toward Grackle and pointed with the sword. "Fly!"

Grackle flung out his wings and leaped into the air. Whistling as he rose, he shot out a burst of white breath and ice pellets that drizzled into the river. When he reached the top of the falls, he flew in tight circles just beyond the hurtling water and logs. Every few seconds, he let out a high-pitched whistle that barely pierced the wall of noise.

"A boat is coming?" Listener took another step into the river. "Do you see a passenger?"

Grackle wagged his head and angled into another orbit.

"Be ready to catch someone anyway!"

Grackle extended his rear legs and made quick sweeps in front of the ledge, as if practicing a catching maneuver.

Listener turned to Matt. "He sees a boat that appears to be empty, but since I hear a song, someone must be inside."

"Hiding?"

"Maybe." She gave his shirt a tug. "Let's get closer."

"Should we get Eagle's help?"

"No time. Hurry!" After sheathing her sword, Listener marched into the river and waded toward the splash point, a large flat stone at the waterfall's base. As Matt followed, the thunder of crashing water heightened, and warm spray grew thick. They climbed onto the edge of the stone just out of reach of the pounding water. The warm spray arced over their heads, veiling their view of the top of the falls.

Listener grabbed the spyglass from its harness, expanded its frame, and aimed it at the watery surge above. As she looked through the lens, her orb pushed into her hair and settled out of sight.

Matt strained to see through the spray. "What are you doing?"

"Trying to position myself. Grackle is not skilled with his claws. I was surprised that he caught you. You're lucky he snagged your shoulders instead of your face."

"If he misses, what can we do? We can't catch someone falling that fast."

"We can try to cushion her fall."

"Her?"

She snapped the spyglass back to her belt and set her arms in a cradle. "I know a woman when I see one."

"But the boat is out of range." Matt faced Listener and copied her pose. "How can you see her?"

"I told you the spyglass has unusual abilities." She blinked away the mist. "It should be any second now."

Matt looked up. Water flowed in spurts, sometimes with a log or two in the flow. Soon, a rowboat eased over the falls and sailed downward. As it flipped, a woman toppled out and fell, slowed by what appeared to be an open parasail.

In a flurry of wings, Grackle clawed at her, but a rush of air caught the sail and jerked the woman out of his reach. She dropped in sporadic plunges and wild angles, like a leaf in a rainstorm.

Matt shifted to a likely landing spot. Listener did the same and locked wrists with him. Finally, the woman dropped into their arms. Her momentum collapsed the cradle and sent all three into the river.

Pressing his feet against the riverbed, Matt stood in chest-deep water, looking for the woman in the flow. Listener rose to a standing position next to him, her clothes and hair dripping. "She's close! Right near our feet. I can hear her song."

"She's singing underwater?" Matt plunged below the surface, grabbed an arm, and hauled the woman up. A leathery wing slapped his face, but the blinding spray forced his eyes closed. "Did Grackle dive in here, too?"

"Just get her to shore!" Listener shouted.

Holding the woman's wrist, Matt trudged to the river's edge and laid her on a grassy terrace. He wiped his eyes and stared. The wings were splayed behind her back. He shook his head hard. Could it really be?

"It's Bonnie!" Semiramis ran toward them, but when Grackle landed in front of her, she stopped. "Matt! It's your mother!"

77

NEW BREATH

Matt wiped his eyes and looked at his mother again. Water trickled from the corner of her bluish lips and spilled over her pale cheek. He turned her to her side and thumped her back between her wings. "Mom! It's me, Matt. You have to cough up the water. Give me something!"

Listener dropped to her knees next to him. "Her song is so weak now!"

Matt rolled his mother to her back, careful to keep her wings from bending. He set his lips around hers and breathed into her mouth. Her chest expanded once, twice. Water surged into Matt's mouth. Just as she began hacking, he jerked away.

He turned her to her side again. For the next few seconds, she coughed up water until her respiration eased into a clear, steady rhythm.

Still dripping, Listener breathed a sigh. "The song's louder. I think she'll be all right now."

"Whew!" Matt let his mother settle again on her back. Her eyes stayed closed, but color flooded her skin and lips.

He dropped to a fully seated position, slumped his shoulders, and let water stream from his hair, nose, and chin. "You keep mentioning a song. I can't hear much of anything over that waterfall."

"That's the other reason my companion called me Listener." She pushed back her hair and nudged the orb from its shelter. "Isn't that right?"

The orb rocked, as if nodding.

Matt pointed at the egg. "You call that your companion?"

"Of course." She prodded it with her finger. "I guess your parents didn't tell you about companions."

He shook his head. "They told me a little bit about Second Eden, but they had so much other stuff to tell me."

"I understand. We all heard about their imprisonment." Listener combed through Bonnie's hair with her fingers. "I believe your story now. Your willingness to risk your life to save someone you thought to be a stranger has done more to convince me of your noble character than could any feat of veterinary heroics."

"Veterinary heroics?" Matt laughed under his breath. "Excuse me, but I can't get over your vocabulary. You and Eagle both seem so … scholarly, I guess. Back where I come from, the people I hang around with give me a blank stare if I use a word that has more than two syllables."

"We read books."

Matt gazed at her expressionless face. Her explanation needed nothing more. Turning to his mother, he looked her over. There seemed to be no wound, no bruises, no blood. Why was she unconscious when the boat flew over the ledge? "Do you feel anything on her scalp? A gash or a crack?"

"Nothing." Listener peeked under Bonnie's sweatshirt, then began feeling her ankles and legs through her loose-fitting jeans. "I don't think anything's broken. She is thinner than I remember, but her muscles have good tone."

When Listener's hands patted Bonnie's thighs, she reached into one of the pants pockets and withdrew a transparent gun. "How odd." She laid it in Matt's palm.

A bright light swirled within its casing, much like the guns the prison guards used. "When I last saw her, she had been shot by a candlestone. I think that's what this gun shoots."

Listener blinked at him. "She shot herself?"

"No, no. Tamiel shot her, and that's probably what's weakening her now. I have no idea why she has the gun."

A deep line dug into Listener's brow. "This makes no sense. Before Bonnie left Second Eden, she learned how to resist the effects of a candlestone. Something else must be wrong."

"If I may," Semiramis called as she approached again. "My son invented those guns. I might be able to help."

Grackle shot a spray of ice crystals in front of her. She stopped and glowered at him. "I am not a caged ape!"

"It's okay, Grackle." Listener rose, again clutching her sword. "Let her come."

Semiramis hurried around Grackle and settled next to Matt. She passed a hand over his mother's mouth, then laid a palm on her chest. "Very interesting. My son spoke of this kind of state as a real possibility."

"Don't try our patience." Listener tapped Semiramis's back with the flat of her blade. "Tell us all you know."

Semiramis scowled at her. "Your lack of respect is appalling. Have you so soon forgotten that if not for me, you would have bled to death on a table of surgery?"

"I know a deceiver's ways." Listener propped the blade on her shoulder. "Now tell us."

"You are not the same humble little girl I once knew." After a stare down with Listener that lasted far too many seconds, Semi-ramis huffed and pointed at the gun. "Mardon invented a weapon that uses candlestones to absorb energy. My guess is that this one has taken Bonnie's energy and left her nearly dead."

"Then we need to get rid of it." Matt drew back his hand to throw the gun into the river, but Semiramis caught his wrist.

"No! Her energy is still within the gun. Just remove it from her presence until we can learn how to restore the energy to her."

Matt stared at the radiant swirl in the gun's casing. Of course Semiramis couldn't be trusted, but believing her story seemed harmless.

A squeal sounded from the cave. Matt jerked his head toward Listener. "Want me to check it out?"

"It's probably just Cheer. She gets excited easily. Besides, Eagle is there."

"True, but maybe Albatross is up. I'd like to know if my patch job is holding."

Without a hint of a smile, Listener nodded. "Go ahead."

"I'll be right back." Matt ran toward the cave. Holding a shielding hand over the gun, he ducked through the wall of spray and ran into the dim chamber. The dragon stood near the back wall, his head low to avoid the ceiling. The children had gathered around him, petting his scales. Their companions flashed like a string of holiday lights.

Eagle knelt by Merit's makeshift grave, a hand on one of the covering stones. He shot to his feet, brushed away a tear, and smiled. "You did well. As you can see, Albatross is on his feet."

"Good." Matt stroked the dragon's neck. "I'm glad to see you're feeling better."

Albatross let out a rumbling whistle that sounded like a cat's purr.

Taking a step closer, Eagle touched one of Albatross's wings. "We won't know if he is fully healed until he is tested in flight."

"That makes sense." Matt glanced at the grave again. "If you want to stay here with the kids, I'll guide Albatross outside and see how he does."

Eagle laid an arm over Cheer's shoulder and pulled her close. "As long as all is well out there, I am content to remain with the children."

"Well, a lot has happened. The water was probably too loud for you to hear all the commotion, but my mother tumbled over the falls in a boat. Listener and I caught her. She nearly drowned, but I think she'll be okay."

Eagle showed no sign of surprise. "I would like to meet your mother." He nodded toward the cave's opening. "Go on ahead. I will be out after I settle the children."

Matt took a step, then turned back to Eagle. "Do you mind if I ask you a personal question?"

"Please do." Eagle gave him a friendly nod. "I have no secrets."

"You and Listener are very different. If you don't mind me saying so, you both look like warriors, but you're laid-back while she's aggressive. I'm just trying to learn your ways, so I was wondering which one is more normal for the people here."

"I understand." Eagle rubbed a hand along his toned forearm. "We are both strong, to be sure, and my, shall we say … gentler ways … are more normal here." He leaned to the side and looked through the cave opening. Matt glanced that way. Listener paced in front of Semiramis, her head down and a scowl evident.

83

"You see," Eagle continued, "Listener has experienced a great deal more troubles in life than I have. When she was young, a unique handicap beset her, one that she mentioned earlier that delayed her ability to speak. An oracle told Listener that her mother on Earth killed her before she was born, and that led to her resurrection here on Second Eden as a newborn."

"Her mother killed her? You mean by abortion?"

"Yes, I have heard that euphemism before. Since it is really killing, we call it what it is."

"Fair enough. Go on."

"Well, learning that her mother cared not to keep her incited her willingness to be a sacrificial lamb. If not for another heroic soul, Listener would have died in an effort to rescue others." Eagle waved a hand. "Those details are not essential, but later events are."

"Okay …" Matt stretched out the word. Maybe someday the details would come to light. "What happened?"

"She later learned that her Earth mother did not kill her. In fact, her mother wanted her very much, but they were both murdered while Listener was in the womb. You see, since most babies arrive here because of such killings, the person who told Listener a falsehood was unaware of the true story and made a faulty assumption. Although the mistake caused Listener no harm, the potential for danger was real. Combining that with witnessing Semiramis's truly harmful deceptions, Listener is now wary and treats any potential deceiver with aggression. Yet, although Listener raises a sword to challenge strangers and proven deceivers, she is kind and affectionate with those who have earned her trust."

"That explains a lot." Matt looked at Listener again as she continued pacing. "Any other long-term effects?"

"Not that I am aware of." Eagle pressed a fist against his chest. "Listener still has the heart to die for a loved one. In that regard, she is an inspiration to me. If an opportunity were to arise to give my life for another, I hope I can summon her courage and resolve."

An image flashed to Matt's mind—a dagger cutting a rope and him flying away from Lauren as she stood atop the tank. "Trust me. If you really love someone, it's not that hard."

Eagle laid a hand on Matt's shoulder. "It sounds as though I need to hear *your* story."

"There's not much to tell. I risked my life to save my sister's, but I don't even know if Lauren's alive." Matt's stomach churned. Thinking about what might have happened to Lauren was too much to take right now. It was time to change the subject. He patted the dragon's neck and forced a lively tone. "Shall we see if you can fly?"

Whistling a cheery note, Albatross bobbed his head. He shuffled to the cave's entrance and stopped in the spray. Shaking his body like a wet dog, he slung soot from his wings and scales, revealing a shimmering white coat.

85

Matt nodded at Eagle. "I'll see you in a little while." Without waiting for a reply, he slid the gun into his pocket and followed Albatross. After this successful healing, maybe others lay in store. If he could fly on the dragon and find the volcano survivors, Listener and Eagle could remain in this valley and take care of Mom. Together they could easily handle Semiramis.

As soon as Matt jumped through the spray, he stopped and looked around, waiting for his eyes to adjust. Above, Grackle flew in a circle, as if patrolling. Blaring a loud whistle, Albatross launched into the air and followed Grackle in flight, his wings beating without a hitch.

Matt exhaled. Excellent. Fully healed.

He trotted toward Listener. She stood near Mom less than thirty paces away, her sword pointed at Semiramis. "Any change?" he called as he approached.

"Only that your mother's song continues to strengthen." Listener stepped closer to Semiramis and pressed the flat of the blade against her cheek. "As I was about to say earlier, it is time that I dealt with this witch. I had to wait for a witness, and now that you have returned—"

"No!" Semiramis backed away slowly. "Listener, I can assure you—"

"Don't try to beguile me. I am not a little girl anymore."

Semiramis's voice shook. "I was always forced to do what I have done. Arramos—"

"Arramos?" Listener twisted the blade, rubbing the edge against Semiramis's cheek. "You are a deceiver. Time and again you have woven a web of lies, promising alliances with us while plotting our destruction. We would be fools to allow you to stay anywhere near us."

"Listener." Matt set a finger on her arm, but she shook his touch away.

"I'm not going to let you spin another web while I'm around."

"Listener!" Matt touched her arm again. "She saved my life."

Her fiery eyes focused on him. "That means nothing. She also saved my life, but in the end she tried to kill us all. She has betrayed us too many times to count. She is a witch, a sorceress, a demon!"

Semiramis widened her eyes, making her look scared and vulnerable. "You have every right to be skeptical. I have, indeed, betrayed you, but I spent more than fifteen years in captivity considering my many misdeeds. My sole purpose has been to conquer Arramos, and I made the mistake of trying to maintain an alliance with him so that I could be close when the time came to destroy him."

"At our expense," Listener said. "You stabbed us in the back to get to Arramos, and at the most crucial time, you tried to take

Acacia so that you could use her blood to build an invincible army. You cared for no one except yourself and your sycophant son. You didn't hesitate to destroy anyone who stood in your way." Her chest began to heave, and a tone of lament blended into her voice. "Because of you, Acacia is dead. Because of you, Yellinia is dead." Finally her voice shattered. "Because of you, my father … my father …" She bit her lip hard and looked at Matt, tears brimming.

Matt touched Listener's wrist and guided the blade away from Semiramis. "Pretty serious charges."

"And completely true." Semiramis lowered herself to her knees. "And now I repent of my crimes and ask for forgiveness. Listener, if you can find it in your heart to show mercy to this wretched sinner, you will see that I have changed."

Listener glared at her, her fingers tightening around her hilt. Her companion zipped to the front of her face and flashed red. Nodding, she took in a deep breath. After drying her cheeks with her sleeve, she spoke in a controlled tone. "I have seen your repentant act before, and I will not be deceived again. You and your arts are not welcome."

"My supernatural arts, yes, I understand, but I am also skilled in the natural art of medicinal potions, as I have proven in the past. I can be of great service."

"Only to get closer to us, as you said you were trying to do with Arramos. Then you sneak up from behind and stab us in the back." Listener set the point of her sword near Semiramis's throat. "We will have none of that."

Matt touched Listener's arm. "Don't you think we should use her help?"

Listener let out a huff. "Her help is poison."

"Didn't she help you?"

Listener spun on the balls of her feet and pointed the blade at Matt. "Your support of this bloodsucker is too persistent for my liking."

The companion flashed again, but Listener paid no attention.

Swallowing, Matt edged away. "Okay … what do you want to do? Kill her?"

Listener narrowed her eyes at Semiramis. "She is already dead, and slaying her here would send her to her rightful place, eternal torment in the Lake of Fire. We would be justified in hastening her journey there."

Semiramis shuddered but said nothing.

Listener's companion floated in front of her eyes, alternating between red and blue flashes. When it blinked off, she let out a resigned sigh. "We will send her away, though I realize the danger. Once she is out of sight, we won't know what mischief she is concocting. But I prefer a hidden stalker over a close betrayer. If she finds her way to the villages and helps people, then so be it, but we should consider her to be a hostile enemy. No conversing with her. No secrets shared."

"So she's free to go?" Matt asked.

Listener nodded. "The way to the village is dangerous. She can either stay here in the valley or risk dropping in the exit waterfall. If she proves herself …" She glanced at her companion. "Then I will reconsider her status among us."

Semiramis rose to her feet. As a tear trickled down her cheek, she backed away. "If forgiveness requires a trial, I accept that. Considering my crimes, I am in no position to demand mercy."

"Just go." Listener clenched her teeth, her sword shaking in her grip. "I want you out of my sight."

"I will not disappoint you." Semiramis turned and strode downstream.

Matt sidled up to Listener. "I guess that was the best decision. If she had stayed with—"

"I am not interested in your opinion, Matt Bannister." Listener kept her stare on Semiramis. Her eyes cold and steely, if a look could kill someone from a distance, Listener's would. Yet, sadness mixed in. Her bent, wrinkled brow quivered, as if ready to slacken. It seemed that she wanted to cry, but her warrior's training refused to allow it.

"Matt?"

"Mom?" He turned and scrambled to his mother's side. Listener joined him and knelt at the opposite side.

Still lying on her back, she smiled weakly. "Hello, Son."

He stooped and took her hand in both of his. She looked fragile, too frail to embrace. "It's great to see you."

"You, too." She massaged his knuckles with her thumb. "The last thing I remember was going to sleep in a boat. I thought I would end up in Second Eden, but I didn't expect to see you."

89

"I didn't expect to see anyone. I thought I was done for." Matt smiled, but he couldn't keep his lips from trembling. "How did you get away from Tamiel?"

"Well, it's a long story. I'll tell you more when I get my strength back."

"Yeah, you took quite a spill from the boat. If not for your wings slowing you down, we couldn't have caught you."

Her eyes darted. "I had a gun. Did you find it?"

"It's in my pocket. We thought it was draining your energy."

"It was, but I'm immune here." Her words spilled out as if she were in a dreamlike daze. "As long as the energy stays in the gun, I don't lose any, but when I inject my energy into people who need it, I will be drained."

"Are you sure you're okay?" Matt waved a hand in front of her face. "You look kind of out of it."

"I feel out of it." After shaking her head, her eyes sharpened. "I was about to say I charged the gun before coming to Second Eden, and I think the pain it caused knocked me out. I feel better, at least for now."

Matt withdrew the gun from his pocket. "Why would you want to drain your own energy?"

"If I shoot someone with it, that person receives the energy." She propped herself on her elbows. "I was told to come here to help people with it."

"Well, a volcano exploded, and we need to look for survivors, but you can't help, not in your condition."

"Since the gun infuses energy," Listener said, "maybe you could shoot it into your mother and help her recover."

Mom shook her head. "I put my energy in that gun myself. It needs to go to those who need it."

"You need your own energy." Matt slid his finger in front of the gun's trigger. "I'll shoot it back into you, and you can rest here while Albatross and I look for survivors."

"No. Only I can use it. It's genetically locked." Mom extended a hand. "Help me up."

"You don't have the strength," Matt said. "As soon as you're able, we can—"

"This is not the time to disobey your mother." She shook a finger, but a poorly hidden smile gave away her mirth.

"All right. All right." Matt grasped her wrist, hoisted her to her feet, and slipped the gun into her hand.

After wobbling for a moment, she steadied herself. Then, her eyes shot open. "Who is that?"

Matt turned. Eagle walked toward them slowly, his gaze upward as he watched the dragons fly. "Don't worry, Mom. He's a friend."

Her eyes narrowed. "He looks so familiar. I think I know him."

"How could that be?" Listener asked, now standing next to her. "Eagle has never been to your world."

"And I haven't been to yours ever since ..." A smile broke out on Mom's face, and tears pooled in her eyes. "Never mind. I understand now, but I think I shouldn't say anything more about it."

Albatross landed in a run, his wings settling as he drew near. Blowing an excited whistle, he nuzzled Listener's cheek with his own.

"Well," she said, patting his neck, "it seems that our healer's works have matched his words."

As Mom stepped closer to Albatross, her own wings flapped slowly. "I trust that this valiant steed can carry Matt and me to the village so I can begin my work."

Albatross whistled a sharp note and lowered his head to the ground.

"He is glad to." Listener drew back and looked the dragon over. "But I am still concerned about his health. Only moments ago he lay dying."

Eagle joined them, his smile gleaming as he extended his hand. "You must be Matt's mother. My name is Eagle."

As Mom took his hand, tears trickled down her cheeks. "I'm Bonnie Bannister." Her voice quivered. "Your eyes. They're so bright and sparkling."

Drawing his hand back, Eagle laughed. "They say I have eyes like an eagle."

Matt tried to read his mother's expression. There seemed to be much more to this encounter than a friendly greeting. "Anyway ..." Matt rubbed his hands together. "It looks like Albatross thinks he's healthy enough. He knows how he feels." He grinned at Listener. "I assume your analytical brain has already told you that."

Listener returned the smile and bowed her head. "I surrender to your superior argument."

Matt helped his mother climb Albatross's neck. He seemed strong and steady.

"I recommend that you stay low," Listener said, "not only to avoid the smoke at higher levels but also to avoid a fatal plunge should Albatross falter." She pointed downstream with her sword. "Once you are in the marshes, you can travel near the river's edge. The lava flowed heavily in that region, but I doubt that it made it all the way to the river. Even if you have to walk, you should be safe."

"What about you two?" Matt nodded at Listener and Eagle in turn. "Are you coming?"

Eagle stepped forward. "Yes, of course." His brow raised, he gave Listener a hopeful look. "I assume you agree."

"I do." Listener pointed at the ground with her sword. "We will follow on foot with the children. There are still a few shadow people in this valley who could overtake them if we were not here. With evening approaching, we need to be careful. The shadow people will come out of hiding as soon as it's dark."

"Evening?" Matt looked at the sun, closer to the horizon than before. "I must have slept longer than I thought."

"Also," Listener continued, "with Semiramis lurking, we'll need to watch for her."

"Semiramis is here?" Mom asked.

"She's somewhere nearby." Matt quickly told the story, from the slingshot ride into Second Eden to Listener's dismissal of the sorceress. She listened intently, neither commenting nor questioning.

When he finished, Mom gazed toward the forest on the opposite side of the river. "Sending her away was a wise decision. She can't be trusted."

Matt turned toward Listener. "If there's an exit waterfall in the way, how will you and Eagle and the children get out of the valley? You can't all fly on the other dragon."

Listener stared downstream. "When we reach the waterfall, Grackle can take us down to the swamp level one at a time, and we can walk from there. I have flown over this region hundreds of times, and Eagle is an expert tracker. We will have no trouble finding our way, but if you have no more need of Albatross when you arrive, you can send him back to help us."

"That should work." Matt climbed onto Albatross's back and settled in behind his mother. As he sat on the white scales, a sensation of warmth radiated into his wet skin and clothes.

Albatross let out two warbling whistles.

93

"He wants to know if that's warm enough," Listener called from the ground. "He'll adjust it if necessary."

Matt smiled. A dragon with a thermostat. Now that was a trait you couldn't find in storybooks. "It feels great. I don't get cold easily. I can regulate my temperature, just like ..." He whispered the rest. "Just like Albatross."

"If you see the flying hospital," Listener said, "signal the pilot to follow you. He might be waiting for someone to let him know it's safe to land."

"Got it." Matt set his hands on his mother's hips. Her wings, now folded in, kept him from getting close enough to wrap his arms around her waist. "Mom, I'll tell you what I know about the hospital on the way."

A child shouted from the cave. "Eagle!"

Everyone looked that way. A boy no more than seven years old staggered through the waterfall's spray, his expression frantic as he wobbled toward them. Eagle sprinted to the boy, scooped him up, and returned with him, setting him down when he arrived. "What's wrong, Blade?"

"Cheer …" Blade clutched Eagle's arm. "Cheer is gone. A woman came and blew some smoke at us. It made me dizzy. When I could finally see straight, the others were asleep, but Cheer was gone."

"Semiramis!" Listener drew her sword, her face flushed. "When I find her, I'll—"

"No!" Eagle grabbed her wrist. "Let me find Cheer. I'm the better tracker, and with Semiramis and the shadow people lurking, we need to get the other children out of this valley."

Listener shoved her sword back to its sheath, growling. "If she so much as leaves a bruise on Cheer, I will scalp her viperous head and use her hair as a foot wipe."

"Don't worry." Eagle's tone firmed. "I will find them both."

Listener's companion again flashed in front of her eyes, but she turned away. "I know, I know. Control my temper." After grumbling for a few seconds, she hugged Eagle and kissed his cheek. "I trust that you will find Cheer. Just take care. Semiramis is far more cunning than anyone you have ever dealt with."

"I will be careful." Eagle returned the kiss. "Let's send our friends on their way, and we can discuss our plans further. We have other options."

"Very well." Listener patted Albatross's neck. "Take Bonnie and Matt to Founder's Village. It might not look like it used to, so be ready to find it by sense of smell. When you're sure they no longer need you, come back to help me carry the children."

Albatross whistled a short trill. With a strong beat of his wings, he jumped into the air. Matt clutched his mother's shirt and held on. "You okay?" he shouted.

"Fine. Save your breath. The air's bound to get smoky."

Matt ached to continue the conversation. Obviously she knew something about Eagle, and she had to be worried about Cheer. Not only that, she never finished telling her story. How had she escaped from Tamiel? Why was she here? Was there more reason for the gun beyond what she explained? If so, why would Tamiel allow her to have it?

Trying to push away the questions, he scanned the sky. To the rear, Mount Elijah, now framed by hazy streaks from the setting sun, still spewed smoke and ash. In front, the river meandered gently toward a waterfall that spilled into an area covered by thicker haze.

Matt blinked at the smoky air. He had lost his jacket and outer shirt, so no breathing filters were available. Maybe the smoke wouldn't get too thick.

Mom lowered her head and let her body undulate with Albatross's. Although her facial expression stayed hidden, her body language spoke volumes. She was no ordinary mother. She was an experienced warrior.

Not long ago he imagined her as a pathetic crackhead, a teenager so desperate she left her baby at a church doorstep. But now? Now he had a mother without equal. She was a woman who had stared down the devil himself. And she was on a mission.

As Albatross flew past the waterfall, Matt set his jaw. He had to make her proud, and most of all, he had to make sure she returned safely to Dad. Nothing was more important.

THE DOOR TO HADES

The rental pickup truck bumped and lurched across the plateau. Lauren hung on to the passenger-side handgrip and leaned forward, hoping to get an early glimpse of a promised crater, but the bounces kept knocking her back.

Dad drove with both hands on the wheel, his brow bent and his lips pressed tightly. Something was bothering him more than bumps and bounces. Obviously Mom's kidnapping weighed foremost on his mind, but something else had cast a shadow over his expression.

She opened her mouth to speak, but addressing him aloud with a familial label still felt strange. She took a breath and forced it out. "Dad?"

He turned and gave her a smile. "Yes?"

"Do you sense danger?"

Looking straight ahead again, he nodded. "It's not much, but we have to keep our eyes open. It might just be a bear or a cougar. I can take care of that."

97

Lauren glanced at the glove compartment. Dad had put a handgun and holster in there when they left the regional airport. The thought of using it magnified their journey's danger. Still, he might have meant that he could use his fire-breathing instead of the gun. Either way, he had said this was a life-or-death mission, probably more dangerous than anything she had ever done. He wasn't talking about the local wildlife.

As her heart raced, Lauren hid a swallow. After getting kidnapped by a winged demon and barely surviving a nightmare jailbreak that included nearly burning in lava, how could she face something even more dangerous?

She closed her eyes. Maybe it would be better to concentrate on the goal—to find her mother by listening to her song, the song of the ovulum. And maybe they could find Matt, though that seemed impossible. If he didn't fall into the volcano, he probably flew into a faraway land no one knew.

Tears seeped past her closed eyelids. *Matt, why did you cut the rope? Why didn't you let me try to pull you in?* Yet, the answer was clear. If he hadn't cut the rope, they all probably would have died in the lava.

After a few minutes, the truck stopped and the emergency brake engaged with a quick series of clicks. "This is as close as we can get," Dad said. "It looks like the edges of the crater have eroded since the last time I was here."

Lauren opened her eyes. They had stopped on a downward slope that plunged into nothingness about twenty paces ahead. Dad pulled the holster from the glove compartment, strapped it around his chest and shoulder, and stepped out on the driver's side. "Let's get a look at the crater."

She unbuckled her seatbelt, opened the door on her side, and pressed a foot down carefully. The ground seemed stable. If a truck could park here without a collapse, walking around shouldn't be a problem.

A stiff, cold breeze gusted toward the edge of the crater. Lauren grabbed her prison-loaned parka from the back and put it on over her hooded sweatshirt as she stepped out fully. Dad didn't bother with getting his coat, though he shivered as he extended a hand. "Ready?"

She took his hand and walked stiff-legged toward the precipice. "Matt never gets cold. Do you have that trait?"

"I'm freezing. I just didn't see the point in bundling up when we have to sling on our backpacks in a minute. A parka will just get in the way." Dad gave her an apologetic nod. "I should have mentioned that."

When they neared the edge, he stopped and pressed the ground with his boot. A crack appeared near the toe. "Don't get any closer. It's brittle."

She clutched his hand more tightly, leaned forward, and looked into the depths. A flat floor lay far below, probably thousands of feet down. The height made her legs tremble, though no tingles coursed along her back. She would have to count on her natural hearing to listen for Mom's call.

After a few seconds, a melody drifted upward, the familiar song of the ovulum, though it sounded stretched out and thin, as if pinched by something. "This is the place," she whispered. "I hear my mother."

"That's great!" Dad stepped back and drew her into an embrace. "We'll find her soon. Just keep listening."

When they pulled apart, she bundled her coat closer. "Now that the truck engine's off, the song's not hard to follow."

"We'll have another engine here in a few minutes." He withdrew a phone from his pocket and pressed a speed dial. "When I was here years ago, the phone service was terrible, but we're using a satellite connection now."

After a few seconds, he looked at a GPS watch on his wrist and shouted into the phone. "Yeah, Dad. You'll have to speak up. Your blades are really loud. ... We're here. The song's coming from the crater, just like I guessed. Do you see my GPS signal? ... Yeah, the tracking chip wasn't hard to imbed. It's almost undetectable. ... Good. I'll text you the coordinates, just in case. ... How are you feeling? ... That bad, huh? Walter should have dragged Mardon back to the prison by now. He promised to give us information about the disease. ... Yeah, we left *Merlin* at the airport, hangar six. They had a four-wheel-drive pickup to rent, and it has a good-sized cab for our gear. ... Right. See you soon."

He pressed the end button and began texting with his thumbs. "I'll copy Walter on this. Once we make a portal jump, we won't have another chance. As Walter once said, there aren't any cell towers in Hell."

100

"Yeah. I guess not." Lauren shuddered. Walter's description of Hell still burned in her mind—the odor of sulfur and roasting flesh, human souls writhing in black fire, like flaming buoys bobbing in a dark sea of horror. He sounded like a sports announcer giving a play-by-play account of eternal condemnation.

Dad snapped the phone closed. "Something wrong?"

She nodded. "I guess I don't like the thought of going to Hell." She laughed inside at her own statement. It sounded like the tearful lament of an actress in one of those cheesy dramas the leaders sometimes performed at Micaela's youth group. They often used fear of Hell to scare people into Heaven, but the script always raised more groans than tears.

"Trust me, I'm scared, too." He laid his hands on her shoulders. "You don't have to go with me. Now I know for sure where her song's coming from, so I can—"

"No." She wrapped her hands around his wrists. "We've been through this. I have to go. I'm scared, but not scared enough to turn around."

He raised his eyebrows. "Are you sure? I can send you back on the helicopter."

She looked into his hazel eyes. Love poured forth, gentle yet strong. When they made plans back at the prison, he offered to take Joran and Selah, but everyone knew he was just trying to protect his daughter from harm. Ashley and Walter needed Joran and Selah's abilities, so that left only one Listener available. Not only that, the lyre had stopped showing Mom's image. It wouldn't be of any help.

She nodded firmly. "I'm sure."

He kissed her forehead, then pushed a lock of hair from her eyes. "I'm proud of you. You have your mother's courage."

"Thank you." She nodded at the phone in his hand. "You mentioned a tracking chip. Is it in the phone?"

101

"That's one signal." He touched the top of his scalp. "Ashley embedded another one under my skin. One way or another, they should be able to track me."

Chopper blades whirred in the distance. Lauren angled her head to find the source. "I hear your parents."

"We'd better get our gear." As they walked to the truck, he gave her a smile. "They're your grandparents. Have you decided what you'll call them?"

"No, but I'll figure out something." Nicknames rolled through her mind—Granny, Meemaw, and Papa, but they seemed so juvenile. If she had grown up using those names, maybe they wouldn't feel so awkward.

Dad opened the truck cab's back door and pulled out a coil of rope and two backpacks, stuffed to overflowing with an extra shirt and pants, cereal bars, bottled water, pens, and knives.

While he checked the supplies, Lauren retrieved an hourglass-like device Ashley had called Apollo and held it by one of its four outer dowels. In spite of the rough ride, its rectangular glass enclosure survived without a crack.

She checked a trio of digital meters on its hockey-puck-like top. The glass over them also appeared to be fine. She pressed one of a series of buttons that programmed Apollo's communications protocols and its ability to generate a portal-opening flash. They were in working order.

She read the meters. Normal. There appeared to be no portal here. On the way, she had read operating instructions out loud while Dad drove. He already knew how an older model worked, but they both had to get up to speed with this new version. The first model needed a supercomputer to read the meters remotely and provide calculations for generating the flashes, but Ashley, before she was arrested, upgraded Apollo with its own processor so the settings could be calculated on-site. In fact, it now had a huge memory that allowed it to collect all light anomalies, including portal splits, both those it created and those it didn't, thereby allowing it to replicate an opening. Not only that, Ashley downloaded the settings from other portal openings accomplished by an older model of Apollo.

Earlier, Dad had told her that Apollo had always been able to physically transport small objects to other realms, but Ashley enhanced its data transfer mode, allowing it to send digital information about objects in its glass enclosure or from a data source plugged into its docking interface. Apollo had become a cross-dimensional data station.

Dad, now wearing a miner's helmet, complete with a light on the front, held a second helmet. "It might be too big, but you'll need it. I also put the night-vision goggles in your pack."

"Super." She took the helmet. "Thanks."

"Do you remember how to use the goggles?"

She nodded. "You're a good teacher."

After she put the helmet on, he held out a backpack. "Need help?"

"Sure." She had to raise her voice to compete with the sounds of the approaching helicopter. "Let me get this coat off."

By the time they stowed her coat in the truck and slid on their backpacks, the whipping air signaled the chopper's descent. Within seconds it landed about twenty yards farther from the crater.

Dad ducked under the slowing blades and opened the front passenger-side door. When Marilyn Bannister stepped out, they embraced warmly.

Jared Bannister stayed put in the pilot's seat, his hand on the steering stick. With graying hair, sunken cheeks, and deeply wrinkled skin, he looked worn and frail, very little like the man Lauren had seen when he picked up Walter not too long ago. Obviously, the mysterious disease had strengthened its hold quickly.

Marilyn slid open the rear door. With the wind beating back her short, gray-streaked dark hair, she waved an arm. "Come on over, Lauren! Jared's not going to shut off the engine. Don't be afraid of the blades."

Lauren hiked up her backpack and, still holding Apollo, jogged to the helicopter. The weight in the pack bounced, but not painfully so, just a heavy but necessary burden. Might this be what her mother felt during her teen years when she carried an uncomfortable weight she had to live with every day?

"Are you sure this is enough?" Marilyn asked as she tugged on Lauren's sweatshirt sleeve.

"Dad says it should be. It has some kind of protective coating for portal jumps, just like our pants, so we don't want to wear anything over them."

"That's true." Marilyn raised Lauren's hood. "But mother hens have to keep their chicks warm, you know."

"I know. I appreciate it." Lauren hugged her, then climbed into the rear of the helicopter and waited for her father to board. When she leaned back, something sharp dug into her skin, but her scales kept it from hurting. Yes, Mom must have felt pain, especially the pain of realizing that the discomfort would never end. With people constantly teasing her about her backpack, she must have had the urge to strip it off and scare them with her wings.

Lauren smiled. *That would teach those losers.*

Dad climbed into the helicopter and sat in the opposite seat. "What are you grinning about?"

She stared at her feet but didn't try to hide the smile. "Just thinking about Mom."

"Me, too." He leaned forward and took her hand. "My father's checking with Larry about radar coverage, so we have time to talk before it gets too loud."

She looked up at him. "Something we didn't talk about on the way here?"

He nodded. "I've been thinking about all the dangers you've faced." His eyes sparkled with tears. "I'm so proud of you. I wish I could tell the world about my daughter's courage."

She blinked. "I wasn't brave. I was so scared I thought I'd pass out at any second. Besides, what you and Mom went through was a lot worse. I mean, you both died, for crying out loud. You've both been to Hades. You've both faced the devil." Laughing under her breath, she shook her head. "*I* couldn't have done that."

Dad patted her hand. "A few days ago, if someone had told you that you were going to face a powerful demon, break someone out of a high-security prison, ride a fire-breathing dragon, and stand on a tank over a volcano while trying to create a musical

104

shield that would keep you from falling into a pit of lava in another world, what would you have said?"

"I would have told them to get a drug test."

"And you would've thought you'd never be able to do it."

She nodded. "I get your point."

"I'm sure you get most of it." He tightened his grasp on her hand, firm but not painful. "Courage isn't always something you plan. Once in a while you know in advance about difficult times you have to face, and you have a chance to build courage beforehand. We need tests of courage like those. But a lot of opportunities to show courage aren't mapped out for you. They come without warning. That's the real test of faith and character—how you react to sudden fear. If danger jumps out at you, of course you get scared. We all get scared. But how you respond makes all the difference."

He averted his gaze, a faraway look in his eyes, as if searching for more words. She angled her head to read his expression. "Go on," she whispered. "You can say anything to me. I won't take it the wrong way."

A new tear glistening in his eye, he returned his gaze to her. "Well, I guess what I was going to say is this. You have a rare opportunity. You know that danger lies ahead, so you can summon courage beforehand, but at the same time, you have no idea how that danger will show itself, so you can rely on the one who will be with you through every danger."

"You mean God," she said with a prodding nod.

"Right." He looked away again, his voice faltering. "I mean God. He's never failed us. ... Never."

Lauren tried to catch his gaze again. He seemed to be trying to convince himself of his own words. After fifteen years of isolation, separated from the love of his life, he had held her again for

105

a few precious moments. Then, a vicious demon dragged her away, promising to make her suffer beyond all imagination. How could even the strongest of men hold up against such a battering ram of horrors? Somehow she had to find a way to boost his confidence.

"I suppose it's like that for you all the time, being ready for danger, I mean. You can sense it coming, so you can look for it."

"True. But when I'm in Hades, I don't always feel it. I have to rely on faith, so we'll both be in the same rocking boat facing the storm together."

She grinned. "I prefer a steady sofa, a mug of hot chocolate, and a picture window so I can watch the storm while curled under an electric blanket."

"Maybe we'll get to do that someday." He reached for her other hand. "Let's pray. We're going to need a lot of help."

"Uh … sure." She wedged Apollo between her legs and took his other hand. "Out loud?"

He lifted his brow. "Not used to that?"

Lauren shook her head. "But that's okay. I want to pray. I mean, I'll listen to you … if that's all right."

"Perfectly all right." He bowed his head, but just as he began, the blades accelerated, drowning his voice in the whipping drone.

She strained her ears. The words *Bonnie* and *help* pierced the noise, and the passion in his tone broke through. As the helicopter lifted off, a tingle spread across her scales, and her father's words crawled into her ears.

"Bonnie is strong. She is brave. She is willing to give her all, a ripened tree ready to feed someone starving for life, ready to plant her sacrificially spilled seeds in the hearts of others so that they, too, can germinate into fruitful trees and restart the cycle of sacrifice and new life that you began so long ago. I know she will face this trial with faith and courage, but will her love be a dagger turned against her? Tamiel is crafty. He knows her weaknesses. Yet you know them even more intimately.

"I will never forget the day I carried her dead body through the perils of the seventh circle of Hades. I thought all was lost. My courage flagged. My strength waned. When Sir Patrick and Devin argued about what I should do with Bonnie's body, my weaknesses overwhelmed me. I couldn't decide, so I just turned her over to you and trusted that you would honor my faith. And, of course, you did."

After taking a deep breath, he continued. "Now again I am weak. I have no control over this situation. We have only a song to follow and a collection of tools that I made a wild guess about. We are so ill-prepared, I feel like we're fishing in the ocean while floating in a teacup and waiting for a hurricane boiling on the horizon."

He gave Lauren's hands a gentle squeeze. "So I turn my beloved over to you once more. Help both Lauren and me find the courage we need to brave this storm. Bring Bonnie home, but most of all bring glory to yourself through our weaknesses." After taking another breath, he added, "In Jesus' name, amen."

"Amen." Lauren gazed at her father's tears, one trickling from each eye. This man was unashamed of his emotions. That took real strength, true masculinity. Even after all that time in prison, he had not grown bitter. No wonder Mom loved him so much.

Soon, the helicopter landed at the bottom of the crater. Lauren, her father, and Marilyn got out. As before, Jared left the blades spinning at half speed. The engine hummed though not loudly enough to force them to shout.

Dad walked several steps from the chopper, eyeing the ground—mostly stone and sand, but a few sprigs of grass grew in depressions where moisture had collected. Snow hadn't fallen here. Apparently the blizzard stayed south of Montana.

Lauren followed, carrying Apollo. Dad had mentioned two possible portals in the crater. The closer one would be harder to find than the other.

After sliding sand away in several places, he stooped and tapped the ground. "I think it was here."

"That didn't take long." Lauren crouched next to him and set Apollo on the spot.

"I thought it might take longer. It's been more than fifteen years, but some events never leave your mind. My mother and I had a reunion here after not seeing each other for four years."

Marilyn joined them, and the three crouched around Apollo. "And then I didn't see you for fifteen years," she said. "We've been apart more years than we've been together."

"When everyone's reunited, we should all go somewhere where no one can find us." Dad slid Apollo a few inches to one side. "The way the connection between Hades and Earth works has always confused me. When the two realms merged, this area was the mobility room in the underground mines, and when the ground above it collapsed, this crater was formed. There was a portal here that led to a cave in the Valley of Shadows in Second Eden. I used it myself. I came back to Earth and found you …" He nodded at Marilyn. "And Yereq camped out in the crater."

"So you think the portal's still here?" Lauren asked.

"That's what Apollo will tell us." He touched its top. "I'll let you practice your spectrometer-reading skills."

Lauren leaned closer and read the digital meter at the center. The default setting, white light, displayed a normal reading for daylight. As she pressed a button that shifted the readout through various frequencies—infrared to ultraviolet to gamma to X-ray—she read the numbers. "The readings are different than they were when we tested it on the way, but they're not far off. Does that mean a weak portal is here?"

Dad raised his brow. "Mind if I look?"

"Not at all." She edged away, still crouching. "I've never done this before."

As Dad went through the same process, he chatted without looking up. "You'll be in charge of sending data to Larry. All you have to do is lay my phone on top of Apollo and turn on its infrared link, then you set it to transmission mode and push its activate button. With the upgrades Carly and Adam installed, we can even send photos and video to Larry from Hades or Second Eden. That way we can stay in touch with Earth."

Lauren grinned. "Good. I gave Walter a hard time about not taking a camera to Hades. Maybe we'll get the world's first photos of that place."

When Dad finished, he picked up Apollo and extended it toward her. "Good job. The readings do indicate a portal, but it's probably too hard to open with Apollo. We would need a big fire, something like Sapphira could provide."

Lauren grasped a dowel. "Disappointed?"

"Not really. This would have been a simple way to get into Second Eden, but the valley where it comes out is filled with creatures called shadow people. I tangled with them way too many times. They can smother you in sticky darkness faster than a tsunami of tar."

Lauren cringed. That conjured a scary image. Dad had come up with vivid ways of describing his ordeals.

"Then on to the mining tunnel?" Marilyn asked.

Dad touched one of his ears. "What does our radar girl think? Which direction is the song coming from?"

Lauren shook her head. "I have to get away from the noise. The engine's too loud."

"Then let's go." Dad jumped up and hurried back to the helicopter. He leaned into the cockpit from the passenger door and shouted, "Going back to the prison?"

Jared nodded, his face grim. "We'll go and get *Merlin* as soon as we confirm your jump through a portal."

"I might be running out of the portal with a demon chasing me, so keep your ears on."

"We will." Jared waved. "Good-bye, Lauren."

She waved back. "Good-bye … um … Grandpa."

A smile warmed Jared's expression. "Keep glowing."

She forced a smile of her own. He looked sick, feeble, in pain. Why would the disease work slowly earlier and now worsen so quickly?

Dad tugged on Lauren's sweatshirt. "Let's see what your ears can pick up."

As the trio walked toward the crater's sheer wall, he whispered to Marilyn, "I sensed danger earlier, but it wasn't a big deal. I thought it might be a carnivorous animal of some kind, but not anymore. I think it's human, and it's getting closer."

She nodded. "Jared has a gun, and he can fly away. Don't worry about him."

"I'm worried about you. Lauren and I might be in a different world by the time danger shows up."

She patted her coat. "I have two guns, and I know how to use them."

"I'll let you know if the danger spikes." Dad stopped at a hole in the wall, too low to walk through. "Quiet enough now?"

"I think so." Lauren trained her ears on the hole. With no tingles erupting on her back, her sensitivity was lower, but the song still came through. "It's definitely coming from inside."

"Perfect." Dad crouched at the entrance. "We'll have to crawl here, but the clearance improves farther inside." He dropped to all fours and shuffled through, the coil of rope dragging in one hand and his backpack scraping the top of the entry.

After he and Marilyn disappeared, Lauren followed on one hand and both knees, holding Apollo with her free hand. Her own backpack scraped at times, but not enough to slow her progress.

For a few seconds, light from outside allowed a view of Marilyn's boots and the seat of her pants, but when they bent around a curve, everything grew dark. After another few seconds, a hand grasped her wrist and helped her rise.

"Well, at least it's easy to see you." Dad's helmet light sent a bright beam knifing around the chamber. "It's odd that your glow is so clear, but it doesn't shed light on anything else."

Lauren touched her cheek. "I don't really know how it works, just that it's brighter when I get emotional."

"It could be a benefit, unless we're trying to hide." He turned on her helmet light, sending a second beam across his. "Put Apollo down so it can get a good reading."

She set Apollo on the floor and sent her beam against the rocky sides of the cave, then on another wall at the back, a dead end.

"Now we'll see what our little friend has to tell us." Dad peered at Apollo's digital meter on its top, its display illuminated from within. "There's definitely a portal here. The spectral readings are through the roof."

"Does it lead to Hell?" Lauren asked.

"To Hades, I think. There is a difference." He pointed his beam at the dead end. "Bonnie told me about this part of Hades before we were arrested."

Lauren read the series of numbers on the meter. White light readings jumped around because of the helmet beams, but the others stayed steady. "Mom said something about Tamiel starting her in paradise. Why would they go to Hades?"

"Other portals are there. My guess is that opening a portal to Hades wouldn't show up on the government's monitors. They're focused on cross-dimensional signals directly from Second Eden, so they wouldn't notice this one. They're ignorant about other paths."

"So Tamiel took Mom to Hades first, then someplace else?"

"Probably. The mysterious part is why the song is still coming from the portal, since it's closed right now. I guess her song is able to travel through anything she passes through."

"I suppose so." Lauren heaved a sigh. "Well, we gotta do what we gotta do."

"Right, but don't worry. I've been to every realm I know about except one, and I survived. And Walter went to the only place I missed, the Lake of Fire, and he's still kicking. I'll be at your side every minute."

Lauren shuddered again. Walter's description returned with a vengeance.

"What's wrong?" Her father touched her cheek. "Your glow is almost as bright as your light."

She laid her hand over his and forced a smile. Telling him the truth about everything was so easy. "My emotions. And my hearing gets better. I can even read unguarded thoughts."

He blinked. *Thoughts? Like this one?*

"Like that one. I guess I didn't tell you before. It's not exactly something people want to hear."

"True, but it could be a big help." He withdrew his hand and looked at Marilyn. "Better stand back. I'm ready to flash Apollo. If the portal's too big, we don't want it taking you with us."

"Will do." She retreated a few paces and stooped inside the low entry tunnel. "What's your danger meter say?"

"Nothing, and that's got me worried. The portal presence might be affecting me."

"In that case …" Marilyn drew out a gun. "I'm ready."

Dad tapped his jaw. "Larry, are you there?"

Lauren tapped her own jaw and listened to her tooth transmitter, but only static came through.

"Nothing," Dad said. "Too much interference."

Lauren opened her mouth, hoping to get better reception, but it didn't help. "Could the portal be causing that, too?"

"Most likely." He rubbed a finger along one of Apollo's meters. "Can you still hear Bonnie's song?"

Lauren touched the cave's back wall. "I hear it better over here, but now it's mixed with a lot of other voices. The others are moaning, but it's not a song at all, just random moans."

"The sounds of suffering." Dad set his finger on a button at Apollo's base. "I'm not waiting for Larry to answer. I'll trust the local processor. Raise your hood and pull your hands into your sleeves."

Lauren lifted her sweatshirt's hood and set her helmet on top.

"Lights off."

She flicked off her beam.

"Here goes." A brilliant flash burst from Apollo's center. Like a splash from a wave, the radiance spilled over the cave's back wall, making a ragged square of sizzling light, as if someone had painted a phosphorescent double doorway.

Dad raised his hood and pinched it closed in front, his hands hidden in his sleeves. As he leaned through the opening, his backpack smoldered on contact.

113

"Dad?" Lauren called. "Are you all right?"

"Fine." He jerked back and batted away the sparks. "We should have put more of Ashley's retardant on the backpacks."

"What did you see?" Marilyn asked as she rose and drew closer.

"Just another tunnel. Apollo's residual light let me see pretty far, and I felt no danger, so I assume it's safe."

"Except that your danger sensing might not be working."

"Right. We'll just have to be careful." He hoisted the rope coil over his shoulder, covered his face again, and leaped through. After pivoting, he looked back, his forehead knitting. "From this side, the portal is a doorway in front of a pile of rocks, like the cave ceiling collapsed."

Marilyn took a step closer. "So there's only one way to go?"

"There's a hole in the pile, but it's too small for me to crawl through." Dad waved a hand. "Lauren, let's go. Bring Apollo with you."

"Coming." Lauren looked at Marilyn. A blend of pride and fear etched her expression. She needed a boost. "See you in a little while, Grandma. I'll take good care of your son."

"I know you will." Marilyn kissed Lauren's forehead. "Stay strong."

Lauren grabbed Apollo, still glowing from the portal flash. She jumped through the hole and stumbled into her father's arms. While he brushed sparks from her backpack, the sizzling doorway shrank further, now about the size of a single door. "Keep your face and hands covered for now," he said. "We want to stay as invisible as possible."

"I won't argue with that. I'm sticking to the shadows."

"Let's check what's ahead." Dad let the rope coil drop to the floor and withdrew his phone.

114

As he looked at the screen, she nudged his ribs. "Any service? Maybe they built a tower since Walter's been here."

"No service." The phone's glow illuminated his smile. "Bonnie once drew a diagram of this place. Carly scanned it for me and sent it to my phone."

"A map of Hades?"

"At least this part of it." He handed her the phone. "Here. Try it. The map has a touch screen interface. There's a map of Second Eden in there, too."

She scanned the glowing diagram of twisting paths and chambers. Using her fingertips, she scrolled along a path and magnified various sections. "It's like a maze."

"It'll help us get to—" He cocked his head, blinking.

Lauren set Apollo on the floor and stood behind him as the portal continued shrinking. "Is everything all right?"

"I feel something."

Tingles spread across Lauren's back. "Danger?"

His answer came in a thought. *Hide!*

Lauren shuffled back into a shadow and crouched. Dad withdrew his gun and pointed it at the tunnel leading to the crater. "Mom! Someone's coming!"

Just as Marilyn extended her gun, a pair of projectiles flew from the low exit tunnel, each with a trailing wire, and jabbed her thigh. She grimaced and dropped to the floor, her body twitching as if locked in a seizure.

Dad fired his gun, ducked low, and leaped across the portal. His backpack sizzling, he jerked a man from the exit tunnel and snatched a taser from his grip. Gunfire cracked—twice, three times. Dad toppled, his face toward the portal. His eyes wide, he shouted with a thought. *Cover Apollo!*

115

The portal, hovering at eye level, shrank to the size of a dog-house door. Still crouching, Lauren grabbed Apollo and pulled it close to her chest.

The second man hauled Dad up by his wrist, forced him to stand, and pointed at the portal. "Does that lead to Second Eden?"

"Hades," Dad said, his backpack still smoldering. "The place you'll fry in if you don't let us go."

The first man, his face scratched and bleeding, pressed a gun against Marilyn's cheek. "One puff of fire and she's dead."

As the portal dwindled to the size of a mailbox, Dad drilled a stare into the second man's eyes. *Lauren, you'll have to do this yourself. You know how to use Apollo. Find your mother or get help in Second Eden. Don't come back here. They're sure to post a guard. Go! You can do this!*

As the opening diminished to a mouse hole, a final thought flowed. *I love you. Never forget that.*

CHAPTER

THE MOUTH OF ELIJAH

The portal disappeared in a splash of sparks. Lauren's chamber darkened. A slight glow emanated from Apollo's glass enclosure, barely enough to illuminate a ten-foot-high pile of boulders that blocked the way back.

Lauren panted. She swallowed hard. What now? Go it alone? Try to find Mom in the depths of Hades? With Dad captured and armed men guarding the entry cave, what other choice was there?

Tingles rushed along her scales. A click sounded. Water dripped somewhere. A skittering of feet raced across the floor. She flicked on her helmet light and pointed the beam at the base of a side wall. A red-eyed rat, black and scrawny, stared at her for a moment before dashing into the shadows.

Holding her breath, she panned the beam across the rock pile, a collection of stones and boulders that sloped upward at about a forty-five-degree angle. Near the top on the left side, the beam passed across the hole Dad mentioned. It was too small for him, like he said, but maybe she could wriggle through.

117

She forced herself to breathe slowly and deeply. *All right, Lauren. Get a hold of yourself. This isn't any worse than driving with a demon in the backseat. At least no one is texting you creepy messages.*

After taking a cleansing breath, she climbed up, careful to step lightly on the smaller, shifting stones. Once near the top, she knelt on a boulder and peered into the hole—a cylindrical tunnel that ran through the pile for about twenty feet, ending out in the open. Not far away, a castle-like house sat atop a steep slope of grass and weeds. Mist hung in the air, and a flowery fragrance passed by.

Lauren replayed her mother's description of where Tamiel was keeping her. It matched that place exactly. Could she be in the house on the hill? Mom had said something about starting in Paradise and descending into Perdition, whatever that meant, so she might have left already. Either way, there was more light outside than in the cave, so it made sense to try to get there.

She slid Dad's phone into her sweatshirt pocket, pushed both arms into the hole in the rubble, and tried to squirm through, but after a few feet, the passage narrowed. She clawed at the walls, but the rocks wouldn't give way. It would take a hammer or pickax to widen the path, and even then the hole might collapse.

She pushed her way back and descended gingerly until she reached the floor. Sweat trickled down her cheeks and back. It was definitely warmer here than on Earth, or maybe she had expended more effort than she had thought. In either case, with only a few bottles of water in tow, staying cool was a priority.

She set the helmet on the ground, aimed the beam deeper into the cave, and took off her backpack. After withdrawing the phone, she removed the sweatshirt and tied the sleeves around her waist. Now dressed in camo pants and a white T-shirt borrowed from the prison, she put the pack on and listened. Mom's song drifted by.

The source lay deeper in the cave, so she probably wasn't in that house anymore.

After donning the helmet again, she hoisted the rope coil over her shoulder and picked up Apollo. Only one option remained—to venture deeper into the cave.

She marched ahead on the narrow descending path, waving her light from side to side and glancing at the phone's map every few seconds. One path was labeled *Exit Tunnel*, her most likely location. If only it had a GPS locator to show exactly where she was on the map, that would help.

Still listening to her mother's song, she slowed her pace. Every movement felt surreal, as if strolling through a dream. Even her shoes grinding pebbles emitted a plastic crunch, artificial, as if the sound had passed through water. Mom's song, however, stayed constant, still somewhat pinched, and wailing laments continued to wash into the music.

As she walked, Dad's explanation about this place came to mind, part of a talk they had while they flew in Merlin. *"When Earth and Hades were merged, a passageway led to a series of tunnels where girls called underborns dug for magnetic ore long ago. Queen Sapphira was one of them, a pitiful waif at the time, and they lived in the depths of Hades without experience of anything beyond their world, though they read about a land without rocky ceilings, a land of sky and sun. Now that the two realms have been split once again, the path between them is sealed, so anyone wanting to go from one world to the other has to go through a portal. An Oracle of Fire can sometimes open an existing portal with flames from her hands, but normal people like us have to use Apollo. Without it, only a huge explosion and fire could open a door to another world, and that's only if the conditions are just right."*

Lauren shuddered. Those poor underborns! But at least they had each other. Walking alone in Hades felt like being marooned

119

on another planet. The oxygen tanks were nearly spent, and the only spacecraft had run out of fuel.

Memories of her father's words continued. *"I know of two portals within Hades. One is in a chamber that held part of a museum. At the top level of the museum, a portal led to a volcano in Second Eden, but I don't know if that portal exists anymore. The other portal is at the bottom of a chasm. It leads to a realm called the Valley of Souls—a holding place for people and dragons who are waiting to get resurrected to Second Eden or to Earth. Your mother and I prefer to call it Abaddon's Lair, because there's a place in Second Eden called the Valley of Shadows, and we sometimes got the two names confused. Anyway, you and I need to avoid that place if we can. Bonnie spent four years there before she finally got out, and she said the master of that land is a pain to deal with."*

Lauren shook her head. If not for seeing a portal to another world herself, Dad's words would be nothing more than a fairy tale, a scary bedtime story, but every bit of his tale was coming true.

Her light ran across a trap-door-sized hole in the floor. She stopped at the edge and shone the beam into the depths, but it revealed nothing but darkness.

She looked at the phone map. At the intersection between the exit tunnel and a wider tunnel, a label read *Caitiff Trap*.

"The ape men," she whispered. She let the helmet's beam knife into the trap's darkness again. If one of them fell into this hole, he could never climb out, could he?

Again looking at the map, she listened to the song. The melody, still mixed with laments, drifted in from the right. She scrolled the map in that direction until it reached the end—a chamber that held a round symbol labeled *Museum Room*. No other labels indicated a trap, so it should be safe to go that way. If the museum room still held a portal, even if it led to a volcano, that might be the only way out of this place.

After bypassing the trap, she quick marched along a level tunnel, then through a series of turns, ascents, and descents, all the while following the song and glancing at the map. Every open area along the way carried a new odor, ranging from musty to biting to perfume-like. Temperature fluctuated as well, though it always trended downward.

Carrying Apollo in one hand and the phone in the other, while lugging the rope over her shoulder and a heavy pack on her back, she kept up the quickest pace she could. With darkness shrouding everything except for the helmet's beam striking the tunnel floor a few feet in front, the path proved to be a dizzying maze. If not for the map, getting lost would have been unavoidable.

After several more minutes, she stopped and shone her beam on a high arch leading into a huge chamber. She looked at the map again. This had to be the right place. The museum room was probably somewhere past the arch. According to a pop-up notation, a flaming tree of life grew in a planter at the center of the museum, though a flood might have doused it years ago.

A light flickered inside the chamber, faint but unmistakable, and the pattering of running feet echoed within.

Sudden fear raised a tingle in Lauren's scales. The footsteps sounded human—no red-eyed rat this time.

She flicked off the helmet light. Now in darkness, she raised an arm close to her face. No glow. But that didn't mean much. While others often saw it easily, her own eyes never detected it.

She slid off her backpack, withdrew the night-vision goggles, and put them on with her helmet still in place. As she tiptoed forward, she scanned the chamber. Darkness had transformed into an eerie blend of phantom images. The flickering light, now reddish,

121

emanated from a circular building, too wide to see around to the rear and too tall to get a look at the top. A pair of broken doors lay open at the building's front leading to the light within. The same light shone through windows higher up, though dimmer at each succeeding level.

A draft brushed her cheeks, cool and moist, and a whisper followed. "Will you be my friend?"

Lauren sucked in a breath and froze in place. Glancing all around, she searched for the source of the plaintive call. Was it a boy? Certainly not a grown man. Maybe a teenager.

The draft returned, swirling around her head. A stench filled her nostrils—rancid, like a soured dishcloth.

"I'm so lonely. Will you stay with me?"

A silky touch tickled her cheek. She whipped off the helmet and goggles and batted the air around her face, as if casting off a spider web. When she lowered her hands, the odor faded along with the breeze.

Trembling, she flicked on the helmet light and panned it across the chamber. The shaky beam knifed through the darkness, striking a bare wall in the distance, then the cylindrical museum room, then another bare wall that wrapped around behind her. Nothing moved. No one was there.

Lauren gulped. Dad didn't mention anything about ghosts, but he probably just couldn't hear them when he last visited this place. Obviously someone had to be adding those laments to the background song. Maybe a condemned spirit broke away from the ghostly choir and now wandered these passages.

She slid the goggles over her head and let them dangle at her chest, then put the helmet on. It wouldn't do any good trying to talk to the poor soul. She couldn't be his friend. She couldn't stay with him. Loneliness would be his eternal shackles.

122

After taking several more steps, the helmet light now leading the way, she stopped at a pair of thin mats on the floor, like gym mats for tumblers and vaulters. Torn in several places, stuffing protruded from tiny holes. She looked at the phone's map. Another pop-up note explained that Sapphira and Acacia slept here.

Lauren stooped and ran her finger along a mat's surface. How could two girls trapped in Hades for untold centuries possibly survive? Most girls on the volleyball team complained about waiting ten minutes for a sibling to get out of the bathroom.

She turned toward the museum. Her angle with the doorway now allowed a view of the inside. A tree at the center stood about five feet tall. With a single tiny flame burning at the end of a branch, it looked like a Christmas tree carrying only one lit bulb.

She listened for footsteps. All was quiet except for the song, clearly emanating from the museum. After adjusting the rope coil on her shoulder, she rose and walked slowly, reverently, gazing at the mammoth building. Inside, the tree seemed to grow brighter and taller as she drew closer, though it was really no taller than herself. The flame flickered vibrantly, as if consuming the greenery, but it made no sound, not even a hiss.

123

When she arrived at the doorway, she stepped through. As she passed, an electrostatic crackle filled the air, though no feeling of static affected her skin, hair, or clothes. The moment her body fully entered the museum room, the noise ceased.

She set Apollo down and dropped the rope near a tall ladder leaning against a wall. How strange. Dad didn't mention a static sound, but, again, he might not have been able to hear it. She slid her arms out of the straps, let her backpack settle next to the coil, and pushed the phone into her pants pocket. Rotating her shoulders, she inhaled deeply. Much better. That load was getting heavy.

She took off the helmet and aimed the beam at the tree. Between the tree's little flame and the beam, the museum room had plenty of illumination. A few rocks and pebbles along with some sand lay strewn across the floor, as if rocky debris had rained from above. A ring of low stones ran around the tree's soil, framing a planter the same width as the tree's five-foot girth.

Tiptoeing, she edged closer to the noiseless flame. Flickering orange surrounded a trio of star-shaped leaves like an undulating glove. How could it keep burning without consuming its fuel? She extended a hand and cupped her palm over the flame, careful not to touch it. Warmth coated her skin. A normal fire would have scorched her by now. Maybe it wasn't real at all.

She touched the flame with a fingertip. "Ouch!" She jerked back and sucked the wounded digit. It was a real fire all right. She withdrew her finger and looked at the tip. Only a slight blister, no bigger than a pinhead. Fortunately, the flame didn't have time to do much damage.

Careful now to stay away from the fire, she skirted the tree and scanned the encircling wall. Flickering light danced along a series of built-in shelves, one on top of another, mostly empty past head height, though shadows of indistinguishable objects stood within the recesses high above. The lower shelves held a scattering of old books and scrolls as well as a few piles of newspapers, magazines, and candles of various shapes and sizes.

She shuffled closer to one wall and reached for a stack of magazines. As her hand passed the shelf boundary, another crackle filled her ears. She grabbed the top two magazines and jerked her hand back. The noise stopped again. Might there be that much static electricity in the air?

She read the magazine covers—*National Geographic* from 1912 and *Life* from 1940, both finger-worn with several dog-eared cor-

124

ners. She slid them back in place, again raising the crackling noise as her hand passed into the cubbyhole.

Backing away, she listened. The melody from her mother's song came through loud and clear, now without the accompanying laments. But from which direction? The entire room seemed like a big stereo system with speakers all around, as if the song bounced off the walls.

After donning the helmet again, she looked above and concentrated on the upper reaches of the room. As her vision climbed the shelves, the beam and the tree's light faded—nothing but dimness and shadows after about five levels. According to Dad, the portal lay up there somewhere.

She picked up Apollo and stepped on the ladder's lowest rung. There wasn't much else to do but give it a try. She climbed, skipping a broken rung near the bottom. When she reached about the twentieth rung, her shoulder brushed a wooden truss. Above, the ladder ended after five more rungs. If a portal existed, it probably wasn't any higher than this level.

She aimed her light at Apollo's digital meters. As in the entry tunnel, the readings indicated a portal, but where exactly? She shifted her light to the center of the room where the truss intersected another at a right angle. That had to be the most likely spot. Climbing out there with Apollo wouldn't be too hard, but if the portal opened inside a volcano, might more debris fall into this room? She shifted the beam to the floor where the rope sat in a coil. Maybe there was a way to create a flash from a safe distance.

After setting Apollo's programming to open a portal based on its readings, she hurried down the ladder. When she reached bottom, she set Apollo down, grabbed an end of the rope, and climbed back to the top. Using the helmet beam again, she searched for a counterweight on the shelves. A scroll came into view in one of the cubbyholes. When she picked it up, again raising the crackling sound, the wooden end clinked against a glass object.

She squinted. Glass in Hades? Strange, but checking on it could come later.

She tied the end of the rope around the scroll and tossed it over the intersection where the trusses met. As she held the other end, she let the rope slide through her hands until the scroll settled on the floor.

Still holding the rope, she shinnied down the ladder, detached the scroll, and tied that end to one of Apollo's dowels. She set Apollo's timer for one minute and, pulling the rope, lifted it toward the trusses. The rope slid easily. In less than a minute, she might have a way out of this place.

Finally, Apollo bumped against the trusses. Lauren tied the rope to the ladder frame and aimed her helmet light high. Apollo swayed under the intersection, slowing with each cycle. By the time the final thirty seconds elapsed it would probably be motionless enough.

126

As she waited, the scene at the prison yard came to mind. The dragons' flames encircled a field of lava. Rocks floated in the super-heated soup, bubbling and steaming. Again, her father's words came to mind. *I know of two portals within Hades. One is in a chamber that held part of a museum. At the top level of the museum, a portal led to a volcano in Second Eden.*

Lauren gulped. An *erupting* volcano?

Apollo flashed. Lauren dove toward the doorway and rolled out of the museum. She flipped to her stomach and looked back. Light poured in from above, and ash drizzled at the center of the room, landing on the tree.

Lauren pressed her hands against the floor to get up, but her fingers slid into something sticky. She lifted a finger. Red liquid dripped from the tip.

Grimacing, she drew back and wiped her finger on the floor. Someone had bled here. And it had to be fresh, unless blood didn't clot as quickly in Hades.

She climbed to her feet and dashed back inside, hearing once again a split-second crackle. From now on it would probably be better just to ignore the sound. It obviously wasn't harmful.

Above, a hole to the sky replaced the entire circular ceiling. All around the hole, smoke rocketed skyward while ash fell like snow. Apollo hung from the trusses, still visible just below the opening.

After removing her helmet and goggles, she began scaling the ladder. As she drew closer to the portal, the air temperature rose, though still tolerable, and the song grew louder. Her waist now at Apollo's level, she lifted her hand into the portal plane, then jerked it back and looked at her skin. A little red, but not too bad. This portal didn't appear to be as electrified as the one she and her father had entered.

127

She untied the sweatshirt from her waist, pulled it on with the hood raised, then stepped up two more rungs and peeked over the opening. The portal barrier sizzled around her shoulders, but the protective coating kept the material from igniting. With her head the only part of her body out in the daylight, she felt like the red-eyed rat peering out of a sewer manhole. Smoke billowed all around, and ash flew everywhere in flashing swirls.

Her throat narrowed, and an acrid taste gnawed at her tongue. She stepped down a few rungs and sucked in clean air. Her throat soon opened again. While she breathed, the portal began shrinking at the outer edges, but not as quickly as the previous one had.

She looked at the place where she had contacted glass earlier. A dark bottle stood next to a clear lab beaker, both about six inches tall. A label on the bottle read "Keelvar Extract – Apply liberally to your mask."

Lauren blinked. Mask? She searched the shelf and found a plastic bag filled with white dust masks, the kind builders used when sanding drywall. She pulled one out, opened the bottle, and poured a stream on the mask. The liquid gave off a pungent, perfume-like odor that hung in the air for a moment before fading.

After securing the bottle, she put the mask on and climbed up the ladder again, two steps higher than before. Her feet at the truss's level, she stepped onto the thick board and slid several feet toward the center to avoid the encroaching portal edges. The barrier again sizzled across her sweatshirt at waist level, but it did no harm.

A breeze pushed the smoke away, clearing her view. Now breathing easily through the mask, she stood directly over a volcano, as if floating a hundred feet above its decapitated peak. Below, lava bubbled and spewed fountains of thick redness. Heat dried her skin, almost unbearable, but the song of the ovulum flowed more clearly. Maybe she could spot Mom from this high vantage point.

She pulled the phone from her pocket and searched for the map of Second Eden. When it popped up on the screen, she compared it to the haze-covered landscape. In the distance, a river spilled into a valley. That could be Twin Falls River. But the rest of the landscape didn't match the map well at all. The forests were mostly gone, replaced by scorched logs, boulders, and lava slowly coursing in fiery paths, like flaming tentacles branching out to consume whatever they touched. Only a few collections of evergreens remained here and there, standing at a level the lava couldn't reach.

In one area, a high wall of lava pressed against a blockade of fallen trees. Flames shot up from the logs, burning them away. It wouldn't be long before the lava dam would burst and send a river of molten rock charging beyond the current boundary.

While scanning the landscape once more, she imagined what she must look like to anyone who might be watching. The top half of a body poked out of nothingness a hundred feet above a volcano. Yet, there was no sign of any life—no animals, no birds, and no Matt or Mom. No one could see her at all. Still, Mom's song played on and on. She had to be out there somewhere.

Lauren turned slowly, recording the panorama with the phone's video camera, though smoke blocked some views. She spoke into the microphone, hoping her voice wasn't too muffled by the mask, and explained her position and observations, but when smoke returned on a shifting wind, she had to stop. Besides, the edges of the portal inched closer to her waist. If she were to keep searching, she would have to slide farther out onto the truss, and that could get treacherous.

She ducked under the portal plane, shuffled back to the ladder, and climbed down two rungs. With light still abundant from the portal opening, the shelves were easy to see all the way to the wall.

After removing her sweatshirt and tying it to her waist, she touched the beaker next to the bottle. Rows of other beakers sat behind it, maybe twenty in all. Long, deep scratches marred the shelf. Might someone have slipped from the ladder and held on until he could set his feet on a rung again? Obviously it was impossible to know.

She grabbed the first beaker and descended the ladder. When she reached the floor, the portal shrank more quickly. Smoke poured down, but the narrowing hole soon pinched off the channel.

She stripped off the mask, draped the goggles' strap around her neck, and put the helmet on. With the tree's flame and her beam the only sources of light, she looked again at the phone's map of Second Eden. The devastation was terrible! How many people died? And there was no way to get down from the volcano to help them, at least not without a dragon. She sighed. What other options remained? Abaddon's Lair? Dad certainly didn't want to go there. It would have to be the last option.

Turning the beaker, she read the measuring lines on the side. This was like the kind she used in chemistry lab experiments. Scorched material lay at the bottom, strands of hair poking up from crusty grit that lined the inner glass. It smelled like burnt leather. Could something like this originate in Hades? Not likely.

After lowering Apollo with the rope, she sat cross-legged in front of it, opened its glass enclosure, and set the beaker inside. According to Dad, Apollo was preset for sending atomic-structure data directly to Larry the supercomputer. If so, Ashley would hear about it as soon as possible.

She set Apollo for analysis and pressed the activate button. A beam of greenish light emanated from the top, covering the beaker. Apollo buzzed for nearly a minute, then shut off. There. That was done. But what next?

She nodded. More data. Sending the video from Second Eden would let everyone know what happened, but adding even more information would be better. She took off the helmet and pointed the beam at herself, then aimed the phone's lens at her face and began recording. For the next few minutes, she provided a summary of all that had happened, including the apparent kidnapping of her father and grandmother. Although she tried to stay calm and stick to the facts, fear kept breaking through. The process felt like scratching a note on tree bark and tossing it into the ocean from a deserted island. Would anyone find it? If so, could they get past the guards to mount a rescue?

After recording the tree of life and the surrounding shelves, she set the phone on top of Apollo, turned on Apollo's infrared receiver, and downloaded the camera's video. When the process finished, she set the instruments for a cross-dimensional data transfer and pressed the activate button. Again Apollo buzzed, this time for longer than a minute. The data file was probably huge, and transmission band-width through the portal had to be pretty narrow.

Lauren sat again with Apollo in her lap. Light from the tree's single flame danced across its glass enclosure and painted a vibrat-ing rainbow on her shirt. At least maybe someone would send a dragon to the volcano in Second Eden and give her a ride out of Hades. But did the dragons make it back to Second Eden? If so, had they become victims of the volcano? If they had to stay on Earth, Sapphira could help Ashley open the portal, so one way or another, the rescue should come soon.

She unzipped her backpack, grabbed two cereal bars and a bot-tle of water, and leaned against a shelf. As she ate and drank, she scanned the room. What should she do now? Try to find another portal? Her gaze stopped at the doorway. *Oh, yes! The blood!*

131

After wolfing down the second bar and draining the bottle, she hustled to the spot and knelt close to the small pool. It seemed too big to have been spilled by a rat. She looked back at the lad-der. If the portal in the prison yard opened over the same volcano, could Matt have fallen in here?

Lauren aimed her helmet light at the floor. A few drops cre-ated a trail toward the archway entrance outside. She clenched a fist. Yes! Whoever bled in here was healthy enough to move. Maybe Matt was alive after all!

She skulked along the trail. Matt's image came to mind, Semiramis pressing a knife against his throat. That had to be where the blood came from. She stopped at a second pool under the arch. It appeared to be fresher, but no trail continued on the other side. Maybe he wrapped his wound with a piece of his shirt. Since he had Semiramis's knife, he could have cut a sleeve and made a bandage.

As her scales tingled, moans drifted past. The sad chorus felt like a heavy weight on her shoulders. She shook her head. The blood couldn't be Matt's. That was just wishful thinking. If he were here, he would have shown his face, or at least called out. The running footsteps proved that whoever was here a few minutes ago didn't want to be seen. Matt would know there was no danger to hide from, wouldn't he?

She shone her light at the museum room. Her backpack lay in view just inside the doorway. Maybe it would act as bait. If she kept quiet, whoever was out there might come to see what was in it.

She entered the tunnel leading out of the chamber, turned off her helmet light, and slid the goggles over her eyes. Crouching behind a rock protruding from the side wall, she watched the museum room through the infrared viewer. New sweat trickled down her back, accentuating the tingles. Someone had to be out there. Maybe a thought would come through and give the person away. He was hurt, bleeding. Might offering help spark a friendship with someone who knew how to get around this place?

As the tree's tiny fire burned on, so did Mom's song. They seemed attached somehow, as if note changes coincided with flickers in the light. It was just imagination, of course, but it was eerie all the same.

The scene conjured images of a solitary lighthouse standing on a promontory in the midst of a gloomy night. Except for the lighthouse itself and its surrounding rocks, everything lay blanketed in blackness.

More thoughts of Matt came to mind, the way he always stepped up to protect her, especially when he cut the rope. He wasn't like any guy at school or even at Micaela's church. He actually seemed to care about her as a person—someone who really mattered. In a way, it would be amazing if he weren't her brother, then …

She shook away the thought. Matt was a perfect brother, exactly what she needed, a real friend who wouldn't care about her glow or her radar ears. Friendship would be enough.

As her emotions spiked, so did the tingles. Sounds poured in. The laments grew louder. Words formed, stretched out and forlorn.

> I daily die,
> Alone and lost;
> I lived a lie;
> I pay the cost.

> Inhale the fires;
> Exhale despair.
> Each day expires
> Without a prayer.

And the song continued, repeating again and again. Although countless voices joined the chorus and sang the words together, each one followed a unique melody, though always haunting. Had the lonely ghost rejoined the choir? Even if so, he probably still had no friends. The singers were together, yet alone, sharing the same torture, but never commiserating. Hades wouldn't allow such comfort.

New voices bounced through the chamber.

"Stop fighting!" A man's voice, sharp and angry.

"No! Please, please! I'll do anything you ask! Just don't—"

Lauren gulped. A young person? The wandering ghost?

As the words volleyed from left to right and back again, Lauren swung her head from side to side, barely able to breathe. No one was anywhere in sight.

"You must! You won't suffer. Death will come quickly."

"I don't want to die! I don't want to die!"

"You'll go in, you little mongrel, even if I have to pry you loose—" A grunt sounded. Scratching noises followed, then a scream.

The scream faded as if carried away by the wind. After a few seconds, silence ensued.

Lauren gasped for breath. What could it mean? Did Hades replay tragic deaths that happened before people came to this horrid afterlife? Might the spirit of that victim be the one who spoke earlier?

The laments continued, as if affirming her thoughts.

She lifted a loose sweatshirt sleeve and mopped her brow. This place was too sad for words. These poor souls would be here forever. Forever! Suffering without relief! No matter how much they regretted their mistakes or prayed for forgiveness, they would never be granted pardon. Never.

She bowed her head. Who were these people? Her foster mother and Micaela probably escaped this place. But her foster father? He had some issues everyone tried to ignore, but they weren't that bad, were they? Was his voice among the hopeless singers?

She laid a hand on her chest. *And who's to say that I won't come here when I die?*

As the laments continued filtering into her soul, her father's final thoughts returned. *I love you. Never forget that.*

"Dad," she whispered, "I wish you were here. It's so lonely in the dark."

She covered her face and wept.

CHAPTER

8

A CALL FROM THE PIT

Joran strummed his lyre, playing the tune that once raised Bonnie's image. Ever since the one success in the jail's medical room, every attempt failed, but it couldn't hurt to try again. A shallow layer of snow covered the prison yard, and sunlight glimmered on the icy surface, creating a glare. The blizzard was long gone, but it had left its mark. Snow and bitter cold were new experiences, unpleasant ones, but it could have been a lot worse.

He squinted through the strings. Only hours earlier, after the battle ended, the snowstorm continued and quickly coated the mud with a blanket of white, hiding tank tracks and boot prints that once gave evidence of a battleground. Now all proof was gone. Equipment and guards vanished through a portal, and Captain Boone, the highest-ranked officer still in the compound, had transported all prisoners to other locations, leaving the base deserted.

Yet the Captain himself remained on duty, now tromping through the snow at the perimeter of the yard away from everyone else, searching for the candlestone bullets the guards had used against the dragons. Chatting on a phone while he walked near some of the demolished barracks, he didn't seem concerned that the prisoners' abodes had been smashed or burned by dragons and tanks, nor did it seem to be a problem that the fence cordoning off the prison's high-security area had been bulldozed. He was at ease—strangely so.

Joran pushed the lyre under his parka, a warm and welcome gift from the Captain, and buttoned the front to keep the instrument in place. The sonic rods were already secure in a pouch attached to his belt. He and Selah might not need them again, but it wouldn't hurt to keep them close.

Several steps away, Selah stood with Walter and Ashley. Her own parka nearly swallowing her, Selah cradled the green ovulum that still held Zohar and Mendallah. Joran smiled at the care she took. She had said earlier that putting it in a pocket might tilt it too much. She didn't want their friends to slide to the edge.

Her prison-issued boots pushing through the snow, Selah shuffled his way. When she arrived, she leaned her head against his chest. "Joran, do you hear what I hear?"

Joran stroked her dark hair. It was soft and smooth and smelled of flowers, a fragrance in the soap from the prison shower. "I don't hear anything in particular."

Backing away a step, she looked up at him. "That's what I mean. Before the Watchers invaded our region, there was always a song in the air. I was hoping that when we finally escaped the ovula we might be able to hear the song again."

He nodded. "Right. The song of the purity ovulum. But Bonnie carries that now."

"I know, and I can't hear her anymore." Tears gleamed in her eyes. "Do you think she's dead already?"

Firming his lips, he shook his head. "I can't believe that. I *won't* believe it. God wouldn't let that happen."

"Like he wouldn't let Father die?" One of the tears tracked down her cheek. "Or maybe we're losing our gift. The lyre isn't working, and we can't hear like we used to."

"I was wondering about that." Kicking through the snow, he nodded toward Ashley and Walter. While Walter punched numbers into a phone, Ashley held a gun-like photometer and aimed it at various angles as she hunted for traces of a portal. With a four-inch purple bruise on her cheek, she looked like she had recently lost a fight, but her determined aspect showed no signs of pain.

"Right now," Joran said, "I can't hear what Ashley is saying to Walter unless I really concentrate." He shrugged. "Before the flood, I could have heard her heartbeat from here."

"Me, too. And I can't hear what Captain Boone is saying on his phone." Still holding the ovulum, Selah spread out her arms. "If we're no longer Listeners, then what good are we?"

"We can sing. I heard you singing one of Father's psalms just a little while ago, and I know my voice is still strong."

Selah let out a forlorn sigh. "Then maybe God will use us in that way. Maybe we can still counter demon songs and make sound barriers with our voices."

"We'll help in whatever way we can." He tousled her hair. "Come on. Let's find out what Walter and Ashley are talking about."

Joran walked their way. When he drew near, his shoe bumped a closed metal box, shaking the candlestone bullets they had already collected. "Any progress?"

Ashley turned off her photometer and bundled her coat close to her body. A gust blew her hair into a frenzy, but she didn't bother to tame it. "Larry's still analyzing. He's taking longer than usual."

Her words echoed in buzzes from Walter's mouth, relayed by his tooth transmitter. Obviously Ashley had inserted one in her mouth as well, though she didn't have any chips remaining for two out-of-place children of Methuselah.

Joran sighed. At least the chips proved that his ears were still sensitive enough to hear scratchy words from inside someone's mouth.

Walter clasped Joran's shoulder. "Something wrong?"

Averting his eyes, Joran shook his head. "Not really."

"Not really?" Walter stepped into Joran's line of sight. "Hey, we're in this together. If something's bugging you, maybe you should—"

"*Are* we in this together?" Joran locked his stare on Walter. "Is there really anything left for us to do here beyond what we've already done?"

They maintained their stare for a moment. Walter's aspect slowly changed from concerned to thoughtful to surrendered. "I guess I see what you mean."

"I hope you're not offended by my question. This is my problem and Selah's, not yours."

"Not offended at all." Walter released Joran's shoulder. "I just wish I could help."

Selah brushed snow from the grass with a boot. "I don't think there are any more candlestones. I have searched everywhere."

Walter picked up the box and plucked a candlestone from inside. "Since Barlow's not in any of these, should I get rid of them?"

"Not yet." Ashley fingered a dial on her photometer. "They might be useful. Just make sure they don't get lost."

Joran stared at the tiny stone. Since he and Selah had been stuck inside a series of ovula for years, it wasn't too hard to believe that a person could live within that little bead. Yet, Ashley's photometer didn't find impurities in any of them. Whatever had happened, dead or alive, Sir Barlow wasn't there. He had been transported to another place or else disintegrated completely.

Walter closed the box and locked it with a key. After setting the box on the ground and pushing the key into his pocket, he turned to Joran and Selah. "Think of any more questions? If I don't know an answer, I can either look it up or make it up."

They both shook their heads. During the past hour, they asked him hundreds of questions about the world—the people, their customs, the government, and faith. Sometimes Walter's answers were funny or sarcastic, but it wasn't hard to figure out the truth behind his humorous quips. In any case, one fact became clear. This wasn't their world. It was blind and deaf, though far from mute. In some ways it was similar to the world they left before the flood, spiritually barren and lost. It seemed that the waters did little to cleanse the land of corruption.

139

Captain Boone tromped toward them, his hands in his pockets and his head low. When he arrived, he looked at Walter, though really past him as he didn't quite focus. "I couldn't find any candlestones. I think I'll go check on Mardon."

Joran narrowed his eyes. The Captain's voice seemed strained, troubled perhaps.

"Sure," Walter said. "No use us all freezing our fannies off."

Captain Boone pointed at the ground. "So all of you are staying right here? Here in this yard?"

"For now." Walter shrugged. "Why? Are you getting some hot cocoa ready for us?"

"I can arrange that." Without another word, Captain Boone marched toward the high-security area of the prison.

Walter laid a hand on Ashley's back. "Did you get a reading on his thoughts? He looked kind of strange."

She shook her head. "I wasn't paying attention. Too many other things to concentrate on."

"Right. The spectral analysis." He stepped back. "Carry on."

Ashley pressed the photometer's button with one hand and her jaw with the other. "Larry, do you have enough data?"

"More data would be better," the computer replied through Ashley's tooth chip, "but based on the samples, it is clear that you are in the midst of a large portal, though it is currently closed. Lois has been comparing the measurements to those of all known portal encounters. The delay is due to wait times generated by other computer systems that are storing the data we need."

"Any matches so far?"

"There are no exact matches. It is possible that this portal leads to a realm you have not visited in the past."

"Maybe," Ashley said, "but there are portals we've been through that you don't have data for."

"If that is the case, then my conclusion is invalid, but lack of data input is not a factor I am able to control."

"We're not playing a blame game here. Let's just stick to the facts." She kept her photometer trigger pressed. "If we had Apollo, could you program a flash to open it?"

"Affirmative, but there is danger. This portal appears to be large, so opening it could cause anyone in the vicinity to be transported immediately."

Walter nodded. "It was a hungry one. It swallowed tanks and a detachment of soldiers. But they fell into lava while Matt flew away into the sky. A deadly plunge into fire or a dangerous slingshot ride into oblivion. Take your pick."

"I am unable to determine the destination," Larry said, "but the presence of lava and sky in the same location suggests a volcano."

Ashley turned her back to the wind. "Got anything else?"

"Our analysis is complete. If you gather more data—"

Silence ensued from Ashley's tooth transmitter. Only the sound of the breeze whispered through their parkas.

"Larry?" Ashley bowed her head, apparently trying to keep the wind out of her ears. "Larry, is something wrong?"

Walter's brow knitted. "I hear someone shuffling papers. The communication line is open. I think I hear Carly's voice, but she doesn't sound upset."

"Larry!" Ashley barked. "Update! Now!"

"I am receiving a stream of data from an unexpected source. Please wait a moment."

"What kind of data? Voice?"

"One more moment, please. I am receiving a second stream. Lois is compiling the results. We will send you video as soon as possible."

"Video?" Ashley retrieved a phone from her pocket and looked at the screen. "Are you able to send it to my phone?"

"Affirmative. Walter provided updated access codes for all communication devices."

"What's the source of the data feed?"

"Hades."

Ashley blinked. "Hades? Did Billy send it?"

"He did not. I will now stream the file to you. Be ready to capture it."

Ashley slid her thumb across her screen and tapped an icon. "Ready."

A video played showing a hazy landscape. As the camera panned from left to right, a muffled voice came through. "This is Lauren Bannister. I used Apollo to open a portal, and now my feet are on a truss near the top of the museum room in Hades while my head is sticking out at least a hundred feet above a volcano crater. I suppose if a dragon flew by, he would see half a girl floating in midair."

Ashley pointed. "That's Twin Falls River. She's in Second Eden."

"According to the map," Lauren continued, "I should be on top of Mount Elijah, but I guess it blew its stack." The camera panned across scorched logs and burning debris in the midst of boulders strewn all about, then down to the crater itself, a cauldron of bubbling lava. "I suppose it's like Mount Saint Helens. The whole top must have exploded and sent rocks flying everywhere. I can't imagine how many people died. I don't even know how many people were in Second Eden to start with. Anyway, I hear my mother's song clearly, so she's probably here in Second Eden."

The video suddenly switched to Lauren's face, now in a darker room with a flashlight beam shining on her. Soot smudged her cheeks and forehead, and orange light flickered in her eyes. "Well," she said with a tremor in her voice, "I have a lot to tell you, but I'd better make it quick. I guess you could say I'm stuck in Hades. Dad and I made the portal jump, but a couple of guys ambushed us. Dad left Apollo with me on the Hades side while he tried to help his mom on the Earth side. As the portal was closing, he told me to go it alone to find my mother, but he also said not to come back through the portal, that they would probably post a guard there. So unless you can somehow signal me that there aren't any guards, my only way out is through the top of the volcano I showed you. I suppose a dragon could fly up and maybe grab me and give me a ride down, but I didn't see any dragons anywhere. I hope Makaidos and the others made it back to Second Eden … or maybe I hope not if the explosion would have killed them."

She held a small glass object in her fingers. "I tried to send this through Apollo. There are a bunch of them on the shelves near the portal opening. Some kind of grit and hair are stuck inside on the bottom, and they smell like burnt leather. I can't imagine why someone would be conducting an experiment up there, unless they needed lava for some reason. Anyway, I thought you might like to check it out, assuming Larry received it. Sitting here alone in Hades, it's impossible to tell what's going on outside. It's just dark … and lonely … and …"

Selah whispered, "Be brave, Lauren."

Joran took Selah's hand and agreed silently.

Lauren bit her lip. With tears sparkling, she continued, her tremor increasing. "I heard footsteps a little while ago. There's a knife in my backpack, but I'm not sure if I should get it. If there's a demon or something in here, I doubt I could kill it, and I don't want it to take the knife from me and …" She swallowed, wiped her eyes with her sleeve, smearing the soot, and went on. "The tree of life is here, and one twig is still burning. I guess the flood couldn't douse all of it." She managed a tremulous smile. "After all, it's the tree of life, right? Anyway, it helps. Its light makes me feel better, but I'm a sitting duck, so I should hide somewhere. Trust me. There are plenty of dark places to choose from."

She glanced from side to side before looking at the camera again. "I suppose if you can't get a dragon to pick me up, the best thing to do would be to clear out the guards from the portal I came through. Of course, I won't know that you succeeded unless you can somehow send a reply to Apollo. I don't know if that's possible or how I would know you sent something, but I'll try to figure out how to download its memory to my phone. I'll just keep checking." The scene shifted to a tree with a single flame at the end of a branch, then a panning view of bookshelves with books and scrolls before going blank.

Ashley tapped her phone a couple of times. "Larry, are you in communication with Apollo now?"

"I am not. I cannot read Apollo's passive data while it resides in another dimension. The digital transfer option requires active manipulation by the operator, so Apollo is able to receive only if Lauren switches it to that mode. I attempted a response to Lauren's message, but Apollo would not synchronize, so we must assume that Lauren is not yet aware of the setting or perhaps something has happened to Apollo."

144

Ashley's hair blew in front of her face, but she ignored it. "If Lauren figured out how to send data, she's smart enough to figure out how to receive it."

"This is a valid assumption," Larry said. "She should be able to set Apollo so that it can receive a cross-dimensional transmission, but she would not be able to access it without a password. If she tried to download data to her phone without a password, the process would fail."

"I hate it when security gets in the way." Ashley slid the phone into her pocket. "Larry, Lauren mentioned sending you something. It looked like a small beaker. Did you get it?"

"Affirmative. It was in the first data stream, but since it needed considerable analysis, I sent the video to you first while Lois conducted a composition test."

Ashley nodded. "Lauren mentioned some kind of precipitate. Does Lois have the results?"

"Preliminary results are ready. She will transmit the details to your phone."

Ashley pulled out her phone again. A series of words and numbers appeared on the screen, lines that scrolled vertically. Her eyes darted from side to side as she read. "The genetic markers indicate cells from anthrozils, but there are some anomalies as well as other organic structures."

"Correct. The sample Lauren sent includes skin and hair from a combination of male and female anthrozils. The genetics were altered in a number of ways. Lois ran simulations to see what would happen to the mixture if it were to be heated quickly to the temperatures one could expect in a volcanic crater."

"You mean poured into the lava."

"Correct again. It was impossible to determine the exact temperature of the lava in Mount Elijah or its composition, so she ran approximately ten million simulations with different temperatures, materials, and known organisms that might live near the volcano. In most cases, the mixture merely burned, but in three hundred and seven simulations, the result was the creation of an invasive, multiplying organism, though really it is a mutation of an already existing species."

"Species?" Ashley's brow shot up. "Then it's not a virus?"

"It behaves like a virus in that it replicates quickly and likely will not be affected by an antibiotic, but it has extraordinary properties indicative of a more complex bug, for lack of a more precise

145

term. Most of the organisms survived the high temperatures for seven minutes before burning up. It would be difficult to battle such a hardy bug. In fact, it would not be detected at all with traditional methods. It leaves no markers normally associated with infectious diseases."

"Do you have any of Jared's tissue samples there? Can you check for this structure?"

"I know of no stored samples, but perhaps—"

"Ashley, this is Carly. I figured out where you're going with this. I'll see if I can collect some skin cells from Jared's bed. It won't be much, but it might be enough."

Ashley nodded. "Good thinking, Carly. When you get the sample, have Lois look for that bug in the cells. If it's there, it'll probably be dead because it doesn't have a host. If she does find it, tell her to get right to work on what kind of countermeasures we would need."

"Got it," Carly said. "I'll be back in a minute."

Ashley clenched a fist. "Mardon has to be behind this. He used Mount Elijah to cook up a bug, or whatever you want to call it, and he sent it all over Second Eden when it erupted more than fifteen years ago."

"Did it infect all the anthrozils there?" Selah asked.

Ashley gave her a grim nod. "As far as I know."

"According to my records," Larry said, "we have reports of severe symptoms in Irene, Dallas, Kaylee, Elise, and Jordan; moderate symptoms in Jared; and no symptoms in those who remained dragons."

"What about Tamara?" Ashley asked.

"She disappeared before the symptoms manifested themselves, but her emaciated condition in her prison

146

role indicates that she has suffered to the same
degree Jared has. Apparently she is not well."

Ashley pulled her hair back from her eyes. "Jared didn't spend
as much time in Second Eden, so less exposure might have been
the reason for his initial resilience, but we heard that he's gotten a
lot worse ever since he came to the prison. So when you combine
all the evidence, you get this possibility—this portal leads to
Mount Elijah in Second Eden, and when Jared came here, he was
exposed to residual environmental factors from the portal opening, which contributed to his deteriorating condition."

"That adds up," Walter said, "but wouldn't that mean the
other sick anthrozils shouldn't be in Second Eden? Was it stupid
to send them there to try to get well?"

Ashley tapped her chin. "Not necessarily. If Jared suddenly got
worse, maybe something happened to the environment when the
volcano blew its top. It could be that Second Eden is worse for the
bug victims now than it was before."

147

"That's probably it." Walter flared out his hands as if to mimic
an explosion. "Mount Elijah blew while we were there during the
big battle. The recent eruption looks a lot worse, so maybe the first
one started the disease by introducing the bug, and the second one
sent ten times more bugs into the air."

"I'm not sure bugs work that way," Ashley said, "but I think
only one person can tell us for certain."

"Mardon?"

She nodded. "If he was behind this disease, he would have to
have known the exact time of eruption during the battle. Otherwise, the bug would have burned up before it could be ejected
from the lava. But if he did know the time, he could have poured
the mixture into the crater a little less than seven minutes before
the eruption. Then, the bug would be created in the hot soup and

blown out into the cooler air before it could be destroyed. Another question is whether or not he used the mixture twice, once for the eruption about fifteen years ago and again for the new one. Semiramis was here for the recent eruption, and the older one happened before she was put in prison in Second Eden, so she might have helped him do it both times. Either way, I don't see how even Semiramis could time an eruption."

"Could he have actually caused the eruptions somehow?" Joran asked. "Then he wouldn't have to worry about the timing."

"Only he would know that." Ashley glared at the high-security area. "Is he still waiting in Captain Boone's office?"

Joran nodded. "Mardon's been there ever since he came back from dropping off Billy and Lauren at the airport."

Ashley's cheeks reddened. "I think it's about time for an interrogation."

"I'll get the weasel to squeal," Walter said. "I don't mind adding a little pain to his miserable world."

"Or a lot." Ashley touched her jaw. "Larry, print out a physical note to send to Apollo. Even if Lauren switches it to receive mode, she might not figure out how to download data to her phone. She'll see a piece of paper."

"What message do you want written on the page?"

Ashley growled. "Instructions on how to receive data from you and the access password, of course!"

"Any particular font? For technical manuals, the most common—"

"I don't care, Larry! Just make it readable!" She let out a huff. "Honestly, these computers can be—" Her gaze met Joran's, and her angry expression slowly wilted. "Sorry. I get really wound up sometimes. We have a pile of emergencies to deal with, and I don't have time to coddle an overly—"

"There is no need to explain," Joran said, waving a hand. "Considering the circumstances, I think you are extraordinarily calm."

"I don't feel calm." As she let out a sigh, her shoulders sagged. "We have to save some dying people and at the same time rescue Billy and Lauren."

"Ashley," Larry said. "I have a priority alert."

She touched her jaw once again. "What is it?"

"I received an emergency signal from Gabriel's phone, but he did not follow with an explanation. I attempted contact with the others in the company returning to Second Eden, but I received no response."

"Did you try contacting their tooth transmitters?" Walter asked.

"Affirmative. Since we altered our encryption algorithms and did not reprogram their tooth transmitters before they departed, they might have extracted them from their molars and decided to rely on their phones. I have since sent signals to their transmitters to reprogram them, but I have no feedback that would indicate success."

149

Ashley pressed her jaw. "Did you switch the encoding in *our* transmitters?"

"Affirmative. Our transmissions are secure, both by phone and tooth."

"Did you try to contact anyone in Second Eden? Karrick? Valiant? Listener?"

"Several times. No one answered. There is no signal emanating from Second Eden at all."

"Did you try to call Yereq?"

"Negative. He was not a member of the party returning to Second Eden, so he was not on my list of Second Eden names to contact."

"Right. He was just guarding the portal." Ashley looked at Walter, her eyes wide. "What do you think?"

"Ambush." Walter pulled a phone from his pocket and pressed it against his ear. After a few seconds, he let out a sigh. "Yereq, thank God you're okay. Where are you? ... Why there? You were supposed to guard the portal. ... Who told you to go there? ... It couldn't have been Jared. He was supposed to transport Billy and Lauren to the crater portal. ... Didn't Larry change your transmitter protocol? If he didn't, then everything we're saying now can be monitored. ... Oh, right. We wouldn't be able to talk to each other now. Good call. ... Well, go to the portal immediately and get back to me with a report. Thanks."

After punching the disconnect button, Walter looked at Ashley. "Larry made the changes a little too late for Yereq. Someone faked Jared's voice and sent him on a wild-goose chase. Anyone getting ready to attack the portal wouldn't want to face him." His face hardening, Walter put the phone away and touched his jaw. "Larry, prepare for lockdown. Highest security. You're probably the next target. Follow invasion avoidance protocol. Carly, are you listening?"

"I'm right here, Walter. I heard everything."

"Prepare to go portable. Put Lois's brain in the docking briefcase and pack all the backup drives. Larry will stay as the decoy. Got it?"

"Got it. Should I contact Adam?"

"Yes, he'll be the operator of the fake headquarters. It's dangerous, but he's up to it. Get cash from my lockbox. Don't use any credit cards from now on."

"Procedures are printing out for Adam," Larry said. "I will shift all secure communications to Lois on your command."

"Do it now!" Walter looked at his watch. "I wonder how long it will take for Adam to get there."

"I already texted him," Carly said. "He's on his way. Probably five minutes."

"Good. If Larry's not the next target, then we might be, so we need to get out of here." Walter scanned the sky. "The transfer of all the guards and prisoners feels diabolical now. An airstrike to cover their tracks isn't out of the question."

Ashley's face paled. "Ten minutes ago I would have said Captain Boone wouldn't approve of that, but now …"

"Right. Don't bet your life on someone who's trained to obey orders without question. If the head is corrupt, the legs and arms will do the dirty work." Walter nodded toward the high-security area. "I saw a weapons room, but I don't know if it's locked. Either way, I'll be back with a Jeep. I know where Boone keeps the keys." He kissed Ashley and sprinted away.

151

Ashley looked at Joran and Selah in turn. "I think we'd better meet him partway. I don't like being out in the open. This portal area is starting to feel like a bull's-eye."

"I think I hear a helicopter," Selah said, setting a hand behind her ear, "but my ears aren't working very well."

As the whir of blades filled the air, all three looked up. Four helicopters swept over the trees and began orbiting above their heads.

Ashley threw the photometer down. "Run!"

The three sprinted toward Walter. One of the helicopters shot a stream of bullets in their path, forcing them to halt. Another followed with a spray of flames that seemed to drip from the sky. Fuel ignited into orange and yellow flares as it fell. When the spray hit the ground, it burst into a wall of fire.

As the helicopters orbited, they added more and more fuel and whipped the flames into a cyclone.

"They're trying to open the portal!" Ashley shouted above the roar.

Selah gripped Joran's arm. "Can you sing a concussion note?"

"I'll try, but from this far away, I don't know how effective it will be."

"Ashley," Selah said as she plugged her ears with her fingers. "Do this, or your eardrums might split. Joran will aim at the helicopters, but it's best to be safe."

As soon as Ashley complied, Joran took in a deep breath and pivoted at the same rate as the attackers flew. He locked his focus on one of the helicopters and sang the highest note he could reach, pouring in all his power. The windows cracked, raining glass into the flames. The pilot grabbed his ears. The helicopter veered into the circle and crashed near the center.

Joran, Selah, and Ashley ducked under a wave of flames, but it quickly diminished. Turning to another helicopter, Joran blasted the note again. This time when the windows shattered, the pilot shifted to the outside of the circle and flew away.

152

"Two more," Selah called, her fingers still in her ears. "You can do it!"

Gasping, Joran shook his head. "No … I can't. … I can barely breathe."

Selah and Ashley lowered their hands. "Can we create a shield?" Selah asked.

"We can try." Joran withdrew the lyre, stripped off his parka, and handed Selah the sonic rods. "Get ready to sing."

Selah set the ovulum on the ground and held the rods far apart, one in each hand. "Do you remember the melody for the mercy song?"

"Just a few notes." He stood in front of her, equidistant from each rod. "I'm hoping it'll come to me. I haven't had a chance to show mercy to anyone."

The remaining two helicopters continued whipping the flames. The snow melted. The ground near the center of the ring had already transformed into lava, forcing Joran, Selah, and Ashley to edge closer to the flames.

"You were merciful to me," Ashley shouted. "Your words calmed me down."

"That wasn't much at all. Anyone would have—"

"No time to argue! Just do it!"

Joran plucked the lyre strings, playing the first few notes of the song, but nothing else came to mind.

"I remember the words we sang when we created the other shield," Selah said. "I will speak them. Maybe it will spark a memory." As the lava expanded toward them, she raised her voice and spoke in singsong.

> Your love protects my soul within
> And shields my heart from shameful sin;
> No flames or fear can steal my love;
> It's safely stored in God above.

A few notes flowed to his fingers, then stopped. It seemed that a boulder blocked the stream. The rods vibrated in Selah's grip, but no shield emerged. She continued quoting the lyrics.

> So now I ask with mercy's song,
> Unfurl a banner, safe and strong,
> The sound of love's enfolding grace;
> We trust in mercy's warm embrace.

A new measure came to mind. Joran quickly played it, and Selah sang the first lines of the next quatrain using the resurrected melody, though she had to resort to singsong afterward.

Although the tempest tosses seas,
And evil men encompass me,
Let grace and mercy be my shield,
And love and truth the sword I wield.

The circle of lava expanded more rapidly, pushing them closer and closer to the wall of flames.

"The ovulum!" Selah dropped the rods and dove for the egg, but it tipped into the lava and burst into flames. Grimacing as she folded her fingers around her hand, she rolled away from the edge and climbed to her feet. "No! It's gone! I should have—"

"Don't blame yourself," Joran said. "You're doing your best, and we can't do anything about it now."

After blowing on her reddened palm, Selah picked up the rods again. As she held them in place, they all backed closer to the fire. Only twenty feet of safe ground remained. Heat radiated from all around. Ashley stripped off her coat and threw it to the mud.

A Jeep with no cover crashed through the wall to their right. It spun, throwing mud in every direction, its wheels avoiding the edge of the lava. As it rotated, it slid toward the trio. Joran pushed Selah and Ashley out of the way, but before he could leap, the Jeep plowed into him and knocked him into a backwards slide.

When the wheels finally halted, Walter stood on the driver's seat. "Joran! Are you all right?"

Still holding the lyre, Joran pushed against the ground, but sharp pain shot through his thigh. Gritting his teeth, he shook his head. "I'm not all right, but I'll try to get up."

Walter leaped to the ground and dropped to his knees at Joran's side. "I'm so sorry. I couldn't control—"

"No ..." Grunting, Joran lifted a muddy hand. "No explanation. All is well."

154

Ashley pressed her fingers around Joran's thigh. New pain ripped through his body, worse than ever. "His femur's broken! If we move him, we might cut his femoral artery!"

"Yeah," Walter said, "but if we don't move him, he'll cook in the lava!" He slid his arms under Joran's back. "Let's get you out of here!"

"No!" Joran raised the lyre. "I remember the melody now. Just help me sit, and Selah and I will make a shield. You and Ashley get to safety."

A shower of bullets clanked against the Jeep, cracking the windshield and ripping holes in the hood and passenger door.

Walter raised Joran to a sitting position. "There *is* no safety. Every option is deadly."

"Then do what you must." Joran set his fingers on the lyre's strings. "I will play the mercy song."

Selah sat behind him and spread out the rods. "I am with you all the way."

"I can't change your mind?" Walter asked.

"I wanted to do something to help, remember? I know what that is now. Let us do it." Joran began playing the tune. It flowed from mind to fingers without hesitation. "Go. Save Ashley and yourself."

Walter firmed his jaw. "There's one chance left." He grabbed Ashley's hand. "Come on!"

Ducking their heads, they jumped into the Jeep. With a new round of mud slinging, Walter drove into the flames, followed by a storm of bullets. One of the helicopters gave chase while the other continued pouring new fuel into the wall and fanning the flames.

The lava crept closer. It would swallow them in seconds.

Selah trembled. "Joran, I've killed Zohar and Mendallah!"

"Not you! The helicopters did it!" Joran squirmed to get into a better singing position. "Now we have to settle our minds, or we won't be able to sing the mercy song."

"You're right." She kissed the top of his head. "I am ready. I will sing with all my heart."

156

9

CHAPTER

ASCENSION

Walter sped the Jeep over the downed fence between the two prison areas and zoomed straight toward the main building. "Walter!" Ashley shouted from the passenger seat. "You'll crash into the wall."

"I know!" Bullets riddled the snowy road at both sides. Walter stepped on the gas. "Get ready to jump!"

"Which way?"

"Backwards! Now!"

They both leaped up and, holding hands, ran over the rear of the Jeep. They landed in a tumble and rolled through snow. The Jeep slammed into the building, smashing a hole in the wall. Now wedged halfway in, its rear wheels spun, slinging muddy water. The helicopter pulled up in a near vertical rise and careened back toward them.

"Let's go!" Walter and Ashley sprinted to the wall, climbed over the Jeep, and vaulted into a dim room.

Gasping for breath, Ashley looked around. "Where ... where are we?"

"Weapons cache." Walter grabbed a shoulder-mounted missile launcher from a bracket. "This place was ready for war. They had more firepower available than they used. Boone had to know this."

Ashley touched an assault rifle leaning against a wall. "They let us win?"

"Hard to say. Maybe Boone held back for us." Walter loaded a missile, climbed onto the Jeep, and aimed it at the helicopter flying over the portal area. "Good-bye, chopper."

He pulled the trigger. With a loud whoosh, the missile shot out, creating a plume of smoke that jetted back and filled the weapons room. The missile slammed into the helicopter and blew it to pieces. Smoking fragments of metal and glass arced toward the ground amidst piercing whistles and crackling flames.

Walter leaped off the Jeep, threw the gun down on the weapons room floor, and grabbed the rifle. "Stay here. I'll be right back."

"No way!" Coughing as she fanned the smoke, Ashley picked up a handgun. "I know how to use this."

They charged out of the room, leaping across the Jeep. Walter aimed at the second helicopter and fired a thunderous volley. Using both hands, Ashley braced her gun and shot again and again. A line of bullets cracked the helicopter's glass and riddled the metal skin from nose to tail.

The chopper dipped at a sharp angle, smoke pouring from within, and retreated ahead of their nonstop gunfire.

When it flew out of range, Walter waved an arm. "Let's go." They sprinted to the ring of flames, now dwindling. Along the way, Walter snatched up a ragged sheet of metal and shouted, "I'm going in!"

158

Just before he reached the wall, light flashed from within. A fountain of sparks flew upward and shot high into the air. The sparks spread across the sky, twinkling like stars, unhindered by the daylight.

Still running, Walter threw the scrap of metal into his path. He leaped onto it and slid toward the wall of flames, ready to jump to the side to avoid the lava, but when the metal pushed across the fire, the circle of lava had receded to the center, now the size of a child's wading pool.

He stepped off and slid the metal sheet back to Ashley, then ran to the spot where they had left Joran and Selah. They were gone.

While Ashley crossed the wall of fire, Walter crouched next to a depression in the mud. This was definitely where he had left them. Had they fallen into the lava? Were they transported somewhere else?

Ashley ran to his side, breathless. "No sign of them?"

"Not unless you mean the sparks." He looked up. The daylight stars had faded away. "I think they transported."

"To where?"

Walter straightened. "All I know is that they're not here, and we'd better transport ourselves before someone calls for reinforcements."

"Do you think Captain Boone called for the helicopters?"

"He asked us if we were staying here, he left, and then the choppers showed up, so, yeah."

"I don't get it," Ashley said. "When he was helping us during the battle, I read kindness in his mind. It wasn't fake."

"I won't argue with that, but that was then, and this is now, and now we'd better get away from ground zero and do some more snooping." Taking Ashley's hand, Walter jumped through a gap in the flames and jogged toward the weapons cache. After crawling

159

over the Jeep, he entered the room, now clear of smoke. Automatic rifles lined the walls in sturdy wooden brackets, ammunition belts and clips hung on hooks nearby, and many varieties of weapons and ammo-filled cabinets and footlockers from one end of the room to the other.

He grabbed a duffel bag and began loading it with grenades, belts, and clips. "Captain Boone could have annihilated us with this stuff, but he didn't, and now it looks like he's betrayed us or at least flown the coop to save his own skin, so we can't trust him. Even Larry could be compromised by now, so we're on our own. When Lois gets back online, we'll see if the security protocol checks out and—"

"Walter, look!"

He spun toward the opposite wall. Ashley stood next to a long, rectangular box made of dark wood. A hinged lid stood open above it. "What's in there?"

"Nothing. That's the point." She ran a finger along the red velvet lining within. "A sword was in here."

Walter touched the box. "How can you tell? A lot of things could have been in there."

She licked her fingertip and used it to scoop red fibers from the lining. "Something sharp scraped the bottom on this end. The hilt end is clean."

Walter squinted at the fibers. "Are you thinking Excalibur was here?"

"If it wasn't Excalibur, why wouldn't it still be here?"

"Right. You wouldn't take a sword to a gun battle." Walter closed the lid. "Can you remember if the sword was in the box when we first came in here?"

Ashley clenched her eyes shut. "I'm playing it back in my memory, but everything happened so fast. If the box was open, I think the red lining would have stood out, and I don't remember seeing it."

"Mardon said he knew where Excalibur was and that getting it back would be difficult. This room was locked tighter than a drum until I made a new door. I'll bet he heard the crash and went to see what caused it."

Ashley used her gun to point at the hole in the wall. "And then he decided to take Excalibur out for a walk."

"Well, he can't be far." Walter stuffed two more handguns and a high-capacity clip into the duffel and zipped it up. "Let's go."

He unfastened three deadbolts, opened the door, and stepped into an empty hallway. Captain Boone's office lay to the left, where Mardon was supposed to be waiting. He cast a thought Ashley's way. *Quietly now.*

Carrying the automatic rifle, Walter tiptoed toward the office, Ashley following. When he reached the open door, he peeked through the gap. Mardon sat in a straight-back chair, his torso erect and his wide eyes darting. Wearing the same ragged jacket and patched jeans he had worn earlier, he squeezed a handkerchief, as if trying to wring it out, and his burn-ravaged face wrinkled with every nervous twitch.

Walter looked at Ashley. *He's here. No sword. Supposedly he and Semiramis are like ghosts unless there's an open portal to Second Eden. If he's a ghost now, he couldn't have taken Excalibur.*

"There was still lava in that circle," Ashley whispered. "The portal is open. At least it was a little while ago. He should be solid until it closes."

Then I have to make this fast. Walter marched into the room and pressed his rifle's barrel against Mardon's chest. "Where is Excalibur?"

Mardon swallowed. "Exca ... Excalibur?" He dabbed his scarred forehead, though it appeared to be dry. "I don't have Excalibur."

"He's guarding his thoughts," Ashley said. "He's hiding something."

"You said you know where it is." Walter pushed with the rifle, forcing Mardon to scoot back in his chair. "Where?"

Mardon tugged on his collar. "There is a weapons room here, and it is securely locked. There were always guards, both in the room and the hall, so I assumed you wouldn't be able to—"

"We had dragons! We had a compliant chief officer!" Walter shifted the barrel to Mardon's eyes. "Don't try to con me. I've dealt with enough liars to know when one is blowing smoke."

Mardon let out a nervous laugh. "Dragons. Blowing smoke. Your metaphors are witty, but they do not alter the truth. I don't know where Excalibur is. In fact, I have been shifting back and forth from a solid state. I could not have carried a sword."

Walter pressed the barrel against Mardon's forehead. "Shall we conduct a test to see how solid you are?"

Mardon's entire body quaked. "If you shoot me, I will not be able to help you find a cure to the disease that afflicts the original anthrozils."

"You're the one who created the disease!"

Mardon gulped but said nothing.

"We found the beakers in the museum room," Walter continued. "I don't know how you timed either eruption, but we know you used the volcano to spread the bug, or whatever you want to call it, and we figured out that the recent eruption made it worse."

Mardon's expression took on a prideful air. "I did create and spread the parasite."

"Parasite?"

"Of course. Your lack of knowledge proves that you need me to counter it. And I didn't time the first eruption; I triggered it. But I had nothing to do with the second one. If it exacerbated the parasite, it was not my doing. In any case, as I hope you remember, the combination of rain and chemicals from the volcano's debris after the first eruption caused the attacking army's rust coat to dissolve, which made them vulnerable to Excalibur's beam. My experiment actually helped you win the battle."

"You're trying to justify what you did by talking about an accidental benefit? You and your witch of a mother have plotted against us for years, all the while pretending to cooperate. Those days are over." Walter's trigger finger twitched. "I ought to—"

"No!" Mardon raised his hands. "Don't shoot me! I'll help you! I promise! There is a genetic switch that …" His hands quivering, he shook his head. "I will not tell you right now. If I do, I will have no leverage."

"Leverage." Walter huffed. "As if we couldn't figure it out on our own."

Ashley laid a hand on Walter's arm. "Good acting job. The stress opened his mind. He didn't take Excalibur."

"I wasn't acting." Walter drew the gun away from Mardon. "Captain Boone, maybe?"

"I suppose, but he wouldn't know anything about its power or how to use it."

"Tamiel would know. Boone could be his delivery boy." Walter waved toward the door with his gun. "Let's go, Mardon. We'll get started on finding a cure."

A smile spread across Mardon's face, bold and confident. "Since you refuse to help me find my mother, I am finished cooperating with you."

Walter aimed the gun at Mardon's head again. "This says you're coming with us."

"Feel free to shoot. I am no longer afraid of you."

Walter rolled his eyes. "I hate it when people do that."

"The portal is probably closed." Ashley pushed her hand through Mardon's body. "He's a ghost again."

Mardon stood and gave them a polite nod. "I must be going now." He turned and walked toward the door. "I will do whatever I can to destroy all of you."

"Stop!" Walter fired, but the bullet zipped through Mardon's body and smacked into the wall in the hallway. Mardon walked on, slowly fading until he vanished.

Walter let his shoulders slump. "Now what?"

"Find Gabriel." Ashley hooked her arm through his. "And Elam and Sapphira and all the others. I think the war is just beginning."

CHAPTER

Valiant

M att slid off Albatross's back and surveyed the area—a land of boulders, fallen trees, and smashed huts. Dark rocks, some steaming and glowing red, peppered flattened grass. Mount Elijah had scattered thousands of superheated stones, as if throwing a temper tantrum. And now that the sun neared the horizon, streaks of red and orange over the volcano made it look angrier than ever.

He helped his mother climb down the dragon's tail. With her wings and shoulders drooping, she appeared to be tired, but a spark of determination danced in her eyes. "This was Founder's Village," she said. "It's been completely destroyed."

"Even without lava." Matt kicked up a door made of wood and straw, but only rocks lay underneath. "Where would the survivors have gone?"

Mom nodded toward the north. "Maybe the birthing garden. It's considered a holy place, so those who couldn't get into the flying hospital might have congregated there."

Albatross whistled sharply and pushed his nose under the wall of a flattened hut. Matt ran to the spot. A little glass egg lay on the ground, similar to those that hovered around Listener and the children, but this one was dark and lifeless. He grabbed the egg and heaved the wall to one side, revealing a black cloak spread out over a large lump.

With a quick reach, Matt pulled away the cloak, revealing a dark-skinned woman lying facedown, her body curled as if shielding something underneath.

Matt handed the cloak to his mother and nudged the woman's shoulder. "Are you all right?"

The woman stayed motionless.

"Ma'am?" He set his finger against her throat, feeling for a pulse. Nothing. "I think she's dead."

"How awful!" Mom pressed the cloak's hood over her lips. "The poor woman didn't—" Her brow dipped. She sniffed the material, then looked at the haze-covered sun through the hood. "It's treated with some kind of chemical."

Matt rubbed the material between his thumb and finger. "I wonder why."

"Ashley formulated a flame-retardant solution that she applied to cloaks. We used it to penetrate a wall of fire years ago. Maybe this woman thought it would protect her somehow. She used it like a blanket."

"Makes sense." Crouching, Matt turned the woman to her back, exposing an infant dressed only in a pink Earth-style onesie. He gulped and cried out, "A baby!"

"Alive?"

"Not sure yet." He set a finger in front of her mouth. She was breathing but appeared to be unconscious, and her companion lay nestled in the crook of her arm, blinking dimly. Swallowing to keep from squeaking, he nodded. "She's alive."

Mom knelt at his side. "Any broken bones?"

"I haven't checked." Matt pressed lightly on the baby's legs and arms. She grimaced but didn't cry out. He shifted his fingers to her skull. Much of it hadn't grown in because of her age, but one side appeared to be cracked. "This isn't good."

"Skull fracture?"

He nodded. "I've healed open wounds, but this is different. It's sealed over with skin."

"We need fire. Ashley and Thigocia healed injuries like this, and they always needed to be coated with flames, but we don't have a fire-breathing dragon or an oracle."

Matt glanced around. "I got the impression that some fire-breathing dragons stayed in Second Eden."

"I don't know who came to Earth or who stayed, but I don't see any now." Mom touched the woman's dark forehead. "Second Eden had people of all races, but I personally knew only one black woman—Mantika."

"Does she look like Mantika?"

With the cloak still in her grasp, Mom slid her hands under the baby and lifted her into its folds, tears brimming. "She's aged quite a bit since I saw her more than fifteen years ago, but I think she's Mantika. She was Candle and Listener's surrogate mother."

"Whoever she was, it looks like she did everything she could to protect the baby."

"That matches Mantika's loving ways." Mom walked a few steps farther out into the field. "I wonder if there are any more companions around here."

167

Matt scanned the ground. Looking for companions would be a good way to search for buried people. A floating egg could dodge flying debris better than a person could, but no other companions glinted in the failing sunlight. "We'd better get that baby to—"

A sharp cry sounded from above. A purple dragon carrying a human passenger dove from the smoke-filled sky. As he came in for a landing, Listener jumped off before the dragon's feet struck the ground. With her spyglass in its belt strap, she rushed to the victim's side. "Mother!" she wailed as she pushed her hand through Mantika's hair. "Oh, my dear mother!" She turned and looked at Lily, still in Mom's arms. "You were protecting Lily. You sacrificed your life to save my sister."

Matt rose and touched Listener's arm. "I'm sorry. She was already dead when we—"

"You're a healer!" Her eyes watery, Listener took his hand and kissed it. "I heard you say she has a skull fracture and you need dragon fire."

"That's true, but where can I—"

"I'll show you!" She grasped his shirt and pulled him close, rubbing their cheeks together as she spoke directly into his ear. "I just came from the birthing garden. Many are dead and injured. Karrick is also injured, but he still has fire-breathing power. He can help you energize."

Matt's cheeks warmed. "What did you do with the children you were going to lead from the valley?"

She jerked back, her eyes aflame. "You take care of Lily. I'll worry about the children."

"All right. I'll do what I can." Matt rolled Mantika's companion into Listener's free hand. "I promise."

As Listener gazed at the companion, her own companion floated close to her eyes and flashed red. After a few seconds, she nodded. "I know, I know. He's doing the best he can." She looked at him, tears streaming. "I'm sorry. It's just that I—"

"Forget it. I understand." Matt stepped back from Listener and drew his mother closer. "Let's find the fire-breathing dragon." He helped her climb onto Albatross's back, careful not to jostle Lily. When he settled behind her, he patted Albatross's scales. "Let's go!"

While Matt held his mother's hips, Albatross beat his wings and skittered across the field, huffing and snorting ice crystals. After lifting over heaps of fallen huts, he flew into another field that appeared to be divided into two halves—one littered with bodies and stones and the other covered with rich soil and a few green plants. A lone man with curly dark hair stood in the soil's midst, his shirt torn, revealing a muscular chest. He wobbled in place, as if exhausted. Yet, a splotch of blood on the back of his shirt told another story. He wasn't merely spent; he was badly hurt.

Moans and gentle cries emanated from dozens of men and women lying in the field. A few hobbled barefoot from place to place, checking on the injured or trying to free them from fallen trees. Blinking companions darted this way and that, and they all appeared to be attached to a human—no loose eggs to signify buried victims.

The moment Albatross landed, Matt spotted a red dragon, its legs and tail pinned under several logs. He leaped off, helped his mother slide safely down with Lily, and ran toward the dragon. The man in the garden jogged in the same direction, but he teetered, as if ready to collapse.

When Matt reached the dragon, he slid his hands under one of the logs and braced with his legs. "What's your name?" Matt asked.

"Karrick, son of Goliath and Roxil." As he grunted painfully, smoke curled up from his nostrils. "But do not help me if there

169

are others you can help. I will not be the reason for any prolonged suffering."

The man from the garden arrived. His companion floated next to his ear, unblinking. "Karrick has refused my help until I finish in the garden. At first I ignored his wishes, but I was unable to move the burdens by myself."

"Maybe we can do it together." Matt turned back to the dragon. "Listen, Karrick, I am a healer, and I need your fire-breathing to help me heal a baby. Will you cooperate?"

"Very well, but I have no strength. My back legs are broken."

"Then be ready to crawl out with your front legs." Matt slid his arms under the closest log. "I'll try to get some of the weight off of you."

The man squatted at Matt's side and added his arms to the effort. "Lift!"

Matt thrust with his legs. The man grunted. His biceps bulged, accentuating his bronzed skin. As the log lifted inch by inch, the dragon clawed at the ground but made no progress.

"You can do it, Karrick!" the man called. "The Father of Lights grants us power in times of trouble."

Finally, Matt and the man threw the log, sending it rolling away. Blood now dampened the man's shirt in a line down his back, and his companion sat on his shoulder as if resting from the labor.

"We have two more logs to move." He crouched and set his arms under the next log. "What is your name?"

"Matt. Yours?"

"Valiant."

"I should've guessed. I've heard you spoken of very highly." Matt squatted and slid his arms under the smaller log. "Say the word."

"Lift!" This time they heaved the log away with no trouble.

Karrick crawled out from under the third log, dragging his back legs and tail. As he emerged, his entire body came into view. Matt scanned him from snout to tail. He looked more like the Earth dragons than did Grackle and Albatross, though he was smaller than Makaidos, Thigocia, and the others.

Valiant wrapped his arms around Matt and kissed his forehead. "Excellent work. Your strength is greater than most I have seen from your world."

With his arms pinned to his sides, Matt nodded. "Um … thanks."

When Valiant drew back, Mom flew closer with Lily in her arms, beating her wings to stay above the debris, but Albatross was now nowhere in sight.

"Karrick," Matt said as he crouched in front of the dragon's snout, "are you all right? I mean, how bad are your injuries?"

"As I thought, my rear legs are broken, but I am confident that I have no internal injuries. I will heal in time."

Matt patted Karrick's neck. "Are you ready to help now?"

Karrick turned his head and shot out a quick burst of fire at the ground. "The power behind my flames is weak, but I will do what I can."

"That's all I can ask for."

Valiant offered Matt his hand. "I must get back to the birthing garden. There are more babies to save."

Matt rose and shook his hand. "Babies?"

"Yes, of course." Valiant turned and hurried away. The splotch on the back of his shirt had doubled in size.

Mom laid Lily in Matt's arms and carefully slid the cloak from underneath. Lily's companion balanced on her chest as if dazed. "Ashley did most of the healing with Excalibur's energy or an oracle's fire. Since you have no scales, dragon fire is much more dangerous."

"So what do we do?"

Mom spread the cloak over Matt's head and back. "Sit on the ground. Karrick will breathe fire on the flameproof cloak, and you will focus on Lily. If your gift works like Ashley's, healing light will come through your eyes. Make sure the light goes into Lily's eyes. Ashley says it hurts a lot, and it will drain all your energy, and I'm not even sure if it will work. Are you up for it?"

"To save this baby's life?" He nodded and lowered himself to the ground. "I'll do my best."

She leaned over and kissed him on the cheek. "That's all we can ask for."

As Matt shifted his back toward Karrick, Valiant came into view in the garden about twenty paces away, picking up stones that had toppled some of the plants. Why would he put such effort into coddling vegetation when so many people were suffering? With his wounds and loss of blood, he might even be risking his own life.

A whoosh sounded. Matt's back grew warm. He focused on Lily, but Valiant's movements stayed in his field of vision. Valiant picked up a broken plant. Two wilted leaves spilled out a white sac the size of a football. As he peeled away the spider-web-like mesh from around the sac, he began weeping. When the last layer dropped away, a little baby lay in his palms, its petite arms and legs limp. A tiny glass egg fell from the baby's fingers and lay motionless on the soil.

Matt's throat tightened. This garden produced babies? How could that be?

As heat from Karrick's flames spread around Matt's body, he couldn't hold back his tears. Why did the little ones have to suffer? The evil in the world wasn't their fault.

Valiant dropped to his knees. He laid the baby gently on the soil. Then, his eyes rolling upward, he clutched his chest and toppled to the side. His companion fell to the ground and rolled several inches away.

Matt lurched, but a hand reached under the cloak and grabbed his wrist, keeping him in place. "No!" Mom said. "Stay where you are! I'll help Valiant!"

She staggered to Valiant and knelt over him, straddling his torso. She laid her ear against his chest. "His heart's not beating!"

Her hand shaking, she withdrew the energy gun from a pocket.

"Mom!" Matt called. "Don't. Get someone to help you drag him to me, and I'll try to—"

"No time!" She pressed the barrel against Valiant's chest and pulled the trigger. Light flashed within the gun and flowed into his body, creating an aura at the entry point. As she held it in place, her mouth dropped open. Her body quaked. Gasping for breath, she looked at Matt, her face pale. "Focus … focus on Lily!"

"Okay, okay!" Trembling, Matt stared at the little girl in his arms. Of course Mom was right. She had to save Valiant, and he had to concentrate on Lily. But at what cost?

After several seconds, Lily squirmed and whimpered. Her companion tipped over and lay dark on her chest. Matt again let out a quiet shushing sound. "It's okay, Lily." His voice shook and rattled. "I know it's getting hot … but you'll be all right."

The words echoed in his mind. Would she be all right? The baby in the garden didn't survive. Many of the people in Founder's Village also lost their lives. And her own companion wasn't responding. What right did he have to tell Lily that she would escape tragedy?

The flow of heat eased. Karrick's energy was nearly spent. Time was running out. Matt again focused on the little girl. Mom said light would come from his eyes, but it hadn't happened yet. This was all so new, so strange.

Still sitting with Lily in his lap, he mentally combined his natural body heat with the surge spreading across the cloak. Concentrating on both sources, he drew the energy toward his eyes. A pair of white beams struck the little girl's face. Moving his head, he shifted the beams to her eyes and opened her lids with his fingers. Light poured in. She jerked, but Matt hugged her closer and kept his eyebeams in place.

Sweat dripped from his nose and chin. His arms weakened, feeling like melting rubber bands. He ran a finger along Lily's scalp. The crack in her skull seemed thinner, as if the broken piece was mending itself in place. Her companion brightened, lifted off her chest, and floated to her cheek, flashing blue.

As burning heat scalded his skin and drilled into his bones, he grimaced but kept pouring in the light. He had to see the healing to completion. No sense in coming this far without making sure.

"You can do it, Matt," a woman called, but she seemed far away, whoever she was.

"Keep it up, Son." The man's voice was strong and steady, much like Walter's, though older somehow.

Finally, his finger detected no crack. "St … stop! I think … she's healed."

The heat on his back evaporated. His arms went numb. He rolled to his side, laying Lily gently on the ground as he keeled over. Blackness pulsed in his vision. A wheezing sound and a deep cough echoed again and again, as if he were in a canyon.

A cool hand touched his forehead. "He is feverish," the man said. "Very hot."

174

"Someone fetch water! I will call the dragons!"

Is that Listener? Matt's thoughts trickled like a slowly leaking faucet. *Yes ... Listener.*

Retreating footfalls thumped the ground, then sharp whistles pierced the air. When they died away, whispers filtered in, close, yet far away at the same time.

"Lily is asleep," Listener said. "She seems fine."

"Praise the Father of Lights. We have two miracles of healing."

Matt tried to blink, but his lids wouldn't move. *That sounded like Valiant. He must have recovered.*

"How is Bonnie?" Listener asked.

"Exhausted. The precious gift she gave me drained her energy. She needs to sleep but refuses to rest. She will be here in a moment."

"She is a holy vessel, a gift from God."

"Indeed," Valiant said. "Few gems compare."

"Help me get the cloak off him."

A frigid hand touched Matt's. He winced. It was cold ... so cold. His body rolled from side to side, but his limp arms and legs couldn't respond. He was at the mercy of these cold but helpful hands.

"Now his shirt," Listener said.

His body rocked again. Coolness spread across his skin, not so icy this time, more like an autumn breeze. Flapping sounds preceded gusts of wind that brought more relief.

"Albatross. Cold breath, but no ice. We have to cool him quickly but without shocking his system."

A bitter wind blasted across his chest, face, and hair. It felt like being naked in a snowstorm. Still, no shivers came. Heat pulsed from within, driving the chill away.

A hand pressed against his forehead again. "He is still dangerously feverish."

175

"It seems that cold air is not enough," Listener said. "Albatross, start with a little ice and add more until I say to stop."

The wind transformed into a wintry blast. Matt winced. He had to move. He had to get out of the blizzard, but his arms and legs stayed numb, as stiff as logs.

"That's perfect, Albatross. Keep it there."

Something smooth massaged his chest, fingers driving the coolness into his skin. A new voice joined the conversation, weak and shaky. "He will recover. It's all part of the healing gift."

Matt tried to say "Mom," but although his lips formed the word, no sound came out.

"Listener, I think we have enough," Mom said. "Please take Albatross away. I'll carry Lily to shelter and see who else I can help."

Valiant's voice returned. "You must save the energy in the gun for yourself. You barely have enough strength to walk. Trust the Father of Lights to bring healing."

"Maybe God is bringing the healing through me."

"I think that is unlikely," Valiant said. "He would not want you to contribute to corrupting your world."

"The people in my world always have a choice. The corruption won't affect them unless they choose to allow it."

"This is true, but I fear that the innocent ones in your world will suffer at the hands of those who welcome evil into their hearts. We cannot employ a healing device that will bring harm to the innocent. Again I say to trust the Father of Lights."

"Valiant, I do trust the Father of Lights, but he also expects us to use the gifts he has given us. Wisdom demands that we—"

"Wisdom demands?" Valiant's tone had sharpened, but after a deep breath, he settled. "Bonnie, I understand your passion, but you must allow me to exercise my wisdom. You are a faithful sojourner who is traveling in a foreign land, a land that is not yours. As long as our king and queen are absent, I must take their place as leader of this realm. You healed me, and I am thankful for your kindness, but I cannot allow you to sacrifice yourself."

"So are you telling me to refrain from saving your people?"

"I am. We will not contribute to the corruption of your world. Use the rest of the energy in your gun on yourself."

After a moment of silence, Mom's voice returned, again weak. "You have the authority to compel me regarding your people but not what I choose to do for myself."

"Agreed. Yet, in your weakened state, it is best not to trust your own counsel. Perhaps you should consider your son's advice. I see in him wisdom far beyond his years."

After another moment of silence, Mom sighed. "I will consider it."

"Then rest while I care for Matt. He needs the remainder of his body cooled."

"I understand."

"I expect the hospital to return before nightfall. Your mother and father are inside as well as the other sick anthrozils, some caregivers, and many of our children. Perhaps you can offer assistance there."

"Thank you. I would love to help as soon as I find a place for Lily."

Wings fluttered and quickly faded. The cooling massage spread to Matt's thighs and legs. "You are surely a son of your mother," Valiant said. "She constantly bleeds for those who cannot repay her, and your willingness to sacrifice yourself for a baby is far greater evidence of your sonship than are facial similarities. You look very little like your father or mother, but your heart is identical. I hope you will honor me with your friendship."

Matt tried to answer, but his lungs had no strength. The surrounding sounds died away. His vision flickered, then brightened. For some reason, he was now driving a convertible with Darcy in the passenger seat. Her auburn hair flowed back in the breeze, revealing a worried expression. Smeared makeup blended with shimmering tear tracks on her cheeks. She wore his cloak, covering her body to her knees, leaving the lower part of her legs bare. She turned to him and said, "You won't regret this, Matt. Your trust, in spite of all I have done to you, means everything to me."

Matt blinked. She sounded just like Semiramis. And hadn't Semiramis used similar words when spewing her deceptive praise?

Smiling weakly, Darcy slid her hand into his. The touch felt electric, yet soothing and good. "Will you take me home?"

"I'll do my best." Matt grimaced inside, but his face wouldn't respond to the thought. How could he say that to Darcy? Taking her home would be like inviting an axe-wielding hitchhiker to dinner with the family.

Darcy pulled Matt's hand to her lips and kissed his fingers. She opened her mouth to speak, but a different voice came out.

"Matt, it's time to wake up." Cool moisture returned, this time across his brow and cheeks. "Your temperature is almost normal, so I think you've recovered."

He blinked open his eyes. Listener knelt over him, swabbing his forehead with a sponge. Its light flashing blue, her companion floated close to her ear. Torches burned in various places, including one within reach, their ends embedded in the ground as they illuminated the twilight scene. As people walked here and there, long shadows followed them, a sure sign that night was about to fall.

"Ah! The healer has awakened!" Listener laid a cloak at his side. "You might need this again."

He touched it with a finger. "I think I remember that it worked."

"It did." She kissed his cheek. "Thank you for saving my sister's life. She would have died if not for you."

Matt braced his hands to get up, but Listener pushed his chest, keeping him in place. "The doctor will want to examine you before you try to walk."

"Doctor?"

"Dr. Conner is in our flying hospital." As Listener turned, her partially unraveled pigtails swayed. "No one has reported seeing it yet, but it should be on its way."

Matt lifted his head and looked around. He lay on a bed of straw under a wooden lean-to, the garden still in sight. Facing him, his mother sat at the soil boundary, her wings wrapped around her body and her head hanging low. A torch to her left spread flickering light over her slouched form and cast a wavering shadow to her right, as if reflecting a troubled dream.

"She's asleep," Listener said. "Exhausted. Also disappointed. She longs to heal people with that gun, but Valiant will not allow it."

"I think I heard that. I hope it's not a mistake. I know my mother doesn't want anyone else to die."

"No one does." Listener stared at the sky, her eyes misty. "I hope Dr. Conner comes soon before any more perish."

"How many have died so far?"

"By my count, thirty-nine in Founder's Village and twenty-seven in Peace Village. Our donkeys fled, so I have no count of them. No dragons died, though Karrick is badly hurt, as you saw. It is difficult keeping him down. It was his job to monitor a portal leading to Earth that was supposed to let Elam and his warriors back to our world, but lava overran the area and closed the portal. Karrick tried to open it again while flying above the heat but

179

failed. We think the lava is somehow canceling the effect of flames, making it impossible to open the portal. Since Elam is probably wondering why he is unable to enter, we have to get a message to him. Because of the eruption, our ground transmitters were destroyed, so we are unable to contact him. We don't know whether or not our hospital radio was affected, but when it arrives, we will find out."

The ground trembled. Matt twisted his body to get a look at Mount Elijah. Only a slight plume of steam rose from its ragged top. More steam would be better, a sign that the pressure inside was escaping through a vent. "I guess Elam and the others are safer where they are, assuming they won the battle."

"True, but they have to return somehow." Listener grabbed the nearby torch and began swirling it as if stirring soup. "In theory, if Karrick were healthy, he could create a fiery vortex and split the portal open, but even if there were no lava in the area, it is too dangerous without knowing whether our people are present at the other side. Portal openings are monitored by the military on Earth, so we would likely soon be greeted by a hostile force, especially considering your world's accelerating corruption."

She jabbed the torch back into the ground. "Can you imagine trying to escape from their machinery? Since we are crippled, we would be captured in seconds, perhaps slaughtered, and Earth's forces could invade and take over our world."

Matt sighed. She was right. They probably would do that. Whatever Earth humans didn't understand, they tried to control or destroy. "But it's also dangerous to stay here."

"Valiant plans to take us to higher ground in case more stones and lava spew out. We have an enclave in a sheltered area where we can wait for the volcano to settle. We didn't have time to get there earlier, and even now we might be exposed to poisonous fumes along the way."

"And carting the wounded to higher ground will be hard enough," Matt added. "It sounds like a no-win situation."

He braced his hands to get up, but Listener pushed down on his shoulder. "You are a persistent one. I admire that."

"Admiration is great, but I prefer that you just let me up."

She laughed. "I'll see if the hospital has been sighted."

As she rose, Matt grasped her wrist. "What about the children? I asked you earlier, but—"

"Oh, yes. You did." Sighing, she knelt again. "I apologize for my outburst."

"It's all right. With your sister hurt, you were kind of stressed out."

"You are kind to grant me an excuse." She glanced in the direction of the valley. "After you left us, I conferred with Eagle. We agreed that for safety and efficiency, it would be best for me to fly directly here so I could send both Grackle and Albatross back as quickly as possible. Between the two dragons, they have already brought five children home, and I sent Grackle once again to help Eagle search for Cheer."

Matt lifted his brow. "Why didn't you stay to search with him?"

"A bold question from a compassionate soul." Listener smiled. "I hoped to stay to help Eagle, but Valiant said no. My mother's dead, and I had to find care for my sister. Besides, Valiant has complete faith in his son, as do I."

"It's really great to see a father and son who love each other so much. I suppose Valiant's wife must really be proud of both of them."

"She was." As Listener's head drooped, her companion brushed against her cheek. "His Eve died only a year ago, attacked by a meadow lion, and he buried her in the birthing garden."

181

"I'm sorry to hear that." Matt searched the hazy field for Valiant, but his reclining position handicapped his view. "I guess that broke his heart."

"Valiant is heartbroken about his Eve's death, to be sure, but that isn't the only reason. Children have perished, including infants in the birthing garden."

Matt nodded. "I saw him crying about a dead baby in the plant. It was like a punch in the gut."

"He is known for his brokenness over suffering children. His surface presentation is multifaceted, but his heart knows only one response. He would die for anyone, both in Second Eden and on your world, and he has diligently taught this sacrificial precept to his son. If Valiant could give his life to prevent someone's suffering, he would do so without question." Her voice breaking, Listener took Matt's hand and caressed his knuckles with her thumb. "Even if his eyes are dry, know that he weeps within. In that regard, we are all one."

"I guess that makes sense." Matt gazed at her tear-streaked face. This young warrior seemed to be describing herself, as tough as steel when confronting a sorceress, yet as soft as velvet when conversing with a newfound friend. Her affection was so sincere, so genuine. It felt good and right. "You said her name was Eve?"

"No, her name was Emerald." She laughed softly. "I apologize. I forgot to tell you about our label for a female spouse." She interlocked thumbs with him. "We say 'Eve.' A male spouse is an Adam."

"Okay, I get it. Adam and Eve." Matt kept his focus on their hands. "I was wondering ... how old is Eagle?"

"How old? For Second Eden dwellers it is impossible to know for certain." She whispered, almost as if praying. "Eagle came to us in the birthing garden sixteen years ago. We think he might be the fulfillment of a prophecy, but I cannot speak of that now."

Warmth rushed into Matt's cheeks. Stepping out of line in this world was way too easy. "I guess I'd better stop asking questions."

"Oh, don't worry, Matt. The man who lets fear of stumbling suppress his desire for knowledge will be a fool indeed." She lifted his hand and kissed his fingers. "Ask as many questions as you desire. We are always gracious to those we love."

More heat flooded his cheeks. Asking the most obvious question was way too difficult. Assuming her affection to be normal for this world would have to do. Valiant demonstrated it as well with his embrace, so it was a fair guess. At this point, almost any other question would be a welcome distraction.

He nodded toward her belt. "Why didn't you give your spyglass to Eagle? Wouldn't it help him find Cheer?"

She pulled the spyglass from her belt and set it in his hand. "See for yourself. It doesn't work very well in the dark, at least when searching for physical objects. With night falling, Eagle will be better off without something extra to carry." She pressed her lips together, but they trembled anyway. "I am holding to faith that he'll find Cheer. There have been too many tragedies already."

183

Matt pulled her hand to his lips and kissed her fingers. "I'm really sorry about your mother. I wish I could've helped her."

A tear glistened in her eye. "I know you would have. Thank you." She slid her hand away, rose to her feet, and jogged into the haze. Seconds later, only her companion's flashing red light remained visible.

Matt kept his gaze on the light until it disappeared behind a boulder. Was kissing her hand a mistake? Maybe her culture allowed her to show affection, but he wasn't allowed to return it. But that didn't make much sense. She was probably just too sad to stay. How terrible it must have been to see her mother and so many others lying dead in this disaster zone.

He sat up and looked at Mom, still sitting enfolded in her wings at the edge of the garden. A tiny light glimmered above her head, like a twinkling star hovering in place. He glanced back, but Listener was nowhere in sight. Her spyglass, however, still lay in his grip. He looked through it, aiming at the odd light.

Through the spyglass, a golden aura surrounded the light, emanating energy. As another tremor rolled through the ground, he pointed the spyglass at Mount Elijah. At the lowest point in its ragged-edged top, fiery lava spilled over and eased down the slope, as if someone had bumped a full bowl of soup.

He followed a billowing plume of smoke that faded as it rose past the lava's glow. More dots of light appeared over the volcano and spread out from horizon to horizon, like the stars of night sprinkled across the sky in unfamiliar arrangements. He lowered the spyglass. The dots were invisible to the naked eye. It seemed that the spyglass worked pretty well, in spite of the dimming skies.

His head pounding, he rolled and crawled toward the garden, keeping the spyglass off the ground. With even more torches burning throughout the field, navigating around the debris proved to be easy. When he reached his mother and paused in front of her, he listened. She breathed deeply and steadily, definitely asleep. Her energizing gun lay close to her side, still glowing with spinning light, the fraction of her stored energy she hadn't yet dispensed.

Matt picked up the gun and tucked it behind his waistband. No use getting it lost or stepped on.

The ground trembled again. Mount Elijah spewed a new billowing cloud, visible only because of millions of sparks swirling in the exhaust. The shake didn't seem to disturb Mom. She just slept on.

The glimmer floated several paces behind her at about waist level. Still carrying the spyglass, Matt crawled toward the glimmer,

184

bypassing two plants, and knelt in front of the light, his torso straight. About the size of a bullet, it looked like a hole, as if someone had punctured the air itself.

He set the spyglass at his side and spread his palm in front of the hole. The slightest hint of warmth emanated from it. Vague silhouettes, barely visible, shifted around the hole, as if people moved behind a projection screen.

He picked up the spyglass and looked through its lens. Golden light spilled from the hole and dispersed. He waved his hand behind the light, but the movement had no effect. With a snatch of his fingers, he tried to grab it, but it passed right through his hand like a phantom firefly.

After setting the spyglass on the ground and sliding closer, he positioned himself in front of the hole and looked through it. A tree blazed within, and three people stood nearby. The flames cast a blinding light over the human forms, making them shimmer.

185

Matt drew away and rubbed his eyes. There was another world in there!

CHAPTER

RETURN OF THE KNIGHT

Lauren's tingles finally eased. Still wearing the night-vision goggles, she focused once again on the museum. How long should she wait? Whoever was there might not come out of hiding, maybe for hours or even days. A resident of Hades probably had all the time in the world.

Soon, an orange form appeared at the left side of the museum room's exterior, creeping around the curved wall. As it edged closer to the front, the frame of a woman took shape, small and trembling, but her face remained vague. With a hand against the wall, she reached the doorway and skulked into the museum.

Keeping her in view, Lauren crept toward the doorway. The woman stooped next to the backpack and rummaged through it. Lauren picked up her pace, but when the woman rose and faced the tree with a knife in her hand, Lauren stopped about twenty steps short and waited. Without a weapon, confronting the stranger could be suicide.

The woman hacked off the end of a branch. As soon as it hit the floor, the leaves began to glow with a golden aura. She snatched them up with a sleeve-covered hand and ran from the museum, retracing her steps around the building.

Lauren followed. This woman didn't look dangerous, just scared, but why would she cut leaves from the tree of life?

When Lauren neared the back of the building, she stopped. A candle burned on the ground about fifty feet away, brightening the scene. She slid the goggles down to her chest and scanned the area. The woman knelt next to a big shirtless man who lay motionless on his back. "I bring leaves," she said, her voice strained and halting. "From … tree of life."

Lauren stepped forward. Although their faces were still out of view, the woman's orange jumpsuit and fractured voice were familiar. "Portia?" she whispered.

The woman didn't turn. Lauren crept closer. Dad had said Portia wasn't deaf. Her real name was Tamara, a former dragon. Maybe she was too focused on helping the man. "Tamara?"

She gasped and pivoted on her knees, the candle now illuminating her terrified face. "Go … go away!"

Lauren set a hand on her chest. "It's me, Lauren."

"Lauren?" She squinted. "Not a … a devil?"

"Not a devil." Lauren pulled off her helmet, flicked on the light, and aimed it at her own face. "See?"

Tamara breathed a sigh of relief. "Oh! Lauren!" Her face twisting, tears began to flow. "I want … want to help … but he …"

"Don't try to talk." Tingles erupting in her scales again, Lauren hurried to Tamara and knelt at her side. "Just direct your thoughts at me. I can hear them."

Tamara blinked at her. *You can hear my thoughts?*

"Perfectly." Lauren put her helmet back on and shone the light on the man's face. "Sir Barlow!"

Tamara nodded, tears still evident as her thoughts flowed in a rapid stream. *Colonel Baxter shot him, and I've been trying to save his life. I found entry and exit wounds, so I think the bullet went straight through. He's lost a lot of blood, and his heart seems weak. I thought leaves from the tree of life might help, but they are too strong to pull off, and I didn't have anything to cut them with. I was ready to bite them off, but then I heard footsteps. I thought devils might be coming. Sapphira told me the tree of life she planted was in Hades, and I thought devils live here.*

Lauren looked at the leaves in Tamara's hand. They glowed orange and gold. "What are you going to do, rub them on the wound?"

"Yes," Tamara said out loud. "Maybe … he chew them."

"I guess it can't hurt." Lauren opened her hand. "I'll try to get him to chew one while you rub the wounds."

Tamara dropped a leaf into Lauren's palm. Shaped like a star, its glow felt soothing, like warm bathwater after walking through the snow.

Lauren shuffled on her knees to Sir Barlow's head and pushed the leaf between his lips. "Chew, Sir Barlow," she said directly into his ear. "You have to chew! That's an order!"

She thrust the leaf deeper and worked his jaw with her hand. "Like this. Chew it up."

"It working," Tamara said. "Not bleeding."

"Think your words, Tamara."

The wound on his stomach stopped bleeding. It's not sealed completely, though.

"Good enough. Apply it to the other wound."

189

I'll need help turning him over.

"Let me make sure this leaf's going to stay." Lauren thrust her finger into his mouth and pushed the leaf as far as she could. Sir Barlow gagged and bit down on her knuckle. She jerked her finger out and pressed his lips closed. "If you don't want that leaf in there, soldier, then swallow it!"

After chewing twice, Sir Barlow swallowed.

"Let's turn him." Lauren slid her hands under his sweaty back, and Tamara did the same. "On three," Lauren said. "One ... two ... three!"

They heaved and flipped him to his stomach, exposing a pool of blood and a pair of gloves on the stone floor. A hole the size of a thumb oozed more blood into a larger smear on his hairy back.

Lauren touched one of the gloves. "I saw blood at the museum room door. Did you drag him all the way back here?"

190

Tamara massaged the wound with a leaf. *He was semiconscious, so I just had to prop him up while he walked. At first we went to a tunnel that looked like it might lead out, but when his bleeding got worse, I knew we couldn't go very far, so I decided to hide him behind the museum. He helped me take his coat and shirt off, but then he fell unconscious on top of his gloves. I couldn't budge him. After a while, I tried to find something to cut a leaf from the tree, but when I saw lights in the tunnel, I ran back to him. I suppose you know the rest.*

"I think so." Lauren spotted the shirt and coat lying in a heap nearby. "Since he was able to walk for a little while, that's a good sign. The bullet must've missed his vital organs, or he would've been dead long ago."

Tamara continued rubbing. *God is with him. He is a good man, a man of faith, a true gentleman.*

"I know. He sure saved my skin."

After nearly a minute, the hole shrank, though, like the other wound, it didn't seal completely. After putting his shirt on, they laid him on his back.

"Whew!" Lauren sat heavily on the floor. "He's no light-weight!"

Tamara raised an arm and flexed her wiry bicep. "He all muscle!"

Lauren laughed. "He's got a lot of muscle, that's for sure."

The two smiled at each other for a moment, but Tamara's expression soon turned serious. *Do you know what's going on? Are we really in Hades?*

"We are. We transported here through portals."

For the next few minutes, Lauren told the story about how Sapphira created a portal and sent the entire laser weapons structure through it. When she explained how they could get out of Hades easily by using Apollo, Tamara's mood lifted, and the warning that guards might be waiting for them didn't faze her. There was a way out. That seemed more important than anything.

191

Tamara mentally recited her experiences, and together they concluded that since the weapons facility was too big to fit in the portal leading to the museum room, it probably fell into the volcano, while she and Barlow dropped through the museum ceiling.

Lauren let her shoulders sag. "But not Matt." Her throat tightened, pitching her voice higher. "Why couldn't he drop in the right place? Why did he have to fall in the volcano?"

"Maybe ..." Tamara rubbed Lauren's shoulder. "Maybe ... still hope."

Lauren set her hand over Tamara's. "You're right. I'm not giving up yet."

While waiting for Sir Barlow to recover, Tamara, again communicating through her thoughts, provided a vivid telling of dragon history. She told of Arramos and Shachar, Makaidos and Thigocia, Goliath and Roxil, and Clefspeare and Hartanna, though the final two never became mates. She described the transformation of dragons to humans, Devin's insane obsession with killing them, and how he nearly succeeded in eliminating the species.

Lauren absorbed every detail. These were her ancestors, her family roots. For years she knew nothing more than a scant, fictitious history of her parents, really just captions under a family album with digitally altered pictures of herself with a fake mother and father—strangers now, though images of her fabricated life still haunted her thoughts.

So, Tamara continued, *it's my fault that Devin was able to find the other anthrozils. Not only did he steal the ovulum from me that led him to the others, but when he came into my house to kill me, he found a message from Valcor, who had become Patrick, a message that I was supposed to destroy immediately after reading. It provided a way to create coded communications between anthrozils, so when Devin took it, he was able to decode secret messages and learn where to find the remaining dragons. Everyone assumed that I had destroyed the message, but since I died, I couldn't tell them the truth. It wasn't until I was resurrected in the Circles of Seven that I was able to tell everyone about my tragic blunder.*

"Why didn't you destroy it?"

It was a terribly complicated code. I had a very hard time memorizing the procedure, and if I couldn't communicate with the others, especially Legossi, I might not survive. You see, back then, I often became confused easily. Some people called me "simple" or even "dimwitted." Whenever I took in information, it would get scrambled before I could understand it.

192

"Like dyslexia?"

A severe form of it, I think. I also couldn't get information from my brain to my mouth efficiently, and that malady continues. In fact, it's worse than it's ever been. I wonder if eventually I'll be able to talk at all.

"How did the input problem get cured? It's obvious that you're processing input very well right now. You seem as sharp as a tack."

I'm not sure exactly how it happened. My mind started getting clearer shortly after the battle in Second Eden, the one in which Acacia died. Tamara's brow wrinkled. *But you might not have heard that story.*

"Yes, I heard about it. My dad told me. Go on."

Well, maybe it was the battle itself that cured me, because right afterward, when I captured Semiramis and Mardon and flew them to the birthing garden, my mind began to clear. You see, Mount Elijah had recently erupted, so I had to fly through a great deal of smoke and ash, and I was worried that I would become confused and get lost, but instead, I found my way much more quickly than I expected. Not only that, even though Semiramis tried to persuade me to let her go by using her deceptive arts, I was able to see through her ploy and complete my task. To this day I am convinced that the old me would have given in to her charms.

"That's very cool. The shock of battle must have made something click in your brain."

I think so, though it didn't happen right away. I could feel the change during the flight, not before, and not long after that was when I noticed that my speaking ability was growing worse at a rapid rate. Anyway, since I felt like a newly hatched genius compared to my old self, after I became human I decided to pursue a lifelong ambition, to be an actress. I began secretly traveling to Earth to study under a lady in England who understood my plight and wasn't bothered by my inability to speak. She said that there were many nonspeaking roles in movies and plays, and she could help me with facial expressions and body language, but when your mother and father were captured, I knew what my first role would be—an infiltrator into the prison.

So when I was sure my acting skills were good enough, I entered the military complex as a prisoner, but I told no one, not even Elam or Sapphira. I was sure they would try to stop me, and I didn't want to risk hurting my chance to rescue Bonnie, so I simply left and went into hiding. I decided to lose a lot of weight, cut my hair in a ragged mop, and stay out of the sun so I could look like a drug addict. Imagine what my friends would have said during that process. It would have been impossible to escape the pressure to give up on my idea. After that, I tried to figure out how to get into the prison system, which took quite a while, but I finally—

"If I am some sort of cat, I think I have used at least seven of my nine lives."

Lauren turned toward the voice. Sir Barlow, now sitting, spat a few leaf fragments into his palm. "Yes, I must be a cat. This hairball is proof."

Tamara shuffled over on her knees and embraced him. "You … feel okay?"

As she drew back, he shook his head. "Not at all, my good lady, but I have felt worse." He pressed a hand over his belly wound and grimaced. "It seems that my efforts cost me a pound of flesh."

Lauren scooted to his other side. "But you saved our lives." She gave him a hug and slid her hand into his. "We're thankful for the courageous knight who sacrificed himself for us."

"Indeed. I will gladly pay that pound anytime." He grinned. "The smiles of two grateful ladies are reward enough."

Lauren peeked at his wound through his open shirt. Only a bruise and blood smears remained. Getting him up shouldn't be too risky. She gave his hand a gentle pull. "Do you want to see if you can stand?"

He nodded. "With a single candle lighting this dark chamber, I get the impression that this is not a good place to stay."

"You're right about that." Lauren gave Barlow a quick summary of her story and how all three arrived in Hades. When she finished, she set a hand behind his back. As she pulled, Tamara helped from the other side. Soon, they had balanced the hefty guard on his feet.

After buttoning his shirt, he picked up his gloves and pulled his pants higher on his waist. "It seems that I have lost my belt buckle."

"You did," Lauren said. "I think all the metal you had on stayed behind."

"Well, then …" Barlow cinched his waistband and tied the two ends of his belt together. "We cannot go into battle with the risk of losing our pants, can we now?"

"I safe." Tamara touched her jumpsuit. "Plastic buttons."

"Then we are all covered." Barlow straightened his shoulders, now perfectly steady. "What is our course of action?"

Lauren nodded toward the museum. "I left a communications device called Apollo in there. It was transmitting a lot of data, and I don't know if it's done yet or not. If Larry got my video, he probably sent at least an acknowledgment and maybe more. I need to know if there are any guards at the portal site."

"I am aware of our electronic friend. I heard there is a new model, so I will be glad to see it." Barlow pulled his pants higher and nodded. "Lead the way, Miss."

Lauren donned her helmet and guided them around the building. When they entered the room, everything appeared as it was before—Apollo and her backpack on the floor and the

195

ladder leaning against the wall, though the knife now lay near where Tamara had cut the tree.

After giving Tamara and Sir Barlow each a cereal bar and a bottle of water from the backpack, Lauren knelt next to Apollo. She pressed the menu button and searched for a setting to check for a received message. While eating and drinking, Barlow and Tamara looked around. As much as her ability allowed, Tamara relayed her knowledge of the museum and the tree of life. Although her cadence was halting and her word choices strained, Barlow seemed able to fill in the details with his usual flair.

"So, they say that money doesn't grow on trees," Barlow said as he bent close to the single flame, "but healing and eternal life are far more valuable."

"Can't argue with that." Lauren scrunched her brow as she scrolled through menu options. *Cross-dimensional transmission. Select mode. Toggle to receive.*

She pressed the final button. "There. That should do it." A diode on Apollo's top turned green. "I think we're getting something."

"Can you read it?"

"Not yet." She set her phone on Apollo's top. A message flashed on the phone's screen. *Enter Password.*

"Password?" Lauren blinked at Sir Barlow. "Any ideas?"

"Since Ashley is its creator, I would suggest words that are meaningful to her. Perhaps *Walter* or *Foley* or *brain choke*."

"Brain choke?"

Barlow chuckled. "You would have to know her as well as I do to understand that one."

"I'll try them, but *Walter* and *Foley* are too obvious." After she punched in the words one at a time, each one failing, a new message appeared. *Security Warning. Next Failed Attempt Will Result in Lockout.*

Lauren let out a huff. "Now what?"

"Maybe it ... temporary." Tamara patted her on the back. "We wait ... yes?"

Lauren nodded. A security warning like that had to be temporary. It would reset eventually.

"What happened here?" Barlow pointed at the tree. "Is a blossom forming?"

Lauren shuffled closer on her knees, blinking at a newly radiant spot. Fresh growth had sprouted from the place Tamara had cut the tree, and the flame blazed brighter than the other one. "This is where the leaves that healed you came from."

Lauren perked her ears. Up until now, Mom's song had stayed consistent in this room, lilting from every crevice, but the source suddenly narrowed to a single point.

She half crawled and half leaped back to the portal. The tree's new sprouts created a vaporous beam that painted a circular glow on the doorway at waist level, as if the air were solid instead of empty space. No bigger than a finger hole, it pulsed with brightness. The song trickled through it, weak and fragile. "Any idea what that is?"

Bending, Barlow looked at the glow. "I have witnessed the formation of a number of portals, strange phantoms, if you will, that hover like this. Since we are in a place that is rife with portals, if I were a betting man, I would wager that this is a hole to another realm, but I wouldn't bet my eyeball that it's safe to look through it."

"My guess is Second Eden. I hear my mother's song directly from the hole." Lauren grabbed a pen from her backpack and poked it part way through. The gap offered resistance, as if the air were invisible wax, soft and pliable. Unlike earlier passages through the doorway, there was no crackle of static electricity.

The front half of the pen disappeared. She let it go. It floated in midair, proving that the edges of the hole were somehow solid enough to support the weight. "It's going somewhere other than here." She pulled it out and examined the tip. No damage, and the wax left no residue.

"It seems that I must take the risk." Barlow cleared his throat. "If you will allow me, Miss, I will see what I can see."

When Lauren scooted over, Barlow knelt and set his eye up to the hole. "Well, this is interesting. I see the birthing garden in Second Eden. When I last saw it, green grass had grown up across its fertile soil, but it seems that they have cultivated the garden once again. There is no mistaking the plants, but I see no humans. There are stones here and there, and one plant is badly damaged." He drew back, his expression sagging. "I fear that the little one inside that plant could not have survived such a crushing blow."

"The little one?" Lauren asked.

"These plants give birth to human infants. I have never understood the process, so I am unable to explain how it works. Suffice it to say that the mysteries of Second Eden are beyond the grasp of Earth dwellers."

"That's for sure." Lauren touched the edge of the hole. It felt rubbery, though her touch did nothing to alter its appearance or position. "So how do we make it bigger? Cut more leaves—"

Apollo buzzed. Lauren jumped to it and looked it over, again kneeling. Within the glass enclosure, sparkling green light emanated from the top platform, though soupy, as if someone had shone an emerald laser through dense fog on a snowy night. While the buzzing continued, light from the tree faded slightly, and the radiance within Apollo brightened. Soon, the sparkles gathered together in a swirl before falling to the bottom platform like spinning green snow. When the movement finally stopped, the glow turned off, and the tree's light revived. A finger-length scroll lay inside Apollo, neatly tied with a blue ribbon.

Lauren opened the enclosure, withdrew the scroll, and untied the ribbon. As she rolled out the paper and read the computer-printed text, Barlow and Tamara looked on.

Greetings, Lauren. I, Larry the computer, have been instructed to provide you with important information regarding Apollo's function. I was going to give you step-by-step instructions regarding how to set it to receive data from me, but I see from Apollo's ready signal that you have already accomplished this step. Now all that remains is to give you the password to access the received data. The password is AmAzing GraCe. It is case-sensitive, so enter it exactly as you see it. Send a confirmation message to let me know if you have succeeded. For your information, we have heard that the dragons who helped in the jailbreak operation were not able to return to Second Eden, so we cannot send a dragon to pick you up at Mount Elijah. We also have no one to send to clear your entry portal on Earth of any guards who might be there. Communications with Jared, Marilyn, and your father have been cut off. The last we heard from Ashley and Walter, they were fleeing military strikes, and we have lost contact. It is doubtful that normal operations will be restored soon. It seems that Earth has declared war on Second Eden, including its allies on Earth.

199

Lauren rolled the paper into a scroll. Tingles crawled across her back. The voices of the condemned chanted their sorrowful song and blended again with her mother's. *"Inhale the fires, exhale despair, each day expires without a prayer."*

Barlow blew out a low whistle. "It seems that we have our backs to the hornets' nest."

Nodding, Lauren slid the scroll into her pants pocket and punched the password into the phone. Apollo's diode turned green again, and a video appeared on the phone's screen. A man and a woman were bustling about in an equipment room of some kind. The woman carried a metallic sphere to a door and paused with her hand on the knob. "My name is Carly. The man is Adam. If you're seeing this, that means you got the update from Larry. What he didn't tell you is that all communications with Larry from now on should be considered viewable by anyone, including the people who kidnapped your father. Larry will delete this video as soon as he sends it, and Adam will try to reroute all cleared transmissions to Lois, but don't count on it."

A loud bang sounded. Adam waved frantically. "Someone's coming! Get out of here!"

The screen went blank.

Lauren stared at Barlow and Tamara. They stared back. Everything seemed frozen in time, stalled without a place to go. Hades now felt like a safe harbor instead of a pit of fears. They might be the only ones out of harm's way, the only allies who could stop the onslaught being poured out against the occupants and friends of Second Eden.

"My advice," Barlow said, "is to solve the mystery of the tree's portal to Second Eden. Perhaps if we enter that realm, we will learn how to counter the attacks. At the very least, we can provide a haven for escapees from the volcano's destruction and from the potential of danger from Earth's forces."

Lauren took off her helmet and goggles and laid them on the floor next to the backpack. "Odd, isn't it? We're offering people who live in a place called Eden a way to escape Earth by transporting them to Hades." She pushed her hand through her hair and grabbed a fistful at the back. "The world is going crazy!"

"Indeed, Miss, but we must cling to our sanity, and I am just the one to lead the way. I lived within a tiny gem for a thousand years, and the pressure to crack was beastly, but my fellows and I kept up our spirits by telling tales as tall as trees and solving mind-bending puzzles we concocted."

Lauren picked up the phone from Apollo's top and slid it into her pocket. "We don't have time for tales. We have to—"

"Yes, of course, but we must solve a puzzle. I have deduced that Tamara cut the tree in order to provide healing leaves for me. That cutting process produced the energetic flame, which, in turn, produced the hole that leads to Second Eden. Therefore, if we cut more leaves, we should produce a larger hole, perhaps big enough for us to crawl through."

201

Lauren smiled. The gallant knight's idea was a good one, the same thing she was going to suggest when Apollo's buzz interrupted her. Even if it failed, at least it would keep him busy while she tried Apollo. "That's a great idea, Sir Barlow." She scooped up the knife and handed it to him. "How much do you think you should cut?"

"Well ..." Like a sculptor studying an untouched block of marble, Barlow surveyed the tree. "I see no reason not to shave it all over. Most trees respond well to a liberal pruning."

"We'd better move out of the way." Lauren grabbed one of Apollo's dowels, rose to her feet, and guided Tamara toward the ladder. "It's liable to make quite a blaze."

"Then I will have to work quickly." Barlow put on his gloves and began hacking at the outer foliage. With every cut, leaves dropped to the ground and began to glow with a golden aura.

As Barlow shifted around the tree and continued cutting, Lauren knelt and slid Apollo close to the portal wall, glancing back and forth between the light meter and Barlow's efforts. Tiny leaves of fire popped forth from the newly sliced stems, making the tree twinkle like a starlit sky. Narrow beams shot out from the leaflets and drew pictures on invisible canvasses in front of the shelves, walls, and doorway. The edges of the tiny hole that led to Second Eden caught fire and expanded from the center. As if burning away a paper covering, the fire revealed more and more of the garden. The crushed plant appeared, then dark soil and stones.

Lauren rose to her feet, Apollo again in her grip. Maybe they wouldn't need Apollo after all.

Finally, a vast land of fallen trees, scattered boulders, and hazy skies covered a quarter of the museum room's wall space. In the distance to one side, Mount Elijah loomed, easily visible in the glow of lava and spewing sparks. If not for the fact that the trees had been flattened, the volcano probably wouldn't have been visible, but now it stood tall, as if proud of the damage it had done.

Between the garden and the volcano lay a scene of devastation. Illuminated by countless torches, boulders and leafless trees lay strewn across a grassy meadow, as if tossed aimlessly by a violent wind. People reclined throughout the field partially hidden by makeshift lean-tos, apparently injured in the storm of debris, and other people wearing torn and dirty clothes walked or limped from station to station, attending the wounded.

A lump sat at the border between the garden and the field. It looked like a woman huddled under a leather tarp. Her head pro-

202

truded from her covering, dipping low. Since she faced the field, it was impossible to tell who she was.

Light from the tree of life's new leaves danced across the portal, as if maintaining the drawing with its radiance. Lauren blocked one of the beams at the edge, but it passed right through her hand without interrupting the scene.

"Let's see if we can get a bigger picture," Barlow said as he continued circling the tree and cutting leaves.

Lauren set Apollo in front of the portal and stood upright. Instead of spreading into the garden, her shadow fell onto the doorway, standing upright, as if the portal opening had physical substance. "Do you think I can just walk in?"

"I advise caution, Miss. I see smoke, which could be poisonous. The people there appear to be in dire straits, perhaps victims of poison."

Lauren sniffed the air. No sign of any fumes. "I don't think it'll hurt to try. I could always come right back." She put on her sweatshirt, raised the hood, and covered her hands with her sleeves. She reached out and pushed through the waxy membrane. Her arm disappeared up to her wrist with the membrane sealing every gap. No sign of sizzling appeared on the protected material.

She walked into the doorway, feeling the wax adhere to her sweatshirt and pants, but as she pushed through, it offered almost no resistance. Without a hint of residue on her clothes, she now stood with her back to the museum, the tree's firelight illuminating the outer chamber and the arched entry leading to the Hades exit tunnel.

She turned to the museum. From this side, everything looked normal within. Sir Barlow continued pruning the tree while Tamara stared at the doorway.

"I'm still in Hades," Lauren called. "Can you see me?"

Barlow paused his pruning. "You vanished. We see only the garden scene in Second Eden."

Another voice made its way to Lauren's ears. *The hole was there a long time before you pushed the pen through.* Tamara's thoughts.

Lauren took off the sweatshirt, retied it to her waist, and walked back in, feeling the same slight resistance. This portal was definitely different from the other two. It didn't burn and showed no sign of shrinking.

She stood next to Tamara and faced the Second Eden scene. "I heard what you thought about the hole. What do you think it means?"

Tamara pushed her hand through the portal. It disappeared on the other side. *Maybe we're able to see the portal right away, and ability to enter comes later.*

"But why would time be the trigger? Maybe it's something else." Lauren picked up Apollo again and turned slowly to the right, glancing at the spectral meter as she rotated. The readings fluctuated wildly.

The Second Eden landscape grew blurry at its edge. Farther to the right, the beams from the tree painted a new scene that covered the second quarter of the wall space. Three men dressed in camo stood in a cave with a spotlight shining toward the portal. An empty backpack lay crumpled next to the light—Dad's backpack. Two men carried what looked like machine guns. The third rested his weapon against a wall while he sat on the ground smoking a cigarette. A portable lantern lit up the chamber and cast their shadows against the walls.

Lauren walked to the portal and reached out. When her arm passed through, her finger touched a shelf and a book behind the image. The portal view made it seem as if she were standing at the cave's back wall where she and Dad had jumped to get into Hades.

The guards couldn't see her, but how long would that last? If the portal eventually opened on its own, she and Tamara and Barlow wouldn't stand a chance against them.

As Barlow continued cutting, yet another scene appeared beginning at the halfway point around the tree.

Still carrying Apollo, Lauren skirted the flames and stood in front of the newest scene. A dragon sat on its haunches in a dim room next to a table. A thick slab of a candle, white and dripping, burned on the surface, providing the only light. The dragon read a huge book mounted at a slight angle on a four-footed stand at the table's edge. Four translucent eggs sat in tripod mounts at the opposite end. Three orange and one green, the eggs were large enough to belong to an ostrich. A foot-tall hourglass sat nearby, its sand piled high in the bottom half. The dragon's eyes flashed blue, and he looked straight at her for a moment before returning to his reading. Strings of smoke puffed from his nostrils and rose toward the ceiling.

Letting her gaze follow the smoke, she scanned the upper sections of the museum room. Each scene continued as far as light from the tree's flames reached, providing a view of the sky in Second Eden; the ceiling in the portal cave, then stone farther up; and a higher ceiling in the dragon's lair.

At the bottom of the lair's entry, a wall of bricks stood, waist-high at the sides and tapering down to knee-high at the center, as if an explosion had blown a hole through a brick wall. At each side, a wooden frame ran vertically with handles attached to partitions that looked like sliding doors. She tried to grab a handle, but her fingers passed through it.

Barlow finished his pruning and showed the knife to Lauren. "I fear that it is quite dull now. The last few cuts were difficult."

"You did great. Thank you." Lauren moved to a spot in front of the final quarter of the surrounding shelves, again checking

205

Apollo's fluctuating meter every few seconds. Soon, the new leaflets painted a high wall with a dazzling white gate. The wall extended upward beyond the reach of the tree's flames, making it impossible to see over the top.

The gate opened slowly. A winged man walked out and flew into the sky at an impossible speed, his wings barely beating at all. In less than two seconds, he was gone.

As the gate swung back, apparently by itself, Lauren squinted to see inside. A street of gold led into a city, but the gate closed too quickly to catch any details.

"Second Eden," Tamara said as she touched the first portal. She walked to the second and set a hand over it. "Earth." She continued the circuit, naming the final two scenes as she pointed at them. "Valley of Souls ... Heaven."

"Valley of Souls," Lauren repeated. "Dad mentioned that place. He called it Abaddon's Lair. People and dragons wait there to get resurrected. My mother spent four years there. He said we should avoid it."

"By the looks of that dragon," Barlow said, "I agree. He seemed quite unfriendly." He nodded at the Earth scene. "I think that one should be high on our avoidance list as well. I am not a coward, but battling three men with weapons like those would be foolhardy, especially when we have only a dull knife and perhaps books and scrolls to heave at them."

"Lauren!" Tamara called from the Second Eden wall. "Look!"

Lauren jogged toward the Second Eden landscape. With a spyglass in one hand, Matt crawled toward them on hands and knees, his face flushed and his hair damp.

"Matt!" She bounced in place, her heart pounding. "It's Matt! He survived!" Cradling Apollo in one arm, she knelt and slid to the portal. Flexing her fingers, she ached to reach out to him, grab his arm and help him crawl, but if she tried, her hand would just grasp the air outside the museum room.

She drew her head closer. Dressed in a black T-shirt and camo pants, Matt appeared to be exhausted, though his muscles bulged through his sweat-moistened shirt. He looked like he had worked beyond his body's limits, and now fatigue forced him to crawl.

When he came within a foot or so, he laid the spyglass on the ground and rose to his knees. He lifted his hand close to the portal as if trying to press his palm against it.

Lauren set her hand in front of his, but the two palms couldn't connect.

He grabbed the spyglass and looked at the portal through it. He reached out, making his arm disappear up to his elbow. As he pulled back, he clawed at the wall as if trying to snatch a bug. He laid the spyglass down again and set his eye to the portal wall.

Lauren's back tingled worse than ever. "He's trying to look through the hole," she whispered. "The one I pushed the pen through."

"I suggest that you not do that now," Barlow said. "You know what they say about a sharp stick in the eye."

"I'm not going to poke him in the eye!" She set her face directly in front of Matt's. "Matt? Can you hear me?"

Matt pushed his finger through the hole, forcing Lauren to draw her head away. The finger appeared in the museum room for a moment, but he quickly jerked it back. *How weird is that? It just disappeared.*

Lauren touched her ear. "I'm picking up his thoughts, but I don't think he heard me."

He set his mouth close and spoke. "Who's in there?" He then eased back.

207

"Did either of you hear him?" Lauren asked. "He spoke out loud this time."

Tamara and Sir Barlow both shook their heads. "You will have to be our ears," Barlow said.

Lauren searched the floor. "Where's the pen?"

"Here!" Tamara scooped it off the floor and handed it to her.

Lauren wrote her name on her left index finger and ran it along the portal plane until it pushed through the original hole and appeared in Second Eden. Matt's eyes widened. He lurched forward and looked at the finger, his lips moving as he read her name. He hooked his finger around hers and spoke toward the hole. "I hope you have your super hearing turned on. If you can hear me, squeeze my finger."

She tightened her grip.

"Great." Matt heaved a sigh. "Where are you? I know you can't write a book on your finger, but maybe another word or two."

Matt jerked away and looked to the side. A man shouted, "A stack of fallen trees was holding back a wall of lava, but it broke apart!"

"Lava's coming!" Matt said as he hooked his finger around Lauren's again. "I have to go!"

CHAPTER

Escape to Hades

Walter held the Jeep's steering wheel with one hand and a phone against his ear with the other. As he and Ashley barreled down a two-lane back road, the Jeep's open top allowing the wind to beat back their hair, he shouted into his phone. "Can you see Billy's GPS signal?"

"Yes," Marilyn said, her voice nearly drowned by helicopter noise. "He's still at the bottom of the crater."

Walter glanced at Ashley. Her slight nod indicated that she could understand Marilyn's end of the conversation. "What happened over there?" Walter asked.

"We think the military picked up *Merlin* on the radar and tailed Billy's rental truck to the crater, because it didn't take too long before they showed up with an assault helicopter. Since it aimed its guns at Jared, he couldn't go anywhere. When he jumped out to warn Billy and me, three guys from their chopper mobbed him and pretty much beat him to a pulp, and another one ripped out his console radio and stole his phone. While they were going inside the cave, he crawled back to his helicopter to try to find a weapon. When the soldiers came out with Billy and me, Billy went on a rampage. He scorched one guy with his breath and set their chopper ablaze. He and I broke away, and while we were running to our chopper, one of them shot Billy in the leg. He yelled for Jared and me to leave in case the military chopper exploded."

A pause ensued. Walter looked at Ashley again. She just shook her head sadly, her hair blowing wildly around her worried face.

"What could we do?" Marilyn continued. "If we tried to fight them, we'd all be prisoners or dead. Since Jared was losing consciousness, I had to get him out of there. When we took off, they shot a bunch of rounds. The helicopter took some dings, and we lost a window, but we got away."

"How is Jared now?"

"Not good. I stopped the bleeding and bandaged his cuts, but with the disease ravaging his system, he's not healing. He looks like one big bruise. I don't think a doctor can help him. Otherwise I'd be at the emergency room right now."

Walter glanced at Ashley again. She winced as if sharing the pain. "Did their chopper explode?" Walter asked.

"I lifted off just before it blew. But as we were rising, I saw that Billy was still okay. He was crawling toward the portal cave."

"So the soldiers had no way out of the crater."

"Not that I know of. If their ability to communicate burned with the chopper, then they're stranded until someone shows up to find out why they're not answering calls. But they have rifles, so I can't go back until I get some reinforcements."

Ashley tugged on Walter's sleeve. "Where was their helicopter in relation to the cave entrance?"

Walter repeated Ashley's question into the phone.

"Maybe a hundred feet closer to the center of the crater," Marilyn said. "Why?"

Ashley snatched the phone from him. "Walter, just drive as fast as you can." She set the phone against her ear. "Marilyn, how long will it take you to get to the portal site, the one Elam and company are trying to get home through? ... You can pick up Merlin? Great. ... Right, it's about a hundred miles from the prison, so we'll be there in a little while. ... Good. We'll see you there in about four hours. Let's hope we can gather some reinforcements."

She pressed the End button and laid the phone in Walter's lap. "If I'm right about where the portals are and what's opening them, we need to get back to where Billy is at light speed."

"Catch!" Still kneeling, Lauren set Apollo down, pulled the scroll from her pocket, and tossed it toward Tamara. When she caught it, Lauren drew her finger back in, wrote the word *Wait* on her finger's upper pad, and flipped the pen to Tamara. "Write where we are on the back of that message!"

Tamara missed the pen but quickly scooped it from the floor. Kneeling, she unrolled the scroll over the uneven stone and set the pen to write. "This will be ... difficult."

"Then get Sir Barlow to help you!" Lauren pushed her finger through and turned the new message toward Matt.

While Matt squinted at it, the people in the field began scrambling to and fro. "Wait? Wait for you to tell me more?"

She wagged her finger up and down. Maybe that would communicate a nod. She pulled her finger back in and slid Apollo next to her knees. "Let's see if we can break through." As she browsed the spectral readings, she shook her head. "The numbers are jumping all over the place. They aren't stable at all."

A young woman ran up behind Matt. Her hair tied in unraveling pigtails, she knelt at his side, breathless. "Valiant says we need to leave right away. The lava will definitely come into the villages."

"Listener!" Tamara called. "My daughter!"

Lauren glanced between Tamara and the young woman. Dad had mentioned Listener, and seeing the pigtails confirmed the connection. "I'll try to get you two together, but Apollo won't synchronize." Lauren looked at the tree. With dozens of lights wavering and flickering, it was no wonder the light stream wouldn't stay consistent. She pushed her finger through the hole again, hoping to signal another "wait."

"How can he be sure the lava will get this far?" Matt asked Listener. "It's never come here before."

"After the dragons returned with the children, Valiant rode Albatross and surveyed the land. Valiant has mapped the topography and knows it intimately." Listener pointed toward the volcano. "When the blockade broke, the momentum carried the lava over some old natural barricades that once protected our villages. Also, the wind shifted, and a huge cloud of poisonous fumes is coming our way. Valiant and Albatross nearly passed out. In fact—" Listener stared at Lauren's finger. "What sort of magic is this?"

212

Matt pushed Lauren's finger back in. "Strange, isn't it? I just discovered it myself. I'm waiting for an explanation."

A glass egg floated from behind Listener's head and hovered near her ear. "What's that?" Lauren asked, pointing.

Sir Barlow knelt with pen in hand while Tamara held the scroll open. "Second Eden natives have floating orbs they call companions," he said. "They speak guidance into their minds."

Lauren whispered to herself, "Companions. How strange." Blinking away the trance, she continued working with Apollo. "Are you making progress?"

Sir Barlow wrote with quick, jerking strokes. "Indeed, Miss, but this surface is not suitable for neatness. The pen has perforated the paper multiple times."

"Just do the best you can." Lauren let her advice echo in her mind. She had to keep trying. Apollo couldn't be expected to analyze something so variable, but maybe it would eventually recognize a pattern.

Listener rose and extended her hand. "We cannot wait. We have to go to higher ground before the lava and fumes arrive."

"We can't haul so many wounded people to higher ground, much less a wounded dragon." Matt pointed at the hole. "This might be a way for everyone to get out safely. It's a portal to another world."

Listener squinted at the hole. Her companion joined her, glowing blue. "I have seen portals open and close in this garden before, so I trust your words, but unless it opens wider soon, we have no choice but to leave. Albatross will help us with Karrick." She turned and walked toward the field. "Make your decision quickly. We need your help."

213

"Finished." Tamara rolled the paper tightly and pushed it through the hole.

When it dropped in front of Matt's knees, he snatched it up. "Wait!"

Listener had crouched at the garden's edge and appeared to be whispering to the woman wrapped in leather. "What is it?"

"They sent me a message." He rolled out the note and read it loudly enough for Listener to hear. "I, Sir Barlow, along with Lauren and Tamara, are in the museum room in Hades."

"Tamara?" Listener jumped up and hurried back. "She's my biological mother."

Matt unrolled the paper to its edges. "We stumbled into creating a portal by pruning the tree of life, but we have yet to figure out how to pass something through it that is greater in size than a pen or finger. We hope to create a bigger hole, but the devices by which we hope to do so will take some time to engage."

He rolled up the note. "Lauren can hear me, but I can't hear her. She has special hearing gifts."

"So do I." Listener scooted close on her knees. Her reddish-brown eyes shining brightly, she tilted her head. "Speak, Lauren. How much time will it take for you to open a way of escape for us?"

"I ..." Lauren looked at Tamara and Barlow. Both stared back with clueless expressions. "I don't know. We have two possibilities. I have a device called Apollo that reads spectral data and creates a portal-opening flash according to what it reads, but the light in here is fluctuating too much for it to work. We also have a burning tree. When we first pruned it, a hole opened to Second Eden, so later we pruned the rest of it, and that created viewports of Second Eden and three other worlds, but we can't seem to enter any of them. The first hole is still here, and things can pass through it, but that's the only spot like that. If I stick my hand through any other place, it just stays in our world."

Listener relayed Lauren's message to Matt. After nodding, he spoke slowly. "Lauren, were there any differences between the first pruning and the second one?"

"Well, Tamara did the first one, and she used the leaves to heal Sir Barlow. He was wounded and was lying outside the museum room. When we came back, he did the rest of the pruning, so the only difference is who did the cutting, but it's too late for Tamara to cut it now. At least I think it is."

Again Listener relayed the message. With each inflection, it seemed that her companion echoed the emotion with varying shades of blue or red blinking lights.

"That's not the only difference. The new leaves haven't healed anyone yet." Matt set his eye close to the hole again. "I see glowing leaves all around the tree. I assume those are the cuttings."

Lauren nodded. He could probably see her gesture.

Matt's face and eye shifted as he scanned the museum room. When he finished, he drew back. "Push some of the leaves through to us, but be sure to send the ones that created this portal, not the other portals. We'll use them to heal people here."

Listener pulled the hem of her shirt and made a basket. "I will carry them."

"Get the leaves." Lauren pushed Apollo to the side and crawled toward the tree. "Just the ones on the Second Eden side."

She scooped up two handfuls of glowing leaves, brought them to the portal, and began pushing them through the hole one by one. As with the pen and her finger, they passed through a membrane that offered some resistance but not enough to bend them.

Listener scooted close and caught them with her shirt. Sir Barlow swept more leaves toward the portal with his meaty hands, while Tamara gathered two handfuls at a time and deposited them at Lauren's side.

"I think we have all of them, Miss. If I were to collect more, I think I would risk getting some that created the Earth portal."

"Good job." Lauren continued pushing leaves through, faster now. "I don't want even a tiny hole for the gunmen to use."

"Well, that possibility exists. I cannot be one hundred percent sure that my feet didn't push leaves into another area while I was pruning."

Lauren stopped with a leaf halfway through. "Sir Barlow, think. Did you always move in a circle around the tree without going back to prune an earlier section? If you did, then your feet wouldn't have swept anything back."

He shook his head. "I cannot be sure. In my day, I was a meticulous gardener, so it is in my nature to go back and prune if I notice a flaw, but I did work quickly, and I don't remember retreating to an earlier section."

"I hope that's good enough." Lauren pushed the leaf the rest of the way and called through the portal. "Listener, take what you have and rub them into people's wounds. If they have internal injuries, force them to chew and swallow the leaves."

"I will try them on Karrick as well." Listener closed the edges of her shirt around the leaves, exposing muscular abs. She rose and ran like the wind into the field.

From the edge of the garden, the woman with the leather covering climbed to her feet, unsteady. The covering expanded into a pair of wings.

Lauren stared. "Mom?"

Mom turned and staggered toward Matt, her legs stiff. He leaped up and helped her settle in front of the portal. The song grew slightly louder, though still fragile.

"Matt," Lauren said, "you didn't tell me Mom is with you. She looks sick."

Matt rubbed Mom's back, but he didn't answer. Lauren winced. Right. He couldn't hear her, and now Listener was gone. No one could relay her messages to him.

While Matt whispered into Mom's ear, Mount Elijah continued spewing glowing ash but no worse than before. The real dangers lay closer, though invisible for now. Soon, they would be overrun by lava and poisonous fumes. Everyone had to hurry. In the field, Listener ran among the lean-tos passing around leaves to the victims. Her bare feet pounding the debris, she was doing everything she could, apparently ignoring the pain from any sharp edges.

"Look, Mom," Matt said as he pointed at the hole. "This is a portal to the museum room. Lauren's in there. She can hear us, but we can't hear her. We think we've figured out a way to make the hole bigger so the Second Edeners can go there for protection."

Her skin pale and her features sagging, Mom blinked. "Lauren, I'm proud of you and Matt." Her voice was little more than a whisper. "What is the mechanism for opening it?"

Matt showed her a leaf. "It's from the tree of life. When a leaf heals someone, part of the portal opens. At least that's my theory." He set the leaf in her hand. "Try eating one. Maybe it'll help you."

She pushed the leaf into her mouth and chewed for a moment before swallowing with a grimace. "If the portal opens, how will you close it after the people get in there?"

"Good question." Matt spoke toward the portal again. "Lauren? I assume you heard Mom."

Lauren blinked. Close it? The thought hadn't come up. Of course they needed to close it. Otherwise, once the Second Edeners came inside, the lava and fumes would just follow them, making the museum room a trap instead of an escape.

Matt turned back to Mom. "I guess she's got a way to close it. She's smart. She's probably thought it all through."

Lauren's cheeks flushed hot. The compliment came with a slap, though Matt didn't intend it.

"What … wrong?" Tamara touched Lauren's cheek. "You … glowing."

Lauren laid a hand over her cheek. "Listener's out there using the leaves to heal people, and that'll probably open the portal, but we have to figure out how to close it again once they get in here."

Barlow waved a hand in front of the tree, but it cast no shadow on the portal. "Hmmm. No effect."

Lauren nodded. "I've already tried that."

"Is it possible to extinguish the flames once they are burning?"

"Probably. Nearly all of it was extinguished a little while ago."

"I will give it a try. With Listener running around like a healing rabbit, the portal might soon be wide open."

"Try it close to the edge." Lauren pointed toward the left side of the Second Eden portal. "We don't want to snuff out a spot in the middle."

"Agreed." Wincing at the light, Sir Barlow walked up to the tree and pressed a fiery leaflet between his gloves. As he rubbed them together, smoke rose from in between, then fizzled. When he backed away, the fire at the end of the twig had vanished. At the portal, a tiny black dot appeared at the left edge.

Lauren breathed a sigh. "Good. At least we know we can close it." She peered through the hole again.

Matt offered Mom another leaf. "You look like you still need a boost."

She shook her head. "I don't think the leaf helped much, if at all. My weakness is not the result of illness or injury."

"I guess it was worth a try."

"It didn't do any harm." She stroked his arm. "When you open this portal, I will have to stay behind with you and Listener."

"What?" Matt drew his head back. "Why? You're exhausted. You need to go to a safe place."

"I had a dream." As Mom replied, her song grew slowly louder. "You and I have to go somewhere else, and we can't get there unless we stay in Second Eden."

"A dream? You can't stay here just because of a dream." Matt's volume also increased. "Dreams are usually senseless. I just had a dream about taking Darcy home in a convertible, but that'll never happen. That would be crazy."

"I heard Matt," Barlow said, "but he shouldn't be speaking to his mother that way."

Tamara swatted Barlow's arm. "He ... upset. ... Pro ... protecting mother."

"Matt!" Lauren shouted. "I think the portal's opening! Can you hear me?"

He looked her way. "Yes. I see more of the tree, but it's like a jigsaw puzzle with a lot of pieces missing."

"I see a complete picture of you and Mom. Can you show me where the holes are?"

After helping Mom rise, Matt reached out. His fingers poked into the museum room, one above the original hole and another through a third hole just below the new one.

Lauren touched one of Matt's fingertips. "I see the holes now, but only because your fingers are there."

"Maybe I can stretch them." Tensing his muscles, Matt pulled against the borders of the holes until his fingers slid away. "No good. The holes feel pliable, but they won't budge."

Flames shot up beyond the field. Smoke billowed, obscuring the volcano. "Look behind you!" Lauren called.

Matt swiveled his head. "The lava's coming."

Mom set a fist over her mouth and coughed. "The fumes ... are getting thicker. We have to get the people over here."

Matt set his hands on Mom's shoulders. "Stay here. I'll round them up." He ran into the field, shouting, but the cries of the others washed out his words. In the distance, Listener grabbed his arm and pulled him out of view, both coughing.

"Masks!" Lauren pointed at the ladder. "Barlow! There's a package of masks up there and a brown bottle. Bring them down."

"On my way, Miss." He ran to the ladder and began a lumbering climb.

"Lauren." Mom pushed a hand through a larger hole. "Come closer."

Lauren took her hand, cold and clammy. "Yes?"

After coughing twice more, Mom pulled her shirt collar up over her mouth and nose. "Remember how we dreamed about Joran and Selah?"

"Sure. I remember. And it was all true."

"That's because you and I are dream oracles. We see realities in our dreams. I learned from a recent dream that you will have to lead the people to Abaddon's Lair. There you will meet Abaddon." Mom aimed her eyes at his portal. "I see that he is already visible. He is a mysterious dragon and extremely odd, so you will have to keep your wits about you. He is sure to test you, and he likely won't help you unless you pass the test. Avoid long conversations with him. He will play with your mind using riddles and alliteration, which might cause you to pay attention to the words instead of their meaning. Don't let him get the best of you. Stay confident. Be assertive. If you wilt under pressure, all will be lost."

"What kind of test will he give me?"

"I don't know, but it will likely involve sacrifice. I realize that sounds scary. It was for me. I was your age at the time, and it cost me a lot of pain and suffering, but God got me through it." Mom squeezed Lauren's hand. "You have amazing strength and courage. You glow for a reason."

"Thank you." Lauren exhaled. "What do we do when we get to Abaddon's Lair?"

"I know only that you must find a woman who is called The Maid, but I can't see the future, only the past and the present, so I'm not sure what she will do to help you."

Lauren tightened her grip on Mom's hand. "Then how do you know I'm supposed to go there?"

"In my dream, I saw The Maid in Abaddon's Lair. She is preparing a dining table with dozens of seats as well as many beds. She is waiting for you and the refugees of Second Eden to arrive."

Lauren looked past the tree to the dragon still reading at the table. He stared at her once again with flashing blue eyes. "I think the dragon is also waiting for me."

"Knowing Abaddon, he probably is." Mom nodded toward the Earth scene. "You have to leave the other portals visible. You will need them eventually."

"Leave them visible? You mean, keep the leaves burning?"

"Or at least make sure you can light them later. It's just something I learned in the dream."

Barlow jumped down from the ladder, carrying the package and the bottle. "I have them, Miss. I apologize for the delay. I banged my head against a rafter of some sort and nearly knocked myself out." He showed her the package. "I counted six masks, hardly enough for everyone."

"They'll help." Lauren touched the bottle. "Sprinkle the liquid over them."

"Gladly." Barlow knelt and began the procedure.

Mom stepped up to the portal and pushed her arms and head through, but her body and wings stayed in Second Eden, blocked by the incomplete sections. She wrapped her arms around Lauren and pulled her close. "I love you, Lauren. I love you with all my heart."

Lauren returned the embrace. Mom's tears moistened her shoulder. As warmth radiated between their bodies, Lauren shed tears of her own. After a few seconds, she took a breath and drew back, wiping her wet cheeks with her sleeve. "Where are you and Matt going?"

"To Earth. Billy needs our help."

221

"And Walter and Ashley and a few more." Lauren nodded toward the ground in Second Eden. "Read the note on that rolled-up piece of paper. It'll give you an update." She pulled the phone from her pocket and slid it into Mom's hand. "I think you'll need this more than I will."

Mom shook her head and pushed the phone back. "You keep it. When I find Walter and Ashley, I can use one of their phones. I'll be fine."

Lauren set a hand on Mom's cheek. "You look so tired."

"Yes, I know, but explaining why would take too long." Mom looked at Sir Barlow. "Noble knight, will you protect my daughter?"

Barlow rose with the dripping masks and gave her a low bow. "With all my strength, Madam. You can count on me."

"I ... too." Tamara hooked her arm around Barlow's and pointed at her head. "I plan ... He talk."

Lauren smiled. They would make a good team. She took the masks and passed them through the portal. "For those staying behind."

Mom took them and slipped one on. After taking a deep breath, she nodded. "I can tell the difference."

A muscular man with a black bandana wrapped around his face ran into the garden, carrying six empty buckets by their handles, three in each hand. A companion zipped along at his shoulder, flashing rapidly. "Bonnie," he called as he set the buckets down. "I know you are tired, but please help me place one of these at each plant. I must collect the babies along with some of the sacred soil."

"Of course." Mom put one of the treated masks over his face, took three of the buckets, and hurried away, beating her wings to boost her along.

Matt bustled into the scene, now wearing a dark cloak and leading a crowd into the garden, some carrying wounded people on litters. All wore makeshift masks that looked like torn clothing remnants.

Listener burst to the front of the line. "I ran out of leaves. I was able to heal Karrick. He's just arrived with the remaining survivors from Peace Village."

Matt slid an arm through the portal, his hand open. "We need more leaves. The portal's not big enough to get a whole person through."

Lauren scooped up a handful and poured them into Matt's palm. "I have more besides these."

"Listener will be back for them." The moment Matt gave Listener half of his handful, she dashed away. Matt turned to leave.

"Wait!" Lauren scrambled to her backpack, pulled out three cereal bars, and hustled back to the portal. "Here." She pushed them through a hole and stuffed them into his pocket. "I hope they help."

223

"They will. Thanks. I'd give you a hug, but …" He nodded at his filled hands.

"I know." She reached through and caressed his cheek. "Thank you for everything."

Mom glided across the garden, her wings fluttering, and landed next to Matt. As soon as she stretched a mask over his mouth and nose, he winked at her, then at Lauren, and ran toward one of the litters.

"Good-bye," Lauren whispered as she offered a weak wave.

"I also gave a mask to Listener." Mom handed Lauren the final two. "For whoever needs them the most."

"Thank you." Lauren touched her mother's hand. She looked pale and dizzy. The fumes were getting to her. "Are you going now?"

She nodded weakly. "Matt insisted that I go with him right away. You know how he is about protecting the ladies he loves."

"I know." Lauren blew her a kiss. "I love you, and tell Matt I love him. I forgot to tell him."

"I will. And I love you, too." She turned and staggered away into the smoke, nearly falling at times before catching herself with her wings.

Lauren let her shoulders sag. Her heart ached. Mom looked so frail, but Matt would watch out for her. He practically oozed heroism. After cutting that rope to save her life, he deserved more than a verbal thanks and a touch on the cheek. If only they could take time to talk, just relax and be friends, but that couldn't be, not yet.

New flames shot up beyond the field, closer than ever. The lava would be there in moments, and the fumes would soon be too dense for survival. A breeze blew the cloud over the garden. Coughs and the sounds of retching flew everywhere. They could never outrun the poisonous fumes. The portal was their only hope.

Listener ran to the portal. Kneeling low, she held her shirt's hem on the ground, pushed her hand into the museum room, and began sweeping the remaining leaves into her makeshift basket. "I hope there is enough space in there for everyone."

Tamara drew closer. "Listener?"

She looked up. "Mother?"

"My daughter!" Tamara slid to her knees, thrust her arms through the portal, and hugged Listener. "I am ... so glad ... to see you."

Listener ran a hand along Tamara's face, then through her hair. "Oh, Mother! The disease has devastated you!"

Tamara clasped her hand and kissed it. "I explain later."

"Of course, Mother. I'm sorry, but I really have to go." Listener kissed Tamara's cheek, rose to her feet, and ran through the haze until she faded from sight.

As more smoke filtered into the room, Sir Barlow grabbed a book and began fanning the cloud back. A bucket filled with dirt and a green plant slid through the portal. A second one followed, then a third.

Tamara pulled the buckets farther in to make room. When all six were safe, a man called out, "Children first! Then their mothers, then all other females."

As coughing blended with the sounds of crackling fire, a breeze stirred the smoke and blew much of it away. The man wearing one of the masks helped a little girl crawl through the portal. "It is appropriate," he said, "that the Father of Lights first provides a small way of escape to remind us of our priorities."

Lauren took the girl's hand and helped her rise. Soot smudged her cheeks and arms, and her tunic was little more than shredded leather, but she seemed healthy. Her companion floated in front of her, blinking a dim red light, as if sniffing out the refuge. The girl turned slowly, her eyes wide. "Where are we?"

"A safe place. I'll explain more later." Lauren put one of the masks on her, then helped a little boy enter, giving him the final mask. Smoke obscured the line of escapees, but the chatter outside and blinking companions visible through the haze indicated that many more waited for entry.

Lauren mentally urged the portal to open further. New holes needed to appear, but that would bring in more fumes. "Tamara, help everyone find a book to fan the fumes away. If anyone is still sick or injured, get a Second Eden leaf and apply it. You know what to do."

The crackling fire grew louder. Terrified cries from the midst of the cloud heightened as well as coughs and sounds of vomiting.

225

"The lava is coming!" someone shouted.

"Run!" another called.

"Valiant!" Listener's voice rose above the others. "We have three more children, then the women."

The man who had carried the buckets looked at Lauren. "Will we have room? The men will not leave for the enclave until they know their loved ones will be safe."

"We have room," Lauren replied. "Are you Valiant?"

"I am."

Lauren helped another child through the portal. "We'll be fine. We just have to hurry."

"Listener!" Valiant called. "Tell the men all is well and to go to the enclave. I need you to go with them to check on our weapons. I will meet you there later." He pointed at another section of the portal. "This hole is big enough. Two lines now!"

Lauren, Tamara, and Sir Barlow helped the final children into the room. Although smoke poured in, those already inside waved books, blocking the flow and sending most of it back out. Women began walking in, lowering their heads to make it through. Everyone crowded around the tree, though not close enough to ignite their clothes. With companions twinkling in the midst of shifting bodies, the scene looked like a mass of floating humanity wearing blinking life preservers.

"Hold your breath as long as you can!" Lauren called, coughing. "And pass the two masks around to those who are sick and have them take turns breathing!"

A breeze again blew the smoke away from the Second Eden side of the portal. A knee-high wall of lava appeared only a stone's throw away. It rolled toward them slowly, devouring everything in its path. Trees and grass erupted in flames. Sizzles and pops filled the air. Nothing could stop it. Death for everyone would arrive in seconds.

Lauren's back tingled. They could battle the smoke for a while longer, but waving books wouldn't keep the lava out. "We have to start closing the portal!"

"Indeed," Barlow said. "The entire tree?"

"Just the part making the Second Eden portal. We need to leave the other portals visible." Lauren helped a woman with a bleeding arm limp through the opening. "And start at the sides. People are still coming in."

As more women filed into the room, Sir Barlow pushed through the crowd and stood in front of the tree. With a clap, he smothered a cluster of leaves. As he rubbed his gloved hands together, smoke rose from between them. His neck reddened. He rubbed more briskly. "Perhaps since the leaves were used for healing," he said through clenched teeth, "the flames are now more durable."

"Keep trying!" Lauren's entire back crawled with tingles. "We have to close the portal!"

"I realize that, Miss." His neck muscles tensed. More smoke rose. Finally, his gloves caught on fire. He shook them to the floor and stamped them out. The leaves' flames withered for a moment before springing back to life. Glaring at the tree, he muttered, "I think we will need another plan."

Lauren pointed at Apollo, still sitting near the left edge of the Second Eden portal. "We have Apollo, but it opens portals. I don't know how to close one with it."

"Then we'd better think fast, Miss. In mere moments, this place will transform from a safe haven to a death trap."

INTO THE DRAGON'S LAIR

Lauren grabbed Barlow's gloves. "I'll try it."

"Very well, Miss, but I assure you—"

"If you have another idea, let's hear it." She cringed. That came out harsher than intended, but apologies could come later.

As she jerked a glove over her hand, a deep voice echoed in the museum room. "Have the souls of Second Eden so soon lost their lesson?"

She spun toward the source. Abaddon had drawn near to his portal and looked straight at her over the heads of the escapees, his blue eyes again flashing.

Letting the gloves drop, she squeezed through the crowd and faced him. "What lesson?"

"When a damsel dissimulated, they desired a dragon. When a flower faltered, they found a physician. When the casualties of conflict climbed, they called for a king." The dragon's tongue flicked out and in. "Remember this riddle. Call to me, and I will answer you. The proverb is your path."

Lauren balled her fists. "I don't have time for riddles. Just tell me what I have to do!"

"Ah! Wouldn't we all wish for wisdom without work?" He raised the green egg in his clawed hand. "Yet I will not acquiesce to answering."

"But children are going to die soon!"

"A song sends salvation. The plants, the proverb, and a prayer produce the promise." Abaddon turned his back and placed the green egg on one of the table mounts. "A wise woman will calculate whom to call."

"Whom to call? The plants?" Lauren turned. Everyone continued fanning the fumes, all coughing as they waved the books. Two children lay on the floor, apparently having succumbed to the poison. Tamara and another woman knelt with them, forcing leaves into their mouths. The lava drew closer. One way or another, the portal would soon be a gateway for a killing wave of fire.

She weaved around the dirty bodies, picking up one of the gloves along the way, and found the plants still sitting in their buckets near the Second Eden portal. Covering her mouth with the glove, she pondered Abaddon's words. *Call to me, and I will answer you.* Maybe she could call for someone who could extinguish the flames, someone with power over fire. But who? He held the green ovulum, but why would it be in Abaddon's Lair? Had it been destroyed?

"Zohar?" Lauren whispered. Could he have died? If so, maybe she could call him from Abaddon's Lair, but what did Abaddon mean about a song sending salvation?

Lauren glanced around. In the distance, a higher wave of lava drew closer, running faster and overlapping the first. Soon it would overwhelm them. The crisis seemed all too familiar. Not long ago, in order to create a protective shield, she had to remember a melody from a dream, a melody that could be recalled only when showing mercy. And now, she needed a song she had never heard at all.

Lauren waved a hand and shouted through the glove, "Those who are healthy, keep fanning! Barlow! Move the sick ones to the back! I have to try something, and I don't know what's going to happen."

"Right away, Miss!" Barlow and Tamara herded everyone away from the portal, about twelve children and twenty-five women. Tamara held a toddler in each arm and shooed a few more back with halting pleas.

Heat shot through Lauren's cheeks. Her delay in closing the portal was threatening the lives of the little ones, and it was all her fault for leading them into danger.

She crouched in front of the six plants. New tingles ran along her back, the worst ever. Every sound heightened—the rumbling mountain, crying children, burning debris, and … a melody?

Lauren looked at the Second Eden sky through the portal. A humming tune passed through the air, riding on the breeze just as surely as did the smoke, someone humming. No. Two people. It sounded like …

"Joran and Selah?" Lauren looked back. With the women and children now pressed to the sides of the museum room and behind the tree, radiance from the dozens of flames flickered over the birthing plants, creating a sparkling aura. As the melody from above continued, words blended in, taking on Joran's distinctive tenor and Selah's lovely alto.

Still pressing the glove over her mouth, Lauren took a deep breath and held it. Then, after lowering the glove, she looked at the plants and sang with Joran and Selah.

231

Elijah's fury threatens death
With choking fumes and lava flow,
While children cry for help above,
I call for help from worlds below.

I call for Zohar, hair of white
And eyes of blue to join our throng;
Arise and quench the endless flames
With words from Heaven's holy song.

The moment she finished, she set the glove over her mouth and coughed again and again. Spasms tightened her throat. Dizziness washed through her head. The poison's effect was getting worse.

The leaves of one of the plants bulged. Something squirmed within. Still crouching, Lauren dropped the glove and pulled the leaves back, revealing an egg, the same size as the one the dragon had put on the mount, transparent now, though it glowed green. Inside, a white-haired boy stood with his arms spread and his hands pressing on the inner shell as if trying to escape. Flames surrounded his body, but he didn't appear to be in any pain.

The combined waves of lava rolled closer, now within a few steps, only seconds away from overtaking them.

"Come on, Zohar!" Lauren clenched a fist. "It's time to hatch!"

The egg swelled like an inflating balloon. Zohar grew with it. Lauren rose and stepped back, giving the egg room. When it reached her height, the shell burst into flames. Fiery fragments broke away. He punched through and spread out his arms. Like a sponge, his body absorbed the flames until they disappeared. His widened eyes darted, blue sapphires sparkling in the firelight. Wearing black pants and long-sleeved tunic, his white hair stood out like a dazzling beacon.

232

Lauren grasped his arm and pulled him closer to the tree. "Don't be frightened, Zohar. We need you to close the portal by putting out this fire."

"Yes, Abaddon let me watch your dilemma." He leaned close and whispered, "I saw Sapphira try to extinguish the tree once, but it did not work. I have far less experience than she does."

She jabbed a finger toward the tree. "We don't have any choice! Just try!"

Zohar turned toward the tree and shouted, "Extinguish!"

The tree burned on.

He shouted again. "Extinguish!"

Still, the tree burned on.

A collective gasp filled the room, then silence. Lauren stared through the portal. The wall of lava loomed, a glowing, slow-motion tsunami. Flames erupted within the flow, making it look like an angry wall of pure wrath. Horrible heat filtered into the room. Fumes thickened. No more than a few seconds remained before they would all be incinerated. Even if they ran for the enclave, the fumes would kill them in short order.

233

Zohar stared at her, tiny flames rising from his hair, apparently the residual effect of absorbing his fiery egg fragments.

Absorbing? Lauren spread out her arms. "Zohar, can you absorb the flames like you did when you came out of your egg?"

"I'll try." He leaped into the burning foliage and clutched two branches. The flames bent toward him and streamed into his body. When he stepped back, every flame from the Second Eden portion of the tree came with him, and the leaves darkened.

Instantly, tiny sparks flew from the portal. With a roar, the surge of lava splashed against it. A few drops penetrated the vanishing holes and sizzled on the floor, but the rest faded as the portal disappeared. Zohar's bodily flames diminished until they blinked out.

Now in three-quarters of their previous light, everyone stood motionless. A few coughs pierced the silence along with a whimper or two. Finally, a husky voice broke in. "Well, that worked better than my gloves did, I must admit."

Lauren laughed. She threw her arms around Zohar and bounced on her toes. "You did it! You did it!'"

Amid sporadic coughing, the women and children joined in the laughter, the children bouncing with Lauren. While they celebrated, the smoke followed the heat upward. Soon, the fumes began to clear.

Zohar pulled away from Lauren's embrace. "Your idea was brilliant and timely. You saved everyone."

"I saved us from my own stupidity." She let out a sigh. "I'm sorry. I shouldn't be so negative. Thank you for the compliment."

Zohar gave her a polite nod. "Gladly given."

234

Sir Barlow stood facing the Earth wall with Tamara at his side. "Something is happening here," Barlow said. "I think these unsavory fellows might see us."

One of the guards walked closer to the portal, his head cocked to the side. "Hey," the guard said, "get a look at this."

A second guard drew near. "A light?"

"Yeah, like a fire."

Lauren let out a shushing sound and motioned for everyone to get away from the Earth portal. Although the men likely couldn't hear them, it made no sense to risk being detected.

As the Second Edeners shuffled back, one of the guards set his eye close to the wall. "I see a burning tree."

The second guard huffed an obscene word and pushed the first guard out of the way. When he set his eye near the wall, he blinked. "There really *is* a burning tree."

The first guard shuddered. "Think it's the same world we saw by the chopper?"

"Don't worry. Those shadow things ain't crawling through this little hole."

Another profanity burned in the air. The second guard picked up a rifle leaning against the wall. "Let's see if I can penetrate this portal."

The gun's barrel protruded into the museum room. Holding her breath, Lauren herded the children toward the Abaddon's Lair portion of the wall. The dragon was still there, sitting on his haunches next to his table, book, and mounts. "Hurry!" she hissed.

Tamara whispered to Lauren, "Heaven … looks better. … Why Abaddon's Lair?"

"Because my mother said they're expecting us in Abaddon's Lair." Lauren glanced at the Heaven portal. "Besides, I don't think you can just march into Heaven without an invitation."

While Sir Barlow and Tamara shooed everyone along, the guard peered over the barrel and through the hole. "I can see my weapon inside that place."

"Fire a round and see what happens," another guard said.

"I see shadows moving and some little blinking lights. Someone must be in there."

"What do I care? Whoever it is must be a Second Edener, right? They have those companion things the sergeant told us about."

"I suppose, but—"

"Get out of the way." The second guard shoved the first to the side and pulled the trigger. A shot rang out. The bullet nicked a twig and smacked into the opposite wall, missing the Second Edeners. The twig's flames continued burning on the floor.

235

"Got part of the tree." The barrel shifted. "I'm gonna see if I can tag one of the shadows."

"But bullets didn't work against them over by the chopper," the first guard said.

"They were scared of fire, and they didn't have companions. These are normal Second Eden scum."

Lauren waved for everyone to squeeze closer to the Abaddon's Lair portal, but the barrel followed their movement.

Sir Barlow leaped for the gun and yanked it toward the room. It jammed and wouldn't pull through.

"What the—" The guard wrestled with the gun, but Barlow jerked it upward.

"Miss! Go through the portal!"

Lauren pushed her hand into the Abaddon's Lair image. It passed right through to the bookshelves. As before, the dragon sat on his haunches reading the book on the table. "How do I go through? There's no one here to heal with the leaves."

The gun fired, sending a bullet into the room's upper reaches. As the guard tried to wrestle it away, Barlow hugged the barrel and kept it in place. "Ask the dragon!"

"Abaddon!" Lauren poised her knuckles over the portal as if ready to knock, but that wouldn't do any good. "Abaddon, can you hear me?"

As two more rounds fired, Abaddon looked up from the book. "I can hear you. You are raising quite a racket."

"How do I open this portal?"

"With prowess you already possess." He returned his gaze to the book, a scowl bending his brow.

Lauren stamped her foot. "What prowess?"

Breathing an annoyed sigh, Abaddon looked up again. "Have you neglected to heed history? Is your perception of portal parting that paltry?"

"If you mean Apollo, it can't synchronize. The light readings fluctuate too much."

While Abaddon stared at her, the three guards joined together and jerked the rifle back into their chamber. Now holding the gun's stock, guard number two cursed again. "Can we shoot tear gas in there?"

"Better than that. I saved the mustard gas before the chopper blew. It'll fit through the hole."

"Get it. Whoever's in there deserves what's coming to them."

"But what about the fire-breathing guy in the—"

"He's buzzard bait by now. Don't be such a coward."

Lauren growled. "Abaddon, just tell me if I'm supposed to use Apollo! We have children in here, and we're going to get gassed if we don't open this portal."

"Then I suggest you open it." Abaddon looked at his book and turned a page.

Lauren drew back a fist, but Zohar grabbed her arm and held it in place. "I am not an experienced Oracle of Fire, but I had the opportunity to watch Sapphira and Acacia open portals many times. Even though I saw them only through a viewing screen, I think I grasped the concept. If I cannot do it, you can try Apollo again. I see no sense in waiting for the dragon to help us."

She huffed. "I guess you'd better go for it. I already wasted too much time with him."

"I will need a firebrand."

"A firebrand?"

"Something that will burn and last more than a few seconds."

Lauren reached through the portal and felt the shelf, but it was empty. "We don't have time to—"

"I found!" Tamara shoved a scroll into Zohar's hands. "Will … this do?"

"Perfect." He raised the scroll and called, "Flames, come to my firebrand!"

The scroll burst into flames. As the Second Edeners moved out of the way, Zohar positioned himself in front of the Abaddon's Lair portal and begin waving the scroll above his head in a circle.

Lauren alternately watched the Earth portal and Zohar. The swirl of fire above his head created a semicircle of flames in front of Abaddon's Lair that began expanding downward like a fiery curtain descending toward the floor. In the Earth scene, the guard, now wearing a gasmask, returned with a canister and spray wand. He handed the other two guards gasmasks and thick gloves and waited while they put them on. "The dragon guy tried to follow me," he said in a muffled voice, "but I clocked him on the head. He's not going anywhere."

Lauren pointed at the portal. "Barlow! Find something to plug it!"

Barlow whipped out a knife and sliced off part of his sleeve. After wadding it into a ball, he jammed it into the hole, but it fell into the Earth chamber. "The gap has no depth. Nothing will plug it." He waved a hand. "Everyone, pass me your books."

Immediately, books began flying from hand to hand. Tamara helped Barlow stack them in front of the hole.

As Zohar continued spinning the flames, the semicircular wall descended to his waist.

Lauren waved her hands downward. "Come on, Zohar. You can do it."

When Barlow and Tamara laid the final book on top, Barlow stood in front of the pile. "Perhaps my bulk will keep them from shoving the books to the side."

"And they might shoot you right through the books," Lauren said.

"I thought of that, Miss, but protecting these women and children is worth the risk."

Finally, Zohar's wall of fire touched the floor. As it swept the surface, sparks snapped and flew, like metal grinding against stone. He stepped toward the portal and pressed his body against it. Then, as if blown away by a gust, the fire vanished.

Zohar stood in front of the wall, still holding the scroll high, though its flames had dwindled to embers.

The Earth guard jabbed the spray wand at the hole, nudging the books, every movement still visible through the portal. "Something's blocking it."

Lauren jumped to Abaddon's portal and pushed a hand through. Her fingers stayed visible. "It's open!" She waved her arms frantically. "Hurry!"

As the Second Edeners funneled toward the portal again, helped along by Lauren and Tamara, an Earth guard pushed the rifle through the hole, bending the stack of books. "This'll clear it."

239

"Barlow!" Lauren shouted. "Watch out!"

He grabbed several books from the top of the stack and set them in front of the hole, front to back. A muffled shot rang out. The books flew from Barlow's hands and dropped to the floor.

Lauren waved again. "Just leave it! We need to get everyone out!"

"I am on my way." Sir Barlow hustled around the tree and stood at the end of the line. The women and children helped each other over the brick wall, slowing the process. Tamara and a few other women hauled the remaining birthing plants through as well.

Abaddon looked up and turned the hourglass over, but he said nothing beyond a smoke-filled snort.

The spray wand poked through the hole. A yellowish gas spewed and spread into the room.

"No time to be soft!" Sir Barlow spread out his arms and herded the stragglers through the portal, shoving them over the bricks. When he, Tamara, and the last children tumbled into the dragon's lair, Lauren grabbed Zohar's arm. "Let's go!" They leaped over the low wall and looked back. The yellow cloud drifted their way, apparently unaffected by the tree's flames.

"Kindly close the door," Abaddon said with a huff. "I prefer no poison in my presence."

Zohar looked at the charred scroll. "It's not working the same as when Sapphira did it. Everyone who passed through the portal had to be inside the circle, and whenever the fire died, the portal closed."

Lauren edged closer to the wall. "The portal Dad and I opened with Apollo shrank on its own. So did the one near the ceiling. But it looks like the portals the tree creates stay open until the leaves are extinguished."

"Then I will absorb the flames again." Zohar stepped toward the portal, but Lauren grabbed his wrist, stopping him.

"No! You won't have a way out! You'll die in there!" Lauren backed away, waving for the Second Edeners to join her. "We'll have to figure out another way."

In her mind, she added, *Or we'll all be dead.*

THE MAID

"Y ou know nothing." Abaddon shuffled toward the portal wall, his long neck and tail swinging. The women and children swarmed out of his path or jumped over his tail. When he reached the portal, he grabbed the partition handles with his clawed hands and slid the doors together, shutting out the gas. "Solutions are simple if you will invoke intelligence. Even imbeciles are able to shut a shutter."

Lauren glared at the portal. Why hadn't she thought of that? She had seen those partitions earlier. "Thank you."

The dragon snorted. "I suppose this glowing guest expects the cultural courtesy of 'You're welcome,' but you are not welcome here. You are the guests of another host. You are free to find her, but do not disturb my domain." He shuffled back toward the table, again carelessly swinging his tail.

Lauren looked at her arm. As usual, her skin didn't appear to glow, but obviously the dragon noticed it. While the Second

Edeners gathered around, she stood between Sir Barlow and Zohar, with Tamara, again holding two toddlers, on Barlow's opposite side. It seemed that everyone was safe, and even those who had fallen sick had recovered.

Glancing back at the wooden shutters, Lauren imagined the museum room. They had collected all the refugees, hadn't they?

She groaned within. Apollo! They had left it behind! She had also left her backpack, helmet, and goggles. Yet, they probably wouldn't be affected by the gas. They would still be there later, assuming there weren't any spirits who could take stuff away.

When Abaddon again sat on his haunches at the table, Lauren gave him a hard look and tried to read his mind. Mom had said not to let him get an advantage, so maybe it was best to use her gifts to her own advantage. Yet, no thoughts came through. He was probably quite able to guard his mind. "Listen, we didn't ask to come here. We were forced—"

"Forced?" Abaddon slid the hourglass close and drilled a stare at her. "Folly! You had other options. You chose to dive into my domain instead of dawdling in danger. How selfish of you to escape harm without considering my privacy."

Lauren resisted a triumphant smile. He began with alliterations, but they petered out at the end. He was breaking. "Stop playing games with me. You know good and well that it's not selfish to save the lives of women and children. I had to—"

"Women and children?" Abaddon looked at Sir Barlow. "It seems to me—"

"Don't even go there!" Lauren jabbed a finger at him. "You're not that stupid. Just show us the exit, and we'll parade right out of your privacy."

Abaddon grinned. "Ah! Alliteration! Admirable!"

Lauren pressed her fingers over her lips. In spite of all her bluster and combativeness, this dragon had scored a triumph. Was this some sort of test, like Mom had mentioned? If so, what kind of sacrifice was she supposed to make? The sand in the hourglass had drained about halfway. Did that signify her allotted moments to complete the test? If so, there wasn't much time left to figure it out.

She surveyed all the wide eyes. The Second Edeners had settled to complete silence, as if hypnotized. Even their companions had dimmed and no longer flashed. Barlow, Tamara, and Zohar stayed quiet as well. She shook off her own growing daze and drilled a new stare at him. "Listen, Abaddon, I'm in no mood to play word games. My mother told me to come here to find someone called The Maid. You said we could go, but if you don't tell us the way, we'll be stuck in this room. I'm sure you don't want that."

"Very well. No more word games, and I will limit my alliterations." Abaddon extended his neck, drawing his head closer to Lauren. "Your mother is Bonnie Silver, is she not?"

243

"Well, Bonnie Bannister, but yes."

"Oh, so she married the young man, did she?" His expression dipped into a frown. "Interesting."

"Interesting? Why?"

"She was hoping for heavenly harmony, but—"

Lauren stabbed a finger at him again. "You said—"

"I know. Habits are hard to … well, never mind. I was merely wondering if her dreams of a blissful marriage have come true, but your presence here is evidence otherwise." His tongue flicked out and zipped back in again. "Am I mistaken?"

"Let's just say that she and my dad have suffered more than she probably expected, but they're handling it." Lauren checked the hourglass. The sand would be gone soon. "Please, get to the point."

"As you wish." Abaddon flipped a page in his book. A hologram arose, creating an image of Mom. Wearing jeans, a white sweatshirt, and a bulging backpack, she looked like a teenager. "I knew her as Bonnie Silver. She came to me twice, once through death and once through a portal. Before her first arrival, my role here as guardian of my lair was routine. If a mother on Earth killed her unborn baby, it would sometimes come here to be reborn in one of Second Eden's birthing plants." Abaddon set a claw on his book. "I recorded each event with meticulous precision, though the details rarely changed. It was routine to the point of monotony. There were a few notable exceptions. Sometimes adults arrived here to be resurrected, such as Lazarus of Bethany, but, for the most part, everyone followed the same path."

The hologram transformed into an image of Dad carrying Mom across a narrow bridge. A dragon perched on the bridge's side, its neck curled as if ready to shoot flames. "Yet, when Bonnie Silver arrived, her case required special attention. I had never dealt with a winged human before, so I suspected that new rules were being formulated and I could expect changes. I was charged with preparing her for a resurrection to Earth, which wasn't unprecedented, but after I sent her back, Billy Bannister came here and then his mother. I also processed her father, her friend's father, her friend's sister, and a ten-foot-tall giant. It seemed that my new routine would be to expect resurrection for anyone remotely associated with Bonnie Silver. I wondered why the Majesty on High would allow their deaths only to raise them up again, thereby making my domain a revolving door." He shook his head. "But who am I to ask such a question? I simply did what I was told and sent them back." The image dissolved and fell like ashes to the book.

"And now?" He scanned the crowd with his blue eyebeams. "And now Bonnie's daughter comes with dozens of followers, as if this is a typical train terminal, and she demands directions to my doorway."

Lauren pointed at him once more. "You're alliterating."

"Yes." Abaddon cleared his throat, huffing out a plume of smoke. "I apologize."

"I don't mind so much. Just as long as you eventually get to the point so we can go and find The Maid."

He gave her an agreeable nod. "My point is purely practical. You must be aware that Abaddon's abode is not to be considered common. To me, you are irritatingly inquisitive intruders, and you are disrupting my decorum. Once Joan joins you, you are to quickly find your quarters and then quietly go about your quest."

"Joan?"

"The Maid."

"Then The Maid's name is Joan."

"Your observance of the obvious is overwhelming."

Lauren let out a huff. "For a dragon who desires our departure, you definitely dawdle—" She again pressed her lips closed with her fingers.

Abaddon's grin returned. "Deliberately." He grasped the hourglass and shook down a few straggling grains of sand. "In this realm, we measure every moment. Make ready to meet the mightiest militant ever to march."

Sir Barlow whispered into Lauren's ear. "You were splendid, Miss, but if you need me to speak to this warrior he mentioned, I will be glad to do so."

"Thank you. I'll let you know."

Zohar leaned close. "Someone's coming."

A light appeared on the far side of the chamber, growing, drawing closer. Soon, it illuminated an arched entry to a corridor.

245

A shadow crawled up the arch, first looking like a huge spider, then taking on a feminine shape.

Finally, a woman walked under the arch wearing a gray hooded cloak. Her body emitted short, wiggling flames from her bare feet to the top of her blonde hair. Young, diminutive, and with fiery white blossoms in her short locks, she looked more like a bridesmaid than a warrior. As she approached, she kept a sharp eye on Abaddon. Her long strides swept her cloak out of the way, revealing dark trousers and a scabbard at her hip.

"Ah!" Barlow said. "A woman who walks like a seasoned soldier."

"Stop alliterating!" Lauren hissed. "I've had my fill of it!"

Tamara squinted. "Is … she Joan?"

"I assume so."

The Second Edeners began whispering, and their companions twinkled in kind, as if awakened from sleep by Joan's appearance—a woman who could walk within an aura of fire without being consumed, almost like an animated tree of life.

She stopped at the table and stared at Abaddon, her shoulders square and her expression hard. "How many have you managed to mesmerize?" Her lovely voice carried a heavy French accent.

Abaddon's tongue flicked again. "Some stayed silent, as if sleeping, but only a solitary soul slipped into spellbinding, though she knows it not."

Joan, her eyes as bright as her body, locked her stare on Lauren. "I see your victim. She has residue, but she is not a statue yet."

Lauren pointed at herself. "Me?"

"Of course, you." As Joan marched her way, the Second Edeners parted to make room, apparently nervous about her fiery form. She halted within two steps of Lauren and looked her in the eye. "Did you not notice your feet of clay?"

246

As warmth from Joan's fire spread across Lauren's face, she glanced down. Dried mud caked her feet and legs. How could that have happened? She tried to lift a foot, but it wouldn't budge. "What's going on?"

Joan offered a courteous smile. "Such is the result when visitors trade words with Abaddon." She drew her sword and batted at the mud with the flat of her blade, loosening it.

"Thank you." Lauren lifted her feet in turn. The mud flaked off and fell to the stone floor.

Sir Barlow gave Joan a formal bow. "I am Sir Winston Barlow, formerly Lord of Hinkling Manor, and I am at your service."

"And I am The Maid, probably better known to you as Joan of Arc, the Maid of Orleans." She bowed her head. "I have heard stories of your remarkable courage, and I am glad to finally meet you."

Zohar bowed as well. "I am Zohar, though I have no last name or office. I was birthed as a plant and uprooted by Joran, son of Methuselah."

"You have eyes like sapphires." Joan ran a hand through his white hair, sending flames from her fingers that danced across his head. "And your alabaster locks give me reason to believe that you are an Oracle of Fire, one of body as well as of spirit. You must be kin to Sapphira and Acacia."

"So I have been told." Zohar's cheeks turned red. "I hope that I do honor to that legacy."

Tamara drew back behind Barlow, apparently hoping she wouldn't have to introduce herself.

Lauren gave Joan a nod. "I am Lauren Bannister, daughter of Billy and Bonnie Bannister. Have you heard of them?"

Joan let out a friendly laugh. "My dear Lauren, I lived here with Bonnie for four years. She became an Oracle of Fire in spirit, and I trained her to be a stellar sword maiden." She grasped Lauren's arm. Lauren flinched at first, but the flames radiated only luxurious warmth, no scorching heat at all. "You, however, are not an Oracle of Fire."

"Am I supposed to be one?" Lauren looked at Joan's grip. Her fingers were stronger than they appeared. "I don't even know much about what an Oracle of Fire is."

Joan stared for a long moment. A thin halo of fire surrounded her blue irises. "You have your mother's clarity of vision but not her maturity in faith. If Abaddon calls on me to train you, I will have to equip you with a sword and shield of a different sort, weapons your mother already had at your age."

"Train me? Are you Abaddon's partner or something?"

"Or something?" Joan laughed. "That is an apt description. We are neither partners nor friends. Ours is a relationship of tolerable cooperation, though he holds the key to my escape from this place."

"Escape? How do—"

"Enough talk for now." Joan pushed her sword back into its scabbard. "I will lead you and these refugees to a safe place."

"Safe? Safe from what?"

Joan eyed Abaddon. "Let us just say that a certain dragon is unpredictable. If you stay here in this chamber, you will become either a statue of stone or one of fire, and I care not to guess which state is worse."

"Then let's go." Lauren shook off more dried mud. It seemed that Abaddon had a statue of stone in mind.

"Come along." Joan pivoted and marched away, her flames growing as she headed for the corridor.

After gesturing for Barlow to follow, Lauren took a little girl's hand and walked in Joan's retreating light. To the rear, Barlow,

Tamara, and Zohar herded the others. As before, everyone stayed quiet. One woman picked up a birthing plant, but Abaddon waved a wing. "Leave those here. I have need of them." She set it down and scurried to join the others, her flashing companion zipping along at her ear.

When Lauren passed by Abaddon, he turned the hourglass over. "Every second the sand slides through, your sibling suffers. The period preceding the prophesied peril precipitates."

Lauren halted, her cheeks hot. "Is Matt in trouble?"

As the others paused behind her, Abaddon narrowed his eyes and whispered, "Almost assuredly."

"How can I help him?" She let go of the girl's hand. "*Can* I help him?"

Abaddon's lips pursed, as if enjoying the drama. "The future is open. The only events that you cannot control are those God has ordained without condition. I merely provide practically perfect predictions premised on the present."

"Stop the alliteration!" Lauren shouted. "This is too important for riddles!" Breathing rapid gasps, she glared at him. "Tell me plainly. What can I do to help Matt?"

"It depends on your decisions … ahem … your choices."

"What choices?" Her heart pounded in her throat. "What do I have to do?"

"I know you have seen one of these." He rolled a green egg across the table. "I suggest we talk alone."

When she caught it, she cradled it in her hands. "Barlow," she said, looking at him through the corner of her eye, "please follow Joan with the others. I'll catch up in a minute."

"If you please, Miss. Your mother charged me with looking after you. I cannot leave you alone in the company of this … well … noble, yet frightening creature."

Lauren looked at Abaddon. "May he stay?"

A sparkle gleamed in the dragon's eye. "Very well, but he must avoid interjecting his, shall we say, intellectually invigorating idioms."

Barlow gave a quick bow. "As you wish. I will stand off to the side while you converse."

While Tamara and Zohar continued guiding the Second Eden-ers, Lauren glared at Abaddon over the egg. "Is showing me this some sort of trick to keep me in your chamber?"

"If a trick, then it worked, did it not?" Abaddon laughed. "But it is not a trick. I want to offer you an option. You know what this ovulum held."

"Zohar and Mendallah." Lauren glanced at her legs. So far, no mud had collected. "Where is Mendallah?"

"She recently perished in a tragic fiery event, and she is now here in my lair. She is a statue outside, a large and noble statue. She is safe, so you need not worry about her. I can revive her from that status at any time."

Lauren took a deep breath. Staying calm was the only way to spar with this dragon. "Okay, so what are my choices?"

"You may remain here in complete safety, though not as a statue. You will rest and recreate with the citizens of Second Eden in comfort, and I will send Joan to your world. I assume you have heard of her prowess in battle."

Lauren rolled the egg back toward him. "Maybe the greatest leader the world has ever known. She led an army when she was only a teenager, and being female made it that much harder. It was a miracle, really."

"Correct." Abaddon caught the egg and set it upright. "Since she is a superior general, she would be able to lead the righteous remnant to victory over the forces of evil."

"And Matt?"

"Matt, being a courageous warrior, would not count his own life precious as he battled to protect the innocent. He would perish early on, so his suffering would end quickly."

She glanced at the hourglass. The sand seemed to drain more slowly than before. "If I go instead of Joan, will we conquer the forces of evil?"

"It is possible, but doubtful. You are not the leader Joan is."

She spread out her hands. "But there is a chance, I mean, the outcome isn't set in stone. The future hasn't happened yet."

"The future is rarely set in stone. Even Joan's victory in your place is merely a high probability, though it is virtually guaranteed. As Sir Barlow might say, 'It is money in the bank.'"

"And my chance of helping us win? I mean, I know I'm no general like Joan, but if I go instead, what are our odds of winning?"

"Perhaps you have heard another idiom about a snowball's chance in—"

251

"Never mind!" Lauren glared at him. Her scales tingled like mad. She glanced at her feet again. Still no mud.

"Yet," Abaddon continued, "your chance of keeping Matt alive is better than excellent. You two as a team would survive, though the war would likely be lost. Perhaps you would even be prisoners, commiserating with each other while in chains, but at least you would have your lives."

She set her hand on the table. It trembled. For the first time in her life, her own glow became visible. She quickly covered it with her other hand. "Why can't Joan and I both go?"

"I never said you could not. I offered you safety so that you could be in comfort while another goes in your place."

She pounded her fist. "I don't care about comfort! Just tell me what our chances are if we both go."

Abaddon looked toward the high ceiling for a moment before letting out a long hmmm. "Joan would triumph, and you would likely suffer a horrible death."

"And Matt?"

"He would be Joan's second-in-command and share in her glorious victory. They would give you a heroine's funeral, and the righteous remnant would bless your name forever, in the same way they do Joan's now. They would compose songs about the girl who glows in the dark, the maiden whose light continues in their minds whenever they have to endure dark days."

Lauren firmed her lips, trying not to cry. "How do you know?" Her voice pitched high in spite of her efforts. "These are all just probabilities, right? I mean, you're just guessing based on what you know, and your knowledge can't be perfect."

"You are correct. Although I am the angel of the abyss, and I have seen the scenes of seventy centuries, I could be contradicted by consequence, but errors are extremely ..." He snorted a cloud of gray smoke. "I apologize for the alliteration. I meant to say that I am rarely wrong."

Lauren glanced at the corridor. Joan's light had almost faded away. "If I decide that we both are to go, should I run and retrieve ... I mean get her now?" She looked at the shutters—solid wood. It was impossible to tell if the gas had dispersed. "And should we go back through your window to the museum room?"

He rolled the egg toward her again. "Take this. It will glow in the dark. Go with Sir Barlow, find Joan, and return here to me without him. We will discuss a new set of options."

CHAPTER

FALLEN COMPANIONS

Matt ran with his mother in his arms, puffing through his mask as the incline steepened. The lava wouldn't follow at this elevation, but the poisonous fumes might. Mom had already fallen unconscious, and her sapped energy didn't allow her body to fight for breath. Only a few shallow wheezes passed through her mask, and even those labored breaths increased her danger. These masks couldn't possibly keep all the poison out. If they didn't find clearer air soon, she would die.

He slowed for a moment and rewrapped her collapsed wings around her body. Every uneven step loosened them, making them flap in his face. The clawed ends sometimes dug in, but he had to ignore the pain and get Mom to safety. For the time being, nothing else mattered.

When they reached the top of a ridge, Valiant signaled a halt. Still wearing his own mask, he scanned the sky. "I see no dragons. They must have joined Listener and the men at the enclave in the hills."

"Then we keep going." Matt took a step, but Valiant held him back.

"You need to rest."

"If I don't find clear air—"

"If you don't rest, your lungs will explode. No man can carry her that far." He nodded at Matt's belt. "Restore her energy, and she can fly."

Matt glanced at the gun, still swirling with light, about half the amount it had before. "I don't think it will work. She said the energy in the gun is tied to her. She doesn't lose it until it's used on someone else. Besides, she wouldn't like it. She wants to save it for other people."

"Her heart is as big as all of Second Eden, and again I say that your heart is a reflection of hers. You are her son indeed." Valiant held out his arms. "I would be honored if you would allow me to carry her for a while."

"Sure." Matt transferred her to Valiant and pushed the gun behind her belt. "I guess she'd better keep it." He rotated his sore shoulders. The cloak added extra weight, but it was too valuable to leave behind. "And thanks for taking her."

A breeze kicked up and carried the smoke toward the valley to the east. The Second Eden moon shone brightly, illuminating the landscape more than the moon on Earth ever could. It looked like daytime during a storm rather than late evening. To the northeast, Mount Elijah stood quietly. Barely a puff of smoke emerged, and the lava on its slopes had dried and darkened, though it still glowed with a dull reddish hue.

Matt lowered his mask, leaving it tied around his neck, and took in a deep breath. Although still tinged with a stinging bite, the air was a lot easier to breathe. "Strange. Everything's settling. It's almost like the volcano chased everyone away, and now it's not angry anymore."

"It is a strange mountain, indeed." Valiant gazed that way. "It is said that eruptions are caused by a human falling into the crater. From what you told me, dozens of men fell in. That surely explains the reason for such a violent explosion."

"You think so? I thought the reason was all the energy that got poured in by the lasers and by the fire that opened the portal. That's a lot more logical than a ..." Matt averted his eyes. He was being as insensitive as sandpaper.

"A superstition?" Valiant smiled, and his companion hovering near his chin flashed as if amused. "I have no doubt that the energy contributed to the magnitude of the eruption, but I am confident that the humans who burned within were the primary cause. Mount Elijah reacts with furious wrath when it is used to execute a human."

"But when it erupts, it hurts more humans. That doesn't make sense."

255

"Your point is well taken. I assume there is an explanation, but I never learned what it is." Valiant nodded at his arms. "I think your mother is waking up."

"Mom?" Matt laid a hand on her forehead. "How are you feeling?"

She opened her eyes, fumbled for her mask, and pulled it down. "Let me stand, please."

Valiant lowered her to her feet and helped her balance. While she took several deep breaths, Matt held her arm. "I guess the clearer air revived you."

"Maybe, but it's more likely because the dream ended."

"Dream?"

"I was being told what to do next." She turned toward the valley, blinking. "The smoke is settling in the Valley of Shadows."

Matt studied the lower elevations. The valley into which he and Semiramis had fallen was now filled with swirling smoke, like a cauldron of boiling gray stew. If Eagle hadn't found Cheer by now, they wouldn't survive for long. "Well, you can't go there, if that's what you mean."

"That *is* what I mean. While I was sitting in the garden with my wings wrapped around me, I was asking God for a dream that would provide guidance. A hologram formed in front of my eyes. Even though it was dark under my wings, I could see everything in full color. I saw a young black man, a woman, and a girl standing at the entrance to a cave. Since the figures were small, and since they were covering their faces with big leaves, at first I recognized only the woman, Semiramis. I also dreamed while I was being carried, and I saw them again, this time closer up but only from the rear, as if I were standing behind them. That's when I recognized Eagle."

"And the girl had to be Cheer," Matt added. "It all makes sense. Eagle found both of them."

Mom tapped her chin. "The puzzling thing is that they seemed content to be together. If Semiramis kidnapped Cheer, why would that be?"

"Semiramis made up a wild excuse, something clever that would fool—" Matt glanced at Valiant, then looked away. "What I mean is—"

"If you are suggesting that my son might be taken in by a lie," Valiant said, touching Matt's shoulder, "you will not offend me. As far as I know, he has never heard one uttered, and if Semiramis is well practiced in the art of deception, Eagle might yield. It is difficult to train a warrior against such weapons when they are not readily available for sparring."

"Good point." Matt swiveled back to his mother. "We need to go and help him."

"We?" Mom slid her hand into Matt's. "If you're volunteering ..."

"In a heartbeat. Try to keep me away."

"I will come as well." Valiant crossed his arms over his chest. "Did you notice anything else? Dangers? Enemies?"

As she nodded, she stretched out her wings. "They were all coughing, even through the leaves, so the fumes were obviously a problem. I assumed they were thinking about entering the cave, but they seemed hesitant."

"The shadow people prey first on little girls," Valiant said, "so Eagle is likely being careful for Cheer's sake. Their numbers have been greatly diminished, but they are still formidable, and the cave is a refuge for them during times of trouble."

"Didn't Grackle go back to help Eagle?" Matt asked. "Why don't they just fly out to escape?"

"That is an excellent question." Valiant scanned the dim landscape. "Since Eagle found Cheer, he would try to leave with Grackle as quickly as possible."

Mom shook her head. "I didn't see a dragon in my dream."

257

Valiant shifted his gaze to the sky. "Listener sent Grackle to help Eagle, because he has more courage than does Albatross, but since he is older, he could have succumbed more easily to the fumes. Karrick and Albatross helped the men carry supplies to our enclave in the hills where Elam and I have hidden many weapons in case of an invasion, and they were told to hurry back to aid us, so we should see them soon."

Matt imagined a cave in the hills and a pile of swords, spears, and battle maces, hardly enough to defend against heat-seeking missiles. Still, these people seemed to have the heart to put up a good fight.

An engine purred somewhere in the sky. Matt searched for the source. Far to the south, a light blinked well above the horizon. "Is that the hospital?"

"It is." Valiant glanced between the light and the volcano. "I had hoped they would come earlier, but they likely waited for Mount Elijah to settle. It seems that they had enough fuel to stay aloft, or perhaps they landed for a while in a safe place. With so many people on board, they cannot fly for very long."

Mom gazed at the hospital as it drew closer. "It has wings now. It didn't before."

"We added the wings shortly after you were imprisoned," Valiant said. "But we had to cut its body quite a bit for balance until we were able to fly without the magnetos we used before that time."

Matt studied the plane. The wing structure pivoted, making it clear that it had vertical takeoff and landing ability. They could settle to the ground almost anywhere in spite of the debris. "That's a really modern aircraft."

258

"While our two worlds were on good terms, we were offered a great deal of technology. Elam was careful, however, with what he allowed to be employed. We heard about your entertainment devices, such as television and computer games, but Elam turned down offers to supply us with that technology, including Internet."

"Well, I like computers and Internet, but I guess Elam knows what's best for you."

Mom pointed toward the hills to the southwest. "Dragons are coming."

Flying low over the slope, two dragons beat their wings while shining red eyebeams on the ground. Atop the larger one, a rider flashed a white light. The smaller dragon carried what appeared to be a saddle pack with long bulging bags on each side.

"Good timing." Valiant used a hand to shield his eyes from the moonlight. "If I am not mistaken, Listener has joined them. That is not a surprise."

Mom lifted her brow. "Because she's such a warrior?"

"That is part of it." Valiant smiled in a knowing way. "She recently announced her willingness to accept an Adam, and there are several men who have shown great interest. The eligible men at the enclave are probably trying to …" He blinked. "How do you say it? Wait on her hand and foot?"

Mom nodded. "And she's too independent to enjoy the attention."

"Indeed. I suspect that not very much time passed before she was too exasperated to stay there."

"How old is she?" Matt asked.

"I am not sure." Valiant stroked his chin. "Twenty-eight? Thirty, maybe?"

"Wow! She looks like a teenager to me."

"Yes, our people do not physically age as quickly as those in your world. Because of your athletic build, you look every bit as mature as her suitors."

Heat filtered into Matt's cheeks. A rush of replies stormed through his mind, reasons why he would never be interested in someone Listener's age, but they all seemed pretty lame. It was best to stay quiet.

Gusts of wind announced the dragons' arrival. His wings beating, Albatross landed in a run while Karrick swept around everyone in a tight circle before gliding to a stop next to Albatross.

Listener jumped from Karrick's back, a flashlight in one hand, her sword in the other, and her spyglass in a belt harness. As she marched with her eyes locked on Valiant and her companion flashing near her cheek, she spoke with a commanding tone. "There is trouble in the Valley of Shadows. Grackle returned without Eagle. He said that Eagle commanded him to return because of the smoke and that Eagle had found Cheer with Semiramis. Grackle is sick from the poison, so I left him at the enclave. He must have flown through terrible fumes."

"Did Grackle say if they were in danger?" Mom asked.

Listener nodded. "His whistles were difficult to interpret, so I have no details, but they are in danger. I think that foul sorceress kidnapped Cheer to make sure someone would come back to rescue them both."

"And now she's guiding Eagle into the portal cave," Mom added. "That can't be good."

"Mom saw that part in a dream," Matt said to Listener. "It's kind of a gift she has."

"I have no argument with assuming the worst about Semiramis." Listener reached toward Albatross and nudged one of the pouches with a fist, making the contents clank. "A sword for each of us to carry, water, bread, more flashlights and batteries, and a few other weapons." She handed Valiant her flashlight, now darkened. "Storing these in our enclave paid off."

260

He flicked the light on and shone it at Karrick. "Since Matt and I are the heaviest, we will ride him, while you and Bonnie ride Albatross. We will eat and drink while we ride. We might not get another opportunity later."

After passing around the bread, Lauren's cereal bars, and flasks of water, they climbed aboard the dragons and launched into the air. As they flew toward the valley, Karrick taking the lead, Matt sat behind Valiant with a protruding spine between them, eating bread and one of the cereal bars.

During the flight, Valiant provided a quick history regarding Karrick and his mother, Roxil, including the fact that Karrick was born from a makeshift birthing garden during the years the swamplands were separated from most of Second Eden. The rest of the story was a blur of dragon relations and transformations, way too much to remember.

When they arrived over the valley, Karrick bent his neck and aimed his eyebeams at Valiant. "The cloud weighs heavily below," Karrick said. "We will dive through quickly, so make sure you hold on. Since breathing might be perilous, prepare accordingly."

Valiant pulled his mask up and fixed it in place. Matt did the same and looked back. Mom and Listener had already raised theirs.

Seconds later, Karrick folded in his wings and plunged. Matt took a breath and grabbed the spine. When they passed through the thick cloud covering the valley, everything fell dark. Water rushed somewhere close, and smoke brought a new sting to Matt's eyes.

After a few more seconds, the smoke cleared somewhat. Filtered moonlight allowed a view of Karrick's spine and scales, though the surroundings stayed veiled in darkness. He fanned out his wings, caught the air, and landed, his clawed feet splashing.

"This is Twin Falls River," Valiant said through his mask. "It is the safest place for a dragon to land. The cave lies within a forest, too dense for dragon flight."

Behind them, more splashes gave evidence of Albatross's landing. Karrick shuffled to the right and lowered his neck. "Dismount," he said. "We are on the beach."

Matt pulled down his mask and breathed in cautiously. The air carried the familiar bite, but he resisted the urge to cough. He checked his danger sensation—low to moderate and vague. The poison in the fumes probably elevated it somewhat, but nothing seemed ready to pounce.

After retrieving the flashlights and swords from one of Albatross's saddle pouches, Valiant, his mask also lowered, flicked on his beam and pointed it through the hazy air. Waving an arm, he called out, "Karrick, come with me. The rest of you follow several steps back with Albatross guarding the rear."

With a flap of his wings, Karrick skittered to Valiant's side, and the two marched into a forest, shuffling through sand, then undergrowth. Matt, his mother, and Listener followed, all with unmasked faces. Each held a flashlight and sword in hand, while Albatross stayed close behind. His eyebeams pierced the smoke and painted two scarlet lines that scanned the ground ahead of them, adding to the four flashlight beams that knifed into the hazy darkness. Albatross whimpered at times, and Listener shushed him. The look in her eyes made it clear that this white dragon was too yellow for her liking.

Matt glanced at the hilt in his hand. Fencing had been part of academy training, so the proper moves shouldn't be too much of a problem, though this blade was thicker and heavier than the ones the instructors provided. An assault rifle would be ten times better. It seemed that Second Eden had no high-caliber weapons at all, or at least they didn't display them anywhere. If Earth were ever able to attack, how would Second Edeners defend themselves against the blitz that advanced armies could deliver? The result would be a slaughter.

Along the way, Listener plucked a large leaf from a vine clinging to a tree. "What's that?" Matt asked.

"I'm not sure, but it might be the leaf I told you about."

"The one that filters poisonous fumes?"

"Keelvar, I hope. I'll ask Valiant to make sure." She folded the leaf and pushed it into her shirt pocket. "I'm taking it in case someone needs protection. If it works, we can always come back and get more."

After a minute or so, Valiant stopped at the entrance to a cave. When everyone had gathered around, he aimed his light through the opening, first scanning the ground where a pile of black goo covered the stone floor. He stooped and fanned strings of smoke

262

curling up from the mess. "Shadow people. Something has already dispatched them."

"They breathed the fumes?" Matt asked.

"The fumes were not the cause of their demise." Valiant straightened. "If they were sensitive to the poison, it would make no sense for them to congregate at a point closest to the outside where the fumes are likely the thickest."

"Semiramis." Listener poked at the remains with the point of her sword. "Whenever she is around, you can count on her as the reason behind any ghoulish mystery. She probably lured them here and had something that would kill them."

"I have to agree," Mom said. "I don't think breathing fumes would make the shadow people smoke like this. Something more violent happened."

Valiant nodded. "Semiramis is a mistress of potions. We should assume that she might use one on us and that she already knows we are here."

"In that case …" Listener motioned for the other humans to join her in a close huddle and whispered, "Because of the danger, we should send Albatross back to the enclave with a report and ask him to return for us in an hour. He is too cowardly to be counted on. It will be a tight fit, but Karrick should be small enough to come with us."

"Agreed," Valiant said.

After transferring the saddle pouches to Karrick and sending Albatross on his way, Karrick bobbed his head. "Allow me to lead. The witch's potions will be less likely to penetrate scales."

When everyone had moved out of the way, Karrick flapped his wings and leaped over the dead shadow people. Matt and Valiant followed first, then Mom and Listener. Again four flashlight beams joined red dragon lasers, piercing the darkness.

As they crept forward, Mom spoke up from behind, her voice low. "Do you feel any danger?"

Matt gauged the sensations. His stomach felt normal, and the edginess had eased. "Actually, I did a little bit out there, but it's getting lower. Maybe Semiramis isn't in here at all."

"She might not even be in this world anymore." Mom brushed her fingers along a wall. "This passageway once led to a portal that opened to Earth."

"Would Semiramis have the power to open it?" Valiant asked.

"I doubt it. She hasn't demonstrated that ability before. Escaping the fumes would be her motivation for coming here. But if somehow it is open, she probably wouldn't hesitate to go through it."

Matt imagined a secondary entrance to the cave well ahead. "If the portal were open, wouldn't the shadow people have gone through it?"

264

"It depends on how much light is on the other side. They fear light." Mom grasped Matt's shirt and pulled him closer. "I'm not sure what we'll find," she whispered into his ear, "but I expect that going to Earth is part of my journey, so if we do happen to go there together, I just want to warn you about something. Valiant and Listener have never been to Earth, so entering a corrupt culture that's probably worse than ever might be a huge shock."

"I can hear almost any whisper." Listener kicked a loose pebble, sending it clicking along the cave floor. "We're ready. Not only do we have our companions, Elam required study of Earth's culture. It was like swimming in sewage, but we learned a lot, including how to use Earth's weapons. And Valiant trained me for battle. Only he is my better with a sword."

"Good to know." Matt focused on Valiant. Looking at Listener might expose his doubt. Expertise with a sword was great, but it wouldn't do much good against guns and tanks. And Mom wasn't as worried about their weapons' expertise as she was about their emotional response to culture shock.

He leaned closer to Valiant. "Since we're assuming Semiramis knows we're here, and since we're assuming she might want to use a weapon against us, wouldn't it make sense to call her name and at least pretend to be friendly?"

"This is wisdom, but we are in search of Eagle and Cheer, not her." Valiant called out, "Eagle! Are you in here?"

"Cheer," Listener shouted, "it's Listener!"

Only echoes of their calls replied.

"I hear something," Listener whispered. "A crackling sound, like fire."

Matt trained his ears. Nothing. But that was no surprise. Listener's ears were far more sensitive.

Soon, a flickering light appeared deep in the cave, dancing on the side walls, and a crackling noise crawled through the air.

"It does sound like fire," Matt said.

Valiant sniffed the air and lowered his voice. "I smell burning fuel."

When the glow from the flame brightened enough to illuminate the cave floor and a curve in the passage, Valiant flicked off his light. Three clicks echoed his, shutting off the last of the white beams, though Karrick's twin red lasers stayed on.

Valiant continued in a whisper. "We should assume the portal is open. The fuel means that an engine is nearby, which might indicate a military vehicle, since the Earth government has been monitoring open portals."

Matt nodded. No use speaking. Apparently no one had been alerted to their presence. The flames might have muffled their shouts.

265

Valiant lifted a hand. "Listener and I will go first to see what lies beyond this bend. The rest of you stay here until—"

"I'm going." Matt flinched. The words just leaped from his mouth. "I'm sorry. I mean, I'd like to join you."

"Of course." Valiant kept his voice low. "I did not want to volunteer for you. I am unaware of how well you are trained in combat."

"I've been training for combat as long as I can remember." Matt swallowed back the next thought, that he was certainly better trained than Listener was, but that would be a stupid thing to say. Although he likely could outshoot her with any gun around, she could probably kick his butt in a sword battle.

"Very well. Karrick will stay with Bonnie."

Listener opened the second saddle pouch and withdrew a rifle of some kind, but the dimness prevented identification. She threw it toward Matt. "Ever use one of these?"

Matt caught the rifle and looked it over. "It's an AK-47!"

"Fully automatic, fully loaded, ready to fire."

"Yeah, I can see that." Matt pushed his cloak back, propped the gun against his shoulder, and looked through the sights. "And I do know how to use one."

"The swords were for the shadow people." She withdrew another rifle, popped in a magazine, and snapped back the charging handle. "These are for the Earth people."

"Good thinking." Matt couldn't suppress a grin. This young woman was getting more amazing all the time.

Listener's companion flashed red briefly, but when she gave it a smiling nod, it dimmed and settled on her shoulder. She turned toward Mom. "How about you? I have more rifles in here."

Mom shook her head. "I am very good with a sword, and I know how to use a handgun, but I'm not sure I can handle that."

266

She touched the candlestone gun behind her belt. "And I'd better keep a hand free for this. Someone might need healing."

After retrieving a rifle for Valiant, Listener collected swords, leaving Mom's in her possession, and returned them to the saddle pouch.

"Bonnie," Valiant said, "you and Karrick follow several paces behind. We want to be sure you are out of gunfire range if we come upon hostile forces."

Matt checked his warning signals again. "I don't sense any danger."

"Do you have experience with sensing danger across a portal?"

"No. I'm pretty new at this."

"Then we will assume the worst and be ready for it." Valiant waved an arm and marched. His companion floated a few inches above his shoulder, flashing blue in a rapid rhythm, as if excited about what lay ahead.

Keeping in step with Listener behind Valiant, Matt glanced back. Mom stood in front of Karrick, her sword ready. Her shoulders drooped, but her eyes sparkled, maybe with tears or maybe with determination. Karrick swung his head back and forth, huffing sparks from his nostrils and shifting his eyebeams all around. Mom would be safe with him.

As they walked, Listener rolled up her sleeves, revealing taut and toned forearms. Her fingers opened and closed around her rifle's grip, and her jaw tightened. Her companion hovered close to her ear and emanated a soft crimson glow.

"Is it talking to you?" Matt asked. "I mean, your companion."

She nodded. "She is concerned about my aggressive attitude and is counseling me to remember that we fight to protect and rescue, not to gain revenge or exact punishing retribution. Vengeance belongs only to the Father of Lights."

"Does her counsel help?"

"Always. When I see you and others from Earth without companions, it makes me wonder how you resist temptations." She laughed softly. "Sometimes wrath boils up inside me to the point that I feel I am ready to explode, but my companion is like cool water, a soothing spring. She tames my temper with a balm of peace. I can't imagine life without her."

Matt glanced between the dim path ahead and the glowing orb. Often he, too, felt a voice inside, what most people called a conscience. Could that be what a companion was, an external conscience? Or was it something more?

When they crept around the bend, flames came into view. At an opening at the end of the tunnel, a heap of twisted metal burned low and weak, apparently soaked with oil, keeping the fire alive. Beyond the fire, flat ground stretched out, ending at a sheer wall in the distance.

As they drew closer to the debris, Matt spotted landing runners, a bent propeller, and two cockpit chairs. "A helicopter," he whispered.

Holding his rifle at his hip, Valiant skirted past the burning chopper. A pop sounded. Valiant jumped back, shaking his hand, though his face showed no sign of alarm. "There is some kind of barrier here that burns on contact."

"Let me go first. Maybe my cloak will protect me." Matt squeezed between Valiant and the helicopter, collecting as much visual data about the craft as possible. With mangled guns barely attached to twisted side supports, it had to be an assault helicopter, definitely military. He reached out a hand. The fire was quite warm but not too hot.

When he passed through the portal with a sizzling pop and emerged on the other side, he turned. Farther back in the cave,

Mom and Karrick came into view around the bend, Karrick arching a wing over her as he shuffled. So far, so good.

Matt shed his cloak and tossed it through the portal. When it penetrated the plane, it sizzled again and fell over Valiant's hands. "Come on through."

After spreading the cloak over his head and shoulders, Valiant stepped past the helicopter, raising a shower of sparks. When he turned, he stripped off the cloak and threw it back for Listener.

Something clinked on the ground. A glimmer rolled past Matt's shoe, an egg-shaped bauble. Valiant dropped to his knees and cried out, "My companion! Where is he?"

Matt scooped up the little egg. Almost completely transparent, it sat in his palm, unblinking, motionless.

Valiant touched it with his fingertip, his eyes wet and his mouth open. He looked nothing like the unflappable warrior from Second Eden. He seemed lost, frightened.

"I am trying to speak to him with my mind, but he is not responding. Could this world have made him ill?"

Matt rolled the egg into Valiant's hand. "I have no idea, but if yours is affected, then …" He spun toward the portal. "Listener, maybe you shouldn't—"

"What?" Listener popped through the gap, the cloak over her head and her rifle tucked under her arm. Her companion teetered on her shoulder, then dropped to the ground. Letting out a squeak, she snatched it up and laid it in her palm. Her rifle loosened from under her elbow. Matt lunged and grabbed its barrel, saving it from falling.

Listener petted her companion with a finger. "What's wrong, my dearest?"

With quick glances, Matt scanned the area. No immediate danger. He stood on flat ground near the center of a cavernous crater, at least a few thousand feet deep. Above, crisscrossing jet trails in the daylight sky, either early morning or late evening, proved that they had entered Earth's realm.

He set a hand on Listener's shoulder. "Are you okay? Is getting separated from your companion dangerous?"

"We aren't separated. My companion is still here with me. I think ..." She shook her head, tears streaming down her cheeks. "I don't know what to think. She has never done this before, not even in the museum room."

Matt pointed at the portal opening. "Maybe you should go back and make sure she revives."

"Yes. Yes, I should." Cupping one hand under the other, Listener kept her face close to her palm and ran like a scared little girl back to the cave. As before, the cloak protected her body as she passed through.

Valiant stepped close to Matt. "I apologize for my outburst of fear. I have experienced many more crises than Listener has, so, although my companion's inactivity is shocking, I recovered quickly. I have my wits about me now."

"That's good. If I had any idea coming to Earth would cause this, I would have come alone."

"Elam had concerns, but Listener tried to persuade him that all would be well. You see, she once went through Mount Elijah's portal to the mining pits of Hades, and the journey had no effect on her. She thought that was enough proof that she could come to Earth. Yet, Elam wanted to take no chances. Since Earth and Hades were combined then, that might have made a difference."

Matt nodded. "So Elam's caution was justified."

"He is certainly wise and experienced." His eyes still misty, yet lucid, Valiant looked around the crater. "I sense great evil here. An oppressive spirit. Perhaps this is a new phenomenon that has caused our companions to suffer."

Matt nodded. *Suffer* was a mild diagnosis. They looked dead. "Maybe you'd better go back with Listener and make sure—"

"We'll be all right." Listener reemerged from the cave and walked across the crater floor, her hand curled into a fist. Her quivering lips revealed relief blended with worry. "My companion revived as soon as I went back, but she didn't say much, only that if I were to continue this journey, I might be on my own."

Matt touched her fist. "But you said you couldn't imagine being without her."

Listener pushed her companion into her tunic's inner pocket, stripped off the cloak, and threw it across the portal into the Second Eden cave. "It's not as bad as I thought it would be." Closing her eyes, she took a deep breath, then looked at Matt again. "I'll be all right. Maybe we won't be here long."

"I agree." Valiant tucked away his companion. "Let us hurry and find Eagle and Cheer. They must be close. They could not have scaled these walls."

Matt turned to the burning wreckage. The portal looked like a rectangular door standing upright without anything supporting it at all. He stepped past the side of the door and peeked around it. From this angle, the portal was completely transparent, invisible. Instead of a tunnel, a bare rocky floor spread from where he stood to the crater's perimeter wall.

After stepping back, he looked through the portal again and spotted his mother and Karrick a dozen or so paces into the cave. "Looks clear so far. I think you can come out. Just be sure to wear the cloak. I'm hoping Karrick's scales will protect him."

Matt gazed along the floor of pebbles and sparse grass until a ragged dark splotch came into view. He kept his voice low. "Follow me." He led the way to an area of moist clay, dark red and bearing two ruts that continued toward a hole in the crater's wall, a low cave entry leading into darkness. As they followed the trails, the ruts became more difficult to see, but intermittent drops of blood along the way made it clear that a wounded person had dragged himself, or had been dragged, to the hole.

Jogging on tiptoes, Matt hurried to the cave and stopped at the entrance with his assault rifle poised. Valiant and Listener closed in, Listener pulling her spyglass from its harness. Back at the portal, Karrick barged through the wreckage and swept much of the burning debris out of the way. Mom, now wearing the cloak, followed in his wake and emerged into the crater, still carrying her sword. She winced and pressed a fist against her stomach.

Matt took a step toward her, but when she gave him an "OK" sign, he relaxed. Valiant and Listener skulked to his side. Valiant leaned over and shone his flashlight into the cave, while Listener aimed her spyglass along the beam. "It is a low passageway," she said. "I see a man lying motionless on his stomach with his feet pointing this way. He is within reach. Beyond him, the passage opens into a chamber with a glowing lantern standing on the floor, battery-powered is my guess since there is no flame. I see three pairs of military boots moving around, but I cannot see above their knees."

"The man on the ground," Matt said. "Can you identify him?"

She shook her head. "I hear him breathing, but his respiration is labored."

"Is there room to crawl through and squeeze past him?"

"Perhaps a child could make it, but no one in our party could get by."

Matt furrowed his brow. Between the burning chopper, the blood trail, and the unconscious body, the clues indicated that the three men were likely enemies of the wounded man, and probably of Second Eden as well. A friend wouldn't leave a bleeding man to die in a cave. And considering his position in the tunnel, he must have been trying to get inside after the three entered. To confront them? Who could tell? In any case, only one course of action made sense.

"I'm pulling him out." Matt laid his rifle on the ground and belly crawled into the cave. When he reached the man's boots, he grabbed his ankles and began a backwards crawl, dragging the man with him. Since the man offered no help, the going was hard.

As soon as Matt cleared the entrance, Valiant reached in and helped pull the man the rest of the way. When the man's head emerged, they stopped and turned him to his back, revealing the bruised and bloodied face of Billy Bannister.

Matt gulped. "Dad!"

"Billy!" Mom jogged toward them, intense pain obvious in her gait. Karrick followed, beating his wings to keep up.

She dropped to her knees at his side, tossed the cloak and her sword away, and withdrew the candlestone gun from her belt. Light swirled within the casing, brighter than earlier, but still not as bright as before she healed Valiant.

"It's … it's not quite charged," she said as she stared at it. "The candlestone inside me is sending energy to it. It won't be long. I want to give Billy as much as I can."

"And then it will drain you again." Matt snatched the gun away. "Mom, you can't do this. You can't sacrifice yourself to—"

"Sacrifice?" She lurched for the gun, but he jerked it out of her reach. "Matt, sacrifice is all I can do. It's what I came here to do."

"Not when I can do it for you." He handed the gun to Valiant and grabbed the cloak. After fanning it over his body, he laid over his father. "Karrick, light me up."

273

Mom grabbed the edge of his cloak. "Matt, don't. It drains you too much. Ashley took days to recover from a healing, and it's been only hours. You don't realize how close you came to dying last time."

"Better me than you." He nodded at Karrick. "Let's do it."

"No!" Mom leaned back as she pulled the cloak. "Billy is my husband. This is not your responsibility."

Matt snatched the cloak away, making her fall back. When she thumped on her bottom, a twinge of guilt pinched his heart, but he shook it aside. This had to be done. "Valiant, please restrain my mother. We don't have any choice. The more she suffers, the worse things will get here on Earth. We can't let Tamiel win."

"I agree." Valiant grabbed Mom's arm, helped her to her feet, and pulled her slowly backwards. "Bonnie, please don't fight. We don't know if Matt is in danger—"

"I *will* fight!" She beat her wings and surged upwards, but Valiant held her in place, his biceps bulging. As she continued flapping and flailing, she cried, "I have to save my husband! I have seen more healings than all of you combined. I know how dangerous they can be!"

"Matt," Valiant said as he struggled, "move Billy away from the cave. The men inside are likely to hear the commotion."

While Matt dragged his father, Listener stood at the cave entrance, her rifle ready. "It's a good thing they have to come out one at a time," she said.

Matt raised his hood and covered himself and his father with the cloak, his head near his father's so he could send his eyebeams in when the time came. After positioning himself, he left a narrow viewing slit between the edge of his hood and the ground. Shuffling noises sounded—Karrick shifting into place. A whoosh followed, and heat pierced the cloak, beginning at the shoulders and spreading downward.

"You don't understand!" Mom said as her voice began to falter. "Enoch himself said I should do this. He said the people I love might try to stop me."

As Matt continued peering through the gap, intense heat radiated across his back. Pain drilled into his bones, as if Mom's cries acted as the drill's bit, and the flames energized the spin.

She settled to the ground and let her wings droop. "That's it, isn't it? You have become my oppressors."

Valiant blinked at her. "What do you mean?"

"I am …" She coughed, then continued in a wheeze. "I am suffering more in my heart right now than I ever could in my body. Even you are being hardened by my stifled song. You can't see the damage you're doing because of the blindness in your eyes."

A rifle shot cracked, echoing in the crater. A man lay at the cave entrance, his body halfway emerged and a handgun in his limp fingers. Blood poured from a head wound. "That's one," Listener said as she trained the barrel on him. "That will probably discourage the other two."

"Listener!" Mom cried. "How could you?"

As heat washed over Matt's entire body, he tried to toss away Mom's words. He couldn't let an emotional entreaty draw him from his duty as a son. Flames spilled across the edge of the cloak, forcing him to close the viewing gap. Not seeing his mother's pleading face would help, though voices might still penetrate.

"He pointed his gun at me," Listener said. "I had to fire."

More pain roared into Matt's bones. Scalding heat pierced his clothes. Dripping sweat made it feel as if his skin were melting. He bit down hard on his lip to keep from crying out. Maybe it *was* melting. But the suffering would be worth it … if it worked. If anyone should suffer, it should be him. Compared to Mom, he was worthless, just a kid who had stumbled through life like an awkward klutz. Even if he did die, at least Mom wouldn't.

"He didn't point his gun at you," Mom said. "He hadn't even looked your way yet."

"I know what I saw."

Matt grimaced, trying to spot any sign of his father's recovery, but he lay motionless, no hint of a stir. Why hadn't the eyebeams appeared yet? Was Mom right about needing more rest between healings? No. More likely, he just wasn't doing it right somehow. He always did mess things up at crucial times. Would this be yet another one of his failures?

"Listener, your senses are being blinded. No trained soldier would risk turning a handgun on someone who's aiming an assault rifle at him. Think! It doesn't make sense. Valiant, tell her."

"I did not see what happened," Valiant said, "but I trained Listener myself, so I know—"

"Not you, too, Valiant!" Mom groaned. "Resist the blindness! Don't let the corruption of my song corrupt you. You still have a choice, but there isn't much time left." Sobs blended into her cries as she shouted, "Let me go! I have to heal my husband! I have to save my son!"

Matt tried to tune out her laments. It was the only way. Listening to crying females had gotten him in trouble too many times. Even Darcy had tricked him with fake tears time and again, and then after luring him into some kind of painful trap, she had called him gullible, a fool for letting emotions get in the way.

"Matt, listen to me." Mom's tone grew calm, her voice smooth and even. "The people of Second Eden are not accustomed to a corrupting influence, and their companions are inactive, unable to help. But surely you have heard the voice of evil many times. You told me about Darcy. You know about Tamiel. You have fought them off before, so you can do it again, only it's harder this time. The song of the ovulum is no longer penetrating your soul to resonate with the law of love that God has implanted within you. The curse upon this land from ancient times is allowing evil influences to conquer those who are unprepared to resist, so you need to fight. Don't let lying whispers blind you to who you are. God made you upright. Only your own choices bring corruption. You must see this. You have to choose to break free from the influences that will bind you in chains."

Using a finger, Matt lifted the hood an inch and peeked through the gap. With Valiant still clutching her arm, Mom knelt, her hands clasped and extended in entreaty. Ribbons of red and black pulsed through his vision, but they couldn't veil her serene visage. Her emotional appeal had vanished, and she was now poised, her face tranquil.

"Matt. Listen to me. Don't give in to corrupting thoughts. We need your courage. We need your strength. I can do this healing, but I cannot be the warrior you can be. If you are going to be a martyr, do so at God's bidding, not Tamiel's ... or Darcy's."

"Darcy's?" Matt clenched his teeth. Heat blistered his body. Pain ripped through his limbs. His heart thrummed in his ears, as if shouting a rhythmic chant, "Fool ... fool ... fool."

He thrust out an arm, his hand spread. "Karrick! No more!"

The flames stopped, though heat continued storming across his skin and deep inside. He threw off the cloak and rolled to his back. "Valiant." He licked his parched lips. "I was wrong. Let her go."

277

PARASITIC BEHAVIOR

Again driving with one hand on the Jeep's steering wheel, Walter listened to the phone pressed against his ear. Ashley leaned close, also listening. Traveling on a snow-covered trail, the ridges and ruts made for a bumpy ride, challenging the Jeep's four-wheel drive.

"Give it to me again, Carly," Walter said. "That last bump almost made me drop my phone."

Carly spoke with careful enunciation. "Lois established contact with the flying hospital in Second Eden. She sent Dr. Conner all we have about the parasite. It turns out that the skin cells I collected from Jared's bed didn't do much good. We couldn't find anything unusual. So I started looking everywhere for more genetic material. That's when I found a used Band-Aid in the trash that had some blood in the pad. Luckily it was Jared's. Lois found a live parasite and analyzed it to figure out what makes it tick. And it's really like a tick, except instead of sucking blood, it sucks energy.

You see, normally an anthrozil's photoreceptors will repel any parasites, but people like Jared and Irene don't have active receptors. They have dormant ones. So the parasites are able to attach to and revive their receptors, but once the parasites are attached, they can't be repelled. Then the anthrozils' bodies revert to using those receptors for energy, and the parasites suck them dry. So the receptors act as agents for the parasites, taking energy from the host and passing it to the leech."

Ashley leaned close to the phone. "So it doesn't work on normal humans, because they don't have photoreceptors."

"Right," Carly said, "and people like you and Billy and Bonnie have photoreceptors, but they aren't dormant, so the parasites can't attach."

A bump shook the phone from Walter's grip, but Ashley caught it, saving it from flying away. After Walter steadied the Jeep, she handed the phone back to him. "We're still with you, Carly. What else you got?"

"Well, Lois ran millions of models based on plausible alterations of the parasite's genetics and found a combination that would create a competing parasite."

"Competing? What would it do?"

"Eat the original one. And she found a genetic switch that will make the competing parasite die after about forty-eight hours. It's the perfect solution, but ..."

Walter rolled his eyes. "I was afraid of that. What's the catch?"

"It looks like the only way to create it is to use explosive heat and quick cooling, just like how the original one was created."

"You mean a volcanic eruption?"

"Unless you can think of an alternative."

Walter gripped the phone through another rollicking bounce. When the Jeep settled again, he turned to Ashley. "As if Second

Eden didn't have enough to worry about, now we have to figure out how to get Mount Elijah to erupt again."

"Lois sent all her findings to Dr. Conner," Carly said. "He's an expert geneticist, so maybe he can work out another option. Now that we're in contact, we can keep each other up to date."

Walter gave Carly a thumbs-up sign, though she couldn't see it. "Right, but let's stick with the phones. Don't try to contact my tooth. I still have it installed, but I think they're too easy to hack."

"Will do."

"Just so I can picture this," Walter said, "how are you transporting Lois?"

"I've got her in the portable station sitting in the passenger's seat. She fits pretty well, but with all the protruding antennae and flashing diodes, she looks like Sputnik at Mardi Gras. I hope she doesn't arouse any suspicion."

"Carly, you're amazing!"

"Yeah, I know. So are you. Anyway, I'll sign off until I get an update. I'm on an Interstate highway without much traffic, so call me anytime. I patched you through to the radio to make it easier for us both to listen in."

"Sounds good." Walter disconnected and handed the phone to Ashley. "Progress, but it feels like two steps forward and three steps back. How can we get the volcano to erupt again? And even if we can, should we?"

"There might be a way to funnel energy to it like we did before. But timing it perfectly so we can be ready to throw in the ingredients?" Ashley shook her head. "Impossible. And it would be suicide for anyone who stirred the pot."

Walter heaved a sigh. "And that's what worries me."

"What? Stirring the pot?"

"No. Suicide. I can't shake this feeling that Joran and Selah burned up on purpose. Remember seeing those sparks flying into the sky?" He lifted a hand and sprung out his fingers. "It was a big whoosh, and the sparks scattered in the air and stuck in the sky like someone threw a bag of adhesive glitter."

"That's a vivid picture."

"Yeah, I thought so. Anyway, I saw a look in Joran's eyes, like he knew it was coming, like there was no future left for him and his sister." He glanced at Ashley. "Have you ever seen a look like that?"

"A few times. But there's nothing we can do to help them." She massaged his shoulder. "It's not Joran and Selah who are bothering you, is it?"

Walter shook his head. "Another brother and sister. When I first met Matt and Lauren, I got the same feeling from them, just not as obvious. It was like they knew they were different and didn't belong, like they were martyrs on a mission just looking for a reason to die for a cause. Do you know what I mean?"

"I think so. I got the same feeling from Bonnie when I first met her in Doc's office. I think it's a sense of freakishness, like you feel so different you know you don't fit into this world. You get a sense that you can't exist here, so you find an exit that helps as many people as possible."

"Exactly, and I especially felt that from Lauren the first time I met her. When I nearly got conked out, I saw her coming toward me, glowing like she was walking through fire without burning, like Moses' burning bush. Anyway, I'll never forget that look in her eyes. She felt lost and freakish, just like you said. I wanted to hug her and tell her everything would be all right." He laughed softly. "But I couldn't even lift my arms then, and I forgot to do it later. Now I feel stupid."

"Don't feel stupid. You've never been a father. You're not used to trying to be one."

"Maybe, but that feels like a lame excuse." As warmth rose to his cheeks, he gazed into her sympathetic eyes. "Is it wrong for my arms to ache to hold her now?"

"No, of course not." She ran her fingers through his hair, tears brimming. After a moment of silence, she intertwined her fingers with his. "Are you sad that we couldn't have a baby? I mean, I know we had only a year before the Enforcers took me, but the tests didn't look promising."

"Mixed emotions. If you had a baby and then went to jail, who knows what would have happened? It could've been terrible for him or her." As tears welled, his throat tightened, pinching his voice. "But when I saw Billy's kids ... especially Lauren ... my heart kind of ripped in half. I felt this overwhelming urge to protect her, to be a dad to her, and knowing she's not my daughter doesn't change that. It's just ..." He tried to swallow down a lump, but it was no use. The words weren't there.

"It's just that you loved that protective feeling, and you want it to be permanent." She leaned close and kissed his cheek, whispering, "You have the heart of a father, and I love you all the more for having it. Maybe someday it will happen."

After a few more minutes, Walter stopped the Jeep at the end of the trail. With tall rocks and deep ditches ahead in the snowy landscape, there was no way to continue on wheels. They would just have to hoof it.

Ashley grabbed a medical bag from the back while Walter checked the Glock in his hip holster. He had stowed the weapons duffel in a lockbox in the back. Taking along another gun and more ammo would help, but carrying it over this terrain might be more trouble than it was worth. He read the GPS coordinates on his phone. "It's not too far. Maybe three miles."

"Not far for you. I've been cooped up in a cell for years. All I could do was run in place, not exactly cross-country training. And the snow will make it brutal."

"Good thing the prison-issue boots are waterproof." He gave her a kiss and took the medical bag. "Don't worry. I won't leave you behind."

After navigating past the rocks and ditches together, Walter ran through the brush, while Ashley hustled a few steps behind. Both wearing multiple layers under thick coats, the race across the Arizona highlands brought sweat and heavy breathing. The snow here wasn't deep, having been blown into easily avoidable drifts.

"Gabriel's close," Ashley called. "I can feel it."

Walter pointed at a rise. "We'll rest up there."

When he crested the rise, he stopped and waited for Ashley to catch up. She ran to the top and halted. As she held a hand over her chest and gasped for air, Walter looked around, shivering in a blustery wind. A stream coursed through a shallow valley with a few trees lining its shore. Beyond that, a flat-topped hill rose about a hundred feet. Lumps interrupted the surface, though failing sunlight made them hard to distinguish.

A human figure rose on the hilltop and began waving his arms.

"I said not to use this, but ..." Walter tapped his jaw. "Yereq, is that you flapping over there?"

"It is I." Yereq's voice buzzed through the tooth transmitter. "Come quickly. I fear that some are losing their battle for life."

"We're coming." Walter touched Ashley's shoulder. "Ready?"

After taking a deep breath, she nodded.

While they ran down the rise side by side, Walter set a finger on his jaw again. "Carly, are you listening to this frequency? We found them. There's trouble, so stay tuned in."

"I'm here, Walter," Carly said through his tooth. "I'm driving through a thunderstorm now, so I might get distracted. I'll find a place to pull over as soon as I can."

"All right. Be safe." Walter and Ashley continued at a jogging pace across the valley floor, dodging shrubs and stunted trees as they high stepped through the snow. When they reached the stream, they splashed through the shallow water and thin ice and hurried on. At this point, a chill didn't matter. There was no time to waste.

After dashing up the hill, they ran across the flat top to where Yereq stood, towering over several bodies, both dragon and human. Makaidos, Thigocia, and Roxil lay motionless with their necks intertwined and their wings splayed over their backs. Gabriel lay curled on his side with his wings crumpled behind him. Elam, dressed only in his Second Eden battle uniform, sat with his head low and his arms wrapped around his legs, apparently unaffected by the frigid wind blowing a thin layer of snow past him.

Ashley dropped to her knees between Gabriel and Thigocia. "Mother! Gabriel!" She spun her head toward Yereq, her voice shrill. "Are they alive?"

"All are alive, though most are struggling to breathe." Yereq reached into his pocket and withdrew something pinched between his thumb and finger. "After sweeping away as much snow as possible, I found several of these on the ground. I assume they are candlestones, so I disposed of most of them, but I saved this one for you to analyze."

Walter studied the semitransparent bead. "Yep. A candlestone bullet."

"So ..." Ashley caressed Thigocia's neck. "They've been shot with candlestones."

"No telling how many times." Walter slid the bullet into his pocket and set the medical bag next to Ashley. "Better get started. I'll find the entry points."

285

"Four in Makaidos. Three in Thigocia. Four in Roxil. Three in Gabriel."

Walter turned toward the voice. Elam had lifted his head. Bruises and bloodstains covered his face, a wide rip in his shirt exposed his chest, and dried blood matted his hair. "How many times were you hit?" Walter asked.

Elam touched a gash on the side of his forehead. "Only once, really, but not by a bullet. I got walloped with the butt of a gun. The blow killed my tooth transmitter. It didn't really matter, though. I stayed out cold until Yereq arrived. That's when I checked out all the wounds."

"Well, if you can move, get over here." Ashley fished through the bag. "I need you to show me all the entry points. If I have to dig out fourteen candlestones, this is going to take a while."

While Elam rose and limped toward Ashley, Yereq crouched next to her. "Do you have transport for everyone?" he asked.

Ashley withdrew a small vise clamp and a knife with a thick blade. "Jared and Marilyn are coming with *Merlin*, so Elam, Gabriel, and Walter and I can go with them. If I can revive my parents, they'll be able to fly on their own. But I don't think you'll fit in the airplane."

Yereq nodded. "Perhaps Makaidos can carry me where I need to go."

"Where is that?" Walter asked.

"To find Sapphira."

Walter slapped his forehead. "Right! Sapphira! I forgot to ask about her. How stupid can I get?"

"Not stupid," Ashley said. "Just distracted. We didn't ask about Legossi either." She raised her brow at Elam. "Where are they?"

"While I tell the story," Elam said, "I'll show you the entry points, and you can work on extracting the bullets."

286

"That'll do." She nodded at Walter. "Grab a towelette from the bag and disinfect your hands. I'll need your fingers."

While Ashley and Walter performed surgery, Elam related the horrific events—finding the portal locked, suffering through the helicopter attack, and trying to prevent Sapphira's kidnapping. During the process, Ashley's healing touch sealed and cauterized ripped flesh and torn vessels, halting bleeding that sometimes became profuse while she probed for candlestones.

By the time Elam finished, Ashley had removed Gabriel's bullets and several from the dragons. Although Gabriel still lay unconscious, his breathing and heart rate were steady.

Finally, Elam let out a sigh. "I left the goriest part out."

Walter tightened a clamp that held two of Thigocia's stomach scales apart, allowing Ashley's fingers inside. "What part?"

"Well, Yereq cleaned up the mess here on the hilltop, but ..." Elam gestured with his head toward the opposite side of the hill. "Legossi was her usual heroic self. This time it cost her her life."

Ashley looked at Walter. Her face twisting, she whispered, "Not Legossi."

"Just keep working." He clasped her shoulder with a bloody hand. "I'll be right back."

"Hurry!" Ashley reached farther into Thigocia's belly. "We have a few more to extract."

"I will." Walter pulled Elam's arm. "Show me."

With hands in pockets, the two walked toward the hill's far side, Walter watchful of Elam's unsteady gait. "What happened?"

"Legossi attacked a helicopter and brought it down. They retaliated by shooting a missile at her." When they reached the edge of the hill's plateau, he pointed at a pile of wreckage at the bottom of the slope. A dragon's wing lay spread over some of the debris, human legs and arms were scattered here and there, and a scaly

287

head protruded between two mangled propellers. Several birds picked at various entrails hanging from a dragon's abdomen.

Walter spun away. Nausea boiled. Clutching his stomach, he dropped to his knees and dry heaved. With no food in so many hours, there was nothing inside to vomit.

Elam patted him on the back. "I had the same reaction. I've seen a lot of death, but who could get used to carnage like that? Especially a dismembered and disemboweled loved one."

Coughing, Walter climbed to his feet. When his spasms settled, he shook his head. "You have a strange way with words."

"Too straightforward, I know. I used to understate the case, but the residents of Second Eden had a hard time understanding me, so I got into the habit of just stating matters plainly. That made me odious in the eyes of your government. They're not accustomed to truth."

"Trust me, I understand. My mouth gets me in trouble, too."

Elam let out a long sigh. "At least Legossi and Angel are finally together."

"Right. Mother and daughter." Walter nodded slowly. "It's good to get an eternal perspective."

"When you're as old as I am, it's easier to do. I'm looking forward to my own heavenly reunions."

Walter turned toward Ashley across the hilltop. Gabriel was now sitting, shaking his head as if trying to wake up. Thigocia's wing flitted at the tip, and two lines of smoke rose from Makaidos's nostrils. Roxil also stirred a wing.

Walter gestured with a flick of his head. "Come on. I have to get back to surgery."

As they walked, Walter rubbed a thumb across his wedding band. "You sure are handling Sapphira's kidnapping well. When they took Ashley, I nearly broke my wrist bashing a limb against a tree trunk. I know it's happened before, but it's got to be eating you alive."

Elam nodded. "It's hard to explain, Walter. When you've been alive as long as we have, and when you've seen as many miracles as we have, there's less urgency about everything. The people who kidnapped Sapphira are afraid of her, so they won't dare open that metal box. I noticed it had air vents and a feeding tray, so they plan on keeping her there until they can move her to a flameproof cell. They'll make a ransom demand, probably access to Second Eden, and I'll delay my answer long enough for us to make a plan to rescue her."

"But you don't even know where they're taking her."

"Oh, but I do. Fort Knox. After the dragons destroyed it, the government worked for years restoring it. I have no doubt that they have been planning a prison cell constructed especially for Sapphira—dragon-proof, if you know what I mean."

Walter felt for the bullet in his pocket. "More candlestone guns?"

"Most likely. We'll have to prepare for the worst."

When they arrived, Walter, Elam, and Yereq pitched in to hold scales apart, pass around instruments, and fetch water from the nearby stream in a metal basin Yereq found in the helicopter wreckage.

After another hour, Ashley had removed every bullet and stitched every wound. When she finished, she reclined on her back with her arms over her face and her sleeves rolled up, revealing blood stains from fingertips to elbows. "I need three ibuprofen tablets and ten hours of sleep. I have the worst headache in the history of the world."

"And your healing reserves?" Walter asked as he dug into the medical bag.

289

"Gone. Kaput. It might take days to get them back. I thought my mother's last wound would never seal."

Walter pushed three pills into her hand. "I'll put some iodine in the water so you can swallow these."

"No need." She lifted her head, popped the pills into her mouth, and swallowed, wincing as they went down.

The three dragons rose to their haunches, their heads drooping at the ends of sagging necks. "You have done well," Thigocia said, her voice low and despondent. "All of you."

"Indeed." Makaidos thumped his tail against the ground. "We are once again indebted to our human friends."

"So what next?" Walter asked. "Who should go with Elam and Yereq to rescue Sapphira? And who should go with Jared to find Billy and Lauren?"

"Thigocia, Roxil, and I will not be able to go anywhere until we regain our strength, especially if one of us is to carry Yereq." Makaidos looked up, blinking. "The sun is well past its zenith, so there might not be enough hours of sunlight to allow for strengthening. Yet, it is critical that we leave as soon as we can. If the people who sent the helicopters decide to retrieve their lost comrades, they will likely send more than they did last time. Perhaps we should retreat to a hidden area and wait there until we are strong enough to fly with passengers."

"Then Jared and Marilyn won't know where to find us," Ashley said.

Gabriel flapped his wings and shot to a standing position. "I'll fly around and look for a place. While you guys take cover there, I can stick around here. I'll be able to get away quick, and I'm a smaller target than the dragons." After taking a breath, he bent his knees and jumped into the air. Seconds later, he was flying toward a high ridge to the west.

"He recovered quickly," Walter said as he followed Gabriel's flight. "Let's hope the dragons do the same. I agree with Makaidos that this place feels like the bull's-eye on a bombing range."

Ashley stroked Thigocia's neck. "Do you know about Legossi?"

"I do." A tear dripped from her eye. "I have lost her before, but seeing the cruelty of not one, but multiple slayers, was more devastating. How could so many conspire to hurt us like this?"

Roxil laid her head on the ground. "At one time, I hated all of humankind. I have to fight to keep those old feelings from returning."

"Earth's corruption is hastening," Makaidos said with a head bob. "There is danger in the air, a heavy, oppressive danger that I have not sensed since my youth, in the days leading up to the great flood. It crawls like a shadow and strikes like a viper, injecting a disease that gnaws at the heart. I witnessed mankind's decay then, and the corruption in the air now is the same rottenness that infected souls in those ancient days."

291

"Could it be the *lack* of something in the air?" Walter asked. "Like a countermeasure? I mean, corruption has been around ever since I've been alive, so it's nothing new. All I have to do is turn on the news or hear a political speech to smell the stench. We're surrounded by greed, lust, and lies all the time. Why is everything falling apart now?"

Ashley nodded. "Walter's talking about Bonnie's song. It's the countermeasure, and it's failing."

"Right." Walter smacked his palm with a fist. "So if we're going to fight this, we need to make sure we take the fight to the source. We have to find Bonnie, and with Joran and Selah gone, the only Listener we have left is Lauren."

"Listener?" Thigocia repeated. "We have a Listener in Second Eden as well."

"That's her name, but we're not sure if she has Lauren's gift. If she does, we don't know if she's able to tune in to Bonnie's song." Walter checked the gun in his holster. "My point is that I want to get to Billy and help him. Since he and Lauren were together, he's probably the key to tracking her down. And if we don't rescue Bonnie from Tamiel and peel his choking fingers from around her throat, we can count on running into more demonized Earthlings than we can shake a stick at."

Elam raised a hand. "Yereq and I will go with Makaidos and Thigocia to Fort Knox to see what's up there. We'll work out our strategy on the way."

"Okay." Walter patted Elam's shoulder. "That's a good team."

Roxil lifted her head. "I will join you, Walter. Just let me know where you are, and when I regain my strength, I will fly there."

"Sounds good." Walter touched his jaw. "Carly, did you pick up everything?"

"Every word … I think. The guy at the toll booth wanted to know what radio program I was listening to, so I told him it was a drama broadcast by satellite. He gave Lois a glance but nothing more. He probably assumes I'm on my way to a geek fest of some kind."

"Maybe you should've dressed the part, like a storm trooper outfit." Walter tried to smile but couldn't overcome the sadness. "Listen, Elam's going to need some cover. Have Lois work on an identity for him. He'll need the usual papers, the same as we did for Sir Barlow. Elam can print them out at an office services depot somewhere along the way. He lost his tooth transmitter, but I can give him mine so you can communicate with him directly. Make sure everyone's synched up on the new encryption. I have the phone, and Ashley will be with me, so we won't need chips."

"Don't forget to clean the one you give Elam." The mirth in Carly's voice was easy to read, but Walter let it slide. Humor felt like a forbidden joy right now, just as it did for the past fifteen years while Ashley was in prison.

"Right," Walter said, trying to loosen the crimp in his throat. "Let me know if you need any input about Elam's identity."

After Gabriel found a suitable hideaway, everyone rested there for about an hour. When Marilyn landed the airplane in the valley, Gabriel fetched Walter and Ashley, leaving Elam and the dragons behind, and the three boarded *Merlin*. Since Roxil also had a transmitter, it would be easy to communicate with her by tooth-to-phone protocol when she recovered.

Ashley and Gabriel took seats in the front row of the plane's passenger section, each leaning into the aisle as Walter crouched close to the cockpit, glancing between Marilyn and Jared in the pilot and copilot seats, respectively. Jared's skin was ashen. Bruises covered his wrinkled face, and a glaze coated his eyes.

293

"Take a rest in the back," Walter said, pointing over his shoulder with a thumb. "Your lovely wife and I can handle this bucket of bolts."

"Thank you." Jared rose, squeezed past Walter, and hobbled down the aisle, his head low to avoid the ceiling. He seemed ready to collapse.

Walter caught Marilyn's gaze. She needed no words. Her knitted brow said that Jared's condition had worsened ... a lot. She feared for his life.

After climbing into the copilot's seat, Walter looked back at Ashley and cast his thoughts her way. *After all that healing, if you feel up to seeing what you can do for Jared, that would be great. One way or another, we have to figure out how to get him to Second Eden.*

If Dr. Conner comes up with that counter parasite, Jared needs to be there to catch it.

Ashley gave him a quick nod and followed Jared to the back of the plane.

"Everyone buckle up," Walter said as he fastened himself in. He slid the communications headset over his ears and looked at Marilyn. Tears glistened in her eyes. When one trickled down her cheek, she swiped it away, sniffed, and slid on her own headset.

"We had some headwinds coming here." She began punching buttons on the console GPS map. "So we should make better time going back if we—"

"Marilyn," Walter said, gently pushing her hand away from the map. "Just relax. Get some sleep. If I need you, I'll wake you up."

As another tear made its way down her cheek, she offered a thankful smile. "Billy needs us."

Walter nodded. "I know. For his sake, for Bonnie's sake, and for their children's sake, nothing on Earth or in Hell is going to stop me from helping them. You have my word."

CHAPTER

RESURRECTED WARRIOR

L auren stood with Joan next to Abaddon's table, her hands folded primly at her waist. The flames on Joan's body had dwindled to tiny firelets, still noticeable but very much subdued. The hourglass sat on the table, the sand about halfway drained— maybe fifteen minutes before it would run out. If it still meant that Matt would meet trouble when the sand spilled through, they had to hurry, but Abaddon seemed to be in no mood to be rushed.

While he used a sharp claw to flip large parchment pages in his book, Lauren scanned the dragon's dim abode. With Barlow, Tamara, and Zohar helping the Second Edeners settle in tents and beds Joan had arranged earlier, it seemed quiet in the huge chamber. Columns lined the walls, and colorful frescoes filled the gaps in between, nondescript designs that resembled modern artwork, unlike the living mosaics in the corridor. Although she didn't get a chance to study those hallway frescoes carefully when looking for Joan, a walking dragon seemed to move along the wall at her pace. Whatever magic this place held, it was enough to incite a chill and a bit more reverence.

Lauren slid out her phone, set it to silent mode, and began taking photos, including Joan, Abaddon, and the chamber. Saving these images for future days might be a good idea, if only for showing friends and family what she went through.

"So many rules broken." Abaddon's neck swayed, but his head remained relatively motionless over the book. "The birthing plant was not in the garden when the call came for Zohar to be resurrected, but the powers that be insisted that I send him anyway. Apparently the garden was virtually destroyed, so they allowed the violation."

Lauren pushed the phone into her pocket and cleared her throat. "I don't know what that means, but—"

"Shhh!" Joan set a finger over her lips. "He is not addressing you. Let him vent his frustration."

"At least he's not alliterating," Lauren whispered.

"That is always for show. It is part of his hypnotic gift."

"And now ..." Abaddon flipped another page, snatched a pen from an inkwell with a clawed hand, and began writing. "And now I am supposed to send Joan back with her full wisdom and knowledge and not as an infant and also with no garden ceremony at all. Of course I did that with Timothy, the most prolific resurrection performer in all history, but at least he appeared in the birthing garden in Second Eden in his human adult form."

Lauren glanced at Joan. Her brow scrunched, her first sign of confusion. Apparently part of the dragon's rant caught her off guard.

Abaddon looked up, as if listening to a voice. Lauren trained her ears. A whisper sounded from somewhere, but the words were indecipherable, as if spoken in a foreign language.

"I know Lauren needs a faithful companion," Abaddon said, "and Joan would be the best companion possible, but I did not provide these options to them earlier. They must know the cost involved. Even now I speak in their language so they will understand my dilemma. With this unique arrangement, the outcome is completely unpredictable. Lauren will be unprepared for what she might face. Will she be like Joan or like Isaac?"

Lauren blinked. Isaac? Who was Isaac?

Again whispers permeated the chamber, this time echoing, as if several ghosts roamed the spacious room and spoke identical words in chorus. The voices crooned, deep and lovely, carrying none of the grief and toil the lamenting voices in Hades communicated.

Abaddon lowered his head and sighed. "Your will be done. I will make the arrangements." Without looking up, he continued writing in his book. Lauren glanced again at the hourglass. It was nearly empty. Only about five minutes remained.

After swallowing through a lump, Lauren leaned closer. "Excuse me, but the sand is about to—"

"You are so much like your mother." Abaddon's tail whipped around, latched on to the hourglass, and turned it over. Sand began spilling once again. "It is a shame that humans rarely understand the nature of prophetic utterances. With rare exceptions, they are conditional. There are many shifting sands in your world, and free will is the greatest of shifters. Yet God's ability to fulfill his purposes is not threatened by freedom. In fact, he delights in it."

Joan pulled on Lauren's sleeve and whispered, "I will explain later."

"No need. I think I figured it out."

Abaddon set his pen back in the inkwell. "The two of you will go to Second Eden immediately. Since Lauren never died, she will not need a resurrection. She will return the way she came, but Joan will need to be resurrected. I will send her to one of the remaining birthing plants. Since she has already undergone a trial by fire and has become a spiritual oracle, she will not need to suffer again in the flames in order to rise from the dead."

"I will explain that as well," Joan said. "It is something your mother had to go through to become—"

"An Oracle of Fire." Abaddon snorted. "It seems that Joan is anxious to begin her role. We will see how she performs when she learns how difficult this role will be, especially when Lauren is faced with her own trial by fire."

Joan's flames erupted, sending six-inch flares curling out like groping fingers. "But you said the outcome of this arrangement is unpredictable. How can you know—"

"One truth is always predictable." Like a striking adder, his head shot forward and stopped within inches of Joan's face. He then turned his sparkling blue eyes toward Lauren. "Those who have the courage to carry the flame of truth without flinching will *always* be consumed by fire, whether it is ignited by their enemies through lies, jealousy, hatred, or fear, or by their own passion as their hearts are set ablaze and they burn in sorrow as others fail to heed their calls."

Turning toward Joan again, he added, "How well you know this."

Joan's chin quivered, but she kept her stare locked without blinking.

As Abaddon drew his head back, he flipped toward the front of his book. A hologram rose from the pages, a woman tied to a stake with flames shooting up from piles of wood stacked all around. Clutching a crude wooden cross against her chest, the woman cried out in agony, "L'eau! Donne-moi du l'eau sainte!"

"Water," Lauren whispered. "She's begging for water." But no one brought water to the Maid of Orleans, and no one rescued her from the flames. All of her friends had abandoned her.

When the hologram crumbled back to the pages, Lauren sucked in a breath. It was so awful! How could anyone face such a cruel execution? According to the stories, Joan of Arc had an opportunity to recant her beliefs and avoid the torture, but she chose truth over lies, and by that decision, she chose torture over comfort.

Tears poured down Joan's cheeks. "Are you saying ..." Her voice cracked, almost shattering. "Are you saying that Lauren will suffer the way I did?"

"It depends." Abaddon closed the book. "If Lauren wants to be an Oracle of Fire like you or her mother, such a fiery trial is essential. At the very least, she must be willing to give her body to the flames, and God is never fooled by lip-service willingness. Like you who withstood the fires of persecution rather than recant your faith, like Sapphira who jumped into the river of lava to infuse the death of Jesus into her bosom, and like Bonnie who allowed me to melt her flesh rather than speak a lie about her purity, so Lauren must welcome her own flames of refinement." He drew his snout close to Lauren. This time his eyes flashed red. Flames erupted in his pupils. "She must sacrifice for the sake of others, a supremely selfless act that will sear her soul. And facing fear of death will defeat all fears forevermore."

Lauren averted her eyes. His stare was too hot, too piercing. Could she do something like that? She wasn't a courageous heroine like Joan. She didn't have the faith of her mother. Believing the sermons about Jesus was easy enough, but could she sacrifice for others, especially in the face of flames?

"Yet, as I indicated earlier ..." Abaddon set a claw on the hourglass. The sand drained even more slowly than before. "The

299

predictability factor is quite low. My experience tells me that sacrifice is inevitable, but some faithful pilgrims manage to avoid the flames. We shall see."

Joan lowered her head. "I assume the possibility that we both will avoid the flames is low indeed."

"Since the two of you will be practically inseparable, I assume you will suffer or thrive together, which will be beneficial for Lauren. When the time comes for her to choose a sacrificial path, you will be there to guide and comfort her. In your incorruptible state, you will not be affected by the current corruption that plagues Earth, so your counsel will be vital. Since you have already taken the path of a martyr, your advice will be better than anyone else's, for what potential martyr can consult with those who have gone before her? This will be a first in history."

Lauren let the word form on her lips. *Martyr.* It sounded so … so morbid, yet … holy. Reading about martyrs had always been scary, the stuff that blossomed into nightmares. Just burning a finger felt like torture, and it stung for days. How could someone subject her entire body to flames? Maybe sacrificing for a close friend was reasonable, even noble, but burning to ashes? It seemed impossible.

"Is the decision for us to go together set in stone?" Joan asked.

"It is not. The offer for Lauren to stay in comfort still stands. If you go without her, you will go as a warrior, and Lauren will enjoy peace while she serves the displaced refugees, which is a fine and honorable position. If you and Lauren go together, you will be her faithful companion, guiding her with the wisdom you are so capable of providing, especially in times of trial. The difference is that you will not be the general that I expected you would be."

Joan nodded. "I see."

"Do you really?" Abaddon's face took on what looked like a smirk. "I think perhaps you do not. You were in a servile position early in life, but you grew accustomed to command. It will be interesting to see if you will adapt to a servant's role again."

"Abaddon, you should know by now that your verbal posturing will not intimidate me." Joan took Lauren's hand and enfolded it in both of hers. Warmth flowed up Lauren's arms and through her body. "I am ready to guide you through this, Lauren. I will neither leave you nor forsake you. If you have to suffer in flames, I will suffer at your side. Yet, you still have a choice. You may stay here, and I will go alone. I have already been through the fire, and I am not afraid to burn."

Lauren looked into Joan's blazing eyes. Such courage! Such love! How could anyone be at peace when faced with torture? As the answer came to Lauren's mind, she nodded. Peace when facing flames comes to someone who has already conquered them. "We will go together, and I will count on you to stay at my side, no matter what."

"Then it is settled." Joan turned back to Abaddon. "What do we do now?"

He nodded toward the portal. "Lauren will open the shutters, take the birthing plants, and return to the museum room. The gas has dissipated, so there is no danger. She will then call upon you to resurrect from a plant. Because of the unusual circumstances, or rule-breaking, as I see it, she will not need anything but a call from her heart to bring you into the plant. There will be no need for special timing or a song. When you rise from the plant, you and she will go to Earth together. Only there will you be able to save Matt and many others from life-threatening peril."

"To Earth through the museum room portal?" Lauren asked. "It has a hole, but it wasn't big enough for anyone to go through when I was there."

Abaddon drew his head closer and lowered his voice. "Let wisdom guide you. If you can discern how to pass through that portal, then do so, but the danger is great, because two enemy soldiers are still at the other side. There is another portal in a cave in Second Eden's Valley of Shadows. That way is clear of enemies, but you will need a winged transport to get there, and fumes from the mouth of Elijah might still rest in the valley. Dragons are in Second Eden who might be willing to aid you—Karrick, Albatross, and Grackle. The two latter dragons are not as intelligent as others, but they are friendly and accommodating."

Lauren repeated the names silently, committing them to memory. Riding a dragon shouldn't be too bad. Still, getting to the Second Eden cave had another obstacle. "Zohar closed the portal to Second Eden. How do I get through it? And isn't everything covered with lava?"

302

"You left your portal-opening device in the museum room. Although it had trouble calculating the necessary settings before, it is able to replicate what it has witnessed."

Lauren nodded. The operating manual had said that Apollo registers and records all light anomalies. She could scroll through the database and find the spectral readings of Zohar's portal-opening flames.

"Once the portal is open," Abaddon continued, "you will have to use wisdom and intelligence to navigate the lava. Although it has cooled greatly, it will burn your skin."

"Thank you. Is there anything else I need to know?"

"Only to be ready for events to unfold in unexpected ways. If not for your mind-reading abilities, you and Joan would be stopped before you take your first step."

"Do you mean I should—"

"That is all I will say." He waved a wing toward the shutters. "Be on your way. Time is of the essence."

Lauren grasped the hourglass.

"Leave that here."

Lauren jerked her hand away. "But how will I know when Matt will face—"

"You will *not* know. That is how faith begins. In fact, with this new arrangement, the time until your brother's peril might not be the one being measured. It is possible that the grains of sand count down to your own peril, or perhaps no one's at all. Such is the nature of the future."

Joan kissed Lauren on both cheeks. "Au revoir, mon amie. I will see you soon. Be brave, and above all remember that from now on there is no turning, no looking back."

"No turning. No looking back. I'll remember." Lauren stepped away, sliding her hand out of Joan's. She strode to the shutters. Next to the wall, five birthing plants stood in their buckets, three large and bulging and two barely sprouted. "Which one do I take?"

"Take them all and leave them in the museum room," Abaddon said. "The tree of life will provide light and warmth, so they will survive. You will call for Joan there, and when you do, you will learn which one to harvest."

Nodding, Lauren turned toward the portal and opened the shutters. A faint odor wafted past, but it carried no bite. With the tree still burning silently, it seemed that the museum room had its own air-purifying system.

She hoisted the plants one at a time over the brick wall, then vaulted in to join them. She looked back through the portal. Staring intently at each other, Abaddon and Joan appeared to be in conversation. Lauren trained her ears, hoping to pick up some words. After all, her own life was at stake.

"J'ai attendue longtemps pour ma résurrection, pour mon retour au combat," Joan said. "Pourquoi maintenant?"

Lauren frowned. Why hadn't she studied harder in French class? *A long time, resurrection,* and *combat* were easy to translate, but the rest was a mystery.

Abaddon's blue eyebeams trained on Joan. "Parce que la guerre est sur nous. Votre résurrection et votre combat ne sera pas ce que vous attendez. Lauren a besoins seulement d'une compagne, pas une guerrière."

"Une compagne?" Joan glanced at Lauren. Even from this distance the flush in Joan's cheeks was easy to see.

Lauren closed the shutters. Joan was clearly troubled, and the presence of an eavesdropper couldn't help. Besides, the French words flew by too quickly to comprehend. Still, Abaddon had said *Lauren,* so she was involved somehow.

With firelight illuminating the room, she bent low and skirted the tree on the Heaven portal side. As she picked up Apollo, she cast a glance toward the Earth portal. Now two men stood inside the cave she and her father had entered, both carrying rifles and pacing nervously. At least they were distracted. They wouldn't be paying attention to the shifting shadows through the peephole. There was no sign of the third man, the one who had retrieved the mustard gas. Maybe he had left to find another weapon to penetrate the museum room.

Lauren set Apollo by the Second Eden portal, then hurried back and forth to Abaddon's shutters, carrying a birthing plant each time. When she had collected all five, she sat with Apollo in her lap and browsed the menu selections on its top. "Let's see," she whispered to herself, "History, Readings, Sort Options, Most Recent." She began reading data and time stamps, pressing a button to scroll from one to the next. Most of the readings appeared to be similar. Since Apollo registered fluctuations, it probably picked up even flickering light from the tree of life. Finally, a much higher reading appeared for ultraviolet and X-ray range. This had to be Zohar's fire.

She programmed Apollo's flash with identical numbers and set it in front of the Second Eden portal. Now to call for Joan.

Kneeling, she gathered the buckets in a circle, setting the largest ones close to her knees. If Joan were to grow as quickly as Zohar did, it made sense that she would start as big as possible. All five had a base stem with two leaves pressed together like praying hands. The leaves bent outward at each side as if they held something within, though the smallest two couldn't hold anything bigger than a hen's egg.

She glanced again at the Earth portal. The men were gone now. At this point, it didn't matter where. They could easily be guarding the tunnel while out in the crater, so going through that passageway to Earth wouldn't be safe.

She searched her mind for a call, something that reflected her heart. Joan's words were so scary, yet so encouraging at the same time. It seemed that Joan encompassed the dark fears of a hundred nightmares while at the same time acting as the awakening voice that shattered the terror and assured the sleeper that it was all just a dream.

After taking a deep breath, she called in a soft tone, "Joan of Arc, my friend, my companion in this journey, come to me and use your light to help me find my way through the darkness we will face on our dangerous path."

As light from the tree flickered across the plants, she scanned each one for any sign of movement. After a few seconds, one of the smaller plants wiggled, and a slight glow bled through its tiny leaves.

Lauren pulled it closer. It had to be the one. Even if it didn't grow quickly, maybe the delay would give the lava more time to cool.

With trembling hands, she peeled back the leaves and let the white sac roll into her palm. She tore the sac away, revealing a glass egg similar to the one that eventually hatched Zohar, though much smaller. Although transparent, there was no sign of anyone inside. With Zohar, he was visible right away.

Two eyes appeared on the egg's surface, blinking, then a blue light glowed within. The egg lifted from her palm and floated toward her until it hovered a few inches in front of her eyes.

Tingles ran along Lauren's scales. A thin beam of light shot out from the egg and struck her forehead with something sharp that penetrated deep inside, as if the egg had launched a harpoon and pierced her skull deep enough to lodge in her brain. Yet, it brought no discomfort.

The eyes blinked again, and a voice entered Lauren's mind, unspoken, a stream of thoughts. *Bonjour, mon amie. As Abaddon promised, I am your compagne ... your companion.*

DISCOVERED

Matt opened his eyes. He sat upright with his back against something soft. Above, stars twinkled in the night sky in a dazzling display. His cloak covered his arms, and a woman clasped her hands loosely over his torso, her arms wrapping around him from behind, barely illuminated by a wavering light. A fire burned several yards away, and a man paced in front of it, making his long shadow cross Matt from left to right, then back again. He appeared to be talking on a phone, his voice too low to detect. With his other hand clutching one of the assault rifles, he appeared to be ready for battle, maybe even expecting an immediate threat.

Sliding his fingers under the clasped hands, Matt lifted them gently out of the way and sat up. The wrapping arms belonged to Listener. She slept with her back against the crater's boundary wall, her head cushioned by a duffel bag. Two AK-47 rifles lay on the ground to her right.

Only a few steps to her left, Valiant reclined against the wall cradling Mom, which meant that the man on the phone had to be …

"Dad?" Matt whispered.

Matt's father spun toward him and lowered his phone. "How're you feeling?"

His joints popping, Matt climbed to his feet. Everything hurt from toes to scalp, especially his pounding head. "Pretty terrible."

Dad lifted the phone again and said, "I'll see you in a few minutes," then slid it into his pocket as he rushed to Matt. He pushed a shoulder under Matt's arm and propped him up. "I heard how you tried to heal me. Thank you for that."

"You're welcome, but I guess Mom's gun really did it, right?"

"Apparently. I'm sure you contributed." Dad pulled away but kept a hold on Matt's arm. "You okay now?"

"Yeah. I'm recovering. Thanks." As Matt steadied himself, he nodded toward Mom. "How is she?"

"Exhausted. Spent. Any word that means totally wiped out. According to Valiant, she shot me full of energy, and the candlestone inside her body absorbed more of her energy and refilled the gun again. He said it was like watching someone getting stretched on a rack. If he hadn't taken the gun away and turned it off, she would have delivered another dose. I'm not exactly a hundred percent, but one dose was enough to revive."

"Where is the gun now?"

Dad patted one of his pockets. "She wasn't in any condition to object. We'll talk about it when she wakes up."

Matt looked again at the dark sky. "How long was I out? Last I remember, it was daylight."

"A few hours. It's good, though. Everyone's getting some rest."

A boiling sensation stewed in Matt's stomach. "I might be getting sick from the healing, but—"

"Danger?" Dad lifted the rifle to his hip. "I feel something, too. It's kind of vague, though. No real direction or closeness."

"Well, we were tracking Semiramis. She might be the cause."

"And Eagle and a girl named Cheer," Dad said, nodding. "I heard. But we never found them. The only way out of here is by chopper. Years ago, we had the world's longest rope ladder that Yereq used to climb in and out, but it rotted. Even if it were still here, they couldn't have climbed out."

"Any other ideas?"

Dad scanned the sky. "I'm wondering if Semiramis was able to call for Arramos. He wouldn't have any trouble carrying all three out."

"Arramos. Yeah, I heard about him. Not a dragon I want to meet." Matt gestured toward his father's pocket. "I noticed you were on the phone."

"Right. Talking to Walter. He's on his way with Ashley and Gabriel and my parents. They'll probably be here in about ten minutes. They flew in *Merlin* to the nearest airport and picked up the helicopter there. Good thing my mother knows how to fly one, but Walter said he'd learn how on the way. They said they had to get my father to Second Eden for a potential cure, something about a cannibalistic parasite, but Walter explained it too fast for me to pick it all up."

Matt gestured toward his father's facial wounds, now sealed and clean, though bruises remained across both cheeks as well as his chin and forehead. "What happened to you? It looks like you got put through a meat grinder."

"It's a long story, and I'll tell it all when everyone is here, but to make it short …" Dad nodded toward the low cave. "Lauren, my mother, and I went in there to find a portal that we thought might lead to your mother. Once I opened it, we got ambushed by the military."

"Military? Do you mean the U.S. Army?"

"Probably a combination of U.S. and U.N. forces. I saw some army stripes, but not on all the uniforms."

"Good guess, then." Matt nodded. "Go on."

"Well, Lauren went through the portal while I stayed here to protect my mother. They beat me and my father to a pulp, but he and my mother got away. But now the soldiers got the worst of it. All three who were left behind are dead. Listener killed the first one, and we gave the other two a chance to surrender, but they came out blasting. Valiant and Listener made short work of them."

"It's good to have some firepower on our side." Matt pressed a hand on his stomach. The feeling of danger wouldn't go away. Still, it wasn't increasing. No use for alarm. "Do the soldiers have reinforcements coming?"

"I assume so. Whoever sent them has to know by now that they were stranded, so we're expecting company. But we can't escape. Until Walter gets here, we're proverbial fish in the barrel."

"No escape?" Matt looked at the fire. "What happened to the portal?"

"It's closed. I think the fire from a helicopter I blew up was keeping it open, but it dwindled at a bad time. Karrick went back to Second Eden to tell Albatross not to worry about picking up anyone in the valley, and when he returned, the portal had shrunk too much for him to get through. I tried restarting the wreckage with my fire breathing, but it wouldn't relight. The combustibles are gone, and there isn't much to burn around here. The fire I have now is burning the dead soldiers' uniforms, but it's not enough to open the portal. It'll peter out soon."

"Did Mom tell you about the devastation in Second Eden?"

Dad nodded. "It's a wasteland."

"That's a mild term." Matt kicked a stone toward the fire. "From what I heard, I think the whole thing was planned."

310

"I thought that might be the case. You can tell me your theory when we all get together."

"Sure, but I don't get why Earth's forces would want to destroy Second Eden instead of just taking it over."

Dad shrugged. "Control. Power. Who knows? Anyway, now that communications are open between the hospital and Lois, we can keep in touch. We heard that Adam's been forced to operate Larry under governmental guidance. They have a goon squad there monitoring every communication, but that works out for us, because we can feed them information that will put them on the wrong track. It's not a good situation for Adam, but he's a trooper. He can handle it."

"Any update on whether or not the government has access to a Second Eden portal?"

"None so far, but Valiant sent word with Karrick for the men to get ready for battle. He says that Elam has prepared them well, and with the women and children gone, their minds will focus on combat."

"Let's hope we can keep the battle away from them," Matt said. "They're a brave bunch, and they have weapons, but they're no match for an all-out assault."

"Agreed. I hope they can concentrate on rebuilding their villages. Valiant said Second Eden is quick to recover from volcanic eruptions, something about the organic material in the lava allowing vegetation to flourish."

Matt jerked his thumb toward the wall. "Did he tell you about the problem with the companions here?"

Dad nodded. "But they're doing better now. As soon as it got dark, the little eggs perked up a bit, though not nearly to the point they should be."

"Maybe the sunlight here does something." Matt scanned the sky again. As before, the stars seemed brighter than usual and countless, though the crater walls blocked all but a narrow view. "Where are we, anyway? I mean, I know we're on Earth, but what part?"

"Montana, near Flathead Lake."

"Montana. I've never been here before, but I've read a lot about it, even a couple of novels that were set here." Matt stepped closer to the center of the crater to improve his view of the stars. "Do the stars look strange to you? There's not much of a view down here, but they look closer somehow."

Dad looked up. "They call Montana big sky country, so it's probably just ..." He blinked. "Hmmm ... They *do* look strange."

While they continued staring, a feminine voice broke the silence. "You did not tell me that your stars sing." Listener stood behind them looking at the sky. She closed her eyes and breathed deeply. "Their song is lovely, too beautiful to describe. I don't understand the language, but my companion seems to be invigorated by it."

Her companion sat on her shoulder, a dim blue light blinking within. Listener turned her head and petted its top. "She's still not quite back to normal, but at least she's communicating with me."

"Is Valiant awake?" Dad asked.

"No, but his companion is. I saw him blinking—" Listener cocked her head. "I hear something. An engine and whipping wind."

"Walter's helicopter?" Matt asked.

"Let's hope so. If it's not—" Dad's brow bent. "I sense something."

The boil in Matt's stomach ignited into a burning inferno. "Danger. I feel it."

Dad kicked through the fire and brushed sand over the flames. As the light died away, he raised his rifle and pointed it toward the top of the crater. "Get Valiant and the other guns!"

"I'm on it!" Matt spun toward the wall, but his legs cramped, sending him into a tumble. As he slid painfully across the rocky ground, Listener ran past him.

"Stay low, Matt! We'll take care of it!" She shifted Mom from Valiant's arms to the ground and hoisted Valiant to his feet. After shaking off his slumber, Valiant grabbed the two guns, gave one to Listener, and ran with her to Dad's side. Their companions wobbled on their shoulders but managed to stay perched.

"Son!" Dad, barely visible now, tossed the candlestone gun. When Matt caught it, he added, "Give it to your mother. I trust her to use it wisely."

While the trio aimed their rifles at the sky, Matt crawled to Mom. His calf muscles clenched, sending torture through his legs, but he had to go on. When he reached her, he helped her sit against the wall with the duffel bag behind her head. She opened her eyes halfway and whispered. "Matt. You're awake."

"Shhh. Don't waste your energy." With only starlight guiding his way, he slipped the gun into her hand. His muscles eased a bit. "Dad says he trusts you to use it wisely."

She nodded. "As I would trust him."

He turned toward their three defenders. "I don't hear the choppers yet, but I guess Listener's ears picked them up from pretty far away."

Mom blinked rapidly, then her eyes widened. "I had a dream." Her breathing spiked to quick, shallow gasps. "We cannot win this battle. We have to surrender."

The roar of an engine finally filtered into the crater, followed by the sound of helicopter blades beating the wind.

"We have three trained warriors with assault rifles," Matt said, pulling up his cloak's hood to better conceal himself, "and they're standing in the dark. An enemy helicopter can't take them out

313

before they shoot it full of holes. There's no way. And besides, it could be Walter. The danger I'm sensing might be Semiramis coming out of hiding somewhere."

"Matt, my dream was blurry." Her words pulsed through rapid breaths. "I saw headlights coming at me, like a hundred cars on the road. It was windy, very windy. My hair was blown about. A voice spoke out of the wind telling me to go with them. I knew if I resisted, all would be lost."

"Just settle down—it'll be all right." He compressed her hand lightly. "Not every dream is a prophecy. There aren't any roads down here, much less cars, so—"

The engine roar heightened. Lights appeared over the lip of the crater—three, then six, then a dozen, looking like drifting stars thousands of feet above.

"Choppers." Staying on his knees, Matt straightened as the lights panned across the encircling wall. "We're trapped."

314

Wearing Sir Barlow's gloves, Lauren picked up one of the fallen leaves from the tree of life and relit it from the tree's flames. Using it like a match, she began spreading the flames across the Second Eden side of the tree.

Joan floated around her head, blinking with blue light and darting from one point to another like a luminescent dragonfly. *Your experience in these matters is beautiful to behold, mon amie. You are wise to restore a view of the portal before attempting to open it.*

"Well, I didn't want lava pouring in here. Abaddon said it's cooled, but he didn't say how cool."

Joan zipped in front of Lauren's eyes. *I enjoy hearing your voice, but remember that you can speak to me with your mind. In times of trouble, silence might be required.*

Lauren nodded. *I understand.*

As she relit one leaf after another, the growing flames seemed to pierce her mind—warm and soothing. After the terrifying journey through Hades, the lonely wait in the midst of wailing laments, and the harrowing escape from the volcano, now seemed to be the first chance to rest, both physically and mentally. For the moment, peace reigned.

Joan brushed against Lauren's cheek. *I sense relief in your mind.*

"There is some relief." With the flames now spreading on their own, Lauren took a step back from the tree. "I still have a lot of questions."

Speak them. I might not have answers, but it often helps to give voice to puzzles.

Lauren spread both hands and let the relaxing glow bathe her palms. "I feel ... well ... inconsistent, I guess. When a demon killed my best friend and I had to ride with him to a prison, I was scared, but I still managed. Looking back, it's kind of hard to believe what I did."

Yes, Abaddon told me about some of your trials before you arrived. Your courage was exemplary.

"I guess so, but when I was sitting alone in one of the tunnels here listening to the laments of condemned souls, I cried like a baby."

Such a display of emotion should not raise doubts, Lauren. Compassion is a beautiful expression of love.

Lauren grasped Joan and let her sit in her palm. As the eyelets on the glassy surface blinked, a blue glow from within pulsed. "I felt sorry for them." Lauren pointed at herself. "But I felt sorrier for me. I kept wondering if I would come here when I die. Why should I believe that I can escape when so many other people didn't?"

Ah! I know these thoughts well. Joan rocked to and fro. *All my life I risked many dangers to serve my Lord, far more than most. Yet,*

I still feared the dark void that lay beyond the fires of execution. When one of my persecutors asked me if I was in a state of grace, I did not know how to answer. Of course, the question was merely a trap. Saying yes would give them opportunity to accuse me of pride, and saying no would be a confession that I am not one of God's children, which would have fueled their accusations that I am a sorceress. Although aware of their schemes, the question became a true quandary. How could I know for certain whether or not I was in a state of grace and preserved for entry into Heaven? So I answered, "If I am not, may God put me there; if I am, may God so keep me."

Lauren blew a breathy whistle. "I don't blame you for dodging the question. It was loaded."

A dodge, indeed, but it was a faithful dodge, a true expression of my troubled thoughts. Joan's light dimmed. *And my thoughts grew even more troubled when I awoke as Abaddon's prisoner. That place surely was not Heaven, and it resembled no paintings of Purgatory that I have ever seen. I wondered out loud if my faith had been nothing more than a mirage. After literally giving my life for the Glorious One, I had still come short of achieving the goal of Paradise. My situation proved my doubts.*

"And do you still have doubts?" Lauren asked.

Shouldn't I have doubts? The egg stopped rocking. *Do you think my current situation is an improvement over my previous one?*

"Well, it's nowhere near Heaven, if that's what you mean, but it's better than dealing with that dragon, isn't it?"

In some ways. Perhaps all will become clear as we continue this journey. Joan lifted from Lauren's hand and rose to her shoulder. *For now, let me consider how I can counsel you regarding eliminating your own doubts. Serving you in this way will be true joy.*

Once the entire tree had regained its blaze, Lauren walked to the portal and scanned the Second Eden scene, still well lit by the moon's bright glow. A sea of hardened lava, black and porous, rose to calf level. Apparently the flow had spread out and covered the field with a foot-high mantle of volcanic material, but if she were to open the portal, would the stuff topple into the museum room?

She shook off the oversized gloves and let them fall to the floor. Probably not. It likely just continued on the opposite side of the portal in an uninterrupted shield.

Although the lava no longer appeared to be in motion, steam rose from holes and fissures throughout much of the black expanse, interrupted by spots of glowing orange. "I guess it's cooler," she said, sighing, "but it still looks hot out there."

Joan floated near the corner of her eye. *Abaddon said to let wisdom guide you, but wisdom and knowledge are inseparable allies. Since it appears to be safe to open the portal, I suggest doing so. That way you can get a better look. Feel the air. Smell the odors. Let all the senses provide the information you need.*

"If there were any holes in the portal, I could hear what's going on over there without opening it. I'm guessing that when Zohar closed it, all the holes went away, and now we would have to heal people with the leaves to poke new holes." She looked again at the Earth portal, still void of guards. Noises filtered in from the hole the mustard gas had seeped through. A distant pop sounded like a gunshot. That route to Earth still wasn't a safer way to go.

Lauren crouched next to Apollo and slid it a few inches in front of the Second Eden portal. She set her finger over the button at the base. "Here goes."

She pushed the button and jumped back. Apollo flashed. A ripple of light ran across the portal from bottom to top, then blinked off. Riding on ash-sprinkled air, a wave of sounds pushed into the museum room—creaking noises, a whistling wind, a warbling trill from far away, and a low growl from even farther.

Inhaling through her nose, she took in the smells. The ash carried an earthy odor, not nearly as foul as expected, and something else tinged the air. What was it? The smell of springtime?

Lauren knelt at the portal boundary and studied the top of the lava shield. Short tufts of grass covered the black field like green whiskers on a dark face. She drew her hand closer to touch the tops of the blades, but the scalding heat made her jerk back. How could such tender grass survive this kind of heat?

"Valiant called this sacred soil," she whispered. "It must have very special properties."

Joan floated down to Lauren's elbow and tipped to the left then the right. *I assume it is special. I have never visited Second Eden, so I know only what Abaddon has told me about the babies who are brought there after dying in their mothers' wombs. For ground to give new life to squandered children, I think it must be sacred and certainly fertile.*

"Then maybe it's safe to walk on." Lauren sat fully and examined the sole of her shoe. It looked thick enough to withstand at least a little burning. She stood and raised her leg, ready to step over the boundary.

No! Joan swept up Lauren's arm and flew in front of her nose, flashing red. *You must walk barefoot on sacred ground, according to the holy word.*

"Barefoot?" Lauren scowled at her. "I noticed that the Second Edeners were all barefoot, but Matt and my mother weren't. And what holy word are you talking about?"

Have you not heard what God told Moses at the burning bush? "Put off thy shoes from off thy feet, for the place whereon thou standest is holy ground." And we have a burning bush here with us. By rights, your feet should be bare already.

Lauren sat down and glanced at the tree. "I think I saw something like that in a movie."

A movie? Joan drew closer to Lauren's eyes and hovered in place for a long moment. Finally, she rocked back and forth as if nodding. *I see that I have much to teach you. Abaddon did not tell me what you lack.*

"What do you mean?" Lauren looked cross-eyed at her. "What do I lack?"

It would make no sense to describe the color of a sapphire to the blind or the sound of a nightingale to the deaf, so I will teach you by experience as we journey together. I told you I would consider how to help you eliminate your doubts, and now the time has come to begin the purging.

"But if I walk barefoot out there, I'll scorch my feet."

And therein lies your first lesson. "When thou walkest through the fire, thou shalt not be burned; neither shall the flame kindle upon thee." I quoted that verse to myself a thousand times while in prison.

"But you *did* burn. You died in flames."

Yet you saw me without the odor of burning flesh or even a scorch mark.

"Right. I assumed that you rose from the …" Lauren nodded slowly. "Okay. I get it. It's a spiritual thing. But that doesn't help me here. My feet are physical, and if I burn them, I won't be able to walk for weeks. I know. I burned a foot once before. It hurts like crazy, and I was on crutches for a week and a half."

Joan flashed red, like a police light's strobe. *Lauren Acacia Bannister, are you trying to educate me about how much pain fire can inflict?*

Lauren blinked at the little egg's eyelets. "Acacia? My middle name is Marie."

319

Your adopted name was Lauren Marie Hunt. Your birth name was Karen Acacia Bannister. From what I have heard, your birth parents have accepted your adopted first name, but you are regaining your middle and last names.

"Oh, so you *do* know quite a bit about me."

I do, but, as I said, I know very little about what you lack. Joan's flashes ebbed. *Lauren, when I underwent my trials, I feared the flames. My tormentors reminded me of them daily, promising slow-burning green wood so that I would suffer all the more. I was terrified. My body quaked. Yet, I did not recant my faith. In a moment of weakness, I did give in on one point, and I am grateful that history has been merciful to me about that, but knowing what I do now, if I were my own companion, I would encourage myself to stand firm and never give in on any point. And do not think that you are putting God to the test with what might seem to be a prideful act of showmanship. You have the gift of heavenly hearing. Listen to his voice crying from the tree itself.* Joan brushed against Lauren's cheek. *Oh, mon amie! I urge you to take my advice. If you can overcome this simple fear and take one step of naked faith, one stride with a heart of courage, the next step will be easier, and you will be well on your way to readiness for greater and more fearful steps.*

Lauren grasped Joan and pulled her down. Opening her fingers, she stared at the little egg in her palm. Why would she be so adamant about this? It didn't make sense. Like she said, it seemed like showing off, not something of real value. Yet, Joan was her companion, called to provide guidance.

"Heart of courage," Lauren whispered. Her father's words returned to her mind. *"Courage isn't always something you plan. … Once in a while you know in advance about difficult times you have to face, and you have a chance to build courage beforehand. … We need tests of courage like those."*

Lauren took in a breath. This was one of those times—facing danger with full knowledge without relying on instinctive actions. If she could do this, whether she flinched or not, the next steps would be easier, as Joan said.

A slight hissing noise emanated from the tree. She cast her gaze on it. It had never made a sound before. Yet, she hadn't really listened to it since Sir Barlow sliced off its leaves. Maybe now …

She rose to her feet and walked toward the tree, keeping her focus on the undulating flames. Joan floated along at chin level and stayed dark and quiet.

As Lauren stared, the fiery leaves formed an image, a person carrying something in an uplifted hand. She stepped closer. A girl? Yes, a girl, and she carried a cross.

Flames from the leaves drifted to the cross, clarifying the rest of the scene, as if the tree had created a viewing portal into another world. The girl, white-haired and barefoot, stood at the edge of a precipice, her cross ablaze.

321

Lauren squinted. Sapphira! Abaddon had mentioned her sacrifice. Could the tree be replaying it now?

Sapphira lifted her gaze high and shouted, "I was born Mara, a slave girl of the earth!"

The words echoed in the museum. Lauren glanced around. The voice and the echo were both so real, as if Sapphira actually stood in the room.

Sapphira shouted again. "And I once knew you as Elohim!"

Her words continued to echo, seeming to wrap Lauren in ribbons of voice, much like one of Joran and Selah's sound barriers. After two orbits around her head, the ribbons flowed into her ears and bathed her mind with pulses of emotion. Ah! Pure joy! Release from chains! The delight of freedom! Could this be what Sapphira was feeling?

Sapphira called out, "But now I call you Jehovah-Yasha!"

More ribbons poured forth, radiant and vibrating. These, too, rode the fire's light and poured into Lauren's mind. Ecstasy surged. She lifted her hands toward the ceiling. Bliss! Light bursting forth and filling the darkness! Had anyone ever felt such glory?

Now Sapphira's voice filled the room with booming resonance. "I finally know what you want me to do! You want me to die! And to be raised from the dead as Sapphira Adi!" She waved her cross over her head in a circular motion, creating a rising cocoon of fire. A cylinder of flames descended from above, and the two fires met, swirling in the air.

Lauren lowered her hands and scooted a step closer, breathless. "You want me to die," she whispered, "to be raised from the dead."

Sapphira stepped to the edge of the precipice. "Now take me where you want me to go, whether to heaven or to hell, to England or to Montana, or keep me here in this tomb forever. I will be content to serve you no matter what you decide … Jehovah-Yasha."

Sapphira lowered the burning cross and hugged it against her chest. The flames spread across her clothes, and the cross melded into her skin. Then, her entire body burst into flames, and she leaped into the chasm. The hovering cylinder shot down after her and wrapped her up in a fiery coil.

The call echoed, "Jehovah-Yasha … Jehovah-Yasha …"

As Lauren stared at the falling fire, she blended in her own voice. "Jehovah-Yasha."

The cross of Christ is in Sapphira's heart, Joan whispered. *If you are to die to yourself and be raised to new life, you must embrace the same fire. It is not enough to mentally accept pulpit sermons; you must join Jesus on the cross. Let him purge your sin with holy fire. Let faith conquer fear. The Oracles of Fire have shown you the way. And take courage, I am with you.*

Her respirations shallow and fast, Lauren focused on a flaming leaf. "This isn't just a spiritual thing. I touched one of the flames. It's real. It burns."

As any fire does. It would be foolish to intentionally touch a normal flame, but this is holy fire from the tree of life. To those who lack faith, it is a consuming flame that destroys, but to those who embrace it with faith, it is a purging fire that cleanses and raises to new life. Have faith, my precious friend. Jehovah-Yasha wants to enfold you in his flaming arms.

Keeping her eyes open, Lauren sucked in a breath, walked between two branches, and grasped a burning cluster of leaves in each hand. The flames burned her skin, but she held on. Heat roared up her arms and across her back. Quaking violently, she cried out, "It … it hurts. Oh, it hurts so much!"

Be brave, Lauren. The fire purges your sin, not your life. Hold on!

Gasping for breath, Lauren closed her eyes and shouted, "Jehovah-Yasha!"

The heat ebbed. The pain eased. Lauren blinked at the tree. The scene with Sapphira had vanished. Tongues of fire brushed against her cheeks and chin, but they felt warm and soothing rather than hot.

She stepped back and rubbed her cheek. No burns at all. "I feel …" She took in a deep breath. "Lighter?"

Ah! An excellent word! Joan zipped around in front of Lauren's nose like an excited puppy. *Fears are vanquished!*

"Fears …" Lauren looked toward the portal. Beyond it lay the sleeping mats outside the museum room where the wandering spirit had spoken to her, though they were no longer visible. "I don't have to fear Hell anymore."

323

Not Hell or anything else. And such fearlessness is freedom to walk in whatever path God leads you, even a lava field.

"Will fire not hurt me now?"

Joan's light blinked red. *You are not invulnerable to normal flames, if that's what you mean. Lava can still kill you, but continue to trust that this walk of faith on the lava field will not.*

Lauren dropped to a knee, untied her boot, and jerked it off, then repeated the process with the other boot. After peeling off her damp socks, she rose again and wiggled her toes as she looked at Joan. "I'm ready."

Joan glowed blue from within her glassy shell. *So be it. The holy ground awaits.*

324

19

CHAPTER

TRAILBLAZER

As Lauren walked from the tree to the Second Eden portal, she eyed the boundary. The rectangular opening had stayed the same size, giving more evidence that the museum room portals didn't shrink over time as others did.

She picked up her night-vision goggles and helmet from atop the backpack and put them on, leaving the goggles dangling at her chest. After removing the clothing, tools, and other items from the pack, she pushed Apollo into the main pocket, zipped it up, and hoisted the straps over her shoulders. It wasn't much to carry, but having her hands free might be helpful later.

Taking a deep breath, she lifted a foot to vault onto the grass-covered lava field. When the heat rose to her bare sole, she stopped.

Do not waver! Joan called. *He that wavereth is like a wave of the sea driven with the wind and tossed.*

"Okay. Here goes." Lauren jumped and landed with both feet on the dark field. Instantly, a sharp burning sensation shot into her soles. She bent her knees to jump back.

No! Joan's light burst like a camera flash. *Do not trust in fears! Panic is the devil's work. Trust in God.*

Gasping for breath, Lauren lifted a foot. The skin stuck to the ground and peeled away. Bullets of pain ripped up her leg and spine, sending jolts of torture pounding into her head.

Walk, Joan ordered. *Keep moving until the trial is complete.*

Lauren gritted her teeth, growling, "What kind of torturer are you?"

Walk! Standing still will be your death!

Lauren set her foot down and lifted the other. It, too, stuck and peeled. More pain sent horrific spasms up her calves. Sweat poured down her arms. Her scales tingled wildly. What did the path behind her look like? A layer of her skin spread across the grass and lava? Gasping, she whispered, "No turning. No looking back."

As she took step after step, more skin peeled, resulting in new pain, though less with each repetition. Soon, the spasms eased. The grass underneath felt soft and cool. A breeze dried the sweat, bringing relief to her entire body.

You may stop. Your trial is complete. You may now view what has been accomplished.

Lauren stopped and looked back. Footprints of blood and skin marked her path from the portal, still open with the tree clearly visible.

Joan floated several inches in front of her nose. *How do you feel?*

"Good." Lauren lifted a foot and looked at the sole. The skin was fresh, pink, and unharmed. "It was terrible. I felt it burning and peeling my skin."

Yet, you are healed.

"But I wasn't before. I burned. It hurt like crazy." She lowered her foot and pointed at the trail of flesh and blood. "There's proof."

Proof indeed. Undeniable proof. As Joan's eyelets blinked, soft blue light flowed like mist. *Lauren, this is the story of the Christ, the theme of life itself. We are of the light, so we sacrifice. We give of ourselves. We burn and let others bask in the warmth of our glow. Their joy brings us joy. Oracles of Fire burn in the flames of selfless service, and unlike the tree of life, our bodies are consumed. We suffer. We die. Our physical lives are but seeds that fall to the ground and perish, but they sprout and grow to life eternal. And our new bodies?* Her light flashed brightly. *Oh, mon amie! Our new bodies are like the tree! We blossom and never wither. We burn but are never consumed. We lift up our fiery hands in praise to the king of all, Jesus the Christ! And the evidence of our sacrifice remains, bloody footprints that will never wash away, a path to guide other newly created oracles. For those who feel the fire burning within will need a guiding lamp. They will be afraid, because they will look around themselves and see that no one understands. Their friends and peers are following the idols of the world, lacking vision, blinded by selfish pleasures destined to perish. Seekers of truth know there is a deeper walk, a holy calling, but unless they are able to see the trail that others have blazed, they will not know how to take those first painful, fiery steps, the walk of faith that cleanses the soul.*

Joan let out a long sigh. *The steps that you have now taken.*

Lauren stared again at her bloody footprints. The wetness sparkled in the light of the moon. Joan's words were so amazing, so filled with meaning. They rang like bells chiming news of liberation. A cleansed soul! How wonderful the feeling! Now everything Micaela had done made so much more sense. She always

327

seemed to go against the flow. It felt so good when Micaela sat down next to her at lunch when no one else bothered to talk to the new girl from Nashville, the girl who seemed to glow in the dark. Micaela didn't care what other people thought, whether they rolled their eyes at the cross she wore around her neck or whispered derisively about the Bible she kept in her backpack. And now …

Lauren bit her lip hard. And now Micaela was dead, the victim of a blazing explosion. Because of her kindness, her willingness to be a friend to a strange girl, she became the victim of her own fiery ordeal. She had blazed a trail of sacrifice. Maybe now she was an Oracle of Fire.

"So …" Lauren swallowed to loosen her throat. "So does that mean I'm an Oracle of Fire now?"

Perhaps. You have merely burned your feet. An Oracle of Fire must be burned body and soul, at least in her willingness to be a living sacrifice. At the tree of life, the fire burned and purified your soul, but your body remains.

Lauren shook her head. "I don't understand."

Of course you lack understanding. You have a long journey left to walk. Joan nuzzled Lauren's cheek and floated to her ear, whispering, *Lauren, I have spoken to you plainly, and I have given you sound wisdom, but I will not always be so straightforward. You have taken a baby's first steps, and I have held your hand. A time will come when I must release your hand, for a child never learns to walk on her own while clutching a supporting finger. Yet, I will always be here when you need me. You might stumble in your ignorance, but I will never let you fall.*

Lauren nodded. "Okay. I get that." She turned and met the little egg's gaze. Joan was right. She had been a mother guiding a baby. It was about time the little girl grew up. "We'd better find that portal."

Joan's glow pulsed. *We will need transportation.*

"I heard a whistle when the portal opened." Lauren scanned the sky. With most of the nearby trees leveled, the horizon was easy to see. Mount Elijah loomed to the north with only a few puffs of smoke rising from its ragged cone. Nearly all the other smoke had blown away, leaving a clear sky in every direction. "I was hoping to find a dragon who could fly us to the Valley of Shadows. Abaddon said we would need a winged transport to get to the cave there."

I suggest calling for one. Abaddon mentioned Karrick, Albatross, and Grackle.

"Right, and he said the latter two weren't as smart. I think I'll call Karrick."

Perhaps you should call all three. Who can tell which one will be close enough to hear you?

"Good point." Lauren cupped her hands around her mouth and shouted toward the volcano, "Karrick! Albatross! Grackle! Can you hear me? I need help!"

She waited, listening. Her scales still tingled, providing excellent hearing. Even the sizzle of cooling lava rose to her ears—a hiss that sounded like a long gasp for breath.

Cupping her hands again, she turned in the opposite direction and called again. "Karrick? Anyone?"

Whirring emanated from somewhere in the field. Lauren pulled up her goggles and looked toward the sound. The form of an elongated airplane took shape about a hundred feet away. With dark colors blending into a dark background, it would be invisible to the naked eye, but the goggles provided good contrast. Why would an airplane be here?

A beam flicked on. Near the center of the airplane, an open hatch created a stairway leading to the ground. A man stood there, holding a flashlight. "Who is out there?"

Lauren pulled down the goggles and turned on her helmet light. She shouted, "Lauren Bannister!"

"Bonnie's daughter?" He shone the light on her face, making her squint again. "How can you stand in the lava field?" The beam drifted down to her feet. "And barefooted!"

"Well, that's hard to explain. I—"

"Never mind." He waved an arm. "Come on in. Let's talk."

Lauren walked gingerly toward the hospital. Although heat rushed into her clothes, nearly blistering her ankles, it seemed to have no effect on her feet. As she drew closer, she whispered to Joan, "Hide in my hair. It's best to avoid questions for now."

I agree. Joan pushed into her hair, nudging upward until she squeezed under the helmet.

When Lauren arrived, the man extended a hand, guided her up the narrow stairway, and ushered her inside. As the stairs lifted to a repeat of the whirring sound, a bank of ceiling lights came to life. The man extended his hand. "Matthew Conner. Bonnie's father." He averted his eyes for a moment before returning his gaze to her. "Your grandfather."

She gripped his hand, then slid her arms around him and gave him a hug. "I'm glad to meet you."

When they drew apart, she tilted her head. "My brother's name is Matthew."

"Yes, I know." He scratched through a mane of unkempt reddish hair, gray at the sides. "Walter assigned it to him during the cover-up operation. He thought it might throw the Enforcers off with a name that was too obvious, if that makes any sense."

"It makes sense. Sort of." Lauren glanced around the corridor. It led to a dark, wider room in both directions. Two beds were visible near the edge of one room, though it was too dark to see if they had occupants. "What is this place?"

"Second Eden's mobile hospital, and I am its resident doctor and part-time pilot. We are in the main vestibule, and we have two dorm areas for patients, one to the front and one to the rear. The pilot's cockpit lies beyond the dorm to the front." Dr. Conner gestured with an arm toward the beds. "Let me show you the rear dorm. I'm sure at least one of our patients won't mind waking up to meet you."

"That would be great."

He reached for her helmet. "May I take that for you?"

She dodged his hand. "No. It's fine. Thanks."

"Okay." A flash of puzzlement crossed his face. "Follow me." When they reached the room, he touched a switch on the wall. Lights flickered on—dim, but bright enough to see twenty beds, ten on each side of the room with one or more people lying on each one. "I won't leave the lights on very long. We're running out of fuel for our generator, and the ground is too hot to get more. When it cools, we'll be able to fill up again."

Dr. Conner touched the foot of someone lying on the closest bed. "Irene, look who's here."

A sheet pulled down from the pillow, revealing a woman with cheeks and forehead so wrinkled, her emaciated face looked no better than skin on a skull. She raised a thin arm and pushed bony fingers through a ragged mop of gray, frizzy hair. She blinked her cadaverous eyes and spoke in a weak whisper. "Who is she?"

"Lauren Bannister. Well, she was Karen Bannister at birth. Now she's Lauren, Bonnie's daughter."

"Our granddaughter?" Her gaze darted past Lauren. "She's even wearing a backpack like Bonnie used to."

"Yes." Dr. Conner gestured with a hand. "Lauren, this is Irene, my wife."

Lauren gave her a friendly nod. "I'm pleased to meet you."

331

The woman's leathery lips bent into a weak smile. "I'd love to give you a kiss, dear, but I know how hideous I look."

Hiding a cringe, Lauren stepped closer. "It's okay." She bent over and kissed Irene's cheek and turned her head to receive a return kiss. Irene's lips felt dry and fragile, barely able to pucker.

As Lauren drew back, she took note of a framed photo sitting on a nightstand. Dr. Conner stood with his arm around a lovely woman, both wearing diving wet suits. With blonde hair and toned body, she looked nothing like the ravaged woman in the bed.

Joan's thoughts seeped through. *Lauren, you have such a tender heart. Kissing that poor woman would have made many girls shudder, yet you did so without hesitation.*

Lauren shifted her eyes toward the helmet. *You can see her?*

I peeked. But I was in no danger of being seen.

Dr. Conner pulled the sheet up and combed his hand through Irene's hair. "Go back to sleep now, dearest. I'm going to show Lauren what I'm working on." He kissed her on the lips. "We'll get through this. I promise."

Irene settled into her pillow and closed her eyes. With a smile on her face, her breathing eased into a deep and steady rhythm.

Lauren tried to count the people. Two to three children slept in some of the beds and only one in others, making it hard to be sure of the numbers. "Are you the only caretaker here?"

"Oh, no. Not at all." He rose and, guiding Lauren by the elbow, walked farther into the room, whispering, "I have some experienced helpers. Steadfast, Pearl, Candle, and Windor, to name a few. Also some of the mothers of the children. Steadfast and Pearl are on duty in the front dorm while the other medical aides sleep."

"When do you sleep?"

"I take a catnap now and then, but I don't see how I can really sleep until I complete my research."

332

"Research?"

Still walking slowly, he waved a hand across the beds. "Many of the sleepers are refugees, women and children who escaped before the eruption. Some are anthrozils who have a parasitic disease that came from the volcano and is now eating away at their energy receptors." He gave her a questioning look. "I assume you know about anthrozils."

She nodded. "And I heard about the disease. It affects the anthrozils who became completely human."

"Correct. And since they are completely human, I assumed they didn't have any energy receptors, so I neglected to look for them. But once I began looking, I isolated a few dozen and found the parasite after several trials. I have dubbed it 'batholith,' which is a volcanic rock formation that has melted and intruded into other strata."

"That name seems appropriate." She caught a glimpse of a woman with a face equally as withered as Irene's. "Are you working on a cure?"

"Most definitely." When they reached the end of the room, he opened a door, touched a switch that turned off the light, and guided her into another room. He flicked on a flashlight and shone it at a table covered with beakers, bottles, and a Bunsen burner with a tube leading to a floor-standing propane tank. The burner's low flame heated a beaker half filled with green liquid.

Dr. Conner touched a laptop on the table and sat on a stool. Several open program windows flashed to life on the screen, each one filled with scrolling lines of labels and numbers. "The overhead lights consume too much energy to risk using, but I can show you what I'm doing." He lit a desk lamp and patted another stool at his side.

When Lauren settled on it, he swept his beam across the laboratory instruments. "I have been trying to replicate a computer model of a parasite that will cannibalize the batholith parasite infecting Irene and five others—Dallas, Elise, Kaylee, Jordan, and Jared. We think Tamara also has it, but that hasn't been confirmed."

"Are they all as sick as your wife … I mean, my grandmother?"

He gave her a gracious smile. "Most are. Jordan is the sickest. Just this evening, we nearly lost her. I don't think she'll live through the night. The others might last a day or two. I hear that Jared is doing the best, but even he is faltering and is trying to get here in time for the treatment I'm working on." He slid the laptop closer and studied the display. "It's as if the most recent eruption enhanced the symptoms, which makes sense. I think the volcanic material aids the parasite, so when it spread through the air, our patients ingested it and fed batholith, you might say, a dose of vitamins."

"How close are you to creating the new parasite?"

"Oh, it's practically done." He picked up the beaker from the burner stand and swirled the thick green liquid inside. "What I lack is the catalyst. I need to subject the raw materials to volcanic temperatures."

Lauren pointed at the burner. "I guess that doesn't get hot enough."

He chuckled. "Not exactly."

"What if someone were to throw the raw materials into Mount Elijah?"

"Wouldn't work. Even if the volcano created the parasite, the heat would kill it soon afterward. The only way it could survive would be for it to escape from the superheated environment within seven minutes after its creation."

"Seven? How can you know that to the minute?"

He pointed at one of the windows on the computer screen that showed an image of a bug-like creature growing and becoming more complex before shrinking again and starting over. "Computer models. A good guess, I think. We can't be one hundred percent certain."

"So if Mount Elijah erupted right away, it might survive."

Dr. Conner nodded. "That's how we think the disease parasite was created in the first place."

"Then the person who invented the parasite must have known when the volcano would erupt."

His expression darkened. "The natives here claim that if a person is thrown into the volcano, it will erupt almost immediately, but in spite of their insistence, I can't rely on superstition. Besides, even if it were true, it would be unethical to ask someone to sacrifice his or her life to create a cure."

Lauren hid a tight swallow. The wandering ghost in Hades! Everything added up. A mad scientist, probably Mardon, manufactured the raw materials to create the parasite, kidnapped a male teenager, and threw him into the volcano from the museum room portal. That's how he knew the precise time Mount Elijah would erupt. But who would believe her crazy theory? Probably no one, especially not a scientist like Dr. Conner.

He slid another beaker that appeared to be filled with soil. "Even if we were able to time an eruption, we would also need a way to deliver the materials safely to the volcano. The necessary enzymes, chemicals, and anthrozil cells require a soil environment with a mixture of organic nutrients, volcanic and nonvolcanic."

"Like what's in the birthing garden?"

"Funny you should say that." He nudged the beaker with a finger. "One of the dragons collected this sample from the garden for me, and it's perfect. It contains dozens of unmodified, native parasites that will mutate into what we need to counter the first batch of mutants."

"How much soil would you need? I mean, if we threw the stuff into the volcano so we could spread the new parasite around, what kind of ... um ..."

"Payload size?" Dr. Conner stroked his chin. "Maybe a large bucketful of soil to go with about two-thirds of the green concoction. Once it disperses, it would spread pretty far, and the new parasites would begin multiplying immediately."

She looked toward the volcano, though it wasn't visible from the lab. "I could take the materials up there, but it wouldn't do any good without the eruption."

"And that's the key to everything." He half closed an eye. "May I see your feet?"

"Um ... sure." She lifted a foot and showed him its now-dirty sole. "Why?"

"Just trying to figure out how you walked out there." He ran a finger along her skin. "That's why I asked Karrick to fetch a soil sample for me. The ground melted the soles of my shoes."

"I guess I have tough calluses." She jumped down from the stool. "I'd better go. I need to get to the portal in the Valley of Shadows."

"Do you know how to open it?"

She touched a backpack strap. "I have Apollo in here."

"Oh, yes. I know about Apollo." He shook his head. "Such a device would have made it easy for Jared to get here, but with the ingredients that enhanced the symptoms still in the air, it is best that he stays away, at least until I can figure out how to simulate a volcanic eruption."

"Maybe we don't need a simulation." Lauren wrapped her fingers around the beaker containing the green liquid. "Can you make more of this stuff?"

"Without a doubt." He lifted his brow. "But why?"

"I'd like to take this beaker and some birthing garden soil to the volcano."

"And pray for an eruption?" He laughed under his breath. "Really, Lauren, that's a noble statement of faith, but it's hardly a scientific approach."

Scientific, Joan murmured from under the helmet. *Someone needs to get back in a training saddle. He's not ready to ride at the front lines.*

Lauren kept a straight face. *Cool your temper, Joan. We're almost finished here.*

"Will it hurt to try? I mean, I could ride a dragon over the volcano and drop it in."

He shrugged. "It is a futile exercise, but I understand the need to want to try every option, even if it's such a long shot."

He grabbed a bottle from the table, poured the beaker's contents into it, and plugged it with a cork. "There. That will travel better."

337

She turned her back toward him. "Will you put it in the outer pocket?"

"Certainly." He unzipped the pocket and set the bottle inside. After zipping it again, he gave it a pat. "All set."

"Do you have something I can scoop soil with? My feet are tough, but my hands aren't."

"I have just the thing. In fact, Karrick used it." Dr. Conner walked to a wall, pulled open a bureau drawer, and withdrew a hand spade. When he returned, he put it in her backpack's main compartment with Apollo. "Now you're ready."

"Except that I need transport. Have you seen any dragons out there lately?"

"Albatross has been on patrol. I suggest calling him."

"Thank you."

He gestured toward a door at the back of the room. "You can leave through the rear access. Better to let everyone sleep. And I will get right back to work."

They walked together to the door. When the hatch opened, letting in a draft of warm air, she gave him another hug. "If you believe in prayer, pray for an eruption at the right time."

"I will." Smiling, he jiggled her helmet playfully. "I'm sorry if I offended you with my overly scientific approach. I will be sure to have the hospital ready to fly on a moment's notice in case the volcano erupts. I kept enough fuel in reserve for an emergency flight."

"I wasn't offended. I understand."

She walked down the stairway, took off her helmet, and jogged slowly toward the birthing garden. Joan pushed out from her hair and floated near her shoulder. *I think I know what your plans are.*

"That's good, because I don't."

EAGLE EYES

When Lauren arrived at the birthing garden, she twisted the backpack around and pulled out the hand spade. Tucking the helmet under her arm, she pushed the spade's metal end into the lava-covered ground and gave it a turn, uprooting a bit of grass. The soil crackled, and smoke rose into the air. "I was going to put it in my backpack, but only the outer material got the fire-retardant treatment. I think the inside would catch on fire."

Joan floated lower as if sniffing the rising smoke. *Very likely.*

"I guess that idea went up in flames." Lauren straightened and put the spade back in the pack. "Almost literally."

You have an innovative mind. Perhaps you will get another idea.

"Either way, I would have to bring Jared first for him to get the benefit. Even if he gets worse from being here, it won't take long to get the cure."

Assuming you can get the volcano to erupt.

"Right. That's not exactly the best assumption, I know."

339

Yet, going to Earth is what Abaddon expected us to do. So let's pro-
ceed and continue to allow wisdom to work out our plans.

"I'd better see if Albatross is around. I've already wasted
enough time." She put the helmet back on and cupped her hands
around her mouth. "Albatross! Can you hear me?"

After calling twice more, she waited. A whistle pierced the air.
Beating wings followed. In the light of the moon, a dragon's silhouette appeared far away in the direction opposite the volcano.
Lauren waved her hand and called again. "I'm over here! Can you
see me?"

Joan flashed brightly, a helpful beacon. Maybe Albatross could
see that.

The dragon drew closer and closer. Soon, his size and color
clarified, a white dragon, smaller than Makaidos and the others.
He swooped and touched down with his claws, then quickly shot
up again with a squeal, tossing Lauren's hair in his breezy wake.

"I'm sorry!" she called. "I know it's hot. Maybe you could just
grab me with your—"

A spray of icy wetness rained on her head and spread across
the ground. Steam shot up along with loud pops and sizzles. Ice
pellets followed and melted on contact with the superheated soil.
Soon, the garden of new grass looked like a sea of fog.

Albatross landed in a slide on the cooled grass. When he
stopped, he swung his head around on his long neck and faced
Lauren, his red eyes gleaming.

"Wait!" Lauren said, raising a hand. "Wait right where you
are."

He blinked, but stayed put. Lauren retrieved the spade and
scooped soil from the area where Albatross had deposited ice. She
lifted the scoop and touched the dark earth with her finger. Hot,
but not scalding. She slid her backpack off, tucked Apollo under

her arm, and began filling the pack, careful to collect soil with shallow scoops.

While she worked, Albatross added more sprays of ice over the area, apparently figuring out what she was doing.

Lauren cast a thought toward Joan. *Who says he isn't as smart as other dragons?*

Not I, Joan said. *He is a most admirable dragon.*

After a few minutes, Lauren had filled the backpack about halfway. Holding a strap, she tested its weight. Not too bad. She could handle it pretty easily.

She pulled the bottle from the pocket, poured the contents over the top of the collected soil, and stirred it with the spade. When it looked reasonably well blended, she placed the scoop and her helmet inside, zipped up the pack, and hoisted it to her back.

Breathing a satisfied sigh, she turned to Albatross. "We need a ride. Will you give us one?"

341

Albatross extended his neck and looked behind Lauren, then withdrew it again, a confused expression on his face.

Joan floated next to Lauren's nose. *I think this good dragon is wondering why you said "we." Since all Second Edeners have a companion, he considers you to be alone.*

"Ah!" Lauren smiled at Albatross. "I have to go to a cave in the Valley of Shadows. Do you know where it is?"

Albatross bobbed his head.

"Can you speak?"

He swung his head from side to side.

"Well, that'll make things more difficult, but at least you can understand me."

He bobbed his head again, this time adding a series of whistles.

"I see," Lauren said, nodding. "You speak with whistles. I suppose the people of Second Eden understand your language."

Albatross cocked his head and let out a whistle with a questioning inflection.

Joan hovered in front of Lauren's nose. *My guess is that he wonders why you speak as if you are not from Second Eden, since you obviously have a companion. I suggest explaining yourself.*

"Right. I keep forgetting." Lauren bowed. "I am Lauren Bannister, daughter of Billy and Bonnie Bannister. I am from Earth, but I have gained a companion by virtue of circumstances I don't have time to explain. I ask you, kind dragon, to provide transport to the Valley of Shadows so I can go through a portal in a certain cave there. It is crucial that I get to Earth as soon as possible. Many lives are at stake."

Albatross lowered his head to the ground. Lauren glanced at Joan and cast a thought her way. *Stairs?*

I think so. Joan descended and hovered close to the dragon's underside. *I am not familiar with dragon riding, though I rode many a horse in my day, but the neck appears sturdy enough to walk upon.*

It's worth a try. Still carrying Apollo, Lauren stepped high on Albatross's neck and climbed up to his back. Once she had settled in place and gripped a protruding spine with one hand and Apollo with the other, she patted his scales. "I'm ready."

Albatross extended his wings and leaped into the air. Lauren lurched backwards, juggling Apollo for a moment before grabbing the dowel again and catching a better hold on the spine.

As the dragon surged upwards, the air cooled, bringing a chill to Lauren's sweat-dampened body. She shivered. Exhaustion had depleted every bodily defense, including resistance to cold. Joan rested on her shoulder, her light glowing blue, though she stayed silent.

Warmth rose from the dragon's scales. It felt wonderful, like forced hot air from a floor vent, and she was a cat ready to curl over the flow and go to sleep. She yawned, then shook her head hard. She couldn't sleep, no matter how exhausted she might be. Fortunately, Albatross rose and fell sharply as he flew, keeping her alert.

Below, Second Eden spread out in all its devastation. Lava fields dominated the landscape, fires dotting the black expanse and a long line of orange in the distance marking the far edge of the lava's march. The huge moon hovering overhead illuminated heaps of logs and stones scattered in every direction. From this high up, it looked as if a child throwing a temper tantrum had kicked his miniature farm set and sent the pieces flying.

The volcano loomed to the left, still spraying a tiny plume of smoke and ash. How odd it seemed to watch it from this vantage point. Not long ago, she poked her head out of nothingness a hundred feet above that very cone, and it wouldn't be hard to go back and do it again since Apollo could easily generate the proper flash. It would be comical to see such a sight now, and it still could serve as another way to enter, though she would need a winged transport to …

She glanced at the dragon's wings as they beat rhythmically at each side. Of course! This dragon understood her words perfectly! She patted his scales. "Albatross, I have something to tell you."

He curled his neck and brought his head close.

"This will sound very odd." She pointed at the volcano. "There is a portal above Mount Elijah. Not long ago, I came through it, my upper body in this world while I stood safely in the other world, but since I was so high in the air and suspended over lava, I couldn't go anywhere. Do you understand?"

Albatross swung his head toward the volcano for a moment, then returned his gaze to Lauren. He gave a quick nod.

"Good." Lauren took in a breath. This would be a big request. "Since you're on patrol, could you keep a watch on that volcano? If someone appears above it the way I described, could you pick that person up and fly him or her to safety?"

Albatross nodded again.

"Wonderful! Please pass that request on to any other dragons you know."

After nodding once more, Albatross straightened his neck and looked ahead. Soon, he descended toward a basin-like feature with a river spilling in from the higher side and spilling out at the opposite end.

Lauren touched the phone, still in her pocket. With the dragon shifting so much, bringing up the map while holding Apollo might be difficult. That river had to be Twin Falls River, though it looked quite different from this angle and distance. Although a thin layer of smoke lay in parts of the basin, it appeared to be blowing away. Maybe the air down there would be breathable.

As they neared the smoke, Lauren lifted her shirt over her mouth and nose and looked at Joan, still perched on her shoulder. *Do you breathe in that little egg?*

Joan's eyelets blinked. *I sense some breathing, and there is something akin to a heartbeat, a pulse of life that thrums like the rhythm of a song. I think it changes depending on your thoughts and mood, which gives me a view into your heart and mind. This will be helpful as I seek how to provide counsel.*

Lauren listened for her own heart. It thumped hard and fast. Was it excitement or terror? In either case, it felt good to know that Joan would be there to help figure things out. *Can you guess what I'm thinking now?*

Perhaps you feel foolish for not bringing one of the masks. We had two extra ones that could have been brought along.

No, but now that you mention it, it was pretty dumb to forget them.

You and I both had many other things on our minds. Joan floated closer to her cheek. *So, what were you thinking?*

Keeping her eyes straight ahead, Lauren smiled. *I was thinking that I'm glad you're with me. I'm glad you're my companion.*

Oh, mon amie! I am glad as well. Joan nuzzled her cheek. *Thank you for saying so.*

When Albatross dove into the smoke, Lauren blinked, trying to find the river again. She patted his scales. "Do you have to …" She coughed, then forced the words out quickly. "To go through this smoke to find the cave?"

Albatross reeled his head back and nodded.

From below, whistles sounded—three chirps and a long warble. Albatross jerked his head back and veered toward the call.

"Wait!" Lauren shouted. "What are you doing? You're supposed to find the cave."

I think he is responding to a higher authority, Joan said. *There is likely no reason to fear.*

Albatross broke into clear air. The river came into view, bright and sparkling in the moon's glow. He landed at the river's edge in a sweeping slide through a stretch of beach sand. When he stopped, he swung his head around, searching all directions. Running water drowned out all other sounds, but the dragon's ears stayed perked.

A whistle sounded again from a forest to the right. Albatross beat his wings and hopped that way. Lauren hugged Apollo and clutched the spine tightly, bouncing with him. The dragon was now like a puppy responding to his master's call, no longer conscious of anything else in the world. Every thump on the ground slammed Lauren's bottom on his scales and shook the backpack. She cringed, hoping the mixture wasn't volatile.

A black teenager dressed in calf-length pants and short sleeves appeared at the edge of the forest. Still bouncing, Lauren tried to look him over. No taller than herself, he stood with his arms crossed, accentuating toned muscles. A flashlight and two daggers hung on his belt, and a companion floated above his ear, drawing attention to his closely cropped hair. With his shirt partially open, a half-dollar-sized medallion glimmered at his chest.

As Albatross bounded toward him, he smiled and clapped his hands, shouting, "Albatross! I was hoping you would come!"

When Albatross arrived, he snaked his neck around the teen and nuzzled his cheek with his own. As he patted the dragon's head, he looked at Lauren. "Who is this young lady you brought to the valley, you silly dragon?"

Lauren set a hand against her chest, trying to catch her breath. With the river's din still high, she raised her voice. "My name is Lauren. I'm from Earth."

"I am Eagle." His smile seemed to light up the valley. "I heard your name from your brother when he came to this world. He seemed concerned about you, so I hope you were able to reunite."

She nodded. "We saw each other for a short time."

"That's good." He angled his head, squinting. "You say you are from Earth, but I see a companion's light in your hair."

Lauren brushed her hair back, revealing Joan. "It's a long story."

"I see." Eagle unraveled Albatross's neck and extended a hand toward her. "I have a long story as well, but it might be best if I learn why Albatross has brought you to this place. This is a time of crisis, not an opportunity to explore."

She took his hand and slid off the dragon's side. "I have to find a cave with a portal leading to Earth. Do you know where it is?"

"I do. In fact, I was there quite recently in the company of a sorceress."

"A sorceress?"

Waving a hand, Eagle laughed. "Don't worry. Semiramis is not a friend."

"You mean Semiramis is here?" Lauren pointed at the ground. "Right here in this valley?"

"She *was* here but not any longer." Eagle gave her a puzzled look. "Do you know her?"

"All too well." Lauren tried to calm down. Getting all worked up over Semiramis's survival wouldn't do any good. "Let's just say she's not my friend."

"As I said, nor is she mine. Our alliance was pragmatic and temporary. We have no allegiances with each other."

Lauren lifted her brow. Pragmatic? Allegiances? This guy had some intellectual depth. "Is the portal open?"

"I don't know. While I was there, the cave had a fiery exit at the back. I hoped that it would provide an escape from the volcano's poisonous fumes, but when I went through it, it burned like fire, and my companion fell to the ground. I decided that following a sorceress into a domain that deactivates my companion would be a very bad idea. I'm glad I left Cheer in the cave so she didn't have to suffer the burn or risk seeing her companion fall."

"Cheer?"

"Cheer is a girl, and I am her protector." He nodded toward the forest. "She's asleep over there."

Lauren looked into his eyes, dark brown, bright and alive. He was so different from most Earth teenagers. "If you don't mind me asking, how old are you? I mean, you look young to be sent here by yourself on a dangerous mission."

He smiled. "I know I look younger than I am. By Earth years, I am sixteen. I am not tall, but my father has trained me well."

Lauren gave his muscular arms a furtive glance. "I'm sure he has."

"I assume that your desire to find the Earth portal is part of your long story."

"It is."

"Then I will lead you to the portal, but I want to avoid exposing Cheer to the danger, so I will ask Albatross to take her to safety."

Lauren nodded toward the hospital. "I just came from your hospital. It's sitting near the garden where the plants give birth to babies. The doctor said he's not going anywhere unless there's an emergency."

"The perfect place." Eagle patted Albatross's neck. "Will you take Cheer to the hospital and return to let me know she is safe? If I am not here, then you are free to patrol."

Albatross bobbed his head with vigor.

"Come." Eagle gestured toward the forest and walked that way. As Lauren followed, the river's noise faded into the background. "When I left the cave with Cheer," he said, "the smoke was quite dense, but since I could provide her with a certain leaf that filters the poison, I thought it better to protect her here than to follow Semiramis."

"What was the pragmatic reason you were with her?" Heat rushed through Lauren's cheeks. "I mean, I know you had no allegiances with her, but ... what I'm trying to say ..."

"Fear no offense, my new friend." Eagle took her hand in his and continued walking. "She told me a convincing story that gave me reason to go along with her for a time, but I soon discerned her wiles. That was another reason not to go to your world with her. She cannot be trusted."

Lauren glanced at their clasped hands. Eagle was so gentle and kind, free with his feelings. Being his "new friend" felt good ... and unnerving. "It sounds like you made the right call."

348

After stepping through dense underbrush, they arrived at a small clearing where a little girl slept in a nest of ferns, the edge of an elephant-ear-sized leaf in her hand. At least ten brightly burning torches had been embedded in the ground around her, making a circle of fire that cast rippling light over her body.

"No shadow people would dare draw near with this fence of protection." Eagle plucked one of the torches and walked through the gap. After tamping out the flame, he dropped the torch, took Cheer's leaf, and folded it into his pants pocket. He then scooped her up and walked out of the circle. "If you don't mind, would you please smother the other torches? There is no need to save any. I have a flashlight."

While Lauren grabbed torches and rolled them over the ground, Eagle spoke to Cheer in a singsong voice. "Wake up, little one. It's time to go dragon riding. You like that, don't you?"

Cheer blinked her bleary eyes and nodded. "Grackle or Albatross?"

Eagle lowered her to the ground and slid his hand into hers. "Albatross."

"Oh, good! He's bouncier than Grackle. I like to bounce."

Smiling, Lauren smothered the final torch. Obviously Cheer was an experienced dragon rider. She would be safe.

After they walked back to the river and sent Cheer and Albatross away, Eagle stood at the river's edge and watched the dragon-and-rider silhouette as it shrank in the moon's light. Tears sparkled in his brilliant eyes. "These are dangerous days," he said, his voice barely audible over the river's rush. "Sometimes I wonder if Second Eden has seen such darkness before, perhaps when I was young, but since King Elam has kept the evils of your world away, I had not experienced such darkness until Mount Elijah exploded and killed my best friend."

His companion zipped down to his nose and began flashing red.

Lauren's cheeks warmed. "Killed your best friend! I'm so sorry!"

"Oh, I am the one who should apologize. My words were not meant to cause sorrow in you." He touched his companion with a fingertip. "He just reminded me that I too often express my thoughts verbally when I ought to keep them to myself."

Joan floated near Lauren's eyes, glowing blue. *Verbalizing the moods of the mind can be helpful. While you search for the cave, lift his guilt by asking him why he wonders about the darkness. It must be something that weighs heavily on his mind.*

Lauren nodded. "Shall we find the cave?"

"If you trust me to hold my tongue." He gave her a sheepish smile. "Stay close."

"Wait a minute." Lauren slid out her phone and pointed the lens at Eagle. "Do you mind if I take a picture?"

"A photograph?" Eagle straightened and smiled. "I am honored."

After taking a picture of Eagle and another of Joan, she put the phone away. They headed downstream at the river's edge, marching side by side. Lauren watched his purposeful strides. With squared shoulders and disciplined gait, if not for his darker skin and shorter stature, he could have been Matt's double.

A hum drifted from his lips, a familiar tune—"Amazing Grace." Lauren smiled. Since he liked that song, it might mean that he had spiritual light within in spite of his dismal words earlier. "Why do you wonder about darkness in your younger days?"

"I have memories." He kept his focus straight ahead. "Dreams, really, so they're vague and fleeting. I see a dark place with jagged streaks of light, much like the lightning you have in your world."

"You don't have lightning here?"

"My father mentioned a time when we had some, before I was taken from the birthing garden, so my dreams must be from the photos I have seen in books brought here from your world. I have not seen any lightning myself."

"Only photos? No videos?"

Eagle shook his head. "We have no video devices, and King Elam prefers it that way."

"I see." Lauren hid a smile. Her friends on Earth would think Elam's policy oppressive and narrow, but if they could see the quality of people here, maybe they would change their minds.

She sighed. No. Even then, they wouldn't change their minds. Most would call the Second Edeners ignorant hicks who needed enlightenment.

"Why the sigh?" Eagle asked.

Looking at him out of the corner of her eye, she smiled. "I'd rather not say."

He turned his head toward her, returning the smile. "I could learn a lot from you, Lauren. Your private manner is wise. You are very much like my father. I am like my mother in that I would ask questions until … What is your idiom? Until your ears fall off?"

She laughed. "Yes, we do say that."

"I will ask another question, and perhaps you will answer when the time is right." He nodded at Apollo. "What is that device you are carrying?"

She lifted it by one of its dowels. "I think it would be better to wait, like you said. It's really hard to explain."

"As you wish."

The glimmer from his medallion caught her attention. "Do you mind if I ask *you* a question?"

"Please do."

"That medallion you're wearing. Does it have some kind of significance?"

He stopped, lifted a thin chain, and set the medallion on his palm. "This is something my father gave me. He wore it for many years and gave it to my mother on their wedding day." He lifted the edge with a fingertip. "See the engraving?"

She read the etched letters—*My gift to you. My life. It is all I have to give.* "So why do you have it now?"

His features sagged. "My mother died about a year ago, so my father gave it to me. I hope to give it to my bride when we wed, to a young lady I would give my life for. As it says, giving my life for the one I love is the only real gift, is it not?"

"It's true. I know I would love to get a gift like that from someone who loved me so much."

And I am sorry to hear about your mother, Joan said without flashing.

"And I'm sorry to hear about your mother."

"I appreciate your kindness." He slid the medallion behind his shirt and continued walking. "Now is it my turn to ask a question?"

"Sure." She shrugged. "I guess so."

"I noticed that your skin glows. Why is that?"

She looked at her hand. No sign of a glow. "It's a genetic thing. It's really hard to explain."

"Well, it suits you. It makes me think of faith and virtue. Those qualities must emanate from within your soul."

Lauren's cheeks flushed hot. "Thank you."

"And if I may trouble you for yet another question."

She gave him a sideways glance. With his expression stoic, he didn't give away any hidden agenda. "Go for it."

"What are you carrying in the backpack?"

352

"It's a mixture of dirt and enzymes and genetic material and parasites, also a hand shovel and a helmet. I hope to throw the mixture into the volcano to create a new parasite that will battle the one infecting the sick anthrozils. I assume you know about them."

"Oh, yes. I have suggested many herbal remedies, but all have failed." He touched the backpack's outer lining. "I think if you throw it into Mount Elijah, you will not create a new parasite. It will just burn. Nothing can survive that heat."

Lauren quickly explained Dr. Conner's theory, finishing with a sigh. "The mutated parasite can survive for seven minutes, so after the backpack gets thrown in, the volcano needs to erupt to eject it into cooler air."

"I hope you will pardon me, but that sounds like one of the fairy tales my mother used to tell me. A volcano can never create life. It only destroys. You might as well hope to spin straw into gold."

"It does sound crazy, I admit, but that's the theory."

"The theory has another serious flaw. How will you make Mount Elijah erupt within seven minutes?"

"Well ..." She looked at the ground. "I was thinking ..."

Joan nudged Lauren's ear. *Do not be ashamed. Tell him. He will understand.*

Lauren looked Eagle in the eye. "How about if I pray for it?"

"Pray?" Eagle clapped his hands. "Excellent. I pray for wisdom all the time."

"Wisdom? Yes, I pray for it, too, but I meant—"

"If you seek wisdom about Mount Elijah, then you asked the right person, because I know why it erupts."

"You do?"

He nodded. "It erupts whenever someone dies by falling into its crater. I heard that this recent eruption was so terrible because many Earth soldiers fell in."

353

"That's true. They did."

"And have you met Listener?"

"I have."

"She has a spyglass." Eagle positioned his hands as if peering through a handheld telescope. "There was an eruption a dozen years or more ago, and right before it happened, Listener was looking through the spyglass and saw someone fall into Mount Elijah. And my father told me about a boy who fell in long before that, an accident when his father took him to the summit. When Elijah erupted, the father barely escaped with his life. After that accident, our prophet Abraham plugged the hole to discourage visitors from coming to see the fire inside."

"That must have been awful!" Lauren lowered her gaze and watched her bare feet keep pace with his. Eagle's words seemed like confirmation from above. Although the theory sounded like a fairy tale, how else could anyone explain the cry for help from the ghostly voice? And the deep scratches in the shelf at the top of the ladder proved that a struggle had occurred—real physical evidence, not just whispers riding on a breeze.

Joan brushed against Lauren's ear. *Abaddon said to let wisdom guide you.*

I remember.

And did you and Eagle agree that you both prayed for wisdom?

Yes. We did.

It seems that the answer to your dilemma was delivered to you as if presented on a velvet pillow.

Lauren nodded. *So you know what I've been considering.*

Of course. Your prominent thoughts are easy to hear.

Abaddon's words flowed into Lauren's mind, burning like acidic bile. *She must sacrifice for the sake of others, a supremely selfless act*

354

that will sear her soul. And facing fear of death will defeat all fears forevermore.

Lauren swallowed hard. *This idea was just a theory. I'm still not sure I can go through with it. Maybe I haven't interpreted everything the right way.*

I see no other way of interpreting it. You knew about this likely result when you chose to come here instead of staying with Abaddon.

I know, but …

But you hoped to escape the fire. Joan's blue light flashed, then dimmed, as if letting out a sigh. *I cannot count the number of times I hoped for escape from my persecutors. Even at the last hour I begged God to bring my compatriots to my rescue, but when the executioner touched the flaming torch to my pyre, and I saw no familiar faces in the panting throng, I realized that my prayers had gone unanswered; at least they were not answered in the way I had hoped. No rescue came. The fire crawled over my body. I burned. I died in torment.*

Lauren nodded. *And because of your death, all of France rallied in your name.*

And they broke their bonds. My sacrifice meant freedom for many.

As tears welled in her eyes, Lauren pushed Joan away. *I need to stop talking about this.*

Very well. Joan settled on Lauren's shoulder and darkened.

From that point on, Lauren and Eagle marched in silence. When they entered a thin cloud of smoke, light from the moon dimmed. Eagle withdrew the leaf from his pocket, tore it in half, and gave her a section. He covered his mouth and nose with his and gestured for her to do the same.

She held her section tightly over her face, trying to close the gaps, and breathed through it. A sweet smell entered her nostrils, similar to the aroma of the liquid she had poured over the mask at the top of the museum room ladder. Although pungent, breathing it was a lot better than choking on poison.

Soon, Eagle guided the way to the left and into the forest. He pulled the flashlight from his belt and shone the beam into the darkness. Never slowing his stride, he marched on.

Lauren slid the goggles up to her eyes. With Eagle watching for anything that his beam touched, she could watch for everything else.

After about a minute, they arrived at an entrance to a cave. He focused the beam on a heaping line of blackness that looked like someone had dumped a wheelbarrow of tar. "Avoid stepping in it," he whispered. "This is the remains of the shadow people who accosted us earlier. Semiramis concocted a potion that burned them."

Lauren lowered the goggles. "You mean, she had it ready before she saw them?"

"She is familiar with the shadow people, so she prepared the potion from roots and herbs as a precaution."

"Hmmm. Resourceful, isn't she?"

"And dangerous." He set a finger to his lips. "Let's stay as quiet as possible from now on. If Semiramis's allies are near the portal, they might be able to hear us. I prefer that we keep our presence unknown to them."

"Just a second." Lauren glanced at Joan, who had stayed quietly perched on her shoulder, and sent a thought her way. *Any counsel?*

Joan blinked at her. *Only that you should continue heeding Eagle's advice. This is all new to me, so he is the better person to consult. I am very impressed with his wisdom and manner.*

Me, too. Lauren nodded at Eagle. "Lead the way. I'll be as quiet as a mouse."

Assuming mice are quiet here, Joan added.

Hush. Lauren followed Eagle into the cave, taking a long step over the shadow people. She left the goggles down. With the cave path so narrow, nothing could escape Eagle's flashlight.

He stopped. "The air is clear," he whispered, lowering the leaf and returning it to his pocket.

Lauren lowered hers and pushed it into her back pants pocket. Eagle flicked off the flashlight and took her hand. "We will proceed in darkness," he said. "A light will give away our presence, so it's a good thing your glow has diminished. If not for my gifted vision, I would probably not be able to see you."

"Yes. It is a good thing." She lifted the night-vision goggles over her eyes. "I have these goggles. They let me see in the dark."

"Then maybe you should lead the way."

She touched the frame. "Would you like to wear them?"

"No. I trust you. I am comfortable staying at your side."

"Okay. I'll let you know if I see anything."

357

As they walked farther into the cave, darkness enveloped them. The slightest of glows from their companions provided contrast for the goggles, allowing her to see pretty well. Eagle's steady hand felt strong and secure. He had been here before and knew the way. Everything would be fine.

Soon, a blank wall came into view. Lauren stopped and set Eagle's hand against it. "Feel this?" she whispered.

"The end of the cave. The portal is no longer open."

"But it was open recently, right?"

"Quite recently."

She ran her hand along the wall. It felt odd, as if charged with static electricity. The scales on her back tingled. Sound trickled in. A gunshot. She flinched. Someone shouted, "Valiant!" It sounded like Matt, yet garbled, as if spoken underwater. More shots fired. Then engines roared, and the noise began to fade.

Lauren pulled away and knelt. She set Apollo on the cave floor and looked at Eagle's dim profile, hoping to keep worry out of her voice. "I guess it won't hurt to turn on your light now. No one's around."

"And since you are glowing once again, more light will not add much to our visibility."

The beam flashed on and illuminated Apollo. She jerked the goggles down and began pushing menu buttons as quickly as she could. "Now I'll tell you what this is all about. It's called Apollo. Among other things, it's able to open portals. I don't know if it's ever opened this one or not, but if it has, the settings should be in a database. If not, I'll just use the readings it detects here."

"Some of your words are unfamiliar to me, but I think I understand."

"Good, because I'm not sure I can explain everything." She ran through the options—*History, External Devices, Apollo, Sort Options, By Label.* She then ran through a series of portal labels— *Glastonbury Tor to Hades, Patrick's forest to Hades, Montana Crater to Valley of Shadows Cave.* That had to be it.

She entered the spectrum numbers into Apollo's flash settings. "If I'm right," she said as she shifted her finger to Apollo's base, "when I press this button, Apollo will flash with a light that will open the portal." She set her finger on the button. "I'm a lot like Listener. I can hear things other people can't. And I just heard some things from the other side of this portal that sound danger-ous, so if it opens, we have to be ready for trouble."

"A flash of light opens the portal?" He crouched and shone the beam on the cave's back wall. "I told you about the fire that was burning when I was here earlier. I detected an odor similar to the fuel we use for our flying hospital, and I know how combustible that is. Could light from an explosion have opened the portal?"

"I suppose it could have. I don't know how precise the light spectrum numbers have to be."

"Then the fire is likely out, but since you heard sounds of danger, perhaps the dragon has returned."

"What dragon?"

Eagle touched the portal wall. "After I came back from your world to the safety of this cave, Cheer and I watched from behind the fire. Semiramis lifted her hands toward the sky and spoke in a strange language. Soon, a red dragon much bigger than Albatross landed. When she climbed up on his back, they flew away. Of course since our companions were at risk and I heard other voices nearby, I couldn't go back to see where the dragon went, especially while looking after Cheer, so we returned to the forest."

"Dragon or no dragon, I think it'll be dangerous on the other side of the portal."

"Then we will face the danger together." Eagle nodded. "Push the button."

359

21

CHAPTER

SURRENDER

At least twelve helicopters descended into the crater. The sound of roaring blades whipped around, their echoes stirred in the cauldron of noise. His legs again cramping violently, Matt knelt next to his mother. "You were right. There's a bunch of them."

"We can't fight that many!" Dad shouted. "We'll have to surrender. Listener, take Bonnie and the guns and hide in the cave. Maybe they haven't spotted everyone yet."

Listener collected the rifles and tossed them into the cave. Bullets ripped the ground in front of Dad and Valiant, but they stood firm. The lights shone on them, crisscrossing from all directions, descending slowly with the choppers.

As Listener crawled backwards into the cave, she extended an arm. "Bring Bonnie to me! Hurry!" Her companion tilted on her shoulder as if ready to topple.

Matt slid Semiramis's dagger from his belt and tossed it into the cave with Listener. "Take this!" It clinked on the ground and bounced close to her hand.

She snatched it up. "Got it!"

He raised his cloak's hood, pushed his arms under his mother, and lifted her into a cradle. His head pounded. Every limb throbbed. Recovery from the attempted healing was way too slow. As he staggered toward Listener, bullets riddled the ground in front of him. He halted. Listener ducked farther into the cave. Her companion fell to the ground, but she grabbed it and disappeared inside.

Swallowing, Matt stayed put. They knew he was there now, so trying to hide Mom would expose Listener. She had the rifles, so maybe somehow she could do something to help, but with so many choppers and soldiers, keeping out of sight would be her best bet.

Helicopters began settling to the floor of the crater, raising clouds of dust and sand. With their lights trained on Valiant, Matt, and his father, the rest of the ground seemed dark by comparison. Matt glanced at the cave entry again. Although dim, movement was easy to detect. A soldier's dead body inched out, Listener's hands barely visible as she pushed it.

Still carrying his mother, Matt limped closer to the landing helicopters, his calf muscles tight. Getting farther from the cave would help Listener stay in darkness, but would his legs hold out? The spasms were pure torture.

"You're brave," Mom whispered as she embraced his neck loosely. "Hold on to that courage. I have faith in you."

Matt took in a deep breath and squared his shoulders. "I'll do my best."

When the last helicopter landed, the lights aimed at the ground in front of them, making the crater floor look like a well-lit stage.

A voice buzzed into Matt's tooth transmitter. "I was almost there, Billy. I saw them just in time and shut down my lights. I guess they didn't spot me, because no one gave chase. I'm hovering pretty high up with Ashley and your parents, but Gabriel jumped out. I have no idea what he might try, but you know Gabriel. Expect something unexpected."

The closest helicopter's propellers slowed, and its engine noise ebbed. A soldier with an assault rifle stepped out. Matt spotted his stripes—a sergeant. A thin man wearing black from head to toe followed him. Breezes from the slowing blades buffeted his curly hair, and the lights made his narrow face appear ghostly pale. He looked like a walking corpse in funeral attire. As he drew closer, the breeze blew open his suit jacket, revealing a shoulder holster and gun.

"It's Tamiel," Matt whispered, hoping the words would transmit to his father and Walter.

His father nodded, also whispering. "Keep providing information. Even if Walter can't hear us, Larry is probably recording everything. They can decipher it later."

"Lois is recording," Walter said. "Larry is —"

"Walter, no!" Ashley's voice broke in. "We're too close. Don't count on encryption."

"Right," Walter said. "Signing off for now, but we'll keep listening."

Matt sidled up to his father, his muscles finally loosening. "Surrendering to Tamiel makes me want to barf."

At least two dozen more armed soldiers poured out of the helicopters and formed a line at either side of Tamiel, their rifles aimed. They all appeared to be army privates.

"I know." Dad caressed Mom's cheek with a finger, making her smile weakly. "But if we don't surrender, we're all dead."

363

Valiant leaned toward Dad. "At what price will we surrender? Even violence toward your wife?"

"I will allow violence toward myself, but if they show any aggression toward Bonnie or Matt, I'll fight to the death and take as many of them as I can with me. I think they want Bonnie alive, so I'm hoping that won't be necessary."

Valiant nodded. "Agreed."

Matt quickly counted the helicopters. At least he could give Walter a blow-by-blow description, even if it sounded strange. "I see twelve choppers."

Tamiel waved a finger at Matt. "Put her down. I want to see how healthy she is."

Matt looked at his father, who gestured with his eyes to do as Tamiel said.

"Okay, I'll put my mother down, but she's very weak." Matt set Mom's feet on the ground and slowly added weight to her wobbly legs. Finally, she stood alone with her arms and wings wrapped around herself. The breeze tossed her hair, and she blinked wearily at the lights, but she seemed steady. "Satisfied?"

"Ah!" Tamiel said. "Very good! She still has some energy left."

"If you so much as touch a hair on her head," Dad growled, "I'll—"

"Spare me the drama. She will not be violated in any way."

"What do you plan to do?"

"I have no desire to tell you, but rest assured that she will be unharmed." Tamiel pulled a long fibrous rag from a pocket and gave it to the sergeant. "Take Billy and Bonnie and the boy. Handcuff them securely, but most of all make sure you plug Billy's mouth with this gag. I advise incapacitating him first, but do not kill him."

"They're going to cuff us and gag my father," Matt whispered, hoping someone was still listening.

The sergeant rammed the butt of his gun into Dad's head, sending him sprawling. He writhed and clawed at the ground for a moment before going limp.

"Dad!" Matt stepped toward him, but another soldier grabbed his arm and held him fast. "You cowards!" Matt yelled. "You just bashed an unarmed man!"

"Don't move!" The soldier cuffed Matt's wrists and pressed a pistol against his head. "Or you're dead."

Mom staggered toward Dad. Her legs buckled. She dropped to her knees, her eyes wide open.

A soldier handcuffed Dad's wrists behind his back, hoisted him over his shoulder, and marched toward a larger helicopter at the rear of the group. The soldier holding Matt shoved him to the side, scooped Mom into his arms, and hurried in the same direction.

"We'll take the kid in a minute." The sergeant nodded toward the crater wall. "The medic checked our three men over by that cave. They're dead."

"You see what I told you?" Tamiel said. "These criminals are butchers. They have no concern for the wives and children these good soldiers left behind. Now they are widows and orphans."

"Yes sir." The sergeant pointed his gun toward the cave. "Do you have any intel about anyone being inside? Someone shot our men, and there are no guns in sight."

Tamiel shook his head. "Gather your men's bodies, and throw some poisonous gas in there or whatever it is you do to smoke someone out."

"You heard him." The sergeant waved at the line of troops. "Three of you get the canisters and see if there's a rat in the hole that needs to be smoked out, and bring our men's bodies."

Matt looked at Valiant. He stood tall in front of Tamiel, his head high and his eyes clear, though his companion was nowhere

365

in sight. Matt glanced upward. The stars were no longer visible, but that could be because the helicopter lights washed them out.

"What do we do with this one?" the sergeant asked, giving Valiant a shove.

Tamiel waved a hand. "Shoot him."

As the sergeant lifted his rifle, Matt lowered his shoulder and lunged at him, slamming into his back like a battering ram. The sergeant's rifle fired, and he toppled forward into Valiant. Matt fell after him. With his wrists cuffed, he smacked his cheek on the stony ground. Valiant wrestled the gun away from the sergeant and began shooting soldiers right and left.

A pop sounded, distinct and clear. Valiant dropped the rifle and clutched his chest, blood pouring between his fingers.

From the ground, Matt lifted his head and shouted, "Valiant!" He bit his lip hard. The scene was too terrible to describe. Walter would just have to figure it out on his own.

Tamiel stood nearby with a handgun. Smoke twisted up from its barrel. He fired again. Valiant toppled to the side and curled on the ground. When Tamiel fired a third time, Valiant rolled to his stomach and lay motionless.

The sergeant climbed to his feet and stomped Valiant's head, but Valiant didn't flinch or groan. With a quick pivot, the sergeant kicked Matt in the stomach. "That'll teach you, brat!"

"Enough!" Tamiel shouted as he returned the gun to its holster. "I need him healthy ... for now. Any suffering he undergoes must be witnessed by his mother."

Nausea boiled in Matt's gut. Pain throttled his head. That monster! How could any soldier follow his orders? Tamiel wasn't even in the military, much less anyone's commanding officer. Why would they so blindly obey?

The sergeant grabbed Matt's collar and jerked him to his feet.

As his head throbbed, the entire scene became a blur of images. Three soldiers ran toward the cave. Each one tossed in a canister. Within seconds, smoke poured out. Matt kept trying to watch, but one of the soldiers shoved him in the back with the butt of a rifle. "Get going!"

With the gun butt constantly prodding him, Matt half walked, half jogged to the larger helicopter. He stepped up into the passenger compartment and sat on a bench facing the rear. With the door still open, the cave stayed in view. Two of the men were now carrying the three fallen soldiers away one by one while the third watched the cave opening with his rifle ready. Listener hadn't come out yet. How long could she stay? Were they using tear gas or something more deadly? She probably still had her mask, but even if it was effective against the gas, it couldn't last forever.

Dad sat on the opposite bench a little more than an arm's length away, his head propped by the side wall. With the asbestos rag stuffed in his mouth, even if he were awake, he wouldn't be able to speak, though a bruise on his jaw and around one eye said plenty. The world was going mad, and they were all helpless to stop it. Mom lay on a cot between them, but with her eyes closed, it was impossible to tell how she was reacting, though her lips moved, maybe in silent prayer.

"Walter," Matt said in the lowest whisper possible. "Dad, Mom, and I are in the back of a transport chopper. I have no idea where they're taking us."

When two more soldiers piled in and began cuffing Matt's and Dad's ankles, the helicopter lifted from the crater floor. As it swung around, the rest of the helicopters came into view. While one

367

stayed put, keeping its lights trained on Listener's cave, the others rose into the air as a single unit. Beams from their lights knifed through swirling clouds of dust, crisscrossing like dueling sabers.

A smaller light flashed on the crater floor. Matt blinked, then squinted. A rectangular glow stood on the ground, like a radiant frame around a gap of darkness. Someone stepped out from the gap and looked up, then darted back in again.

Matt averted his eyes. With all the lights dancing around, maybe no one noticed the newcomer. The light had to be a portal, but who could that person be? And what would happen if someone spotted him?

When the soldiers finished clasping their prisoners' ankles, they sat on the benches, one next to Matt and the other next to Dad, each one with a rifle clutched in front. They stared straight ahead, expressionless, though their tight jaws gave away their anger. Since they thought their three buddies had been murdered by their prisoners, it probably wouldn't do any good to talk to them.

The soldier sitting next to Dad winked. The other soldier winked back. The first raised his gun and rammed the butt into Dad's ribs. Dad groaned but kept his eyes closed. "Oops," the soldier said, grinning. "I'm so sorry."

"Accidents do happen." The other soldier lifted his gun. "Sometimes more than once."

Matt tried to block with his arm, but the handcuff held it in place. The gun butt rushed toward him, pain rocked his skull, then blackness filled his vision.

Lauren pushed the button and jumped back. Apollo flashed. A wave of light splashed against the cave's back wall and coated it with sparkling yellow radiance. The light coalesced into a rectangle that opened into another world.

On the other side, beams of light whirled everywhere, while engine noises and whipping wind burst through the portal like a tsunami of sound. Lauren reached out and touched the portal plane. It sizzled on contact.

"Wait here." She untied her sweatshirt sleeves, pulled it on, and jumped through the portal. Helicopters buzzed above like a swarm of angry dragonflies. About ten steps from the portal, a body lay on its stomach, probably a man. Near a wall in the distance, three men with guns stood at the entrance to a cave. Smoke poured from within.

Lauren leaped back inside and pulled Eagle into a crouch several feet from the portal boundary. Gasping for breath, she clutched his hand. "They have helicopters … and rifles."

"I saw them. Can you close the portal?"

"No, but I think it'll close by itself." She took in a deep breath, hoping to calm her racing heart. "I don't know how long it'll take."

The portal hole began to contract, now the size of a single door. At this rate, it would be closed in about a minute. "Before I opened it, I thought I heard gunshots, and then I heard Matt call Valiant's name. If that's Valiant lying out there, maybe he's been shot and—"

"My father?" Eagle jumped up and leaped through the portal. When his body made contact with the plane, his shirt and trousers caught fire. He dashed to the fallen man's side, hoisted him over his shoulder, and ran back, slowed by the weight.

"You there!" someone shouted. "Halt!"

A shot rang out. A bullet smacked into the cave's side wall. Eagle dove in through the shrinking hole and rolled with the man on the ground. Blood from the man's chest wound sprayed across Lauren's clothes. She leaped up and helped Eagle to his feet, batting away the flames on his pant legs and shirt sleeves. "It *is* my father!" he said, his voice hoarse.

369

Lauren looked at the portal. It had shrunk to the size of a car door, though it was still big enough to provide light for the cave. A man leaped through and fell into a somersault, barely missing Valiant as his momentum carried him along.

Another man appeared at the portal, trying to crawl through. Eagle whipped out his dagger and slung it at him. The blade impaled his chest and sent him falling backwards. The portal contracted further and closed with a sparks-filled pop.

Two flashlights flicked on, one in Eagle's grip and the other in the hand of the man who leaped through the portal. "If you have a weapon," Eagle growled, "drop it now. I have another dagger, and you have seen how accurate I am."

The man lifted a hand. "Cool it! I'm on your side."

Eagle's light fell across the man's standing form. A pair of wings spread out behind him.

Lauren gasped. "It's Gabriel! He's a friend!"

"Good." Eagle dropped to the ground next to his father and pressed an ear against his chest. "Father? Can you hear me?"

"Where did you come from?" Lauren asked Gabriel. "Were you just flying around out there?"

Gabriel brushed sparks off a sweatshirt sleeve. "Dropped out of a helicopter. Walter, Ashley, and Billy's parents are still in it flying near the crater."

"Jared's out there?" Lauren grabbed his sleeve. "We need to get him into Second Eden. We're close to a cure, but he has to be here."

"I'll give them a shout as soon as we get back to Earth." Gabriel pointed his flashlight at Valiant. "How is he? I saw them shoot him."

Eagle lifted his head from his father's chest. As he rose, he displayed something in his palm, a companion in a pool of blood. It lay motionless and dark.

"Is he …" Lauren bit her lip. The words stuck in her throat.

"I heard a faint heartbeat," Eagle whispered.

Valiant's companion flickered, then tilted upright and floated in a meandering path to his chest and settled there. Valiant blinked his eyes open, but swollen bruises allowed only narrow slits to appear. "Eagle." His voice gurgled as he gasped for breath. "You almost … lost something."

"Lost something?" Tears trickled down Eagle's cheeks. "What?"

Valiant opened his hand. A companion lifted from his palm and flew to Eagle's shoulder. "It fell … when you picked me up." He grasped Eagle's wrist and drew him closer. "Do not fear death … neither for me … nor for yourself." Blood oozing from the corner of his mouth, his voiced weakened to a whisper. "We go to a better place. Remember that."

Eagle's tears dripped to his father's chest. "I will remember."

Valiant closed his eyes. After a final exhale, his chest stopped moving. His companion rolled off and clinked on the floor.

His chin quivering, Eagle picked up the companion and set it back on Valiant's chest. "My father is dead. The great warrior has fallen."

Gabriel stooped next to Eagle and laid a hand on his shoulder. "I hate to say this, but we'll have to grieve later. Your father would want you to keep fighting. This is far from over."

Nodding, Eagle rose, his legs unsteady. "What do we do?"

Gabriel pointed his light at Apollo. "Can we fire up that thing and open the portal again?"

"I suppose so." Lauren crouched next to Apollo. "The settings should be the same, but I don't know if it needs time to recharge. I've used it a lot."

"Ashley's new model can flash a bunch of times without plugging it in. It can also recharge on ambient light."

371

"What of the soldiers?" Eagle asked.

Gabriel withdrew a handgun from a hip holster and touched his jaw. "I picked up a lot of info from the chatter, and I think Listener's in another cave in that crater. We have to help her. It looked like they were trying to gas her out."

"And I can get Jared into Second Eden from in there," Lauren said. "There's a quick way to the hospital and Dr. Conner."

"First things first." Gabriel checked his ammo clip. "We'll have to clear out the opposition."

Eagle withdrew his other dagger. "Let's go."

"What about your companion?" Lauren asked.

"Since my father thought it was a good idea to fight out there, I will follow his wisdom. I think I will not need a companion." With a gentle hand, he took his companion from his shoulder and pushed it into an inner tunic pocket. "I am ready."

"Okay. On three." Lauren hiked her backpack higher and set her finger on the button. "One ... two ... three!" She pushed the button. Apollo flashed again. Radiance splashed over the wall, this time covering an area the size of a bedroom window.

After hooking his flashlight to his belt, Gabriel leaped through, firing his gun. With a beat of his wings, he vaulted into the air. Eagle stowed his flashlight and jumped. Again flames slithered across his clothes, but he quietly batted them away. Lauren snatched Apollo and ran in his wake, protected by the flame-retardant sweatshirt. Since she and Eagle passed through with so little noise, maybe Gabriel's covering gunshots kept anyone from noticing them.

Lauren and Eagle dropped to the ground, Lauren careful to keep Apollo safe. The soldier Eagle had impaled leaned against the wall near the other cave with the dagger still in his chest, his shirt now off. The other two stood, aiming their rifles at the sky, alternately shooting and shifting their aims, while the wounded man shone a flashlight into the air. "Someone must be in the cave," he shouted, "or the dragon freak wouldn't be coming after him!"

"No one could survive the gas that long," one of the others snapped. "We'll drag him out when the gas clears."

From above, a shot rang out. A bullet smacked into the ground next to the wounded man's foot. He shifted his body away and pointed the flashlight. "There! I think he's there!"

"Gabriel is keeping them occupied." Eagle pressed a leaf over his mouth, muffling his voice. "I'm going in. The darkness will conceal me."

"I'm coming with you." Lauren pulled her leaf from her pocket, shot to her feet, and skulked at his side, carrying Apollo. When they neared the cave, Eagle bolted for it and dove inside.

"What the—" One of the soldiers aimed his rifle at the opening, but another batted the barrel away. "He's dead meat. Let him stew."

Lauren looked up. Gabriel was nowhere in sight. With the soldiers focused on finding him, it was now or never. She heaved in a breath and ran for the cave. Hugging Apollo and tucking her body, she rolled into the opening, then, still holding her breath, crawled the rest of the way, pushing Apollo along. Her backpack scraped the ceiling, halting her progress once, but with a strong kick, she broke through.

Behind her, someone laughed. "These idiots really have a death wish, don't they?"

Lauren slapped the leaf over her mouth and stood in the chamber, her eyes stinging. The soldiers' lantern shone dimly, illuminating white gas that swirled with her movement. Listener sat against the back wall with her eyes closed and her mask on, while Eagle crouched at her side, his flashlight beam pointed at her chest.

"She's okay," he whispered through his leaf as he blinked. "Her eyes are burning."

"Mine, too. Let's get out of here." Lauren set Apollo next to the back wall. "Please help Listener move out of the way, and then give me some light."

After Eagle guided Listener toward a side wall, he shone his flashlight on Apollo. Lauren scrolled through the recent data settings, barely able to see them through her tears. She and her father opened this portal once before, but it led to a mining tunnel in Hades. This time it needed to open into the museum room. Since this cave was visible from there, it had to be possible.

She ran a finger along the wall until it poked through a small hole. "Eagle, look." She blinked her stinging eyes. Her mouth burned. Words had to stay at a minimum. "Do you see a flaming tree?"

Eagle peeked through the hole. "Yes," he said, his voice muffled. "What does it mean?"

"Sorry. Can't explain." She set her fingers back on Apollo and continued scrolling through data. She had to set the flash with the spectral numbers she used to open the portal while inside the museum room instead of the numbers Dad used to go to the mining tunnel. Finally, the settings appeared.

Lauren transferred the database entries to Apollo's current settings. "Ready?"

Eagle stood with his shoulder under Listener's arm. Both breathed through their filters. "Ready."

"Here we go." Lauren pushed the button. Apollo flashed and painted its usual rectangular door on the wall, though even smaller this time, no taller than her shoulders. Still, it was big enough. The tree of life burned brightly, and gas flowed through the portal, sizzling as it ran across the tree's flaming leaves.

Ducking low, Lauren picked up Apollo and walked into the museum room, followed by Eagle and Listener. Listener dropped to her knees, stripped off her mask, and began coughing and dry heaving.

Eagle knelt beside her and patted her back while rubbing his eyes. "Inhale deeply through your nose. Exhale through your mouth."

After setting Apollo down and stuffing her leaf into her pocket, Lauren pushed the edge of her shirt sleeve into one eye and absorbed the tears, then repeated the process with the other eye. They still stung horribly.

As Listener's spasms eased, Eagle looked at Lauren. "I think she'll be all right."

"Good." Lauren nodded toward the portal. "We need to get the guns."

He leaped back to the Earth cave and returned with three rifles. As with the other portals attached to the museum room, this one didn't shrink.

375

Lauren picked up Apollo. "We don't have any time to lose, but I have to see if I can recharge Apollo, at least a little bit."

Pushing the menu button, she ran through the settings—*Maintenance, Charging, AC Power.* She altered the setting to *Ambient Light* and pushed Apollo close to the tree. She checked its power meter. It was already increasing. Maybe a few minutes would be enough.

Although the portal window to the Earth cave maintained its size, very little gas drifted through, mainly what was drawn in by their bodies when they rushed from Earth to the museum. Inside the cave, the soldiers' lantern dimmed. It probably wouldn't last much longer.

While Listener sat on the floor, still coughing at times, Eagle again consoled her. Lauren walked to the Second Eden portal and gazed at the cooling lava field she had so recently walked upon. Her prints remained in a line of six foot-shaped splotches of blood and skin.

As Joan floated closer, Lauren sent a thought her way. *I can't take Eagle and Listener that way, can I?*

Not as long as it stays as hot as it is. Joan blinked red a single time. *That was your trial, not theirs.*

"Right." Lauren looked at the Earth portal. "If we go back that way, the soldiers will pick us off as we come out of the cave."

I assume so. Their anger was filled with malice.

Lauren continued in her thoughts. *I can't leave Gabriel to fight those guys alone, and I have to get Jared into Second Eden.*

Of course, but how will you do that without getting yourself and Eagle and Listener killed?

Lauren let out a sigh. *By going without them.*

BURNED

Lauren stripped off her backpack, retrieved the helmet from inside, and scooted the pack close to the ladder. She retied her sweatshirt sleeves around her waist. Since it was probably still pretty warm out there, her T-shirt would be enough. "Eagle, stay here and watch over Listener. I'll be back as soon as I can."

"Are you going to help Gabriel?"

"That's my plan." She picked up one of the rifles and grabbed Apollo. After checking to make sure her goggles' strap was still secure around her neck, she stood in front of the Second Eden portal. "We can't escape safely from the cave we just came through, so I'm going to the Valley of Shadows. I'm the only one who can walk on the lava field, so you two stay here and get your strength back." She nodded at the Earth portal. "Look for me there in a little while."

"Do you know how to fire that weapon?" Listener asked.

Lauren looked at the rifle. "Pull the trigger, right?"

"You took mine, so it should be set." Listener pulled down her mask. "Do you know how to be ready for recoil?"

"Recoil? What's recoil?"

Listener struggled to her feet, picked up another rifle, and pressed the butt against her shoulder. She set one foot well in front of the other. "Lean into the shot when you fire. Otherwise, it will kick you off balance."

"Got it." Still holding Apollo, Lauren put the helmet on and gave Eagle and Listener a one-armed embrace. "Please pray for me."

"We will," they said, almost in unison.

Lauren stepped through the Second Eden portal and walked across the field, unaffected by the heat. Joan floated near her shoulder, humming an unfamiliar tune. Might it be something French from her era? It would be interesting to hear the words, but would it ever happen? Probably not this side of Heaven, not with what the future likely held in store for both of them.

When Lauren reached the end of her bloody footprints, she looked at the hospital, still barely visible. A tiny light appeared from a gap under a window shade. Maybe Dr. Conner was working on how to simulate a volcanic eruption.

She shook her head. The poor man. His dear wife lay dying, maybe within hours of succumbing to the batholith, and he labored feverishly, desperate for a cure. With his mind battling between science and faith, he likely knew that only a miracle could heal Irene, but he had to rely on science while he waited for God to act. No one who really loves someone twiddles his thumbs while his beloved is suffering.

She turned toward the volcano. As trickles of lava crept slowly down the mountain's sides, the entire area glowed. Could a miracle come from the mouth of Elijah? Maybe everyone would find out soon.

Cupping a hand around her mouth, Lauren called, "Albatross! Can you hear me? I need another ride!"

Something scratched her shoulders, caught the back of her shirt, and jerked her upward. She gasped. Her helmet flew off. Two fingers clung to Apollo's dowel, and one lodged in the rifle's trigger. It fired, sending a bullet into the ground. After juggling Apollo and spinning the rifle for a moment, she hugged both against her chest. Her fingers touched the goggles, still in place.

A dragon's head appeared at the end of a long neck that snaked underneath a white, scaly body. Albatross blinked at her, his face upside-down. He blew a whistle that sounded like a question.

Lauren let out a relieved sigh. "I'm okay, Albatross. I appreciate the quick response. Now, if you don't mind, please take me back to the cave in the valley." She added in her mind, *A little warning would have helped.*

379

Albatross let out a happy squeal and extended his neck forward.

Joan emerged from Lauren's blowing hair. *It was wise to hold back that thought. There was no need to dampen his joy.*

Right. I'm just glad I didn't shoot anyone.

Take courage. You might have to shoot someone if you wish to rescue Gabriel.

Lauren swallowed. *I know. It won't be easy.*

I commanded soldiers who killed many men, and it was never easy. Freedom for the righteous oppressed often comes at great cost.

Lauren nodded. Joan was right, as usual. The cost was high, but freedom for Gabriel and restored health for Jared were worth even more.

As Albatross flew on, Lauren's shirt rode higher, exposing her abdomen up to her ribs. Cold air chilled her skin. At least this flight shouldn't take too long.

Behind her, Mount Elijah's crater retreated, still smoking and bubbling. She breathed in the relatively clean air. Had she been holding her breath? Everything happened so fast! This merry-go-round of portal jumping was enough to make anyone dizzy, and it wasn't over yet.

Soon, Albatross dropped Lauren off near the river and landed in a run. After running out her own momentum, she set Apollo and the rifle down and straightened her clothes. As the dragon shuffled toward her, she raised the goggles to her eyes and shook back her hair. Joan slid out from her flying locks and settled on her shoulder. "Listen carefully, Albatross. I need you to do something very important."

He extended his neck, bringing his head close. Blinking, he gave her an expectant look.

"Back where you picked me up in the birthing garden, you'll see a trail of human footprints. I need you to cool a path from the first footprint all the way to the hospital. Some people are going to walk on it. Do you understand?"

Albatross nodded and let out a long whistle, as if indicating what a difficult job that would be.

"I realize how much ice that will take. Do you think you can do it?"

He rolled his eyes upward for a moment, then nodded again.

"Great!" She picked up Apollo and the rifle. "I'm glad you're always close by. Keep watching for me. You never know where I'll show up next."

She turned and ran toward the cave, dodging rocks and roots. Even with the goggles in place, the obstacles were often hard to see.

When she reached the forest, she tucked the rifle under her arm and walked in. The shadows seemed to merge, as if moving and blending. Might living shadow people still be around? If so, what did they look like when they were alive? No one had described them.

At the cave entrance, she stepped over the pile of dead shadow people and marched on. When she came across Valiant, she gazed at his lifeless body, barely visible even through the goggles. After heaving a sigh, she averted her eyes and stepped around him. Tears could wait. Lives hung in the balance.

After putting on her sweatshirt and raising the hood, she set Apollo at the back wall and, reading the illuminated display, retrieved the settings for this portal. Without hesitation, she pushed the button, jumped away, and pressed the rifle against her shoulder. When Apollo flashed and created the portal opening, she stepped into the Earth crater and looked around. The helicopter's lights shone on two soldiers as they stood under its slowly spinning propeller, one pointing a rifle at Gabriel, who knelt with his head low and a wing sagging.

Lauren lowered the goggles and took aim at the soldier with the rifle. The other soldier pointed at her and shouted, "Look!"

The armed soldier swung his gun around. Lauren fired but missed. The rifle kicked her backwards, sending her stumbling. As she fell to her bottom, bullets whizzed over her head.

Gabriel lunged at the gunman and tackled him to the ground, knocking his rifle to the side. While they fought, Lauren jumped up and ran toward them, keeping her head low. The other soldier grabbed Gabriel's wing and threw him back. She stopped, braced her feet, and fired again, this time nailing the standing soldier in the hip. While he toppled, the soldier on the ground sat up and grabbed his rifle. She swung her barrel toward him and shouted, "Drop it!"

He snapped open his hand, letting the rifle fall.

"Move away from it!" While the soldier slid on his bottom, Lauren kept her aim on him, searching with darting eyes for the third soldier. She spotted him nearby, lying in a pool of blood, probably a victim of Gabriel's aerial shooting.

Gabriel struggled to his feet, his wing still sagging. As he limped toward Lauren, he touched his jaw. "They took out my transmitter. I couldn't call for help."

She nodded at her pants. "I have my dad's phone in my pocket."

Gabriel fished it out, punched a button, and set it against his ear. "We're all clear, Walter. Land your buggy right away before the rats return."

A tinny voice emanated from the earpiece. "Ten minutes. I had to scoot away when the rats took off earlier."

"Ten minutes." Gabriel punched the End button and slid the phone back to her pocket.

Lauren passed the rifle to him. "If you don't mind."

"Not a bit." He took it and kept it aimed at the remaining healthy soldier. "You did a great job. I'm sure you could watch him as well as I—"

"That's not it. I have to—" She gulped. "Apollo!"

She dashed toward the portal. Still radiant, it had shrunk to the size of a softball. She dropped to her knees, covered her hand with a sweatshirt sleeve and thrust it into the hole. She let go of her sleeve and grabbed Apollo, but when she tried to pull it through, it wouldn't fit.

She pushed it back a few inches and ran her fingers down a dowel, searching for the activation button. The settings were the same, right? Just pushing it should open the portal again.

With each shift and stretch, her sleeve rode up toward her elbow, exposing her forearm. The portal closed around her skin.

A jolt burned her arm and drilled into her bones. As she gritted her teeth, dark spots coated her vision.

"Leave it there!" Gabriel shouted, still guarding the soldiers. "We'll get it another way!"

"There *is* no other way! I have to use it one more time!" The jolt spiked. Pain ripped through her body, stiffening her limbs. Numbness crept from her forearm to her wrist to her hand. Her fingers cramped. Stretching them in spite of the pain, she set a fingertip over the button and, sending all her strength toward that point, pressed down.

In a spray of sparks, the hole expanded to the size of a cabinet door. Her arm fell limp, buzzing with numbness. She reached into the hole with her other arm and drew Apollo from the cave. Rising to her knees, she dragged her injured arm up and let it hang at her side. "I got it."

"I see that," Gabriel said. "I'll just trust you that it was worth it."

383

"It was." After blowing out a pain-filled sigh, she leaned close to him and lowered her voice so the soldiers couldn't hear. "When Walter and company get here, bring Jared to the cave they gassed. There's a portal at the back that'll get him to the hospital in Second Eden."

"Got it." He lifted his injured wing, grimacing. "What are you going to do?"

"I have to get back to Listener and Eagle. I'll meet Jared inside." She walked in the helicopter's light toward the cave leading to the museum room. She let her wounded arm dangle, still aching and buzzing with numbness. Sighing, she looked for Joan. *At least it's my left arm. Since I'm right-handed, it could have been worse.*

Worse? Joan floated in front of her eyes. *There was no need to risk so much to get Apollo. The portal to return to the museum* room is still open, as is the one from the museum room to the birthing garden.

Lauren hugged Apollo close to her chest. *I know.*

Then why did you—

I'd rather not talk about it.

Very well. I understand. Joan blinked at her, then floated to her shoulder. *You have made your decision.*

When Lauren arrived at the cave, she set Apollo on the ground and withdrew her phone. After taking a picture of Gabriel and the cave entrance, she pulled the filter leaf from her pocket, held it over her mouth and nose, and crawled in. Guiding Apollo in the crook of her arm as she held the leaf, she pushed against the ground with her legs. In spite of her efforts to keep everything in place, the leaf slipped, allowing a biting odor into her mouth and throat. Still, she couldn't slow down—there was too much to do. At the same time, she couldn't hurry. Without any light, there was no way to tell where the low tunnel opened up into the larger chamber. A wrong move could mean getting a nasty cut.

Yet, maybe there could be light.

Joan, Lauren called with her mind. *Will you please get excited about something and light up this place?*

Joan's glassy surface rubbed against Lauren's cheek. *It is difficult to generate real emotions without a real reason.*

Well, I read your story a couple of years ago, and I got emotional when no one came to save you when you burned at the stake. Your own people abandoned you. It made me cry.

Yes, I shed many tears. Joan glowed, altering between red and blue. *I gave my all to save my king and my people.*

Lauren continued scooting through the low tunnel, now illuminated with Joan's dim glow. She dropped the leaf, then snatched it back up and held it over her mouth. In its mangled condition, would it still keep the gas out? *What Cauchon did to you made me so angry! The trick about wearing men's clothing was pure treachery.*

As Joan's light strengthened, now all red, Lauren pushed with her feet, then slid Apollo, repeating the process again and again. With one arm not functioning, the going was slow and tedious. The cylindrical passage seemed to spin one way, then the other, as if someone were rocking it back and forth. The gas was probably getting into her system. She took in a deep breath and held it. The end of the tunnel had to be close.

Joan's thoughts continued. *I wore trousers only for battle and for protection against ... well, violation. And I cut my hair for a similar reason. I did the same in preparation for our journey today, though I did not know I would be in this form.*

The red glow grew brighter and brighter. Lauren finally pushed out of the tunnel. Someone grabbed her good arm and wrenched Apollo from her grip.

"Don't worry," Eagle said. "I've got you."

Someone else clutched her injured wrist, and the two helpers dragged her the rest of the way into the cave's inner chamber.

Lauren clenched her eyes shut and cried out with a loud moan. The pain was too horrible for words.

"I'm sorry." Listener's voice seemed to travel under water. "We'll carry you."

Lauren felt her body rise into the air, every limb supported, though her middle sagged. Joan's light pulsed blue, looking like a police car strobe light. *I am here, Lauren, as always. I will not leave you.*

Soon, her body pressed down in a sitting position, bending forward. Her arms settled at her sides, and someone crossed her legs for her. Her wounded arm ached, worse than ever.

She opened her eyes and took in a deep breath, clean and warm. Eagle and Listener crouched next to her, one at each side,

385

and Apollo lay in her lap. She sat facing the border between the Second Eden portal and the Earth portal. Sprays of ice splashed across the birthing garden, raising plumes of vapor. Albatross swooped into view, then zipped back up. A few pellets rolled into the museum and melted into tiny pools near her backpack.

In the Earth portal, everything was dark, and no sounds emanated from the cave.

Eagle slid his hand into hers. "How are you feeling?"

"Somewhere between terrible and horrible." She tried to smile, but her lips barely moved. "Thank you for helping me."

"We didn't see the rifle you took," Listener said. "Did you succeed?"

"I saved Gabriel, if that's what you mean. He has the rifle now." She extended a leg and pointed with her foot toward the Earth portal. "Keep watching. I hope more people show up."

Eagle nodded toward Second Eden. "Albatross has been busy. I didn't bother to ask him why he is doing that. Since he picked you up, I assumed you told him—"

"You assumed right." Lauren pushed Apollo out of the way and offered Eagle her good arm. "Help me up, please."

He gripped her wrist and pulled her upright. As she fought off a round of dizziness, he held her in place.

"I'm all right," she said, pulling away. "I'm fine."

Listener edged closer to the Earth portal. "I hear something."

The sound of coughing filtered in. Light glimmered in the Earth cave, then Walter appeared, pulling one end of a stretcher, a beam on his helmet leading the way. As the stretcher emerged from the low tunnel, Jared came into view lying motionless on it.

Eagle jumped through the portal and helped Walter guide the stretcher into the chamber. At the other end, Marilyn crawled out and climbed to her feet, then Ashley did the same.

All four coughing, Walter, Ashley, Marilyn, and Eagle pushed the stretcher through the portal and, with Lauren and Listener's help, set it on the museum room floor.

Kneeling at the stretcher, Lauren brushed back Jared's hair. He breathed in fitful gasps. With a leathery face similar to Irene's, he didn't look much like the Jared Bannister she had met not long ago. The batholith's effects had spiked in him as well.

Marilyn knelt at his side, her hands wringing. "Gabriel said you wanted us to bring him here. I heard that coming here might make it worse, but he was getting worse anyway."

"You did right. He needs to be here to get the cure." Lauren rose to her feet and pointed toward Second Eden. "Go through the portal and turn left. Follow the path of rising vapor. That should take you to the hospital. Dr. Conner will meet you there."

"And he has a cure?" Her intertwined fingers and kneeling position made her look like a beggar hoping for a slice of bread, but Marilyn was begging for just a crumb of good news.

"He has a model to generate a competing parasite that should destroy the invading one. He'll explain what I'm talking about." Lauren nodded toward the portal. "Walter and Gabriel can carry Jared, and Listener and Eagle will guide you. I'm too dizzy to walk very far."

"Eagle should stay with you," Walter said. "We tied up the surviving soldiers out there, but I can't guarantee they won't get loose or that reinforcements won't arrive soon."

Eagle picked up one of the rifles. "I will be glad to stay and protect Lauren, though she has proven that she needs no help."

"Better to have two than one." Walter raised an end of the stretcher, while Gabriel lifted the other. "When I get back, maybe you can tell me what's going on in this place."

"Real quick …" Lauren pointed toward the opposite side of the room. "The Second Edeners went through a portal over there to Abaddon's Lair. Sir Barlow and Tamara are with them. And straight up …" She gestured with her head. "There's a portal leading to the top of the volcano."

"Good enough for now. Tell me more later. We'd better go."

Listener led the way through the portal, walking on newly cooled ground. Walter and Gabriel followed with Jared on the stretcher between them, while Ashley stood at the portal, waiting for Marilyn.

Marilyn paused and turned to Lauren, her face awash in worry. "He's fading so fast," she said, obviously fighting back a sob. "I don't think he would have lasted more than an hour." She kissed Lauren's cheek and whispered, "Thank you for everything. If not for you, my one and only love would have died. Now I have hope."

When Marilyn passed through the portal, Ashley stood in front of Lauren and gazed into her eyes. "Your mind is very troubled. What's wrong?"

Lauren looked away, blocking her thoughts. "I can't tell you. Please, just go. I'm sure Dr. Conner will need your help."

"You're worrying me, Lauren." Ashley compressed her shoulder. "But you're right. I need to go."

As Ashley hurried to join the others, Joan nuzzled Lauren's cheek. *You avoided telling them all you know. Dr. Conner has a model but not a method.*

Lauren nodded. *Is that the same as lying?*

Sometimes. As one who was asked to recant in ways that would be technically true yet still deceptive in my heart, I had to face similar decisions. Joan pushed into Lauren's hair and nestled close to her ear. *Only you can know if you intended to deceive.*

I didn't deceive her. Lauren hobbled to her backpack and picked it up. *I just have to provide the method.*

She pulled out her phone. "Eagle, would you mind giving me a little privacy? I have a personal message to record."

"What of the potential danger?" He pointed the rifle toward the Earth portal. "The soldiers."

"Don't worry. If they come, I'll scream. Just stay within shouting distance."

"I can do that." He stepped through the Second Eden portal, hesitating at first as his bare foot touched the lava field. Then, he walked toward the hospital, fading quickly in the thick fog.

Lauren shook her hair. "Joan, if you don't mind, please hover close. I want you in the video."

Very well. Joan pushed out from Lauren's hair and floated next to her cheek. *What do you intend to do?*

"I thought you already guessed."

I have. I was seeking verbal confirmation.

"Are you worried about what's going to happen to you?"

Not at all. I fear for you, not for me.

"I'm sorry, but I think it's the only way."

I agree, but that is not what I mean.

"What do you mean?"

Do you remember when I told you that I would not always be so straightforward, that after your baby steps, I would need to release your hand?

"I remember. You said you would always be with me, that you would never let me fall."

Releasing your hand means that I will not always teach you in a straightforward manner. I will bide my time and tell you what you need to know if necessary.

"Suit yourself." After clearing her throat, Lauren tried to smile for the camera, but her lips wouldn't cooperate. No matter. Smiling now would be deceptive.

She pressed the record button. "Hello, Mom, Dad, and anyone else who's watching. I am in the museum room in Hades. Here's the tree of life next to me." She turned the lens toward the tree briefly. "I don't have much time, so I'll just say I love you. I know what I am about to do will break your hearts, but …" Her lips trembling, she swallowed down a sob. "But it's my turn to sacrifice."

She wiped a tear with a knuckle, blinked away more, and steadied her voice. "Mom, you did it, and Dad, so did you, and Grandma, so did you. Tamara told me about Makaidos and Karen and Naamah and Acacia, and I saw Sapphira leap into the lava, not knowing for certain if God would save her." Finally able to smile, she touched Joan with a fingertip. "And Joan of Arc sacrificed, too. You all considered the lives of others as more important than your own, and you knew you had to do what was necessary to help other people, even if it meant dying to save a few. Only Sapphira didn't die, but she proved her willingness. I guess some people get saved in time, and some people don't."

She heaved a deep sigh. "Now I have to save Grandpa Jared, Grandma Irene, and the other anthrozils who are being killed by this terrible parasite. I am probably the only person in any world who even believes this will work, so I am the only option."

You haven't told them what you plan to do, Joan said.

Right. I know. They will see for themselves. Forcing another smile, she lowered the phone close to her chest and angled the lens upward, hoping to show the dark ceiling while she stayed in range of the lens. "After I sign off here, this is the next view you'll see. Just show this to Eagle, and he'll explain."

She glanced at her bloody footprints on the lava field. "If this works, then I will have followed in some noble footsteps. If it doesn't, then I will be a fool who hoped for the best. Either way, I don't really have a choice."

Wiggling her fingers, she gave a little wave, tensing her muscles to keep from crying. "I love you all."

She turned off the camera. As she stared at it, a spasm forced its way into her throat. A sob broke through. Tears dripped.

"No!" She clenched a fist and swiped away the tears with her sweatshirt sleeve. "I don't have time to cry!"

She tore the goggles over her head and hoisted the backpack on. "I'm ready."

Are you? Joan floated in front of her eyes, staring with her eyelets open. *I am not so sure.*

Lauren's head pounded, and dizziness returned, but not too bad. "Well, I can't wait until I'm fully recovered, if that's what you mean. If I don't go now, I'll change my mind." She set the phone on the floor, aiming it at the ceiling, and turned the camera on again. "Let's go."

She picked up Apollo and limped to the Heaven portal. The room swayed twice before settling. If only the effects of the gas would stop, this would be a lot easier.

The ladder stood near one edge of the portal and rose into the dim reaches of the museum room. Tucking Apollo under her sore arm, she gripped the ladder's side and climbed toward the top, her shaking body making the ladder quiver.

Joan hovered close to her ear. *There is still turmoil in your mind.*

Shouldn't there be? Trying not to grunt, Lauren trudged up each rung. It wouldn't do to make too much noise and bring Eagle running back in.

There was none in Sapphira. She pressed the cross into her bosom, and it set her heart aflame.

Lauren continued climbing until she reached the truss. *I saw that. I did sort of the same thing.* She set Apollo on top of the truss.

True. You are very similar, but Sapphira did not die.

I remember. What's your point? With a quick leap from the rung, Lauren vaulted to a sitting position on the truss. After rising to her feet, she picked up Apollo and shuffled toward the center where the trusses intersected. With every movement, Joan stayed close, her light glowing bright blue.

As she edged farther out, Lauren slid her feet, now glad that they were bare. The skin-on-wood contact helped her grip the truss and maintain balance. The effort felt like balance beam practice in gym class.

She whispered to herself, "Three more paces. Slide, don't lift."

My point is that you have great faith, but not every faithful servant of God is called to give up her life. Even with a set of identical twins, Acacia and Sapphira, one was called to die, and one was not.

Lauren's head continued to pound, making Joan's words spin in her mind. They made almost no sense. "I realize that, and I'm glad Sapphira didn't die. She's still doing a lot of good." When she reached the center, she crouched low and set Apollo on the trusses' intersection. Using its backlit display, she browsed through recent portal openings, found the one for the museum room ceiling, and programmed the flash settings.

Joan floated between her face and Apollo, as if trying to block her view. *Do you know what Jehovah-Yasha means?*

"My mother was praying the first time I heard it. She said, 'Jehovah-Yasha, the Lord my savior,' so I guess that's what it means." With a gentle push, she guided Joan out of the way. She set her finger on Apollo's button, looked to the side, and pressed it. A flash brightened the area, then vanished, and a glow washed over the trusses.

Above, Second Eden's moon shone brightly overhead. Lauren raised her hood and looked down. The phone lay on the floor, a tiny light flashing to indicate recording mode.

Spreading her arms for balance, she straightened. Now higher than she was before when she stood on the ladder, her entire body from her thighs up protruded into Second Eden. Yet, the portal's edges didn't extend as far to the sides. Apollo's energy hadn't quite recharged.

Joan settled on Lauren's shoulder. *Your mother was right. A person who calls out Jehovah-Yasha is trusting in God to save. It is a valid call for both physical and spiritual deliverance.*

Lauren crouched low again and ducked under the portal plane. She grabbed Joan and held her between her thumb and finger. "Listen, my head hurts, I'm dizzy, and I can hardly keep from falling off this truss, so I can't handle riddles right now. If you're trying to tell me I shouldn't do this, then just tell me, but you'd better include another way to save Jared and the others. I have lives to save and no time to waste. The portal's going to close."

I ... I know of no other way to save them.

"Then I guess you're done." She set Joan back on her shoulder. "I hope you're not offended."

I am not offended. I am troubled. Perhaps I am not the companion you needed. I know intimately the pain you are about to embrace, and my emotions are shouting at me to stop you from destroying the wondrous life you could have in service to the greatest of kings. Joan's voice grew somber. *I assume you know that suicide is forbidden. It is murder of yourself.*

"This isn't suicide. This is sacrifice." Lauren sharpened her tone. "Don't tell me you haven't marched straight into death to save the life of another person."

It is true. I have. I cannot deny it. Joan's light darkened. *Do what you must. I cannot make this decision for you.*

"I don't think I have a choice." Lauren reached for her backpack strap, but when she pivoted, her hip bumped Apollo off the truss. It plunged and clattered to the floor, breaking two dowels and smashing the interior glass.

She pounded a fist on the truss. How stupid! Now if the portal closed too quickly she wouldn't be able to open it again.

With a quick lift of her shoulders, she let the backpack straps slide off, then spun it around her body and set it on the truss. She unzipped the main pocket, tossed the hand shovel out, and checked the soil level. It seemed that none had spilled, but something sizzled deep inside. Warmth emanated, along with a foul odor.

"What are you doing?" The voice came from below.

Lauren looked down. Eagle stood next to Apollo's remains. "I … uh … I'm throwing the parasite-making stuff into the volcano. I told you about that." She glanced at the portal opening. It had shrunk to about four feet wide.

He walked to the bottom of the ladder, passing by the phone. "You didn't say when to come back, so when I heard the crash, I decided to check on you."

"Thanks. I appreciate it. I knocked Apollo off. Pretty clumsy, right?"

"Accidents happen." He gripped the side of the ladder. "Do you need help?"

"No! I mean, help would be great, but there's not much room up here, and I have to hurry."

"Lauren, your words trouble me." He stepped up to the first rung. "Since I knew you would take a little time to finish recording your message, I ran to the hospital to see how Dr. Conner would heal Jared, but he has no cure yet. It's all on a computer. Poor Marilyn fell to the floor sobbing. Jordan is already dead, and Dr. Conner thinks Jared and Irene will die in mere minutes. They are failing quickly."

"I know. That's why I have to throw this stuff into the volcano."

"Then why didn't you simply tell us that's what you were doing?" He took another step up the ladder. "Mount Elijah won't erupt unless someone falls in. I told you that."

"I know. I believe you." Hugging the backpack, Lauren rose to her full height and gazed out over the volcano crater. Lava boiled and bubbled below. Even from a hundred feet away, the heat scalded her cheeks, worse than last time. She swallowed. No turning. No looking back.

"No, Lauren! Don't!" Heavy footfalls sounded from the ladder.

"Eagle!" Listener's voice broke in. "What's going on?"

Lauren turned her head toward Joan. She sat motionless, her shell darkened. "Thank you for being with me all the way. I'll see you in Heaven."

Joan nuzzled her neck. *I hope so, mon amie. I hope so.*

Lauren took a deep breath and jumped over the portal edge. As she plunged toward the lava, she closed her eyes and cried out, "Jehovah-Yasha!"

23

CHAPTER

TRIAL BY FIRE

Falling facedown, Lauren opened her eyes and clutched the backpack. Joan plunged with her, hovering close to her shoulder. Death would come quickly. The suffering wouldn't last—

A whistle sounded. Something snagged the back of her sweatshirt and stretched it. Like a rubber band, she snapped upward and sailed away from the lava.

Lauren jerked her head around. Albatross flew toward the sky, his claws embedded in her sweatshirt as he beat his wings furiously. He flew past Eagle, who stood in midair over the volcano crater, his shirt smoldering. "Eagle!" she screamed. "Tell him to let me go! I have to create the parasite! I have to make Mount Elijah erupt!"

Setting two fingers in his mouth, Eagle blew a shrill whistle. "Albatross! Bring her to me! Hurry!"

Albatross circled back. With every beat of his wings, the tips came into view, blackened and smoking. As he closed in, Eagle appeared to be marching in place. His pant legs had caught on fire, and the edges of the portal brushed his thighs. When Albatross passed, Eagle leaped, grabbed one of his rear legs, and hung on, dangling next to Lauren.

Squealing, Albatross dipped. His wings beat out of sync. He and his passengers dropped closer and closer to the lava. The portal closed with a splash of sparks. Lauren gasped. There was no returning now.

"He's not going to make it!" she shouted. "Tell him to let me go! It's his only chance."

"There is one other chance." He wrestled the backpack away from Lauren and yelled, "Albatross, make sure she gets to the hospital safely!"

Eagle let go and plunged toward the lava. The release sent Albatross skyward. Eagle dropped into the volcano with a silent splash. Fire erupted at the entry point and quickly settled.

"Eagle!" Lauren cried. "Oh, Eagle, how could you?"

A low rumble emanated from the crater. Dozens of fountains spewed lava. Geysers of smoke shot out from each one. Albatross's wings beat out of sync again. With every flap, he dropped closer and closer to the shooting spray.

He stretched out his neck and dipped his head down to Lauren. With a snap of his teeth, he grabbed her sweatshirt, swung her up, and set her on his back. She hugged a spine and hung on. Still, he floundered. In seconds they would splash in and be consumed.

"Fly, Albatross!" Lauren patted the dragon's scales. "You can do it! We have to hurry! This thing is going to blow!"

He lifted over the crater's ragged edge and descended toward the plunging slope—sharply angled and still covered by super-heated lava rock. Shooting a torrent of ice out in front, he dropped to the slope and slid down on his own carpet of frost. Lauren bounced hard on his back, making her slide off to the side. She hung on to the spine with her right hand, her body dangling as she slammed against his scales with every bump and twist. Vapor shot skyward all around. Sizzles and crackles ripped through the air. Sooty mud splashed Lauren's face, hot and slimy, though cooled by Albatross's ice.

Albatross rocked forward, then back. He beat his wings to keep from tipping over, slinging Lauren in all directions. With Joan floating an inch from her eyes, Lauren dug her feet into the dragon's scales, lunged upward, and latched on to the spine with her other hand. Pain roared through her sore arm, but it couldn't be helped. Flexing her biceps, she pulled with both arms, pushed with her pedaling feet, and scrambled back in place, again hugging the spine.

Finally, Albatross reached level ground and slid for another hundred feet or so before coming to a stop. He huffed a few more jets of ice around his body, raising more skyrocketing walls of vapor. With a final heave, he shot out a wheezing spray of drizzle and slumped to the ground, his wings splayed.

Gasping for breath, Lauren looked around. To the rear, behind a veil of mist, Mount Elijah coughed billowing clouds of smoke and glowing ash. In front, an expanse of huge boulders and piles of smoldering logs stretched out across the hazy landscape, impassable on foot for at least a couple of hundred yards. With an exhausted, crippled dragon as her only transport, there was no escape.

The mountain rumbled. The ground shook. Lauren wiped grime from her face with her sleeve. "Oh, Albatross! What are we going to do?"

He curled his neck and laid his head on her lap, whimpering. As her tears flowed, she petted his scales, pushing back his pointed ears. "I know. I know." A sob erupted from her gut, but she sucked it back in, allowing only a lamenting tone to break through. "I saw what happened to Eagle. He was so brave. So sacrificial."

Joan floated down and rested on Lauren's petting hand, as if joining in the effort to comfort him. *Discouragement is the greatest crippler of all. No human or dragon can struggle through suffering without a reason to believe that his efforts will make a difference.*

Another rumble shook the ground. A loud crack sounded. To the left, a split in the rocky floor opened wide. A boulder toppled into the gap, and a pile of fallen trees cascaded behind it.

Lauren fought back another spasm, gasping between phrases. "I know you'll miss Eagle … but we have to keep going somehow. … Mount Elijah might erupt at any minute … and if it heals the anthrozils, no one … no one will ever know … about what Eagle did to save them … if we don't survive to tell the story."

Albatross looked up at her with unblinking eyes—sad, exhausted eyes. Then, with a low groan, he lifted his head slowly. He nuzzled her cheek with his and stretched out his neck, aiming his eyes again to the front.

As he lifted his wings, the ground quaked. Lava shot from the volcano in a towering geyser. It rained over the upper part of the slope in splattering fiery globs and ran downward in a boiling avalanche.

Lauren spanked Albatross's scales. "Hurry! The lava's coming!"

Walter stood hand in hand with Ashley between two beds, one holding Irene Conner and the other, Jared Bannister. Both patients gasped for breath, their mouths hanging open, accentuating their macabre faces—gaunt, wrinkled, and pale.

Dr. Conner crouched at the opposite side of Irene's bed, combing through her straw-like hair, while Marilyn sat on Jared's, her eyes sad and wet. Gabriel lay awake on another bed, curled on his side to keep from compressing his injured wings. Adhesive bandages covered gashes and cuts on his face and hands, a temporary stopgap while he awaited stitches.

With the lights on in the hospital's dorm cabin, several women and children sat up in their beds, most with troubled faces. It seemed that death stalked the room with a sharp sickle, ready to reap at any moment. Candle paced the aisle, his long dreadlocks swinging every time he reached the end of his route and spun to go the other way, ready to jump if anyone called for help, but so far there was nothing to do.

Walter leaned close to Ashley and whispered, "How long has Listener been gone?"

"Only a minute, but it seems like an hour."

He added a thought. *Dr. Conner's story about Lauren seems too wild to believe. Does she think throwing a bunch of supercharged soil into—*

401

"Shhh. I know, I know. Just be patient for another minute. There's something I need to do." Ashley slid her hand away from Walter's and cleared her throat. "I have to interpret for Jared," she said, loudly enough for all to hear. "He is trying to speak to his wife, but he hasn't the strength."

Marilyn blinked at her. "You're reading his mind?"

"Quite easily. He's thinking straight at me on purpose." Ashley knelt by the bed and stroked Jared's head. He stared at her with wide eyes, his mouth still open. "Go ahead, Jared. Pour your heart out. I won't leave anything unsaid."

Ashley grasped Marilyn's hand and interlocked their thumbs. "Like this?" Ashley asked as she looked at Jared. "Oh. Okay." She shifted her hand around and intertwined her fingers with Marilyn's. "Like this. Got it."

Marilyn pressed her lips together and choked back a sob.

"That's fine, Jared," Ashley said. "Take your time."

Jared swiveled his head toward Marilyn and looked at her, though his face stayed locked in a hideous mask.

"Marilyn," Ashley said, closing her eyes as she continued stroking Jared's head. "My darling. … You often worried that you would grow old without me … that you would become wrinkled and gray while I stayed young. … I promised that I would love you no matter how you looked. … Remember? For better or for worse? Till death do us part?"

While Jared continued his gaping stare, Ashley chuckled. "But now look at me. … I am the one who looks like a zombie … while you are as beautiful as ever."

Marilyn pressed a hand over her mouth. "No, Jared, I think you look—"

"Shhh," Ashley said. "Don't waste words. I am hideous. There is no denying it. … Here is the reason I wanted Ashley to speak for me. … We have not yet finished this race. Billy needs us, so I'm going to keep fighting this disease, no matter what. I have been weak and impotent, and my inability has stabbed my heart, especially my failure in the crater. But the spirit of Clefspeare still lives in this decaying shell, and when I recover, I will go to war to save our son."

Marilyn caressed Jared's wrinkled cheek. "That's my Jared. But it might take a long time for you to get your strength back."

Ashley nodded. "There is a way for me to recover more quickly. I put the information in an encrypted file in Larry. I believe Lauren will be successful, so when I begin to heal, ask him for the data."

Jared closed his eyes. His breathing grew shallow and rasping.

"Jared?" Marilyn stood and slid an arm under his back. "Let's boost him up so he can breathe better."

Candle leaped to the other side of the bed and helped her lift Jared to a sitting position. Within seconds, his breaths came easier through his gaping mouth, though still rattling.

"He's asleep," Ashley said. "I'm not getting any more thoughts."

Marilyn sat again and held Jared's hand. "Thank you, Ashley. That was very helpful."

"Can I get you anything?" Candle asked.

She nodded. "Water. Thank you."

Candle hustled to the vestibule and closed the door behind him.

Ashley drew back and pulled Walter away. "We'd better leave them alone for a while."

"I agree." Walter swiped a tear with a knuckle. "I thought for a minute there we were going to lose him."

"Me, too. At first, I thought he wanted to communicate a final good-bye. I don't know if I could handle that."

Walter nodded at Irene. "Maybe you should see if she wants to say anything to Doc."

"Ashley!" The door to the vestibule burst open, and Listener ran into the room, breathless. "They're gone! Lauren and Eagle!"

Walter caught Listener's arm. "Gone? Through a portal?"

Nodding along with her flashing companion, Listener pointed up. "Through the museum room ceiling. They just disappeared, first Lauren and then Eagle. It was too dark to tell what happened to them. The portal hole closed, and they were just gone." She withdrew a phone from her pocket and held it in her trembling hands. "I found this on the floor. I was wondering if it might—"

"I'll look." Ashley snatched the phone away and began pressing buttons with her thumbs. "The camera's recording. Let me see what it's captured." After a few more clicks, she called out, "Found

403

some photos!" She stopped pressing buttons and squinted at the screen. "I can't believe it!"

Walter shifted behind her and looked over her shoulder. A photo of a young black teenager appeared on the screen.

Ashley's eyes opened wide. "Derrick?"

"Derrick?" Walter blinked at her. "The boy who anchored the candlestone dives?"

She spun to Dr. Conner and showed him the screen. "Doc! Isn't this Derrick?"

He turned away from Irene and looked blankly at the phone. "Yes, that's Derrick." His voice was melancholy, barely above a whisper. "He's Eagle now. I watched him grow up here. When he was about fourteen, I knew it. No need to tell anyone. It seems that resurrections are normal here." He sighed. "A true irony, I think—a blind boy becomes known for his sharp vision, which explains why he often hummed 'Amazing Grace,' though I think that song is foreign to the people here."

Staring straight ahead, Ashley whispered, "I once was lost, but now am found, was blind, but now I see."

"Weren't we all?" Dr. Conner nodded and turned back to Irene, again stroking her hair. "He saved a wretch like me."

Blinking away tears, Ashley began pressing phone buttons again. "I found a video. It's the last thing on here."

She pushed the play button. On the screen, Lauren climbed the ladder, wearing a backpack and carrying Apollo. Something to the side sent a wash of light over her.

Candle hurried back in and gave Marilyn a bottle of water, then watched the video with Walter and Ashley.

"Lauren's carrying the soil," Walter said. "She's heading up to the portal leading to the volcano, right?"

404

"Right." Ashley sped the video to double speed. Lauren climbed onto a support beam, slid out to the center, and made Apollo flash. The portal opened to a moonlit sky. Lauren knocked Apollo over, sending it tumbling. When it clattered, Ashley winced but said nothing.

"So she's going to throw the stuff in." Ashley pointed at the backpack. "But Doc told her it needed an eruption. Timing it would be impossible."

Listener squeezed close to Candle and peered at the phone. "Not if she jumped in," Candle said.

Walter turned toward him. "What?"

"Mount Elijah erupts when someone falls in. That's what Valiant always told us."

"She …" Listener pressed two fingers over her lips, her voice quavering. "She must have jumped in. She disappeared, just like I said."

"Look, Walter." Ashley pointed at the screen again. While Lauren stood on the beam, Eagle scaled the ladder, churning his arms and legs. Garbled words shot from the tiny speaker. Lauren leaped from the beam and disappeared.

Ashley gasped. "Walter! She *did* jump!"

"I know!" Walter stalked away from the phone and paced in the aisle between the two rows of beds. "I can't believe this. Valiant's dead. Legossi's dead. Billy and Bonnie and Matt are missing. And now Lauren's …" Choking up, he couldn't finish. He just stuffed his hands into his pockets and kept pacing the floor.

"Oh no!" Ashley stared at the phone, her mouth agape.

"I was right! Eagle jumped, too!" Listener dropped to her knees and covered her face with her hands. "How can this be happening?"

While Candle helped her up, Walter stepped toward them. The ground shook, knocking him off his feet. The beds rattled but stayed in place, their bolts holding fast to the floor. Whimpers and gasps filled the room. Doc held Irene in place, while Marilyn hugged Jared close. Gabriel shouted from his bed, "Everyone hang on!"

A rumble sounded, deep and long. Walter leaped up, ran to the vestibule, and looked out. In the distance, lava spewed from Mount Elijah high into the night sky. More lava rolled down its slopes, red and glowing. "It's blowing its top!" He stalked back to the dorm. "Let's get this hunk of machinery off the ground!"

Albatross beat his wings frantically. No longer shooting ice, he lifted over a boulder, touched down for a moment, and bounced over a mound of smoking logs. He repeated the bouncing and touching again and again, screaming in agony every time his feet and wings brushed the ground. The ends of his wings smoked, then caught on fire. He continued his sporadic leaps, banging into burning logs and scraping the tops of boulders.

Lauren hung on with all her might. With every bump, Albatross's body twisted and lurched. Gut-wrenching screams burst forth, but he surged on—flailing, bouncing, and heaving gasps. Fire combined with the moon to cast bright light everywhere.

Lava stormed down the slope and spilled over level ground. From the crater, flaming rocks spewed in every direction, like missiles arcing to the ground and exploding into thousands of fiery fragments. Hot pebbles rained on Lauren's back and slid off her flame-retardant sweatshirt. She raised her hood and shouted, "Go, Albatross! Go!"

Albatross leaped over the final boulder and skittered across flat lava rock. Sizzles erupted at his feet. He tripped and fell to his chest, sliding and scraping. His momentum slung Lauren forward.

Flailing with her arms and pumping her legs, she flew through the air. She landed with a thump on her bare feet, absorbed the impact with her knees, and ran until her momentum eased.

She spun back to Albatross. He lay twitching on the field, smoke rising from his burning wings. Lava approached, drawing closer and closer. She took a hard step toward him, but the ground shook once more. She lurched in reverse, backpedaling on the burning rocks to keep from falling.

Lava poured over Albatross's body. Flames burst from his scales and covered him in seconds. More fiery missiles rocketed down from the shattered cone, hurtling toward Lauren.

She stood and stared, her legs locked, her arm and head throbbing. She whispered, "Albatross?"

Joan zipped up to her nose, flashing red. *Run! You have to run!*

Holding her hood up, Lauren spun and ran toward a rising slope in the distance. Joan zoomed with her, floating above her shoulder. Explosions rocked the field. Flaming grit rained all around, pelting Lauren's head and back. An ember struck Joan and drove her to Lauren's shoulder.

407

She snatched Joan, clutched the heated shell, and sprinted with all her might. Finally, the storm of debris stopped. Lauren slowed, turned, and walked backwards, her legs stiff. While staring at the lava flow, now turning toward a lower elevation, she opened her hand to let Joan cool. Smoke poured over the field like a morning mist, blinding but not caustic.

She stopped and drew the egg close to her eyes. Something sizzled. Although the ember hit Joan pretty hard, the shell hadn't caught fire, so the noise couldn't be the crackle of flames. Yet, the outer part of the shell formed tiny bubbles, as if wrinkling from heat. "Joan!" Lauren's hand shook uncontrollably. "What's happening? Are you all right?"

The egg pulsed with a dim blue light. A bare whisper emanated, fragile and quivering. *I am unsure, mon amie ... I know not what is happening ... I hear voices ... Joyful singing ... Someone cried out with rapture that ... that your fiery ordeal is complete.*

The egg split from top to bottom, revealing a blinding light within. "Joan!" Tears spilled from Lauren's eyes. "You're breaking! What do I do?"

Nothing ... All is well ...

The egg crumbled, leaving only a figurine—Joan with her arms outspread and her face to the sky. *I see angels ... My precious angels ... Oh, mon amie! They have finally come to take me home!*

Sobbing, Lauren stared at the lovely little image of Joan, so beautiful as she stood on tiptoes and reached toward Heaven. *Lauren! My glorious Jesus has spoken to me. Now I know I am in a state of grace, and so are you! Forgiven! Welcomed into his embrace! Let us rejoice!*

Joan lifted from Lauren's hand and floated slowly upward. As she ascended, she turned to Lauren, her smile wide and her arms still outspread. *I will see you in Heaven, my dear friend. Be brave. Death is a conquered enemy. All fear is gone.*

Lauren swallowed through a tight lump. "Good-bye, Joan. I ... I love you."

Like a feather taken by a breeze, Joan floated into the sky, her light slowly fading as she flew out of sight. With tears dripping, Lauren stared at the glow, her hand still open.

When the light disappeared, she dropped to a crouch, wrapped her arms over her head, and sobbed. "Oh, Joan! My dear companion!" Spasms throttled her chest, forcing halting gasps. "What am I going to do now? ... How can I go on without you? ... I lost my mother ... my father ... my brother ... Eagle ... and now ... and now you! ... I've lost everyone! ... I was supposed to ... to be the one to sacrifice … the one to face the fire, but now … but now I'm still alive … and Eagle is dead … and no one even knows to look for me."

As she wept, images flashed to mind—Joan striding into Abaddon's chamber, white flowers in her hair; Albatross squealing with delight when she complimented him; Matt collecting leaves as he worked desperately to heal the Second Edeners. All three marched forward in their faithful journeys without knowing what lay ahead. Two had perished in flames. But what had become of Matt?

Wiping tears, she straightened and turned away from Mount Elijah. A bare field of cooling lava from the previous eruption stretched out ahead. A few fallen trees and boulders lay in sight as well as a thin curtain of smoke. In spite of the visual obstructions, the hospital shouldn't be too hard to find if moonlight kept the way illuminated. Maybe Matt was there by now. Maybe the new parasite had already floated that far, riding on the wave of smoke.

She breathed in the sooty air. Although it carried a choking odor, it wasn't as bad as before. Maybe this eruption carried healing along with harm. Time would tell. So far, it had brought only death.

Tears still trickling, Lauren kissed her palm. "Au revoir, mon amie. I will look forward to seeing you again." Then, squaring her shoulders, she limped into the smoky field.

Dr. Conner jumped up and joined Walter in the aisle. "It'll take just a minute to lift off. If you'll secure everyone, I'll—"

"Wait!" Listener called. "Don't leave! There's no more top to blow off. The lava shouldn't come this way."

"Shouldn't?" Walter pointed toward the volcano. "Listen, that lava means business. We can't afford to take a chance."

"But we want the anthrozils to breathe the fumes," Ashley said. "If the eruption expelled the new parasite, it's their only hope."

Walter smacked his palm with a fist. "Then we fly right into the smoke."

"Our patients can breathe it." Dr. Conner strode toward the rear of the dorm. "But we'll need filters for the others. I have surgical masks."

"Doc, no!" Ashley pointed toward the front of the hospital. "Get us off the ground. I'll take care of the filters."

"Then secure everyone. There are belts on the beds." Dr. Conner hustled toward the front of the hospital.

Walter and Ashley hurried from bed to bed, lifting straps over patients and refugees and buckling everyone in, including Gabriel, Irene, and Marilyn, who was now lying with Jared.

Listener ran toward the vestibule. "I'll get the other dorm. Steadfast is there. He'll help me."

"Tell everyone to get under the covers," Ashley called as she worked. "Everyone except the anthrozils."

"We will." Listener grabbed Candle's wrist, and the two hurried through the doorway and out of sight.

With all the beds full, Walter pulled Ashley to the floor and grabbed a bed frame. "Just like riding a dragon. Hold on tight."

Ashley curled an arm around the leg of a bed and leaned her head against Walter's. "I suppose Listener will be all right."

"She's been riding dragons since she was little. She'll be fine." She half closed an eye. "Will *you* be fine?"

"Me? What do you mean?"

"I know you too well. As soon as we're in the air, you'll be at the door searching for Lauren and Eagle."

He smiled. "You're right. Anything wrong with that?"

"Only that they're both probably dead, and you shouldn't risk your life. I know that won't stop you, so …" She kissed him on the cheek. "Just be safe."

The airplane engines roared to life. Propellers whirred. The hospital shifted for a moment before lifting from the ground.

Walter slid his hand into Ashley's. "Let's go breathe some parasites, shall we?"

Lauren staggered through the darkness, coughing and gasping. With smoke veiling the moon and the land covered with lava rock, the entire world looked dismal—shadowy outlines on a deep purple canvas. Only the barest light glowed from the volcano, now far to the rear. How could anyone possibly find the hospital or the portal to the museum room without more light, especially in such a strange world? It would be like trying to catch flying bats while blindfolded.

Her bare feet padded on the spongy soil. Hot air shot up her pant legs and across her arms, making her sweat. Earlier, the flow from her pores had been profuse, but now very little trickled. With the sweatshirt again tied around her waist, she rolled up her short sleeves, hitched up the shirt's hem, and tied it at her ribs. But not even that did much to cool her parched skin. The torrents of hot air from below wouldn't relent even for a second.

She licked her cracked lips. With no more fire danger, maybe tossing the sweatshirt away would be best. Still walking on stiff legs, she began untying the sleeves. Her wounded arm ached and tingled with numbness. Every movement hurt. Lying down was out of the question. The lava rock would burn her to a crisp.

Finally, a slight breeze cleared the smoke somewhat, making breathing easier. A buzzing noise came from above. Plodding slowly, she looked up and searched for the source. Barely visible through a hovering layer of smoke, a blinking light passed by, floating along with the drifting sound, but nothing took shape. It seemed to be heading toward Mount Elijah, so it couldn't be the hospital. That wouldn't make any sense at all.

Her toes slammed into something hard. She staggered back and squinted. A pile of fallen trees stood in a head-high pyramid. She touched one of the logs at chest level—warm but not hot.

Lifting her leg high and grabbing the stub of a limb, she hoisted herself up and climbed to the top of the pile. As she balanced, the pile shifted but quickly settled. She sat with her legs dangling over the side, untied the sweatshirt, and hung it on the stub below.

She rolled up her pant legs and lay on her stomach. With her cheek pressed against the bark, she hugged the top tree. A breeze blew over her half-exposed back. Ah! That was better! Finally some relief! Still, with no water, she couldn't stay long. She would die of thirst.

As she rested, she looked at her shoulder where Joan usually perched. In the hazy moonlight, her gaze met only a bare arm protruding from a rolled-up sleeve. The void plunged a dagger into her heart. Was Joan happy now? Surely she was, finally resting from her labors. She had hoped for Heaven for centuries, and now she likely rejoiced with the other martyrs who had blazed a trail before her.

And what of Eagle? Since he was here in Second Eden, that meant he had lost his life for a second time. Maybe he, too, would go to be with God forever. With such a sacrificial heart, the young man who hummed "Amazing Grace" would receive grace, wouldn't he? And finally, what about Valiant? Maybe all three were already celebrating their heavenly resurrections, wondering why people on Earth and Second Eden were so worried about their troubles. It all ended in a glorious reunion for everyone who understood the meaning of Jehovah-Yasha.

Lauren heaved a sigh. Yes, all would be well. Even if she died here on this pile of logs, she could go be with them. Like Sapphira, she had burned the cross of Christ in her heart and sacrificed everything for him.

Consciousness began to drift away. Lauren whispered, "Jehovah-Yasha" and fell asleep.

CHAPTER

LIFTING THE LOST

Walter stood at the hospital's door, the stairway hatch open below his feet. As smoke filtered in, he coughed through a surgical mask. Although thin, the mask helped. At least it kept him from choking while he searched the ground for any sign of life.

Dr. Conner ran by, giving Walter a high five as he passed from the front dorm to the rear. Also wearing a surgical mask, he didn't bother to speak.

"Is that hand slap a good sign, Doc?"

"Ask Ashley. She's on her way." He disappeared behind a door.

Walter smiled. With Steadfast now piloting the plane, Dr. Conner was free to care for the patients, and his energy level had to mean good news.

Ashley walked from the front dorm, her mask below her chin, revealing a wide smile. She pulled down Walter's mask and gave him a kiss.

"Now *that's* a good sign!" Walter grinned. "What's up?"

"We think it's working. Doc's been taking blood samples, and he's spotted a new bug on some receptors. Jared and Irene are already improving."

"That's fantastic!"

"Yep! Great news!" Walter and Ashley joined hands, and both gazed out over Second Eden's devastated land. Steadfast had already flown to the volcano, back to the birthing garden, and then to the volcano again, and now he had just turned toward the garden once more. This would be the last segment, their final chance to search the area.

Walter sighed. No sign of anyone. Like Ashley said, Lauren and Eagle probably both fell into the volcano, and now they were just fragments scattered from one end of Second Eden to the other. It would be better to focus on the good news. "Any long-term prognosis for Jared and company?"

"Should be good. What we still don't know is what will happen to the receptors once the original parasite dies. Since Dr. Conner set the appropriate genetic key, we assume the new parasite will die along with the one it consumed, but since the receptors were revived, will they stay revived? It certainly would help if they did. The way their bodies aged, they need some restoration."

"Might they develop any dragon traits? They didn't have any as humans before, but ..." He scratched his head. "I don't know how it would work."

Ashley shrugged. "Maybe. We'll see. One step at a time."

Walter reached toward the door controls. "I guess I should close up now and do something useful."

"No." Ashley pulled his arm back. "Keep looking. I don't see any reason not to."

"You don't think it's hopeless?"

"After all I've seen, nothing is hopeless." Ashley kissed his cheek. "Call if you need anything."

When she closed the dorm door, Walter crouched and stared at the dark ground, partially veiled by smoke. As it passed underneath, an occasional orange glow drifted by, remains of burning debris, but no sign of a human, either walking or dead. Since the hot surface would burn up anyone down there, it probably was hopeless, in spite of what Ashley said. No one could survive a fall into a volcano … no one.

Near the edge of his field of vision, a white glow drifted into view, dimmer than the orange ones. As it drew closer, it appeared to break into segments, almost as if covered here and there by …

Walter blinked. A shirt? Pants? He began to straighten, his voice rising with his body. "Ashley!" He pounded a fist on the airplane wall and shouted, "Ashley!"

She burst out from the dorm. "What is it?"

"Look!" Walter pointed at the ground. "See it?"

"See what?" She peered out the door. "I see something white. A phosphorescent rock, maybe?"

Walter clutched her wrist and rubbed her skin. "Lauren glows in the dark!"

She stared at him, her mouth dropping open. "Lauren survived?"

"Not sure. Gotta check it out. I haven't seen any movement."

"Can we land here?"

Walter shook his head. "Too close to the volcano. Too hot to risk it. We can switch to vertical propellers and drop down close."

"Keep your eye on her. I'll tell Steadfast!" She ran toward the front of the cabin.

"Doc!" Walter called into the rear section. "I've spotted Lauren! We'll need water! Lots of it!"

Dr. Conner replied from the dorm. "For drinking or for washing?"

"Both! And tell Candle to get a rope over here. Hurry!" Walter turned toward the front. "Listener! I know you can hear me. Go with Ashley. I'll shout directions, and you can relay them to Steadfast."

Pounding feet ensued. Shouts clamored throughout the cabin, some commanding and some joyous.

"Walter!" Gabriel yelled from his bed. "Maybe I could fly down there and—"

"Stay strapped in!" Walter pointed at him. "You can't fly in your condition! You might get you and Lauren both killed!"

Gabriel sighed. "You're right. Just be sure to relay updates. Everyone will want to know what's going on."

When the hospital flew directly over Lauren, Walter called, "This is the spot! Switch to chopper mode!"

Candle arrived with a coil of rope. "I hope this is long enough."

"It'll do." As the hospital slowed, Walter grabbed one end of the rope, whipped it around his waist, and jerked a knot in place. "Loop the other end around a bed frame. Then get Doc and come back with that end to help with the pulling."

"Yes sir!" Candle scrambled away.

"Listener! Tell Ashley to get back here to help. I'll need her muscles and her mind reading."

Footsteps sounded again. "I'm already here, Walter!" Ashley burst into the vestibule. "What do you want me to do?"

"Wait a sec and I'll tell you."

Dr. Conner and Candle bustled in, Candle holding the end of the rope.

"Ready, Walter," Doc said. "And I have a basin and five bottles filled with water."

"Perfect. Now all three of you pull the rope tight and hang on. I'm counting on you."

"Why the rope?" Ashley asked. "Can't we just hover down and pick her up?"

Walter shook his head. "This plane is too clumsy for that. If we get close, turbulence might make us drop on top of her."

Candle reeled in the rope, forcing it to slide around the bed frame, until it tightened.

Ashley checked the knot at Walter's waist. "Anything else?"

"Just this." He gave her a kiss. "We've done this once before. Remember?"

She nodded. "When you slid down to the mobility room. That was a long time ago."

"Yep. That was the first day I realized I loved you."

"Okay, Romeo." Smiling, Ashley lifted his surgical mask over his nose and mouth. "You'll get another kiss when you're safely back up here with Lauren."

"That's good incentive." Walter winked. "Now everyone hang on and let it slide easy. Maybe twenty feet. That should be enough for a safety buffer." As he backed toward the door, Ashley, Doc, and Candle fed the rope through their hands. He climbed down the stairway and leaned out. "Can Listener hear me all right even with the engine noise?"

Holding the rope with both hands, Ashley bent toward him. "She's fine. Steadfast spotted Lauren, so he knows where to hover. You'll just need to shout elevation adjustments."

"I hope my voice can penetrate this mask." Still leaning back, Walter looked down. Lauren lay prostrate on top of a pile of logs about two hundred feet below. "Yep. We're right over her."

Ashley gave him a firm nod. "Let's do it."

Walter pushed out. As his three anchor people let the rope slide around the bed frame, he descended. The plane lowered as well, bringing him closer to Lauren at a rapid clip. "Listener!" he shouted. "Not so fast!"

The descent slowed. The vertical propellers pushed smoky air over his body, sending him into an elliptical sway. More rope would make it worse. "Ashley! That's good! Hold me right there!"

The line stopped reeling. Walter looked down again. A hundred feet to go. ... Seventy. ... Fifty.

"Listener! Slower!" The hospital's drop continued at the same rate. Letting go with one hand, he ripped off his mask and shouted at the top of his lungs. "Slower!"

The descent eased. Hot air from below mixed in with the swirling wind. Walter swung through a five-foot arc, sweat dripping. This place was an oven, maybe two hundred degrees. If Lauren was still alive, she had to be roasting.

Shifting his body to a horizontal position, he reached down. Twenty feet.

Lauren's body clarified. Her sleeves, shirt, and pant legs had all been rolled up to expose her skin. Had she intended to create a beacon, or was she just trying to cool off?

Ten feet.

"Listener! Hold it right there!" The hospital stopped and hovered, swaying as it dipped and rose like a log dangling from a rubber band. In a downward surge, Walter's outstretched hand swiped just inches from Lauren's back before shooting up again. "Lauren! Can you hear me?"

She lay motionless. It was too dark to tell if she was breathing. If she was dead, taking a bigger risk wouldn't be worth it, but if she was alive ...

420

Walter looked up at Ashley as she leaned back against the rope, her head protruding from the doorway. "Are you getting any thoughts from Lauren?"

Ashley squinted, then nodded, a smile breaking through. "She's alive! She keeps thinking 'Jehovah-Yasha' over and over."

"That's all I needed to know. Put me down on the logs."

As the rope fed out, Walter reached with both hands. The first touched the back of Lauren's shirt and the second a log next to her hip. When his feet pressed down, one on each side of her legs, he tried to stand.

The logs shifted, then toppled to the sides. Walter grabbed Lauren's shirt and held her dangling over the ground. As the logs rolled, their bark ignited. Flames shot up, brushing her bare feet. Her shirt began riding up to her shoulders and slipping over her head.

With a quick twist, Walter jerked her up, swung his legs around her waist, and wrapped her limp body in a scissors hold. "I got her! Haul me in! Listener, get us out of this heat!"

Grunts sounded from above. Engines whined. The hospital rocked, slowly ascending. As they rose, Walter reached down and slid his hands under Lauren's armpits and shifted her higher in his grip. That was better. Not even Arramos could snatch her away now.

Above, Ashley and company pulled. Walter and Lauren rose in hesitating surges. Only a few feet to go. Listener appeared at the doorway, one hand reaching as she walked down the stairway, the other hand clutching the rope. "All I need is her wrist!" she shouted.

Walter slid his hand down Lauren's arm, lifted it, and jerked backwards to a horizontal position, giving her an upward boost.

Listener grabbed Lauren's wrist and hauled her in. After laying her on the vestibule floor, Listener scrambled back down the stairs and locked forearms with Walter. Helped by the rope's pull, she hoisted him up to the stairway. Their momentum sent them flying into the cabin.

Walter rolled onto the floor and sat up against the wall. He pulled Lauren into his lap and leaned her head on his shoulder. "Water!"

"It's right in here!" Dr. Conner dropped the rope and ran into the dorm.

Candle fell to his knees, panting. Ashley sat next to Walter and brushed Lauren's hair from her eyes. Skin peeled on her forehead and face, reddened and sooty. "Oh, Walter! She looks awful!" She pressed her palm on Lauren's cheek. "At least a hundred and four. I'll have to sponge her down."

"It's a miracle she survived." He nodded toward her bare feet. "She's got to have terrible burns. I can't imagine how she walked on that ground."

422

Ashley shifted over and ran a hand along one of Lauren's soles. "They're filthy but not burned at all."

Walter stared at Ashley. "How could that be?"

"I have no idea. I—"

"Here." Dr. Conner thrust a water bottle into Walter's hand. "Start her slowly. You might have to dribble it over her lips at first. I'll keep watching for any sign of Eagle."

"Sounds good." As Walter let the water trickle over Lauren's lips, it spilled down to her neck and over his shirt, cool and refreshing. Her lips pursed, then opened, letting the water in, though her eyes stayed closed. As she drank, tears welled in Walter's eyes. He looked through the doorway at the clearing night sky. "Jehovah-Yasha," he whispered. "Thank you for saving this amazing girl."

Matt drifted through the air, floating above the clouds, vibrating, aching. Loud noises—rumbling roars, metallic clanks, and airy hisses—rushed in and flew past. The slow, sometimes bumpy hovering lasted for hours and hours. Could it all be a dream? Probably. With no wings on his back, how could it be anything else?

A gray cloud rolled overhead, growing darker and darker. Thunder boomed. Chilly wind penetrated his clothes. A torrent of rain splashed in his face.

He opened his eyes and shook his head hard, slinging droplets. One of the helicopter soldiers, now wearing a parka, held an empty pail. "Wake up, pretty boy."

As a cold breeze swirled around Matt's head, he pushed against gritty pavement and rose slowly to a sitting position, rubbing a knot just above his ear. The pain wasn't too bad, and the water barely dampened his cloak's hood, not enough to raise a chill, since he so rarely got cold.

Setting a hand on one of two single-story wooden buildings that sandwiched him in a narrow alley, he glanced around. Only one door interrupted the buildings' blank walls, and no signs gave evidence of what might be inside. A Mustang convertible with its top open sat between him and the alley exit, its engine running. Someone wearing a backpack and a hood sat curled facing left in the rear seat. Brown hair protruded from around the hood, veiling the person's face. About a hundred feet beyond the car, a narrow street ran perpendicular to the exit. Dim light in the sky made it appear to be early evening or morning. "Where am I?"

423

A new voice broke in. "I'm sure you've seen an alley before."

Slowly turning, Matt found the speaker—Tamiel, still in the same dark garb, his suit jacket open again, making his shoulder holster obvious. He extended a hand. "May I help you up?"

Matt glanced at the soldier who had splashed him with water. He now stood with a pistol at his hip, obviously ready to fire. Trying to grab Tamiel and disarm him would have been easy otherwise.

"I can manage." Matt climbed to his feet. His head pounded. With his cloak so wrinkled, the hem barely fell past his knees. "Where are my parents?"

Tamiel pushed the toe of his pointed boot into a half-frozen puddle. "Your father is too dangerous to be involved in this little experiment, so we are transporting him to a safe place."

"Experiment?" Matt rubbed his head again and squinted at the car's passenger, maybe his mother, if the backpack meant anything. She was probably all right. Otherwise, they wouldn't have positioned her so carefully. "Now I'm a guinea pig?"

"In a manner of speaking. Soon you will join your mother on what you might call an impossible mission, though with your talents, I have faith that you can accomplish it."

Matt growled. "What do you know about faith?"

"Well, I see that your pain hasn't diminished your spunk." Tamiel chuckled. "That's good, because you're going to need it."

Nodding toward the Mustang, Matt tempered his voice. "I assume that's my mother. If she's hurt, I'll—"

"Don't be so dramatic, Matt. She's fine, as you will soon see."

"Okay." Matt tightened his hands into fists. "Where's Lauren?"

"I honestly have no idea. Since I no longer have use for Lauren, I am letting others deal with her."

Matt studied his expression—cool and calculated. Maybe what Semiramis said was true. He was staying away from Lauren because touching her would mean his death … and hers. "So let's get on with it. What's the experiment all about?"

Tamiel withdrew a mobile phone from his pocket and ran his finger across the screen. "You will find seven addresses in the database, and you are to visit each one. This unit has GPS mapping capabilities, but it cannot be tracked. Also, don't bother trying to use the phone for calls. It doesn't work except for communications with my phone, both voice and text." He handed it to Matt, a smile wrinkling his lips. "We removed the transmitter between your molars, so I'm sure you will be more comfortable now."

Matt snatched the phone. "You act like this is a game."

"It *is* a game—the ultimate showdown."

Matt scrolled through the list of addresses with his thumb. They appeared to be locations in multiple states. "Care to explain?"

"I will, but not now. When you get in the car, tune your radio to FM eighty-seven point seven and set the phone to broadcast the first message in the inbox. I'm sure you can find the proper application. Then you and Bonnie will be able to listen to my explanation together while enjoying the sights."

Matt slid the phone into his pocket and looked at Mom again, still sitting motionless in the car. Might she be asleep? Still exhausted from the candlestone's effects? "Where are we?"

"I'm sure you will figure that out as well." Tamiel withdrew a wallet from an inner pocket. "Driver's license, credit card, and cash, all untraceable." He tossed the wallet to Matt. "And you will find food and drinks in the backseat."

He caught the wallet and rifled through at least thirty bills inside. The driver's license had his photo but a different name, issued by the state of Nebraska, definitely authentic looking. The credit card bore the same name—Michael Foster. Apparently since this mission covered multiple states, it would require checking into motels under an assumed identity. "So why do you think I'll go along with this screwball charade?"

"Two reasons. First, we hold your father. Second, your mother's compassion will drive you more surely than will your hands on the steering wheel." Tamiel lifted his brow. "Which reminds me. Are you an experienced driver?"

Matt resisted a smirk. After driving military Jeeps through muddy swamps and mountain trails during training, he could drive anything. "I'm experienced."

"Good. We expect you to arrive in each locale by a time that I will provide through text messages. You will check into a motel by that time using the credit card, and you will visit the address the next morning. When you arrive at the address, Bonnie will know what to do. After you finish, you will drive to the next town."

"So you'll know we're on schedule when we use the credit card."

"That is one method. We have other ways of tracking you."

Matt slid the wallet into his back pocket. The Mustang was probably equipped with a GPS locator. There was no escaping their watchful eye as long as he drove it. "What happens if we're late?"

"Your father will suffer the consequences. The severity of the punishment will depend on the circumstances." Tamiel patted Matt's shoulder. "Yet I think you will—"

Matt jerked away. "Don't patronize me! I've seen enough deceivers to know when one's trying to play me for a fool!"

"Ah! Yes, you are less gullible than most. Darcy has, indeed, opened your eyes to betrayal."

Matt pressed his lips together. The statement was bait. Tamiel wanted to show off his knowledge of Darcy and maybe expose other raw wounds, but that bait would just have to dangle. He jabbed a finger at Tamiel and growled, "Just don't."

"Very well." Tamiel swept an arm toward the Mustang. "Be on your way."

After glancing at the soldier again, Matt walked toward the driver's side, his head still throbbing. When he reached for the door, Mom's face came into view. Her eyes shut, she sat motionless, her face pale.

He opened the door, reached in, and touched her cheek. Her skin felt normal—the right temperature, smooth and not too dry. "Mom?" he said softly. "Can you hear me? It's me, Matt."

The phone chimed in his pocket. He looked back at Tamiel. The demonic scarecrow smirked.

Matt snatched the phone and read the message. "She will wake up only when you follow my instructions in the audio message."

With quick thumbs, Matt typed, "Listen, jerk." Then, sighing, he cleared the message. The phone beeped again.

He switched to the incoming message and read it. "I almost forgot. I have something to show you." He looked back at Tamiel. The soldier opened the building's door and coaxed a girl out at gunpoint. Wearing a low-cut, spaghetti-strap top with one strap broken; a short, tight skirt; and high heels, she kept her head low and turned away, shielding her face.

"Las Vegas," Tamiel said as he laid a hand on her bare shoulder. "It took a while to hunt her down, but we finally found her at a seedy street corner at midnight."

Matt scrunched his brow. Why would Tamiel bring a streetwalker here? It didn't make sense. Whatever the reason, she had to

427

be freezing. He slid off his cloak and walked toward her. "Here. I don't need this as much as you do."

As he draped it over her shoulders, she turned her head toward him, revealing her face, heavily rouged and painted with dark lipstick, mascara, and eye shadow. Yet, no amount of makeup could hide her identity.

"Darcy?" Matt staggered back, leaving the cloak with her.

She nodded. "Yes, Matt. I'm glad you still recognize me."

"Let's make it easier." Tamiel nodded at the soldier. "Clean her up."

While Tamiel watched with his gun drawn, the soldier dipped a handkerchief in icy water and wiped Darcy's face, smearing her makeup. After a few swipes, he dropped the rag into her hand. "I'll let you finish."

Her body shaking, Darcy dabbed at her face with the rag.

428

Tamiel shoved her toward Matt. As one of her high heels broke and fell off, she stumbled out of control. Matt lunged and caught her under her arms, keeping her from falling. He quickly set her upright and let her go. "What's this all about?"

"Darcy fulfills a role that you will understand soon. Yet, you are free to take her with you or leave her here. If you leave her here, however, I will kill her, because I have no other use for her. Since your mother is asleep, she will never know that you made that choice."

Matt looked at Darcy. Those familiar evil eyes stared back at him, and her attire and vocation proved that nothing had changed. There wasn't a shred of decency in her. Yet, leaving her here to die at the hands of a demon would make him even worse than she was. "She'll come with us."

"I expected as much, but be aware that we are tracking her as well. If you decide to leave her in what you consider to be a safe place, we will find her and kill her. She must stay with you or die."

Matt glanced again at Darcy. Had they implanted some kind of GPS chip in her?

"Start driving." Tamiel waved his gun toward the car. "As I said, I will text the arrival time while you are on your way. Do not waste even a minute."

After helping Darcy into the front passenger's side, Matt settled in the driver's seat, pulled the floor stick to the drive position, and rolled out of the alley. When he stopped at the vacant street, he started the phone's GPS program and accessed the first address, a place in western Kansas, drive time six hours.

He glanced at the car's console clock. 3:00 p.m. Since it was the middle of the night at the Montana crater, he must have been out cold most of the next day. But where was he now? He studied the map. A little town in western Nebraska. Why Nebraska?

As he drove onto the street, Darcy turned his way. "You won't regret this, Matt. Your trust, in spite of all I have done to you, means everything to me."

Matt's throat tightened. Hadn't she said that before? Yes! In a dream. It had faded away but now came roaring back—the cloak, her bare legs, the smeared makeup. It was all the same, even the words she spoke, a near duplicate of Semiramis repeating the phrases word for word. Might Darcy be Semiramis in disguise? Maybe, but how could he test that theory?

Darcy slid her hand into his. In the dream, the touch felt electric, much like a touch from Semiramis, but now her skin felt cold and clammy, a sign of fear. Maybe she wasn't Semiramis after all. "Will you take me home?" she asked.

His dream answer came to mind, *I'll do my best.* It was a good answer. It made sense. But letting the dream control their destiny didn't. "I'll … I'll do everything I can to get us all home safely."

"Thank you." Darcy drew his hand to her lips and kissed his fingers. "I'm sorry for all those pranks I pulled on you. They were mean." She let go and clutched the cloak closer to her body, shivering. "You could have let them kill me, but you gave me your own cloak and took me away with you. I have no idea what's going on, but … thank you."

Polite phrases ran through Matt's mind—you're welcome; no problem; we were just kids back then, so forget about it. But he couldn't force any of them through his lips.

"I guess you're cold." He found the convertible control, closed the top, and turned on the heat and the radio. After setting it to 87.7 on the FM dial, he pulled up the recorded message, chose the broadcast option, and began following the GPS directions.

"Good evening, Mr. Bannister."

Matt cringed. Tamiel's voice had become a rusty hinge, and now his earlier reference to an impossible mission made sense. He was imitating the opening of every *Mission Impossible* episode ever made. How could that demon know about his favorite classic TV show?

He glanced at Darcy and nodded. *That's how. They really are in this "experiment" together.*

"As I told you earlier," Tamiel continued, "I want to explain the situation to you and your mother at the same time. So if you will examine her neck, you will find a small button-like tab adhering to her skin. Remove it, and she will soon awaken."

Matt pressed the pause button and stopped the car. Reaching back, he slid his fingers around Mom's neck and found the tab. He pulled it out, pivoted to his seat, and studied the white, dime-sized button. A tiny needle protruded from one side.

"We'll see if that helps." He laid the tab on the floorboard and touched the play control, reviving Tamiel's voice. "We noticed that Bonnie's energy level had dropped too low for her to continue this mission, so we removed the candlestone bullet and provided her with a boost. She should be quite energetic when she awakens. From what I have observed, the initial phase of the experiment produced such dramatic results in what I hope to achieve, I decided that the energy-drain was no longer needed. What she will experience in the next few days will be sufficient to continue strangling her song."

"Matt?"

"Mom?" He paused the audio again, reached back, and patted her arm. "Yeah, it's me. You're all right. We're both all right."

"Your hair's wet." Her tone seemed confused, and her eyes wandered, as if she were still in a dream.

He touched his hair. "I got a rude wake-up call. I'm fine. I don't get cold easily."

"Where is Billy?" Her eyes sharpened. "The last I remember—"

"We were in that crater in Montana," Matt said. "Some military thugs beat us up and shipped us here to Nebraska. Dad's a prisoner somewhere, and they let us go so we could conduct some kind of experiment. Supposedly, Dad's safe unless we don't do what we're told." He lifted the phone and showed it to her. "I'll play the explanation when your head's clear."

"It's clearing up. I feel a lot better." Mom smiled at Darcy. "May I ask who you are?"

Darcy glanced at Matt before answering. "Um ... I think I'll wait for Matt to explain. I have no idea what's going on, so ..." She faced the front and folded her hands in her lap. "Yeah."

Matt looked at Mom through the rearview mirror. She caught his gaze and gave him a questioning tilt of her head. "I guess we should start unraveling this mystery." She nodded at the phone. "Let's hear it."

431

RECOVERY

Lauren awoke to the sound of a vibrating rumble. Her head pounded, and her left arm throbbed. She opened her eyes. Dim lights illuminated a small airplane cabin. An IV tube led from her sore arm to a bottle hanging from a stand in the aisle next to her seat. Ashley sat in the adjoining seat to the right, her head leaning against a shuttered window. In the cockpit, Walter sat in the pilot's chair, and a section of a dragon's wing indicated that Gabriel sat in the copilot's.

Lauren touched a stinging spot on her forehead. The ends of threads meant someone had stitched up a deep wound. She sat up straighter and looked out the front windshield. Only blue sky and clouds came into view.

After clearing her throat, she whispered, "Walter?"

Walter turned and nudged Gabriel. "She's awake, Try to keep us from crashing."

"No barrel rolls?"

"Wait till I'm buckled in." Walter rose, walked the two steps to Lauren's seat, and stooped next to the IV stand. "How are you feeling?" His voice was low and soothing.

"Okay. Kind of weak."

"Well, you've been out for a while. Dr. Conner wanted to keep you in the hospital, but I thought you'd want to help us find Matt and your parents, so I"—he drew quotation marks in the air—"persuaded him to let you come."

She smiled, but even that effort hurt. "Thank you. I do want to help."

"Great. We'll need your listening ears. Our other Listener stayed in Second Eden. With her surrogate mother dead, a baby sister to take care of, and most of the other women gone, she couldn't come. Besides, her companion doesn't do too well here."

Lauren glanced at her shoulder, now covered with a sweatshirt. The companionless void hurt … a lot. It ached worse than her head and arm combined. As tears welled, she cried out in her mind. *Mon amie! Are you watching me from above?*

"We're tracking your father's GPS chip," Walter continued. "It's embedded under his skin, so we're hoping they don't notice it. We're assuming your mother and Matt are with him, but we're not sure. It looks like he's in western Nebraska traveling east, so we're heading that way. I saved some weapons and ammo from the prison base, so we'll have some firepower, especially when Roxil joins us. Right now we have no idea why Tamiel took Billy to Nebraska, but nothing's going to stop us from finding out and rescuing him."

"That's my Walter." Stretching her arms, Ashley yawned.

"Sorry," he said. "Didn't mean to wake you."

"No problem. Shall I finish the rundown while you fly this bird?"

"Be my guest. You're good at a quick summary."

Ashley smirked. "Spoken by the king of telephone fast-talkers."

"Who, me?" Grinning, Walter laid his hand behind Lauren's head and kissed her cheek. As he drew back, his blue eyes sparkled with tears. He whispered, "You are absolutely amazing. Your idea saved a lot of lives." He bit a trembling lip, turned as he rose, and walked back to the cockpit.

"Thank you." Lauren's cheeks grew warm. Walter's emotions seemed to penetrate her own.

"I'll just give you a quick rundown." Ashley set a nutrition shake on Lauren's seat tray and opened it. "After you drink this, you need to sleep more."

Lauren tipped the shake up to her lips and took a long drink. It was so refreshing—cool, sweet, and smooth.

"Good girl." Ashley raised a finger for each news item as she continued. "After the men of Second Eden bury Valiant and give him and Eagle a funeral, they'll work to restore their villages. With Karrick and Grackle helping, the work should go pretty fast. We decided not to call the women and children back until their homes are ready. We're also in communication with Elam, Yereq, and some of the dragons while they try to rescue Sapphira, but the details on that can wait. Like Walter said, Roxil will be joining us as soon as we figure out where we're landing, so we'll have dragon firepower to go along with the weapons."

Taking a breath, she looked at Lauren. "We were wondering about Tamara. She looked pretty bad in her photo, so we assume she needs to be treated. Doc saved some of the new parasites, so it won't be difficult."

"Tamara's fine. She looks thin and washed out on purpose, but let me tell you more later. It hurts to talk."

"No problem. She must have an immunity for some reason." Ashley folded in her fingers and restarted her news-item count.

"We don't know where Joran and Selah are, but we think they were transported into some kind of ethereal existence where they can sing and help us out. We have no clue where Semiramis and Mardon are, but we're sure they'll cause as much trouble as possible. We can't communicate with Billy or Matt, probably because their tooth transmitters were taken out, and I don't think Bonnie ever had one. Jared and the other anthrozils are recovering slowly, and Jared and Marilyn are on their way to Castlewood to get a file from Larry. They can't risk getting it remotely, because Larry is a communications decoy and is being monitored by the government. We're doing the real work with Lois. She's the one who ran the models on the stuff you sent in the beaker, and that gave us our breakthrough in beating that parasite."

Lauren tried to sort out all the events, but her brain felt fried. "Well, I'm glad I did some good."

"Some good? Sweetheart, if not for you, a lot more people would be dead, including my own brother." Ashley leaned over and pushed a lock of Lauren's hair away from her eye. "Like Walter said, you are an amazing girl."

Lauren pressed her lips together, trying not to cry. If not for her bungling, Eagle and Albatross would still be alive. How could anyone be happy trading lives for other lives?

"Oh, Lauren!" Ashley set a cool hand on Lauren's cheek. "I know what you're thinking. You have to put those thoughts away. You did everything in your power to save as many lives as possible. We found Albatross's remains, and we figured out what Eagle did, because …" She dug into her pocket and withdrew a medallion on a chain. "We found this in your pocket. I studied the phone video and saw that he was still wearing it when he climbed the ladder, so I assume he gave it to you after that."

Lauren pushed her fingers under the chain and lifted the medallion. As it twirled slowly, the engraving came into view. *My gift to you. My life. It is all I have to give.* Eagle's words flowed like a lovely echo. *"I hope to give it to my bride when we wed, to a young lady I would give my life for."*

"I hope it's all right that I read your mind a bit. I figured out that he took your place in the volcano."

Her throat tightening, Lauren squeaked, "It's all right." She hugged the medallion to her chest and wept. *Oh, Eagle! You'll never have a bride! Why did you give your life for mine? I could have done it! I could have died to stop the disease! Why did it have to happen this way?*

"Why?" Ashley brushed Lauren's cheek with the back of her hand. "I can't say for certain, but maybe because we need a Listener to save your family. Only you can do that. Eagle did his part. Trust me. I know him better than you realize. Doing his part is all he ever wanted to do. And now you have to grieve while you can and then fight past it. There are too many more lives to save."

Sniffing back the tears, Lauren looked into Ashley's eyes. She was right. For fifteen years she and Walter suffered but kept fighting. She had blazed a bloody trail of her own, though not on a hot lava field. It was time to follow in her footsteps.

"By the way …" Ashley withdrew a phone from her pocket and gave it to her. "This is yours."

"Thank you." Lauren looked at the screen. Ashley had brought up Eagle's photo, probably thinking it would complement the medallion somehow. It was a nice thought, but Eagle's eyes pierced too painfully. Maybe someday his image wouldn't hurt so much.

She switched to the next photo—Joan in her companion form. Glowing blue and staring with narrow eyelets, she hovered in place. For some reason, without her penetrating thoughts, she seemed to be no more than a floating bauble, artificial and unreal.

With two clicks back, Lauren pulled up Joan's photo in Abaddon's Lair. Dressed in battle array, she stood with her legs set and shoulders square, her eyes sharp and clear. Yes, this was the real Joan, a sacrificial warrior, the best of companions.

Tears welled in Lauren's eyes. Her image, too, brought a stab of pain—another friend, short-lived but more precious than life, swept away too soon. What did their sacrifices mean? They had given their all, each one dying to feed someone starving for life, each one spilling seeds in the hearts of others that would germinate into fruitful trees and begin the process all over again, but only if the new soil would let it grow.

Three people had faced death—Joan, Eagle, and herself. Two had succumbed. Now, as Abaddon had said, facing the fear of death had defeated all fears forevermore. Since Jehovah-Yasha had rescued her both physically and spiritually, there was simply nothing left to fear. That kind of security might go a long way in battling the likes of Tamiel.

Taking a deep breath, Lauren brushed away the tears and hung the medallion around her neck. "I'm ready, Ashley. Let's go find my family."

438

The **Dragons in our Midst®** and **Oracles of Fire®** collection
by **Bryan Davis**:

RAISING DRAGONS

ISBN-13: 978-089957170-6

The journey begins! Two teens learn of their dragon heritage and flee a deadly slayer who has stalked their ancestors.

THE CANDLESTONE

ISBN-13: 978-089957171-3

Time is running out for Billy as he tries to rescue Bonnie from the Candlestone, a prison that saps their energy.

CIRCLES OF SEVEN

ISBN-13: 978-089957172-0

Billy's final test lies in the heart of Hades, seven circles where he and Bonnie must rescue prisoners and face great dangers.

TEARS OF A DRAGON

ISBN-13: 978-089957173-7

The sorceress Morgan springs a trap designed to enslave the world, and only Billy, Bonnie, and the dragons can stop her.

EYE OF THE ORACLE

ISBN-13: 978-089957870-5

The prequel to *Raising Dragons*. Beginning just before the great flood, this action-packed story relates the tales of the dragons.

ENOCH'S GHOST

ISBN-13: 978-089957871-2

Walter and Ashley travel to worlds where only the power of love and sacrifice can stop the greatest of catastrophes.

LAST OF THE NEPHILIM

ISBN-13: 978-089957872-9

Giants come to Second Eden to prepare for battle against the villagers. Only Dragons and a great sacrifice can stop them.

THE BONES OF MAKAIDOS

ISBN-13: 978-089957874-3

Billy and Bonnie return to help the dragons fight the forces that threaten Heaven itself.

Published by Living Ink Books, an imprint of AMG Publishers
www.livinginkbooks.com ✦ www.amgpublishers.com ✦ 800-266-4977